ON PAIN

OF

DEATH

ON PAIN OF DEATH

Nah then, mayat.
No more bogglin' abowut.
Fer frim folks, it's taim to
larn yersen abart Linkisheer.

Cary Smith

ON PAIN OF DEATH

Copyright © 2023 Cary Smith

ISBN: 978-1-916696-33-4

You can contact the author on Facebook
For more details visit Amazon and search for Cary Smith

We are here on Earth to do good to others.
What the others are here for, I do not know

1

Jake Goodwin knew from bitter experience to follow his dad's instructions implicitly. Even so, he was not at all sure he'd found the right place. So far he'd seen no sign of a farm, even the tarmac had ended and he was now onto potholed gravel.

Why does Sod's Law always do its best to choose the most inopportune moment to strike? Like all cops the Detective Sergeant didn't enjoy coincidences, so whatever this was leading to had to be something else.

A weekend away at his parents with Sally and son Tyler helping them celebrate another wedding anniversary at their place in the village. No more than a good stone's throw from the farm he'd been told to head for.

Suspicious death and Code Red phoned alert. Acute instructions from his dad and here he was spotting at last the battenburg decals on the Roads Policing Unit's Skoda, with one of the cops gesturing for him to halt.

Window down, Warrant Card. 'Jacques Goodwin, Detective Sergeant. We have a body or so I'm told.'

'Yes guv. Easy best you park behind us for now and walk.' Jake peered at the gravel road ahead. 'Long way round by road Sarge. Think best if you park here and head off that way,' he said as he gestured in between bushes. 'It's where you'll find Shaun and the farmer.'

'Thanks.'

'And his dog.'

Momentarily Jake's body sank down as he sighed to himself. How many times had he been called out to similar rural situations to be greeted by some dear old soul out for walkies with a dog who just happened to sniff out an abused body? Jake parked up close behind the police car.

'Body's in the middle of a field sarge, and it's all a bit odd. You'll see when you get there.'

'All I need on a Sunday morning, thanks.'

1

'Right funny business up there. Just follow your way and you'll see Shaun.'

The route the traffic cop pointed out as a path of sorts, was little more than just downtrodden grass and nettles. Each side of him as he trudged were wildly overgrown shrubs and weeds. He was pleased after a while to see the pathway turn sharp left when he thought he was about to be heading through thorny bushes and gorse spikes. Then within twenty metres there was light ahead through a break in the trees and an opening between two and a rusty iron fence some kind soul had knocked down flat. Stepping over steadily in his best jeans and trainers there before him was who he assumed to be this Shaun.

'Hello gaffer. Bit of a trek eh?' he was greeted with as he showed his card again. 'There he is,' dark haired, tall fully kitted up Shaun said pointing to a figure in shadow set against the skyline a good seventy or more yards away.

'This seriously the best way in?'

'Road for what it's worth goes right through the farm, out the other side to the far end of two fields away. Be the way an ambo'll have to come I guess.'

'Thanks fella. D'you know any more?'

'Dog found him and that's Herring the farmer waiting. Not in a very good mood to say the least.'

'Nor am I. Got dragged out before breakfast.'

'From Lincoln?'

'No. Stayed local for the weekend. Now that's that buggered.' Jake blew out a breath. 'What else is new in this game eh? Thanks,' said the DS and set off across an open expanse of field with green crops growing in perfectly straight rows ahead of him.

He walked carefully head down to avoid stepping on whatever the plants were to avoid increased aggravation. As he approached, the man was stood legs astride hands on hips, and there beside him was a Collie, tongue hanging out panting.

'Right sir,' Jake said as he looked at the body of a man and at one peculiar aspect in particular. 'Detective Sergeant Jake Goodwin. Major Incident Team from Lincoln.'

'Nah then. Least yer got a shift on, pleased some bugger has.'

There was no point in explaining why he was there so quickly. Next thing he'd ask about his dad, talk about them seeing each other in the shop and they'd lose focus on the priorities. He made do with. 'Mr…?'

'Herring. David Herring.' He waved a hand about like an umpire confirming a four and Jake could only think of fish out of water. 'This here's me bread an' butter, son,' was unmistakably glottal Linkisheer, which could easily have provoked sarcasm from Jake about green bread being mouldy. This was not the time. 'Need this old bugger shifting a bit sharpish, son.'

'And these are what exactly?' the DS asked pointing to a row of plants.

'Cabbage. Spring Cabbage,' he said as if it was obvious. He was a tubby man who Jake guessed to be in his fifties with an equine face, a disheveled mop of thinning brown hair at the front of his head with little beyond.

'How d'you come across him?' Jake Goodwin asked as he realized the cadaver's face was known to him. What some these days call an environmental influencer. Widely recognized not only to him but the whole damn nation. Despite years of experience in dealing with some very strange and nasty rural situations, he'd never come across anything like it before in his life. Eyes closed but eyelids are where rigor mortis starts its work.

'All downta Spike,' he was told but Jake was too preoccupied with what he was looking at. Intent on trying to get a flavour of what had happened. 'Got no sheep these days but allus had a dog. Old Spike's bit long in'tooth now but he's more a pet. Out for me morning look round and silly bugger scampers off top side o' bottom meadow here. Chasing rabbits an' all sorts usually's his game. Heard him barking like, but he'd not react to me whistles. Came all the way up here and its a fair walk an' that's what he'd got. Old Alerick there, poor bugger.'

From experience Jake was fully aware he was alone with a possible suspect, even though what Herring claimed was entirely possible.

'What're they bringing? Paddy wagon, to cart 'im off in?

'I've no idea,' Jake admitted. Looking all around he knew it would be a good trudge with a stretcher whichever way they came.

'Not want it up here. Needs to come from o'er that way,' he gestured with big chunky fingers. 'Gate at far end there,' Jake couldn't even see. 'They can park it up an' walk. Not ruining this bloody lot that's for damn sure lad.'

'How big is this field?'

'Good seven acres and a touch more.'

'Has Spike touched the body?'

'Just barked for ages. Fair good walk to get here to check wha' all the fuss were about.'

'And you. Have you touched him?'

'What wi' that on there?'

'You know him then?' said Jake gesturing to the man on the ground in what looked like the sort of trousers old Colonels still wear and expensive but battered brown imitation brogues.

'Lives a mile or two off up his big manor place.' A fact Jake already knew as the victim was somebody his father regarded as a neighbour with some pride. 'You seen his missus?' Jake shook his head. 'Tidy piece that and no mistake', and he whistled which was hardly a polite reaction with her husband lying there dead. 'Me lad'll be here soon. Wan' us ter get him an' give us a hand shifting him?'

'Don't you dare!'

'Hang on,' was said back crossly. 'In case yer not noticed this be a working farm mayat and…' his voice to degree was full of sarcasm turning into desperation.

'Excuse me,' was forthright Goodwin. 'This, in case you haven't noticed,' was Jake's own derision. 'Is a crime scene. We'll have a pathologist on his or her way. Nothing happens without their say so. Understand?'

'What'll I do then?'

'What exactly had you in mind for this field today?'

'Well,' he blew out a breath. 'Nowt actually, jus bogglin' abowat…'

'Thank you. This field stays exactly as it is. Do I make myself clear?'

Herring was contemptuous, turning his back on Goodwin and his next remark was to his dog. 'C'mon Spike me ol' son. That's all the thanks we'll get.' He patted the dog's back. 'Ave a word with Eddie, he'll sort the buggers out and ge' yous breakfast.'

The brown shirt dead Keating–Price was wearing had been cut off at the right shoulder and that bare arm was carefully laid out between the plants.

4

Jake looked up to watch David Herring and his dog Spike in the distance walking off the way he'd indicated the farmhouse was situated. He pulled out his phone. 'Nicky,' he said when she answered. 'You at work?'

'Yeh.'

'Am I doin' this on my own?'

'How d'you mean?'

'I've got that Keating-Price bloke dead in a field of cabbages. Anybody on their way d'you know?'

'*The* Keating-Price?'

'Sure is.'

'Wow! Only me and Jamie in as yet.'

'What about the boss?'

'You're kidding.'

'Know all about delegation and we can handle it, but Inga'd take an interest. Not always racing to the scene, but this is going to be high profile. Not heard a dicky bird from him.'

'You know what he's like,' Nicky suggested.

'Yeh, that's the trouble.'

'Sandy's been in, heading your way.'

'Thank goodness.'

'Anything else?' she asked.

'No. We'll be good.'

The popular environmentalist's uncombed hair was thin and turning grey in places. Far too long at the back but although it was hidden from view Jake knew there'd a be a ridiculous ponytail. Unless somebody's chopped it off for a lark

Too conventional even for his age, with seriously dated clothing you'd struggle to find at the majority of retailers in town or on line.

DI Oliver Bristow'd not replaced Inga Larsson that long ago, but he was never a hands on sort of boss. Living close to Grantham meant in a round about sort of way the cabbage field was not that far off his route. Why not poke his nose, in Jake wondered?

According to one of Jamie Hedley's contacts he'd only been at Grantham as a DS for not much more than a year. They understood he'd moved from somewhere down south and then got promoted and moved to MIT.

Tended to keep himself to himself unlike Inga now the force lead as a DCI covering rape and serious sexual offences. She'd talk about her husband Adam and her daughter. Jake had been to her house a few times. With Bristow all they knew was his mother owned a vineyard in France.

Back to the cadaver, Jake was so aware you only get one shot at a crime scene, in a constantly evolving and improving world.

With Keating-Price's arm bandaged from wrist to shoulder and sealed with duct tape top and bottom, there was a bulge in the crook of his bare arm. As if that wasn't enough, stuck to the arm in a clear plastic bag with a yellow and black well known skull and crossbones image were the printed words:

Do NOT Remove

ON PAIN
OF DEATH

2

As he looked down at the cadaver Jake was reminded how the main injuries in such cases were down to two things. Blunt force trauma and stabbings. These were usually accompanied by massive haemorrhage or bleeding out, resulting in death. His head was unharmed and there was surprisingly no sight of blood.

In this case for the pathologist, there'd be no pondering about the size and width of a sharp blade. Was it a kitchen knife, a heavy sharp sword having been wielded with intent to kill?

In the mood he found himself in, when Jake Goodwin pulled out his phone he was momentarily tempted when the boss answered to simply ask *'Why the hell aren't you here?'*

'Hi boss. Sorry to spoil your Sunday morning. You're not going to like this one but guess you know the basics. Certainly Category A and easy be a major incident. Anybody else on their way apart from Sandy d'you know, because I need bodies?'

'Just got in,' said Detective Inspector Oliver Bristow. 'Sandy's heading your way,' he repeated what Nicky Scoley had already told him. 'Why what's the problem?' he then asked.

'It's Alerick Keating–Price,' with no reaction, he went on. 'He's that climate change guru, the environmentalist. Vegan odd ball, always spouting on the telly. But,' he hesitated. 'Lying in a seven acre field of cabbages with his right shirt sleeve chopped off and a sign taped to his bare arm, saying,' he glanced down at the cadaver to get it right. 'Do not remove under pain of death. With a skull and crossbones hazard sign.'

'What's that all about?'

'You tell me.'

'Who else is there?'

'Just me and two traffic lads and one's back at the lane as far as I know. Need a pathologist and fast.'

'He is dead is he?'

'Sorry guv but I'm not touching it. Yeh, got gloves on but that warning's a bit too much for me. No sign of rigor or decomposition as yet, that I can see. '

'What d'you think it could be?'

'In the crook of his arm there's obviously some sort of padding, and the whole of the arm is bandaged up from his wrist right up to his armpit with duct tape holding it in place. If you're not coming I'll send you a photo now. Call me back eh?'

'Will do.'

'Got to say, some of these climate change people can get up to some bloody annoying things at times, but this looks to me like somebody's fed up to the back teeth with their disruptive antics and done for their poster boy. Photos on their way.'

'Be like some bunch of vegans stopping the traffic when some poor sod's got a chemo appointment.'

Jake stepped back to take a full length photo of the body from several feet away. One of the arm and then as close as he dared of the hazard sign and message. He waited longer than he expected, all the time looking across the acres for any signs of assistance.

Jake was aware it was not unknown for someone to kill another on the spur of the moment, to then be overcome with shock and vomit.

The message on the arm said premeditation and a lack of visible stomach content ended those trains of thought.

Not for the first time the behaviour of the DI had bemused him. Oliver Bristow lived in Grantham. From there to Lincoln was thirty miles, but Anwick just down the road was closer. Why not pop in on his way?

Was he inexperienced with crime scenes, so deliberately avoided embarrassing himself? In the few months he'd been with MIT he'd not attended one crime scene. Just headed for Lincoln Central. Good for Jake and Sandy MacLachlan to be able to work without interruption, but still a tad odd.

At times such as this Jake did wonder if one day his Sally would finally become sick and tired of their lives being constantly disturbed. It was only the aftermath of his parents wedding anniversary but knew back in the village they'd be putting all the plans for the day on hold. Once again.

He was, after a fairly long spell of nothing with only a cadaver for company, sorely tempted to call his boss back.

'Jake,' was DI Oliver Bristow on his phone before he could. 'Sent your photos to the Darke boss. He says major incident and he's onto it for us. Could be anything he reckons. People already talking about Counter Intelligence Team, so you could get more than you bargained for.'

'Be serious guv! This is Keating-Price not the bloody Taliban.' He blew out a breath even his boss must have been able to hear. 'Alright for you, I've got my old man to deal with. Kitted out armed Counter Intelligence lads buying a pint of milk in the village shop's all I need!'

'Be one of those climate change doom merchants if I've got the right one.'

'Farmer knows him, lives local apparently.'

'Darke says can you set up a hazard site, clear the field and don't let anybody anywhere near it? And Jake don't be tempted. Nobody touches him, understand? I don't need a dead hero and nor does your wife.'

There was a degree of empathy about the man and he'd bought Jamie Hedley a bottle of quality of wine for his birthday. Some of the gloss had gone off the gesture when Nicky Scoley somehow discovered Bristow's mother owned a vineyard in France.

'Yes boss,' he sighed. 'But, it's seven acres and there's just me. Traffic lads probably got enough tape for a big square but what d'we tie it to, cabbages? Got to be a good two hundred yards one end to the other if not more. Can't even see the farmhouse from here'

'Who discovered him and how?'

'One guess,' he sighed to himself. 'Dog,' he paused. 'But to be fair it's not the sort of muppet we normally get. Sheepdog Collie from the farm, but they've got no sheep, thank goodness.' As he stood there he'd noticed copper Shaun disappear from view. 'Any chance you can get a message to the traffic lads, they're back over at the cart track in, they need to know what's cracking off and which way to send the troops. Moaning farmer reckons any vehicles need to go through the farm. Had to push my way through bushes and all sorts to save time.' *And I missed my bloody breakfast.*

'I'm at Central setting up the systems, but keep in touch. Phoned Sandy, he reckons fifteen minutes.'

'Farmer. A David Herring could you get somebody to check him on PNC. Bit of a yokel's got the idea we'll have this sorted in no time and we'll remove Keating-Price without disturbing his cabbages pretty sharpish. Twice he's reminded me they're his bread and butter.'

'If this is real bad Jake, chances are he'll lose the lot, but that's for higher authority,' Bristow told him. 'When you see him might be good policy to warn him.'

'Locals coming for a gander worry me if we don't get some uniforms here soon. Good chance he's now calling all his buddies even though I told him to stay schtum...on pain of death to coin a phrase,' his boss laughed at. 'If we're not careful bloody trolls'll have him all over the net if they come in force.'

'Local coppers almost with you I would expect. Called in a few favours with Grantham's help.'

'Thanks.'

'Need what you can find soon as. Phone, wallet...'

'No chance,' stopped him. 'Not touching it. Start rifling through his pockets anything could happen. Brought a Faraday Bag across with me and a couple for evidence. Still in my pocket, unless you fancy a few cabbage plants.'

He knew examples of detectives not being prepared with phones being remotely wiped out. Set to factory setting before they'd got their hands on them or left them unprotected.

Jake just stood there looking all around in case of news, but this dour copper was expecting more bad. He called wife Sally and explained what his situation was without any detail. She offered for his dad to bring him a flask and a bite to eat but he explained how it was not at all a good idea under the circumstances.

Waiting_there alone among the plants with what they call an environmental activist, though to Jake he was just an annoying spouter. Sort who go on about carbon footprints, adaptive capacity and bore you with talk of people's individual climate emissions. Some pretentious odd bods praise him, but in truth chances are they have no idea what he's talking about.

Stood there musing the situation Jake knew statistics on deposition sites indicate killers drive their victim's bodies a maximum of thirty miles from the crime scene, thereby avoiding the chance of being stopped or having an RTC. Lincoln, Spalding and over the border to Newark were all inside that circle. Fortunately

Keating-Price he knew, lived not much more than a good stone's throw from his final resting place.

Before he considered that, was there an egress route he knew nothing about from the farm?

Would that Herring take pity on him and the two lads and bring out a flask they could share? Would pigs fly?

Two crows Jake had been watching suddenly rose cawing into the air. The reason was soon clear when there was the welcome sight of DC Alexander 'Sandy' MacLachlan, their burly Crime Scene Coordinator traipsing across towards him between two of the rows, closely followed by Connor Mitchell the CSI photographer.

He was popular in the force in that Sandy took jokey banter about Scottish football with good heart. Just what the awful political correctness brigade saw fit to banish at every turn. A good six foot two or three and solid with it, most would not dare to mess with.

In the main Sandy tended to modify his Galashiels accent, dropping phrases he'd been so used to using back home. Jake knew he'd have something to say about this situation, with words he'd not easily understand.

'Och.' he uttered with his breath. 'Strange shenanigans d'ya reckon?' was not as broad or bitter a reaction as Jake was expecting. 'Gaunie take a bit of sortin' this.'

Both of them were staggered by the sight laid out in front of them. Connor was quickly taking photos galore he was enthusiastically punting back to all and sundry in Lincoln and making video of the whole scene.

To reticent Bristow back in Lincoln, Sandy and Jake as a pairing were ideal in these situations. Hard working, level headed, good coppers and conscientious. Working in tandem was as good as it gets.

'Nae boss again?'

'Inga during her time left us to it mostly, but you'd think he'd have been at one site in the early months of his reign.'

'Especially as he passed by kinda.'

'If only to check up on us.'

Interesting sight next for Jake was Shona Tate the Forensic Scene Manager heading her team of men and women in white and blue trimmed oversuits, blue protective shoe covers, rubber gloves, face masks with hoods up all trooping single file close behind her. Like something out of a sci-fi movie.

'Pete's brought you a suit,' she said as a greeting. 'Best be on the safe side'

'Thanks.'

'D'you know Professor Urquhart? Wait till you see him if he can walk this far, got the whole regalia on and brought an assistant with him,' she said without taking her eyes off the body of a national treasure.

'Regalia?' said Jake as he walked away to remove his shoes.

'Putting on a Hazmat suit when we left.'

'You're joking. What's he think…?

'You guess is as good as mine,' she shrugged as Jake struggled to pull on the white trousers over his jeans. 'Can't get my head round the reasoning for this Jake,' she suggested as three of her team walked back the way they'd come to unload the incitent. 'This is that old guy off the telly, so why do this? And what's with all the pain of death danger business? Surely to God he's anti coal, oil and gas if that's what this is,' she said as she struggled to delve into her white garb for her phone. 'Bryan, need a geiger counter,' made Jake take a few steps back and remove his jacket.

Everything was doubly difficult with attempting to avoid the small cabbage plants.

Two hooded men in cumbersome outfits were slowly heading in their direction followed closely by another similarly dressed taking the utmost care to avoid trampling on the cabbages. A sight he'd never seen before for real.

'Good morning, or maybe not,' said the first heavily clad man with a brief case in one gloved hand. 'Professor Tom Urquhart, Home Office Pathologist from Nottingham,' no handshake, no elbow punch. 'And my colleague Dr Bradley Johns from Boston Pilgrim. Right,' he nodded at Jake. 'What apart from the obvious do we have here then…er?

'Detective Sergeant,' Jake filled in for him. 'Jacques Goodwin, I'm the Senior Investigation Officer.' Jake then set about briefing the two pathologists with the full story from his perspective as they both were intent on viewing the prostrate Keating-Price. Jake waited for them to finish their viewing they followed with a quiet conversation together then they both stood looking down at the nacreous pallor of the well-known whiskered face.

Urquhart turned back to Jake. 'I suggest we can all understand such public fury against this time-rich elite cult of protesters having their livelihoods damaged and in some cases ruined. This however as we all know,' he said looking down at Keating-Price again, 'is the voice of reason.'

'Might I suggest,' said Johns. 'On the other hand. If this was some of the lunatic activists surely they'd have put their name to it for the publicity they crave.'

'Strange indeed,' added Urquhart ruefully.

'But then we should be thankful for small mercies. Had this been that Thunberg girl we'd have been knee deep in local didicoys taking their blasted selfies.'

Just for a fleeting moment Jake wondered to himself how much a tabloid might pay for one photo of Keating-Price? Only momentarily though.

'Right Sergeant…' brought him back.

'Jake.'

'Certainly Jake. Nobody in and nobody out of this field without my specific instructions.'

'We've got our incitent coming,' Shona butted in.

'Not today. Fresh air is a priority as we have no idea what we're dealing with,' made Shona blow out a breath and pull out her phone as she stepped away treading on a cabbage as she did so.

'And I've ordered up a geiger counter,' she admitted as the two pathologist looked at each other. She lowered her phone. 'Want me to cancel that as well do you?' was slightly sarcastic. 'What about stepping plates?'

'Fine. Can't do any harm you never know with situations like these.' Urquhart turned back to Jake who imagined his normal everyday look would have oozed neatness and vanity. He could envisage all that business would have been drummed into him at his private school. 'I'll be honest...Sergeant. We need Health and Safety. Bradley will deal with if you can organize one of your POLSA teams to search the entire field,' he said waving one of his thick unwieldy arms about. 'This could easy be deadly, and once we have the surrounding area fully checked he'll need to go to Queen's Med at least,' he said gesturing down at Keating-Price, 'but I'll arrange the necessary transport.'

'How deadly?' Jake had to ask with Connor Mitchell stood close listening. Urquhart's Hazmat outfit to him was not at all good for his image.

'Million dollar question Sergeant,' he managed. 'Could be anything from Sarin,' he pulled a face. 'Very toxic, colourless and odourless liquid. Palonium they can slip into somebody's tea as we know, and there's an outside chance this is Novichok. The one used by the Russians down in Salisbury if you remember?'

'Yes.' was all Jake could manage as his brain did its best to digest.

'Remember it was a perfume bottle killing the woman in that case, but so far we're looking down the odourless route.'

'Covid?'

Another grimace as he screwed his eyes up. 'Possible, but is that sign really necessary I ask. Why not Covid in big red letters?'

'Farmer wants his field back.'

Dr Johns chuckled. 'This month, next month, maybe never depends on contamination of soil, crops and a whole host of other elements such as the water course. Sorry.'

'Thanks for that,' said Jake. 'Guess that bad news chat is down to me.' His phone beeped. 'Jake.'

'Sitrep please Jake,' was once more the annoying voice of DI Bristow. 'Darke boss has already called Health and Safety, talked to their regional boss man. Be them littering the place next.'

'Hang on,' he said. 'Excuse me,' he aimed at Urquhart. 'Our Detective Superintendent has already spoken to Health and Safety apparently.'

'We'll do it from our perspective. Thank you anyway.'

'D'you hear that boss?'

'Who was that?' Oliver Bristow asked.

Jake carefully stepped over four rows of cabbage plants. 'Professor Urquhart Home Office Pathologist' he said quietly. 'Here with a Dr Johns from Boston. Reckon the boss must've organized them.'

'What else?'

'Talking about the cadaver needing to go to Queens Med only place who can deal with it. Shona Tate has organized a geiger counter and we're all stood well back.'

'Geiger counter!' he almost shouted.

'We've no idea what the hazard is, do we? Shona plans to use it in detecting ionizing radiation. And that's not the half of it. Professor's talking about all sorts, such as that Sarin and even...Novichock,' Jake dared as he walked further away. 'There's

14

no witnesses apart from the dog, remember. No CCTV, no tyre tracks apart from possibly on the gravel roadway in.' He knew would all make a difference to the investigative command. The only reaction was silence for five seconds to hint at his disbelief.

'Listen here Jake. Keating–Price will be on the front page of every tabloid tomorrow and every news bulletin from the BBC to Fox News. What must not happen Jake is, finding ourselves alongside him.' Sighing Jake guessed budgets and image would inevitably inveigle their way in. 'This is now a pathology and HSE issue, it could easily be security services or even the damn MI5 if we're not careful. We withdraw to reduce the chances of a cock-up. Do you hear me?'

'It's still a murder investigation,' he tried. 'Or is that suddenly not our remit?' he then wanted to drag back.

'Do as I say, or tomorrow the Sun'll have a picture of you picking your nose wasting taxpayers money money just standing about in a cabbage field. No thank you. Remember, this is not some peroxide blonde prostitute nobody gives a fig about, taking a short cut down some alley on her own. This is a Cat A situation and he is what people like you term, your national favourite or somesuch.'

'Don't include me.'

'You fancy a Sky News cameraman following you home to Sally? Then go ahead and make their day.'

'On my way,' he sighed, and angry at being spoken to like a child.

Through experience Jake remained ostensibly calm yet he could have swum in the waves of frustration. The tone from Bristow was most certainly not at all what he had become used to with Inga Larsson over the years.

'Still stuff to organize this end. '

'Leave it to Sandy, he's big enough and ugly enough. He's a good coordinator unless you know different?'

'Hang on a sec guv,' he said, as Shona Tate gestured to him. She passed on the latest news from her perspective. 'According to Shona our friend Luke Stevens is talking to East Midlands Specialist Unit and he's onto the National Crime Agency as well. That lot all turn up'll make a bloody good mess of the cabbages.'

'He can turn it into coleslaw.'

The only part of the normal meticulous routine they'd undertaken was photographing and videoing by Connor.

'Got jobs to do,' said Jake. 'Such as, Pathologists suggesting it may be ages before Herring the farmer boy can get his field back. Somebody's got to break the news and he's in a bit of a strop anyway. Expects us out anytime soon. Probably the sort phoning his MP as we speak.'

'Do that then. Organize Sandy and head back here.'

'Be a while guv. Got to find this farmer boy and I've not had a bite to eat yet. Need to pick up Sally and Tyler and with a bit of luck get brunch, or at least a decent coffee.'

'Make sure you do,' Bristow said. 'Tell you what. This is not likely to be heading off at a fast rate of knots with all that going on. First tranche of uniforms being drafted in as we speak. See you in the morning bright and early. Thanks Jake.'

Jake just stood there looking at his phone. Another thoughtful gesture, yet Bristow appeared not to be one for making small talk. Over the weeks the team knew very little about him and he appeared keen not to elucidate.

Once the danger had been dealt with, state of the art technical resources would discover what had attached itself to the last days and hours of Keating-Price's life. Any drug and drink used would be covered by the autopsy, out of place DNA, foreign loose fibres and other unusual elements.

'Good morning Jake,' on his phone was Detective Superintendent Craig Darke.

'Morning boss.'

'What's the situation now?'

Jake then went through the process and as he did so Bristow once more came to mind. He'd briefed the DI well, so why had he not passed all that onto Darke? Had he even seen the photos?

'Good man. Anything else I can help with?'

Jake sucked in his breath. 'May be speaking out of turn here boss, but,' he hesitated but then ploughed on regardless. 'Any reason why the DI's not here? It being high profile and that message taped to him, I'd a…'

'You saying you can't cope Jake?'

'No, not at all, it's just…'

'Your best bet is to get yourself back here.'

'Yes boss.'

DS Jake Goodwin turned off his phone and just stood there looking at it.

3

DI Oliver Bristow knew avoiding an early discussion with his boss would have been asking for trouble, bearing in mind what he had that morning been advised by Jake.

'Body in the cabbages, sir,' he said as he sat down in the office along the corridor. 'As we know is the much admired Alerick Keating-Price.'

'Now in the morgue over at Queen's Med, and good luck to them. Be like handling a scalpel wearing boxing gloves I imagine.'

'Did you know he was once a member of a band?' Bristow posed. '*Rockapelt*, I think it was using the name Rick Howard? Went round the village like wildfire apparently, and it was Jake Goodwin's mother who came up with the bit about him being in a band at one time.'

'Group it is actually not a band.' and Darke was thoughtful for a moment or two, elbows on his desk, finger tips touching. 'Andy Fairweather-Lowe got away with it, but I guess Alerick reckoned chances are he never would. Pop star called Alerick Keating-Price is never on, at least back then when they were still proper rock stars.' Darke just shook his head and Bristow was surprised by his knowledge. 'All we get these days is nonsense such as Ghostface Killah and Big Boi. At least Alerick to some extent was real, had basic stage craft and presence, not made up like some we get today. But hey,' he shrugged his shoulders. 'That's before the music died. Been a fair while since I've heard anything about them.'

'D'you know any more, sir?

'Be mid to late-90s at a guess. *Sheer Delight* I'm sure was his. On Radio 2 every now and again' He hesitated. 'How did Jake's mother know?' he returned to.

'Village jungle drums and she was telling Jake there'd been an old friend of ours knocking on doors asking about Keating-Price recently,' Darke waited for the reveal. 'A female called Molly Jackson.'

'How odd,' he frowned. 'What's she doing there for crying out loud?'

'Who might she be?'

'Private detective's assistant, and probably more if you get my meaning.'

'Thanks. Can I just say before you slap Jake for discussing the case with his mother. It was this farmer Herring, who found the body, making the most of his fifteen minutes of fame and spread it all round the village.'

'That'd be how it's all over the tabloids this morning. Somebody's made a pretty penny no doubt'

'Apparently this Molly Jackson woman was poking her nose in last week.'

'If she left her name, some crafty sod could've easy have phoned her.'

'May well be right.'

'Apparently,' said Darke. 'As well as being known as Rick Howard rather than Alerick Howard Keating-Price. Sometimes uses his wife's name in an attempt to remain anonymous.' Bristow couldn't help but shake his head. 'Heard he also lets his pony-tail run loose and wears glasses in an attempt to be incognito. '

'Ex-wife that is,' Bristow said. 'Or rather his estranged apparently, according to Jake, or more than likely his mother, Keating's wife left him and just disappeared. Story was she went to Italy. He'd got a new fancy piece in tow according to the media.'

'So I read this morning.'

'Mention of a pony tail and they all knew according to Jake, or rather his parents.'

'How might I ask are they involved.'

'He spent the weekend there. Left them just as they were about to start breakfast when he got the Code Red.'

Detective Superintendent Darke nodded then chuckled. 'How ridiculous. He's not world famous on the music scene as much as it is these days, and he's certainly not Bernie Taupin! *Rockapelt* had one very minor hit, if you can call lower forties a hit.' The chief stopped to chuckle. 'These days of course most of the dross'd not make the top thousand back then. Then their *Sheer Delight* got an unexpected boost and got shoved onto LPs as a filler track ever since.'

'You saying Bernie Taupin lives down there?' Oliver Bristow grimaced his query in an attempt to follow the boss's thought process.

'No, no,' said Darke as he shook his head. 'Comes from Anwick nearby originally, before he linked up with Elton. Lives stateside now I believe.'

'Reason I'm asking, sir. Need your expertise if you'd be so kind, give us everything you know about this Keating-Price.'

'You think the group's involved?' he asked. 'All must be close to or in their fifties now I guess,' he chuckled. 'All that pain of death warning nonsense is a bit much even for a long retired bass player.'

'Background really, and in order for the team to be au fait with the back story before we tackle this Molly Jackson.'

'When was she poking her nose in did you say?'

'This last week so I'm told.'

'Interesting,' arrived with a grimace. 'Not her scene at all, surely she's all to-go Latte Macciato and hip-hop hipster wine bars.'

'And unintelligible rap?'

'Enough said,' and he stopped to think and grimace. 'More than just some local Eco enthusiast. He's a respected environment guru nowadays you know. Dear oh dear. Just very sad, and if you can say that about the dead, unnecessary. There has to be better ways of getting your message across than shutting down Dover for four hours and blocking roads to Heathrow.' He just sat there thinking again. 'Be fascinating to discover why and how. No marks on the body you say?'

'According to Jake no blood, no sight of cuts or bruising just the sleeve ripped off and the message stuck on his arm. Didn't touch him of course and when he left the high-flying pathologists were still doing little more than looking and discussing likely cause and how to move him from a big field full of crops.'

'Tell you who will be well miffed. Dr Bronagh O'Connell. This is a big one she missed out plunging her scalpel into.'

'Call from Sandy later on, is the only reason I know they've moved him to Queen's Medical.'

'Secure, in total isolation, I'm told from on high,' he pointed at the ceiling. 'Almost treating him as if he'd got Covid.'

'At least they've got plenty of PPE now.'

Oliver Bristow was never sure the protest nonsense some of the enviro types go in for was the correct way to achieve their objectives when they put the public's backs up rather than engendering their support. His mother spends half her life living in France and at one time told him polls showed in elections the environment issues polled around 1% of interest.

'See on PNC he's been arrested a good few times, more than once for trespassing when trying to destroy GM crops and all the rest of his…'

'Recklessness.'

'Think we're lucky. Your predecessor Inga had that young Thunberg she had to admit to.'

Darke had a situation report to finish for the higher echelons before he appeared in the Incident Room to brief the troops later in the morning.

After DI Bristow had given a reason for being there for anybody unaware of the Detective Superintendent's extensive popular music knowledge, he explained how he knew next to nothing about Rick Howard's recent history.

'First things first. We've been allocated Operation Oldfield and before there's any bright ideas, they've moved us onto names of policemen from the past.' They all knew random words are used to hide the target of the operation from the actual code word. Jake had often wondered who came up with the names to go into the system. And wondered if that was all he or she did all day? 'Right.' Bristow went on.'We're delving into his recent past on social media,' he said, 'with the assistance of DS Goodwin's mother and her friends from the village.'

Darke held up a printout he'd obviously taken off the internet of a posed publicity shot of a group back in their heyday. 'We're talking here about a bunch of people who never ever got things quite right. They were on the verge of the big time, they toured with a whole host of major artistes back in the late nineties but when it came to the elusive hit single it never quite happened. Wouldn't listen to management, went with the wrong producer so I'm told, made a hash of their first single making it all too fast by a long chalk. In fact one guy I spoke to reckons the best thing they ever did was a single made after their contract wasn't renewed. Only reached the demo stage alas.'

Darke sipped coffee Michelle had provided, to wet his lips as he looked down at his notes to continue. 'Let's start with the name. Rockapelt was said to be a 19th century word for a noisy person, and to be fair the group was loud. Except. The word is actually spelt with an A. Its rackapelt, but they changed one letter so it included the word rock. One thing they got right. Second mistake, they weren't a rock group as such, if anything they were R&B with a helping of heavy country at times. We're talking proper rhythm and blues not the inept silliness you get nowadays.'

'People reckon they had a number one, boss.'

'Hold on a minute,' said Darke and gestured the instruction. 'All the band members used their own names, but in good old rock and roll tradition this Alerick Howard Keating-Price the lead guitarist decided to change his.' Darke then held the picture up again and pointed at one of the youths, at least a good six inches taller than the others. The sort where his centre of gravity is too far from his big feet so he can't dance, or do much more than just lope about. 'Didn't change his name to anything sensible, not to something like Rory Storm or Billy Fury which was all the vogue in 60s but to Rick Howard, an adaptation of his own name. The front man, would be the obvious one to seek out a groovy macho name and had the looks to go with it. He kept his own.' Darke pointed to the blonde and checked his notes again. 'First single into the charts at 47, then a week later it bombed out never to be seen again. But, a sleazy glossy mag had them in their chart at 20, but really it meant nothing, except upped their price.'

'Why does it matter he changed his name?' DC Michelle Cooper asked.

'Because these days after one change of name all that time ago he's now been using his wife's name as a way of wishing to be incognito at times, for some reason best known to himself,' Jake advised. 'What's that all about?'

'Alisha,' said Darke and nodded to her.

'From what I've been able to find out so far, sir,' said the team's new tall slim dusky brunette. 'He became a vegan donkey years ago before it became fashionable. When the group broke up he lived in a hippy commune for a year or two and was where he met his wife apparently.' She hesitated to read from her iPad 'She is Katherine Arbiter, the only daughter of Lord Arbiter or... Gregory Marmaduke St John Arbiter to be precise,' brought about chuckling.

'Certainly go in for odd ball names eh?'

'But,' DC Alisha O'Neill went on. 'When they first met she was years younger than him. Too young in fact and got hitched years later. They lived in Gorgie Hall,' she continued reading from her monitor. 'I say lived because she walked out about eighteen months or so ago and story is she went to Italy to live with a young lover. Keating-Price was living there with the one the media can't get enough of. Bryony Furneaux. Her odd name comes from a French background.' She stopped to just sip her coffee. 'According to social media they have a gardener and a cleaner and the web calls her a socialite at best. Think I should mention at this point how they have never married because apparently Keating-Price and his wife have never divorced.' She looked up from her screen. 'I'm now hunting down where this Furneaux woman popped up from. Two or three versions of events are circulating.' The dark boss went to speak. 'Just a warning, sir. This Furneaux woman is a social media celebrity, spouting and blogging to millions of followers on Twitter, YouTube and the rest. So, we need to be careful. Proceed with caution.'

Jake Goodwin was sat there pondering coincidences. His own mother is French from the Dordogne. Newish boss Bristow's mother owns a vineyard over there and now there was this Furneaux allegedly with French connections.

'Thank you, appreciate that.' To Darke that was exactly why Alisha O'Neill had been introduced to the team with her serious insight into all aspects of social media. 'Anybody here ever heard of him before his body was found?' Darke looked around the room.

'Of course...' said Nicky Scoley.

'Ah. But what about as Rick Howard, or using his wife's name Arbiter,' pulled her up short.

'Only the climate change one using his proper name. Others are news to me,' said DC Jamie Hedley. 'On the radio spouting about the end of the earth if I don't put my cardboard in the right bin.'

'To know how a man died,' said Bristow. 'First you need to know how he lived,' he said stopped and shook his head. 'Except in this case not only do we know, so does everybody else.' Nicky Scoley looked across at Jake.

'That surely is their big problem. Stuff they spout and way they protest means people finish up making remarks like Jamie's just done,' was Nicky Scoley's next contribution. 'When they should spend their time getting the message across not creating havoc so we all turn off.'

'Most people I know have no idea what biodiversity means, probably because it's not on Tik-Tok or Netflix,' Michelle offered.

Jake knew full well who he was, according to his mother and agreed with Nicky's version.

'That's exactly the issue,' Darke confirmed. 'But in his defence I do have to say he was not as far as I'm aware breaking the law and causing untold damage and chaos on the roads, outside factories like some do. Nor was he responsible for all the rail strikes. Climbing up bridges. Being fined and jailed in some cases seems to have little effect. But then the majority involved have more money than sense. And probably no job.' He looked around. 'Maybe, just maybe this'll bring them to their senses.'

'Knew there was somebody around those parts had written a hit song,' Jake smirked. 'But I couldn't have told you his name or he was the environmentalist chappie.'

'Going back to his real name would have been enough.'

'Can I just say,' said Michelle Cooper interrupting. 'No talk of notorious drug induced loud parties, in fact quite the reverse apparently, according to the locals. Keep themselves very much to themselves and neither of them need to work apparently.'

'We're talking nineties,' Darke went back to his favourite subject. 'We're talking Guns N' Roses, U2 and Dire Straits and record companies splashing out money on the next big thing and then of course wanting to get their money back. They reckon back then the major labels needed to sell a few thousand product to get into profit, and one way of doing it was to release big UK hits abroad with a lesser known artiste on the B side in an attempt to recoup their initial outlay for the smaller artiste.'

Somehow the Detective Superintendent's image belied the man behind it. Not for him some quirky odd-ball hobby such as photographing sundials or collecting jars of marmalade as some do. Whenever anybody accepted a lift in his car the blast would still catch passengers by surprise. No Mozart, Haydn or even Britten for him.

The moment Darke slipped in his ignition key the stereo racked up and sound hit hard with progressive rock forcing the speakers to shake, the bass thumping powerfully through a passenger's body.

'How did they compare with somebody like Metallica?' big Jamie asked.

'They didn't,' he said with a grin. 'Having said that we're talking about the beginning of the end for classic rock, we're looking at the last decade before the utter pap and rap came in. We're now of course in an era where people are producing less than average product they're trying to sell to people who don't buy records. Like trying to sell beef steak to vegans. We've almost made nil point at the Eurovision our standard. Like coming up with a brand spanking new sandwich you can't sell because people don't eat bread; and the reason people won't eat bread is because the manufacturers created tasteless rubbish.'

'What happened to…them, with the B side business?' Michelle Cooper was curious to know.

'It happened to the song written by Rick Howard as he called himself then. A number one by another group sold over a million in the States and yellowbelly Rockapelt with *Sheer Delight* were on the B side.' Darke shrugged. 'What they did back then as a promotion tool.'

'And he made a few bob?'

'A few grand. A great deal more than the other members of the group because he also wrote it.'

'Money is a regular motive,' Bristow slid in.

'Not over much,' Darke chuntered. 'Few grand back in the nineties. How much is left now?'

'Doesn't sound as if he needs any now.'

'Don't prog rock and marijuana always go hand in hand?' was not the cleverest thing for Jamie to ask him.

'Speak for yourself,' said Darke instantly. 'And they were not prog rock. Better than we're likely to get these days of course,'

Nicky prayed he wasn't about to go off on one about modern music yet again. 'What was it I heard on the radio this week? Some bunch of no-hopers were said to be,' he waited a moment. 'Dub-soul romantics with integration of samples and beats, on their new album.' He laughed. 'Apart from such utter bilge, it turns out their sound is slightly worse than garbage...'

'What happened to the rest of the group?' Bristow rushed in to stop him.

'I've got people checking for me,' said Darke after another drink. 'All I've come up with so far is one lives in Nottingham, but not sure which as yet, the drummer finished up as a self-employed bricklayer and a big mouth and Nathan Tyson the singer the only one with a grammar school education has been running a fairly successful chain of estate agents for a good few years. My secretary's checking for me, but it's most probably one of those all done on line these days like those *Purple Bricks* people.'

DS Nicky Scoley sat quietly wondering why the Darke boss felt he always had to mention irrelevant nonsense about one going to grammar school. Old boss Inga Larsson would have told her it was the British obsession with class.

'Can I just say,' was Jake. 'Appreciate the help my mother has given, but please remember all the stuff I've got is really no more than just village chit chat, volunteer-run community shop gossip.'

'None of this explains why anyone would want to murder an environmentalist, and leave him in that state. Except nobody's safe these days. That wildlife bloke Packham has suffered arson attacks and all sorts from people unhappy he wants the Royal Family to turn their thousands of acres wild, handing them over to beaver and suchlike. Rather than hunting, grouse shooting and deer stalking.'

'Been on the telly again about too many deer, suggesting Lynx be introduced to cut the numbers.'

'But, having said that,' the DS continued. 'According to my mum he could be a real nasty piece of work forever spouting in the community shop about them daring to sell pork sausages or demanding to know where fresh raspberries have come from. How many miles the carrots have had to travel. She reckons a few years back he was in there having a right go about David Attenborough, about him being a hypocrite because of the carbon footprint he causes by flying all over the world for the telly and giving lectures on climate change.' He looked down at his notes. 'More than one mention on the web, lists him as having links to eco-terrorism but it's the climate change business he can quickly bore you to death with apparently.'

Darke stood up and smiling to himself made his way to the door. 'He'd say no to a Big Mac but offer him weed and he's all for it,' masking a face as he smiled. 'Despite that, fourth estate will be onto this in no time, so be warned,' he said. 'Local boy makes good be just right for the *Leader*. Eat more greens'll please the farmer boys,' and he was gone.

'Not sure anything would please that David Herring idiot. What's the betting Sandy's still getting an earful this morning.'

'Fourth estate?' Alisha had to ask Jake quietly.

'Media, press, newspapers,' still meant she was none the wiser.

'This could well be high profile,' said Bristow. 'Spiking an unhealthy interest from the media. So team, we don't rest until we find his killer. Understood?'

'Except as yet we have so little to go on. And PM results?' he asked the DI.

'Today I'm told, but tox and histology will take a good few days of course, so we need to venture down a different path. Starting with a visit to Gorgie Hall and taking this opportunity to poke our noses into all his, "we don't inherit the earth from our ancestors we borrow it from our children" business.'

'Hang on, hang on guv,' was Jake Goodwin. 'Have I missed something? We're talking here about the possibility of Novichok and ionizing radiation in the same breath as talking to a cheep skate private eye.'

'I'm not asking you to interview him,' he grinned. 'Not yet anyway.'

4

Gorgie Hall like so many big old houses was the sort of place Jake Goodwin always knew existed, but he'd never actually had any reason or inclination to visit.

He and Sally had never been the sort to spend their precious free time together wandering aimlessly around people's homes full of illgotten gains as some folk do. Jealously peering up at paintings of scurrilous ancestors and walking in defined roped off areas and stopping off for weak tea in silly dainty cups and a badly baked and scandalously priced cream scone.

Added to which, there was no way they'd demand Tyler suffer for an hour or two. Except he'd probably enjoy a jam doughnut in the cafe.

Whereas most people count their reception rooms as two or if you're very lucky on three single fingers, this Hall looked as though they counted theirs in dozens. When he was still living at home Goodwin's family had lived in Western Avenue in the city, not out in the village where his parents now resided happily. Life back then had been in line with the kitchen, two reception rooms, three bedrooms and bathroom norm of the urban semi.

Offer of early retirement, enhanced big lump sum and pension had suited Reg and Celeste Goodwin down to the ground and a move to escape into the country appealed to them both. Well away from the hustle and bustle of an increasingly tumbledown society.

Big wrought iron gates were already open with weeds and long grass giving the impression they had been that way for a very long time. Immaculate dry stone walls cither side must have taken some building. Such a pity so much was hidden by unkempt sturdy thick sycamores and bushes was his first impression. When Nicky Scoley under Jake's instructions pulled off the road from the village, it was to take them along a lengthy meandering narrow drive through between beech and sycamore close to the road, then they grew less abundant before a bunch of huge oak trees with their canopy blotting out the weak sun and then all of a sudden they came out into the brighter light and a huge swathe of grassland clearing.

As he and DS Scoley appeared from between the last two oaks there it was Gorgie Hall in full view on a rise above and beyond. A massive tired looking neo-Georgian house flanked with regimental cypresses and glorious banks of shrubs masking almost everything beyond. The sheer size gave the Hall an air of class, privilege and of money, together with responsibility.

All set in acres and acres of rolling countryside off to their left, with an unmistakable huge wind turbine to the rear.

The driveway finally opened out into a parking area in front of the big house with just one car parked. It was an imposing property built well before there were cars to fill that designated space.

'How the other half live, eh?'

There was no sign of life save for the one car. Jake said 'Hybrid's a surprise,' as they walked past. No people, no hint of movement and no lights they could see inside. A huge pair of oak doors fronted by three stone steps and framed by a pillar each side. An echoing hefty knock on the wooden door seemed a pointless exercise, but Jake gave it a good thumping before both he and Nicky just stood back and waited. Nothing.

It was all very much *Downton Abbey* based on servants below stairs doffing their dirty caps, slaving away for the rich owners and their ungrateful friends, for a pittance. Nicky wondered if anything had changed.

Was it surprising under the circumstances? This Bryony Furneaux was a young blonde full-breasted beautiful woman, who dusky Alisha O'Neill had provided the whole team with an opportunity to view on her PC.

The Family Liaison officer tasked with informing her of Alerick Keating-Price's untimely death in a field, had admitted being incapable of contacting anybody. She had been replaced by two Response officers in a decal liveried Volvo who had proved more successful in discovering the lady of the house.

'Excuse me!' Goodwin heard as he gazed up into the windows for signs of life and spun round and saw a woman traipsing around the corner of the house in their direction. He and Nicky made their way towards her.

'Ms Furneaux?' she hoped.

'Who's asking?' was to DS Goodwin suspiciously abrupt. She looked at the pair with a cool, clear and disinterested gaze.

'Good afternoon,' said the detective and the pair set about making their introductions with warrant cards apiece.

Time for the pair to go through the laid down procedure for dealing initially with bereaved relatives.

There was a degree of incongruity about her get-up. The jacket looked more Primark than Barbour, yet the tight jeans probably cost more than most people earn in a week.

She appeared not to bat an eyelid, simply turned and gestured for them to follow her back around the side of the house and with her striding away she led them a fair way between old stables, across a yard and eventually through a small copse to an old stone brick built rundown cottage set some way back. Grubby weather-beaten walls and mossy flagstone roof tiles in need of attention. Jake imagined it to be the sort of ghostly place where the stairs would creak. Next door there were virtually derelict outhouses which could at one time have been home to pigs, sheep or pretty much anything.

The building they approached was decidedly scruffy but set against the area around and about at least it had not been given over to the cultivation of weeds. This woman most probably resided in this out of sight cottage, to hide from the common people, the plebs.

'Here we are,' this Furneaux woman said as she walked in the front door, kicked off her wellies and held the door open. Scoley and Goodwin decided to remove their shoes and then followed her through into an old country kitchen. There was the delicious aroma of freshly baked swirling around to tempt the taste buds. Before he fully entered Jake had glanced back to notice the big house was not visible from where they were by then.

'I'm sorry we have to do this Ms Furneaux...'

'Bryony,' was a pleasant surprise for the pair. 'And you are?'

'Detective Sergeant Nicola Scoley,' the blonde repeated what she'd said previously, as the woman gestured for them to both pull out bentwood chairs and sit at the sturdy well-worn scrubbed wooden table. 'As I was saying, we apologize for our intrusion at a time like this, but under the...'

'Tea, coffee?' she was asked which brought Nicky up short, suggesting the poor woman simply wished to avoid the subject.

'Coffee please,' Nicky responded. *Don't suppose there's any chance of a double shot skinny latte?*

Her hair was simply a cascade of mingled shades of brown. Unless the DS was much mistaken the drinks were likely to be that incorrigible vegan silliness she expected. No matching twin set or mandatory pearls for this beauty and Scoley guessed by her body language and calm exterior she was not at all surprised to see them.

Her slender shape, immaculate facial features told Nicky she must be somewhere around thirty at the very most. Getting on for a three decades younger than Keating-Price.

Despite how she was dressed in the image of an organic-gardener Bryony was elegant and calm. Too calm possibly under the circumstances, but Scoley only had what she'd read in the society pages of magazines at the dentist to go on. Always all about her support and absolute devotion to her partner.

'Make it two please,' was Jake Goodwin.

Even the shirt was not a basic Next offering. It was the image of somebody they'd disturbed from working in the extensive garden, yet it was almost a contrived look of the sort the fashion industry are likely to deck a reality 'star' out in.

Any lingering suggestion from some internet trolls about this Bryony Furneaux wrecking Keating–Price's first marriage badly enough for Katherine to disappear to Italy or goodness knows where, would now end. Public opinion as they sat there was already getting up a head of steam to swing hastily in her favour. Women like the one with her back to them making coffee Scoley knew, are very adept at wringing volumes of piteousness from tragedy.

How often had Scoley pushed her way through the no tweed, no pearls style and costly make-up to discover nothing underneath? Not in this case she bet herself.

'Good choice,' said Bryony and turned away. 'Can I just say,' she said unhooking two cups from under a cupboard. 'I'm really not into all this grieving business, sorry just can't be doing with it. Always wonder how women got so wishy washy?' She turned to look at Scoley. 'Surely from an early age every one of us knows we will eventually die. In my case I've had enough years knowing life will pan out with the death guarantee at the end. For almost as long I knew about my fate the same was true about Alerick. One day he would die, so what is the point of grief, when something you know damn well is going to happen, comes to fruition? Sorry, not got time for all these insipid attitudes, when so much work needs to be done. Business we get of some folk laying down bunches of flowers for people they don't know without even removing cellophane, I see as a horridly offensive gesture. Same with dopes blubbing on television news. Sorry,' and this busty silky haired lovely was back to the task in hand, filling her very old and battered metal kettle and getting on with making coffee in three chunky tin mugs as the police officers sat in silence, looking at each other with confused gestures.

Nicky Scoley couldn't imagine this female would be the sort with enough confidence to use such utensils for visitors as the norm. Glasses from Poundland and ill-matching crockery. Then it dawned on her. This was all very much Katherine's world.

The woman boiling a kettle in that ramshackle cottage of sorts was younger and most certainly fresher than her predecessor. Katherine Arbiter had birth class rather than the bought-in version and Nicky wondered if this tea lady had any idea what that meant in some quarters.

In these situations Goodwin knew from experience the grieving one can become distant, almost disengaged, but not in her case. This woman was remaining as dispassionate as possible, and to Scoley this was a great example of the British stiff upper lip even though half-French Jake would remind her of the woman's family tree.

At this stage experienced Goodwin would expect the journey of grief for Furneaux to have only just begun, but doubted whether it ever actually would.

'You always lived over here?' Goodwin checked for something to break the ugly silence. Bryony explained how Alerick had lived in the cottage since his wife had moved out rather than waste energy lighting and heating such a huge monstrosity. The room smelt musty and stale. Perhaps he decided it was food remnants he could smell or was it just odd-ball vegan delights?

'Your…' Scoley almost said husband, but somehow stopped herself. 'Partner. Just out of interest, did he have any enemies that you know of? Received threats of any kind maybe?'

'Plenty of cranks obviously including one previous President of the United States who shall remain anonymous and a number of socialist crackpots. Not what you'd call enemies as such, just people who cannot give of their time. Helping the environment, doing our level best to save the world for future generations rather than heaping more and more money on top of their ill-gotten gains.'

'President of the United States?' Goodwin had to query.

'That Trump clown you remember, said climate change was a hoax at one time I do believe. That is of course, if you can believe anything you hear on the news these days. You watch it at all?'

'Headlines,' said Goodwin.

'Covid of course had the same set of intellectual dopes saying some thing about the campaign to vaccinate everyone rather than just an elderly few in care homes was an extraordinary case of mission creep in political history.'

'You think people would actually attack Alerick because of his environmental beliefs?' seemed implausible but Scoley asked before the woman went off on one again.

Nicky Scoley was pleased with the interaction when she knew by what Jake had said some of the local born and breds in the village would if they still wore them, doff their caps or curtsey to this woman. Just the way they'd been taught for generations tending not to greet frim folks too earnestly. Even so, Nicky was in no doubt in overall terms the locals would be good people.

They'd not be happy with the confident, educated movers and shakers the media are adapt at calling new arrivals. Determined to change the character of the village and ride rough-shod over centuries of history. Stop the church bells ringing and cockerel crowing to ensure their hungover Sunday mornings are not disturbed

'My partner was a grassroots activist as well as being a foremost social and economic conservationalist. Alerick had no time for corporate dominated politics where the alcohol lobby holds greater sway than those favouring the basics of human life such as clean water for millions of desperate children.'

Bryony ironically poured boiling water into all three mugs as she went on. 'In Alerick's world there would be no fossil fuels. Have it replaced almost overnight by renewable energy, the energy given to us by our Lord. He was always campaigning for sustained and organized resistance to the overpowering corporate control of our lives.' She turned to plonk a milk container onto the table.

Scoley who smiled internally when noticing it was a plastic bottle, had come across all this clean food business with nonsense like alkaline eating and talk of dairy being a hate figure in some people's minds.

Jake was still interested in Furneaux as a woman as a human being. Her clipped accent had come from her mother's knee or drummed into her at Alma mater.

'Have you any idea who may have done this?' Goodwin tried.

A surprising 'Hashtag how would I?' was quite unnecessary.

Needing to change the subject. 'Do you have family to be with you at this time, children maybe?' Scoley tried as she struggled to remember whether or not normal semi-skimmed milk was vegetarian.

'I'm sorry...detective, but there really are far too many people in this world of ours already,' and the DS had to suffer another tirade. 'Millions and millions of people we cannot feed. Every time you walk through somewhere like Lincoln there they are. The scruffy unwashed pushing huge great prams as if it's the only thing they've not ticked a box for this year.' The woman then began an audacious mimic: 'I see her at number eight's got her fourth like, fink it's time we had a shag for another Wayne an' that.'

Jake was well pleased his drink had not arrived at his mouth as spluttering over such an audacious outburst, would not have gone down well.

'I take it you have no children?' Nicky Scoley had no idea how she'd said it without a chuckle.

'Certainly not,' Arbiter tossed back. 'We put as little strain on our damaged environment as is possible,' she said as she turned to pick up a patterned tin mug to place it on the table. 'That's what comes of allowing people to be selfish. Must have the big television, the ghastly new diesel guzzling huge car, what next oh yes,' she grinned. *And a plastic milk container*, Nicky wanted to add. The tin mug put in front of Nicky had a Yes I Get Enough Protein slogan in red. Then one for Jake saying King Of the Allotment and pictures of gardening tools. 'Time for another sprog the world really cannot afford, rather than spending their money on solar power. Then taking their damn kids off on a plane in term time even during that awful pandemic. Selfish people make me so angry.' She sighed and shook her head. 'What is it these idiots don't understand?'

By choosing to talk about everything and anything but her dead partner was similar to previous meetings with close relatives of the recently killed, Nicky usually put down to shock and grief reaction.

Not in this woman's case it wasn't. There were absolutely no signs of anguish, certainly not total misery or of somebody suffering inconsolable distress. Far from it.

DS Scoley started talking again. 'Would you have liked a family?'

'I don't have a dog, I never had a guinea pig nor do I have a goldfish and I don't have brats.' The detective prayed when she added a small plop of milk and then lifted the white tin mug up to her lips, but lowered it without taking a sip. It was cow's milk, and not anything untoward like from a goat she had imagined it could be. Probably organic she'd realized which meant pricey. 'Yes there are many things I don't have in my life, but jealousy is not something I ever suffer from. However I have had a great deal of which I am truly proud. One of those was Alerick'

DS Scoley ignored it. She'd dealt with witnesses and family members a great deal more annoying than this woman on many occasions. Could be she had no real idea how to be a supporting partner and it was quite possible she'd done the woman a disservice. Maybe, just maybe the milk was purer than the stock supermarket stuff and the plastic had been simply been an oversight and those bamboo milk jugs they advertise was her norm.

As she was speaking Nicky Scoley took the opportunity just to glance around the kitchen of this stone clad flagstone floored cottage without making it too obvious. It was small and very cosy, be the sort of place she and Connor would thoroughly enjoy as a holiday cottage. No lazy blinds and chintz in sight. No

Forever Dewdrop matt emulsion and pristine glittery cushions all plumped up and crease free.

A place to live day-to-day though was something else, not quite her cup of tea without a proper tour and nothing she could see was ever likely to be the work of a skilled artisan.

They then waited for Bryony to deliver another tin mug to the table before lowering herself onto a chair opposite Nicky as she wondered how tin mugs were related to this vegan lifestyle. Wouldn't wood be better for the environment or was that too much about chopping down trees in the Amazon?

The blonde DS had seen no signs so far of the modern ignorance of some. Such as those who quaff water from a bottle, then apologize with *"Sorry, do you water?"* Who invents such garbage she always wanted to know in order she can furnish them with a good slapping given half a chance? Fortunately this woman obviously came from better stock than to take on such internet nonsense.

'Do you ever use the big house?' Goodwin tried once he'd added a spot of milk and sipped his hot coffee. This woman had the smug look of a Tory constituency party committee member about her. The type who'd voted for that Liz Truss failure. He guessed she'd never turn up there in her Country Casuals attire, plastered in bespoke make-up, pearls and twin-set. Everything Jake's dear mother Celeste down in the village despised with good reason.

'There is an ancient Arbiter covenant set up by one of his wife's ancestors. Generations back Lord Arbiter I think it was, which stipulates who is required to retain the house and land.'

'How did Alerick feel about it?'

'The house, well everything, is to be left to his wife alone in trust being the last in the Arbiter line, and Alerick did not believe in handing down worldly goods. He actually owned nothing whatsoever except perhaps the clothes he stood up in. So in truth it meant nothing to him, had no qualms about irritable matters like pervasive possessions.'

'This cottage is an essential ingredient of what she owns, I take it?' Goodwin checked as Nicky realized this Alerick had probably not been bumped off for his money. Bryony nodded, then drank her coffee. *When his missus walks back in she can kick you out.*

Nicky Scoley was pleased there was no silliness like copper saucepans hanging from the ceiling by a fish hook or a brass hunting horn strapped to a wall some consider fashionable. Set against it was the fact the room was untidy and layers of paint were peeling.

'Alerick always felt the world was too obsessed and preoccupied with possessions and he had always been quite the opposite, which to a certain extent I admired him for. Just because the chappie down the road thinks a 75" television is some sort of status symbol, doesn't mean we all have to be so crass in the manner in which our mind implores us to show off. I'm sorry, people we mix with would never be impressed by such debauched shoddiness.' She took another good sip. 'People we socialize with are more concerned homelessness exists right alongside empty property the length and breadth of this nation of ours. We advocate fairness for all and economic and ecological justice and respect. Alerick was never controlled by the three things so many people live by. Money, money and the greed to fuel it.'

Said somebody with what two hundred metres away was quite possibly a huge empty property dozens of people could live in. This don't do as I do, do as I say attitude really annoyed Jake, but biting his tongue at that juncture was something he got used to with the job.

'What else was Alerick involved in?' Detective Sergeant Goodwin posed. 'Did he belong to any local groups or organizations?'

This woman intrigued Nicky Scoley. Not all women are overly obsessed by their looks she knew, with Jake's Sally only using make-up for high days and holidays and frequently not even then. Like so many of her kind this Bryony would tell you she had more important aspects to her life.

Scoley as yet had not tried the dark coffee, but guessed a degree of this spouting had a liberal dollop of re-hashed New Age half-truths and conspiracy theories about it, but the woman was not finished by a long chalk.

'He was an excellent debater of course,' was not quite what Goodwin meant and didn't answer his question. 'How I first met him. He was guest speaker at a...' she grinned. 'A vegan dinner I went to with my parents. Sort of turning point in my life. Living at home I obviously had to obey all the vegan traits, but to be fair

I'm a real cheese and wine person, so it was never a good fit. Then just after his wife left he was a weekend guest at my uncle's farm.' she grimaced. 'The rest as they say is all across those beastly tabloids.'

'How did Alerick feel about you eating real cheese and drinking wine?'

'The cow didn't die as a result of it. With wine of course it needs to be unrefined and unfiltered to comply although my parents still avoid it, but as most wine producers use sterile filters it's vegan.'

To Nicky she was spouting the sort of nonsense to make her angry. She could vividly remember when some skinny pale vegan blogger was allowed to win some obscure Porridge Making Competition by not making proper porridge. She concocted what in effect were deep fried balls of risotto using oats, mushrooms she'd picked wild and vegan cheese.

Scoley was trying hard to discover a way back to the death of Furneaux's partner, but the woman was on a roll. 'Solar and on-shore wind power has its detractors unfortunately, but they'd not win a debate with my Alerick. They are adding more to the global economy than shale oil production did at one time. We need these to begin bending the emissions curve, is what Alerick would tell you if he were here. We need to scale up to the mass market and grow customer acceptance.'

She went on to describe the characteristic instinct fostered by capitalism of seeking to acquire more and more. Billionaires doing their utmost to hoard more and more to increase their personal wealth often admired by the insanely jealous who themselves have next to nothing.

Nicky Scoley was aware how in some small communities there can be a poisonous atmosphere based upon a torrid mix of nasty gossip and prejudice. She knew from what Jake had already mentioned, tongues in the local village would be wagging about the death of Keating-Price and there'd be more than one or two locals spreading rumours about how the mighty had fallen, More than likely starting with Herring the farmer.

5

'Just out of interest have you had a visit from a private detective?' DS Jake Goodwin asked the Furneaux female. The coffee Scoley tried was unnecessarily bitter and certainly unusual but not one she'd want on any sort of regular basis. She was certainly not at all sure Craig Darke their in-house coffee aficionado would approve.

'No,' introduced a slight chuckle. 'Advantage of living round here. I can easily ignore the door knockers, hawkers and peddlers.' *But not the dopes on Twitter.*

'How come you spotted us?' Goodwin asked.

'Heard you. Just out mushrooming actually. After those two very nice policemen found me out in the garden, I knew officialdom would come calling so when I was out back I heard a car, had a sneaky peep and you looked official.'

'And the media?'

'Gutter press?' she chuckled. 'No,' she said. 'And woe betide them if they try.' This was most certainly not home to velvet monogrammed curtains, ornamental clocks and silver candlesticks. Rough and ready in estate agent speak. Very rough.

Scoley became serious. 'I'm afraid as in any case of unexplained death, there will need to be a post mortem, and it may be a while before we are able to release your Alerick. I'm afraid Bryony, we'll need you to identify the body.'

'My solicitor will deal with it,' she said abruptly.

'We would prefer…'

'I want to remember the Alerick I knew. End of. Please understand if you will, my solicitor will deal with all that side of things.' She sipped her coffee. 'What I pay him for after all,' she then downed at least half of her mug in one foul swoop to give herself a caffeine boost. 'It will be a very private funeral. Absolutely no commercialization of cars polluting the atmosphere and ornate coffin, not held in the cradle of those religions of hate based on myth with a seedy vicar in residence. My Alerick will be buried here in our grounds along with many of the Hall's ancestors. His wishes are specific, but basically it will in essence be a green burial with a wicker biodegradable casket.'

Scoley picked up on what she'd said if there were indeed ancestors buried in the grounds. Unless she was very much mistaken they'd be the forebears of his wife Katherine Arbiter. Plus Lord Arbiter or another one she couldn't for the life of her remember, from the murder board back at Central.

'Could you please ask your solicitor to make arrangements to identify the body for us?' Goodwin asked, and this woman just nodded as if it were an everyday occurrence.

'Your coffee's unusual,' Scoley fibbed. She wondered what the odds were on this woman chomping on a hefty wedge of époisses after slurping down oxtail soup on the quiet with her organic man now out of the way. Or what was to stop the likes of this elegant young woman hunting down a back street kebab shop with her partner a gonner and still claiming vegan rights?

Goodwin took the opportunity to switch his focus away from the Furneaux woman to scan the room without moving his head.

'So glad you like it,' she came back complete with a disingenuous smile.

Nicky had been aware early on how this Bryony appeared to have no desire to discuss the subject of Alerick's death right then, and the circumstances surrounding it. Talk about anything and everything was not unusual. No tears as yet though, and a chat about crap coffee was her route of choice.

'In general terms Secondary Alliance coffee. We always follow the environmental, social and ecological guidelines set for sustainable agriculture.' *Not to my taste* Scoley wanted to tell her. Not go down at all well with two pals she met up with in Starbucks now and again. Enough already and fortunately Jake came to her rescue.

'Can we ask about the pop group?' he posed. The look he received suggested she was nowhere near his wavelength. 'Rockapelt'

'Dear me,' she sighed and shook her head. 'Why on earth would they have anything to do with all this business?'

The scenario would move on, once MIT had gathered more data, produced more forensics to point them in the right direction and had completed background checks. Nicky knew from experience how then it would be a much better time to fire questions at the woman if need be.

To her sort, image was everything, as it was to the millions of dunderheads following her every word and action on social media. Revelling in the knowledge the death of Alerick would keep her in the limelight for a good while.

'Rockapelt,' Jake reminded. 'Part of his life, his past history might I suggest?'

'We've moved on I'm afraid. Dear me.'

'Was he still in contact with other band members?'

'Goodness me no,' she chuckled. 'Whatever gave you such an idea?'

'Just wondered,' Scoley queried. 'Part of his life. We have a requirement to look at every aspect of your partner's past under the circumstances.' Furneaux's look said she could not fathom the reasoning. Jake Goodwin still had a head full of questions to ask. 'You didn't report your partner missing. Any reason why?'

'Missing?' she threw back and smiled. 'What d'you take us for? D'you seriously think he was at my beck and call all the time? Had to ask my permission to get up from the table to go out? Had a time to be home like some naughty runny-nosed kiddy?' she chuckled. 'Wilberforce it was I think who got rid of slavery.'

'But you must...'

'We don't all want to be shackled to men. Certainly not in this day and age, not that a Keating-Price would ever wish me to be. Always remember, controlling is the basis of domestic violence.'

'But you must have,' Scoley tried again. 'Some idea what he was doing, where he was going maybe?'

The DS swore under her breath as there was so much somebody needed to say to this woman, but her role in life meant it could not be her. Not right there and then anyway.

'Not that sort of relationship,' said this grinning Bryony with the fine bone structure, as she held her arms out wide. 'You're not on one of those dreadful sink estates now you know,' and allowed her hands to plop down into her lap as she cultured a look of utter disdain.

'So, when did you actually realize something was amiss?' Goodwin queried. While Scoley was disgusted by her instinctive prejudice.

'Didn't,' she frowned. 'Why would I?' She blew out a breath of annoyance. 'Thought I'd already covered this sort of thing. We facetimed quite often.'

'I'm sorry,' DS Goodwin said. 'Each day, when you were home you mean?'

'No.'

'But at some point you must have realized you hadn't seen him.'

She shrugged. 'Probably when those police people called.' Something was wrong. It immediately struck Nicky how this increasingly obnoxious woman might now be claiming to have spoken to Family Liaison. The very people failing to gain access.

'You spoke to our Family Liaison?'

This blonde Bryony Furneaux made a face, shook her head slightly and her hair swayed gently. 'No.' made no sense. 'Do I look as though I need a babysitter?' she considered amusing.

'His car,' said Goodwin, to switch emphasis. 'Did Alerick take his car?'

'How would I know?'

'Is it missing?'

'You tell me.'

'What make is it?'

'One of those Land Rover things is it?'

Jake Goodwin was surprised at her admission. When he had expected some peculiar all electric he'd never heard of. Colour and model Jake guessed was a waste of time. Her phrase was to him particularly annoying. 'Do you have the registration documents to hand?' he asked. 'We didn't see a vehicle as we came in.'

'They'd be in the car I would suggest.'

'You saying he kept the car registration documents and things like insurance actually in the car?'

'Where else?' she grimaced.

Jake sighed to himself as he questioned the logic. Why do one trick ponies like this bozo Keating-Price get so uptight and obsessed about a subject yet just ignore the basics of their own vulnerability, was a question he often asked.

Chances are this dopey sod would carry his driving licence in his wallet. Means pickpocket would not only have access to his bank and credit cards, but could also prove he was who he claimed to be with full name, address and date of birth. Be what Sandy always calls bampots of the sort you see with a phone stuck in their back pocket.

'I'm sorry to say, we will need a buccal swab for DNA purposes,' made Furneaux frown. 'As you'll appreciate we need to eliminate your forensic features from all those our teams will have collected. If you'd pop in some time, just give us a call first if you wouldn't mind, or I could arrange for somebody to call.' Nicky Scoley expected a reaction. 'Just a quick wipe inside the mouth, only takes a couple of minutes.'

No reaction, no comment, just a sullen look. Jake Goodwin had by then made his mind up to bring this all to an end, when Nicky asked Furneaux about his phone she decided that was it.

Scoley knew her sort would take advantage of their largesse given half a chance. People like this Furneaux were not cultivating all this vegan and environmental business for no good reason unless it was her heart's desire to one day be stick thin. Never knowingly doing something for nothing was a sure bet. Knew that more than likely there was always a motive behind whatever she did, and more often than not it was money. The filthy lucre these types loved nearly as much as themselves.

She had to sit there while poor Jake was forced to persuade the woman to hand over her phone to allow him to get her number and then to scan down to find "Rick's" mobile number and have a quick peep to see who else was on it.

'One last question if you will? Do you have Katherine Arbiter's number or address maybe?'

'Why would I?'

'Did Alerick?'

'After the way she behaved?'

'Many couples although separated do keep in touch,' was answered with a slight shrug. 'Indeed unusual if they don't.'

The woman was being as obstreperous as she could and Inga knew there had to be a reason why, and was absolutely determined to discover the issues. She'd had her fill of her for now, but knew at some point she'd find a dank interview room and really set about her.

The Detective Sergeant was on her feet. 'Thank you,' Scoley said. 'We'll see ourselves out. It's been good talking to you,' she lied.

Outside as they strode purposefully to where they'd parked the car back up by the house if they could remember the way, Jake just stopped to look back to remind himself it was just a rough looking tired stone cottage nothing more, nothing less. If anything at a guess he reckoned it could have once been a piggery and looked too small for a milking parlour.

'Did you smell anything?' Jake asked casually. 'Always reminds me of musky treacle.'

'Hops. Smell I often get. So many smells in there, whole place needs a good blow through. Pleased there was none of that Del fry business.'

'Only what you'd expect I suppose, folk like her acting all fancy dan, then smoking a bit of weed on the sly.'

Jake was so good to bounce her ideas off.

Front door he'd noticed on the way in had flaking brown paint with the previous blue showing through in places. At one side it looked for all the world like a pigsty and the wire netting suggested a chicken coop but both lacked residents.

Back at the car Jake just looked up at the size of the place. 'What's the betting that's not insulated,' he chided. Back when so-called House Insulation Campaigners had caused traffic chaos blocking the M25 Jake knew it was the very same unruly mob once more attacking the public and a week later were chuntering about HS2.

'Always the same,' said Nicky looking from side to side. 'As per usual, do as I say not as I do.'

'Only people who suffer is the man in the street, or those trying to get to work. Folk desperate for a hospital appointment or at your wit's end to turn up on time for chemotherapy. Urban terrorists somebody called them.'

'Rich kids with nothing better to do. Guess he was seriously rich when his wife was about and seriously frugal.'

'What's the betting our friend Alerick was an antivaxxer?'

'Can't see him wanting to glue himself to a plane though, can you?'

'With people like him obsession with Eco is a form of addiction like gambling, chilli and alcohol.'

Perhaps Nicky wondered to herself sat beside him as he pulled away, a second opinion was required about the sweetness and light village where Jake's parents lived.

'My guess is,' she said to Jake. 'That's a lonely woman.'

'Think your guess is right.'

'But just because Alerick to some extent must have been a bore to live with. He'd endlessly demanded we all fly less, close airports, holiday within a mile of home or drive our electric cars to spend a fortnight in a tent. Is that any reason to kill him?'

'Surely electric cars are an issue. Coal fired or oil fired power stations to produce the electricity to run these foreign cars. No better than petrol or do I not understand?'

'Does anybody?'

'You know what some are like,' Jake responded. 'Stripped to the waist almost, at the airport. Flip-flops on, garish shorts, fish and chips and throwing pints down their throats is something he was hell bent on putting a stop to. Could for some be a very good reason indeed.'

'Jamie was telling me the boss had a word in his ear for taking the piss out of the climate change wally's like Keating.'

'And he's not here again today, when Inga would have loved someone like her.'

'A form of delegation by default. Think I've said it before but I worried he'd walk in and change everything. At least we're still doing it the Inga way, and with him living down near Grantham he's never likely to just pop in.'

'Great Gonerby,' Nicky corrected. 'Lives in the family home with his mother.' She had a quiet snigger. 'Copper I met on a course keeps in touch now and again. He was telling me.'

'Interesting.'

Jake drove on through the big trees to the road. 'What did you think of all that?' he asked Nicky. To his mind it'd not been the sort of place boasting a utility room or dressing rooms upstairs off the master, but no doubt the big house they'd passed had more than enough. It was never a farm he surmised or at least it hadn't the smell, mud and muck one associates.

'Very interesting,' said the blonde DS. 'All reeked of calm prosperity, hidden from the road and the locals. Yet up here within touching distance it's plainly obvious to me.'

'You'd not creep up on them for sure.'

'Should have told her she'd mistaken me for somebody who was in the slightest bit interested in where she gets her awful coffee from.'

'Everything she talked about was from Alerick's perspective. His beliefs, his opinions, he was the vegan, he had no money. Where does she stand on all this climate change business, is she happy living in a little dump of a place, riding a donkey and cart to market or whatever she does? When I asked her if she would have liked a family she didn't answer.'

'Control freak you thinking?'

'Vegan tree-hugger more like, but tin mugs bother me. Shouldn't they be wattle and daub?' She sighed softly. 'Nasty, lying…but for why?'

'That one was certainly different. Why else was our conversation about what her partner said and did, what he believed in, what he fought for? Why was there never any mention of *us*? What was all that facetime business?' Jake wondered out loud

'I'm never very happy dealing with the grieving relatives as you know, but now I'm not so sure. I found it quite unnerving her being the way she was. No crying, no bloodshot eyes, no face puffy through tears, no sodden handkerchief grasped in her paw and all the rest you normally get.'

'A distinct lack of questions about where and when is interesting.'

'What did one vegan say to another vegan?' Jake didn't bother to respond. 'We should not *meat* like this!'

'Very good,' he chuckled.

'What did you think of the way she looked?'

'Apart from why is somebody like her living in a hovel?'

'Furneaux herself, her look.'

'Good bone structure. Look quite glamorous all dolled up. Not at all what I'd expected. Creatures like her tend to follow a laid down procedure, but she certainly didn't.'

'Excuse the phrase, but was she the reason his wife buggered off?'

'Interesting thought,' said Jake as he pulled over and stopped the car in a layby. 'Press conference,' he reminded her as he turned on the radio. The pair sat there waiting and then went through needless introductions covering almost the life history of Keating-Price before they went over live. The pair sat there listening.

'What's going on?' Jake asked at the end and looked at his colleague.

'How d'you mean?'

'Question one. Where was Bristow? Question two, why Luke Stevens who knows next to nothing about it?'

'Is that a problem?' Nicky asked.

'In essence no. But, somebody as well known as Keating-Price found dead in a cabbage field with that note pinned to him. Our case is all over the papers, but he's not mentioned. Why didn't he pop in to the farm for ten minutes on Sunday on his way from home? Now, as the SIO, why was he not at the press conference?'

'He ever been to a crime scene?'

'Not here.'

'What about Grantham?'

'No idea, Could get Jamie to ask his pal down there.'

'He not like the sight of blood? He all box ticking admin based?'

'Darke wasn't and Inga certainly attended her fair share. Not at every one to be fair, but anything slightly odd she'd at least poke her nose in. Get the feel of it.'

'And this one's as odd as I've known.'

'This the Darke boss you think, making him take a back seat for some reason?'

'But why?' Nicky posed.

'When I was out there Sunday morning watching the cabbages grow, Darke rang me, asked for an update. Then wanted to know if I needed anything. I asked why Oliver'd not been near the place, and he chopped me off short.'

'That because you were questioning what he was doing?'

'Felt as though I wasn't allowed a voice. Anything I can help you with he said, then slammed the door. It's been a drip feed of all these bits and pieces since the guy arrived. Has he got a partner? Brothers, sisters? Why live alone most of the time down there?'

'Mother's house somebody said.'

'Mother's house not parents?'

Nicky shrugged her answer. 'Girls even asked me if he's gay.'

'Has he got any interests?' Jake asked. 'None we know about. Not taken any holiday since he's been with us is mighty odd.'

'Talking of odd. Had Davie Kemp, DI from Cambridge onto me week or two ago, asking if a chap called...Nugent had joined us.'

'Who's he?'

'DS he knew from way back. Carl, I'm pretty sure he said. Carl Nugent.'

6

Within minutes of returning to the Incident Room for Jake to collect DC Jamie Hedley and headed off out again, Nicky received a call from the Desk Sergeant. She was advised how while she'd been away, a Todd Wood had called. Saying he was seeking information on Rick Howard.

She stood in the DI's doorway and explained the call and who Wood was. "Wondered if you fancied poking your nose in?'

'Why not.'

TJ Private Investigation Services First Floor said the plastic nameplate on the door in Silver Street. DS Scoley had no need of signs or satnav to locate TJ. She knew from experience and previous visits exactly where she'd find the man they call Marmite almost to his face.

'Look what the cat dragged in,' came from Todd Wood after the pair had climbed the dirty stairs and been ushered through into the inner sanctum. The moment Scoley walked into Wood's crummy office although the smell had gathered pace, the stench of his aftershave and other potions slammed into their noses. The receptionist had followed her and DI Oliver Bristow in and started whimpering about how she'd tried to stop them, before Woody just dismissed her with a wave of his hand and Bristow closed the door behind her.

'First question,' said Scoley calmly as she plonked herself down on a saggy black leatherette chair without being offered. 'What are you doing knocking on doors asking about Rick Howard aka Alerick Keating-Price?'

'Which one d'you want first?' Wood quipped.

'Just answer the question,' said Scoley with Bristow stood with his back to the door trying to figure the source of the aroma.

'He's new,' Todd chuckled with a glance at the DI. 'Outside your bandwidth eh fella?'

'Tell you what,' said Bristow. 'We've got a very cozy interview room, how about you come with…'

'Shut up for God's sake!' Wood blew out a breath. 'When d'ya flog yer sense of humour? Hope yer got a bloody good price matey,' was typical of this smarmy and self-opinionated bag of wind.

'This is not a joke,' Oliver Bristow looked all about. 'But the same can't be said about this bloody place?' He wanted to ask what the smell was. He knew where from, just not what fragrance the pong was.

'Got your Beamer parked outside have you? What about yer villa in Madeira, and a hot tub? Got yoursen one yet?' Wood chuckled. 'Not on your crap pay, I bet. How many Michelin chefs d'you know personally eh? What was the last musical you saw on Broadway then...eh Mr Policeman?'

'I make do with a very prosperous vineyard in Alsace,' surprised even Nicky.

A hand went up from disconcerted Wood. 'Need to check with our client, sorry. Would like to help the long arm of the law as you know, but...'

'Please,' Scoley sighed. 'Don't come out with your usual bollocks for goodness sake. Just spit it out.' Bad body odour would be better than what the pair were wallowing in right there and then.

'Been sworn to secrecy, sorry missy. But there yer go.'

'Enough now,' said Nicky Scoley and pushed herself to her feet.

'No names. No pack drill, understand?' Wood said quickly to avoid what just might be next especially from this tall new guy he'd need to find out about

'Why'd you message us about him?'

'We've been hired by a big multi-national and it's all to do with a top secret product they plan to launch just before Christmas. I tell you and it'll be all round the cop shop and in the *Sun* tomorra before they bloody kick us into touch.'

'Are you linking Rick Howard and a multi-national?' Scoley grimaced as Wood nodded. 'Sorry but the two seriously don't go together,' the DS chuckled.

'Why the hell not?'

'From what I understand he hates them. Can't abide anything to do with big business. He and his woman are died in the wool environmentalists, vegans and all the rest of the tosh. Virgin,

Apple, Huawei, Google and stuff like nanotechnology are all an absolute scourge of the world as far as people like him are concerned. A complete anathema to the pair of them. Anyway why would such people want anything to do with somebody like him?'

'Look,' said Wood and leaned forward onto his desk pointing. 'Keep this to yourself for crissakes,' he said and looked up at DI Bristow momentarily. 'All to do with a song.'

'What song?' Scoley snorted. 'Look fella, if you're…'

'Shut up and listen!' Wood shot back. 'Molly!' he hollered rather than getting off his slumped backside. Bristow moved aside as they waited for the door to open and when it did this thing appeared.

'Yeh?' she just managed, chewing gum as she did so.

'What's the song called?'

'Wha' song?'

'The one we've been chasing Keating-Price for,' highlighted his exasperation.

'Oh him, yeah,' this Molly nodded. 'Thought you said it was hush-hush like. Don't breath a word and that.'

'Just tell me,' Wood insisted.

'Sheer Delight.'

'And why have you been knocking on folks' doors?' Bristow asked her, but Todd Wood answered instead.

'Their legal boys wrote to him and got no reply. Sent some flash git all the way up from down t'smoke and found nobody in, sent registered letters…nothing. Return to sender, is another song,' he thought was clever.

'So in utter desperation they called on you?' smiling Scoley queried with a huge grin. 'Be serious,' she chuckled.

'Hang on a tick. Not in bloody desperation,' Wood insisted.

'Are you asking us to find him for you? Got enough mispers of our own to deal with. Thought you were the detective.' Nicky Scoley turned to Molly with her face scrubbed clean she knew not to expect a Lancôme exponent but expected more than she saw. Torn jeans, nails all painted different colours, eyebrows shaved off and lips lathered in Dulux gloss. Particularly messy bright red hair which she knew had to be a wig. 'Thank you, that'll be all,' she gestured to the female to leave and Bristow opened the door wider for her and she made a face before sauntering out, chewing.

Despite her odd-ball look she was a slim, fit woman in her mid-twenties.

Bristow closed the door and again stood across it. 'Reason we've reacted and why I'm here,' Scoley said to Todd Wood then hesitated to create more effect. 'He's dead,' left the recipient with his mouth open. 'Alerick Keating-Price is no more. Like the proverbial parrot.'

'Shit!' was thrown out and mouth remained open.

'Unexplained death.'

'You're fuckin' joking man!'

'Be in the press in the morning I guess. Probably on line as we speak.'

'Crissakes how that happen?'

'PM and tox will take a while.'

'Bugger all to do with us matey,' was sharp. 'We've not bloody seen him. Hang on, hang on…'

'Did I say it was anything to do with you?' Bristow queried.

'You're not bloody pinning it on me matey, no fuckin' way.' he insisted loudly. 'We could'nt soddin' find him.'

'Somebody sure enough did,' said the DI.

'Why not ask his missus?'

'Heard that little madam of yours has been poking her nose round the village and we're looking into everything. So Todd, what else do you know about Rick Howard or whatever you want to call him? Which multi-national, the song, the whole works, let's have it all.' Scoley paused momentarily.

'Now!' Bristow shouted.

'Be that buggered then,' the smelly one sighed. 'Bloody hell,' he blew out a breath of frustration. 'Oh shit! All gone down the bloody plughole, that's for sure.'

'Bang goes the yacht eh?' Scoley just had to chuckle to herself enjoying the surprise packet of her DI.

'All I know is, it's a sugar free sweet tasting special drink for teens up to Millenials. With none of the sugar and additives they get all fussed about with obese kids and the like. Gonna be bloody huge and the advertising bods want to use his song in the adverts. On telly. In cinemas, on the net and we understand the record company's looking to release the single. Could be bloody massive.' He blew out a breath and shook his head. 'What's the chances that's all gone to buggery now? Bollocks!' and Todd Wood slammed a fist down on his desk.

'Why d'you say that?'

'They're calling the drink something from the song.'

'Such as?'

'Top secret. Could be absolute bliss,' Todd chuckled. 'This is an absolute delight,' he said slowly and deliberately. 'But I never told you, right? I'm in love, I'm in sheer bliss. Just imagine what they can do with song phrases like that.'

'And he wouldn't answer the door d'you say?' Scoley asked.

'About the size of it. Nor his new missus. Now there's a tart an' a half.' He sucked in his lips. 'You reckon the silly sod was already a gonner when Molly...?'

'Don't think so.' Scoley moved away. 'If the company turned up in their bloody great cars, there's no way he'd answer the door to them anyway. Absolutely not their scene at all. Chances are they live on grass sandwiches and quinoa on toast rubbish, don't even have a coffee machine. Heck of a rum place where they live too, let me tell you. Your lass with red hair'd be welcomed with open arms. Not.'

'Big house. Bloody massive Molly was saying.'

'You can say that again.' Nicky Scoley had no intention of putting the goon straight about where they *actually* lived. Knocking on the hall door was a waste of time as she and Jake had discovered.

Looking at Wood it reminded Nicky of the lengths some men are going to these days in the vain pursuit of physical perfection, hardly ever matched by any mental adequacy. No doubt for his image if nothing more he'd be in the gym first thing, walloping along like a lump of lard on a treadmill. Just so he could throw *when I was in me gym early doors* to impress the inadequates.

'Wonder where it leaves us eh?'

'Not a word,' said Nicky with a finger to her lips. 'I'm being serious now. Keep a lid on it.' She pointed to the door. 'Keep schtum about his death until its official and on the news or you'll be paying us a visit.'

'How bloody long?'

'Today. Evening news, tomorrow maybe, but post mortem bits'll be a while.' Scoley took a step closer. 'I'm being bloody serious.' she said pointing down.

51

'We should be working together more.'

'I agree,' said Bristow at the door. 'But you need to sort yourself out first. We may need to come back for your contacts about the song business.'

'Why are some blokes just complete arses?' Nicky asked walking down the High Street heading for the Cornhill and car park by the bus station.

'He always?' Bristow asked.

'You don't know the half of it. Him and Keating-Price are not exactly poles apart. Eating low carb and downing vegetable shakes they say is as unhealthy as salt and sugar, but if its image you're after like him, then you do just as your preening bible tells you.'

'Not sure what the smell was, but I reckon he'd bathed in the stuff.'

'Something with coconut I reckon. Bet it cost an arm and a leg. Weekly visits to the barber is too over the top to make any sense to most people. But an absolute must for Mr Marmite our metrosexual male there.' Nicky looked at her boss. 'He'll be all for this sickly drink. Probably shower in the stuff!'

'Marmite?'

'Typical gym bunny. You either love him or hate him and I read some place how this extreme grooming puts people like him at greater risk of STDs.'

'What?'

'Grooming the nether regions,' left Bristow looking perplexed.

'Sheer bliss eh?' Nicky chuckled.

'With any luck he'll drink himself! Coffee?' the bearded DI asked.

First time for everything, and as far as Nicky knew no other member of the team had been with the DI away from the confines of Lincoln central.

Over his black coffee, his remark about a vineyard had been explained to Nicky, with his mother having been left a vineyard in France by a distant relative. She told him about Jake speaking French having been brought up by his French mother Celeste. Without poking her nose in too obviously she had news for the team. At least he'd not admitted to a useless and unexpected daft hobby.

7

Not smarmy, not over eager, not drenched in his own charisma or any obnoxious overpowering lotion. Nathan Tyson appeared to be a good, attentive and welcoming host into his office.

When they'd entered the estate agency the pair of coppers had faced two suited and booted young men and one young woman in similarly coloured blue suits, sat at identical work stations peering at matching monitors. The young woman introduced herself as Cheryl and then ushered DSs Jake Goodwin and Nicky Scoley through to a glass encased office at the end where this Nathan Tyson was sat.

A bull-necked man in that he didn't have one. What struck Nicky first was, with his tie loose at the neck and top button undone she wondered how big his pale blue shirt collar must be if he could ever get it done up.

Her mother would regard such as an element towards being unkempt, but then she'd also not be happy with Bristow having a beard. Well trimmed and tidy it may be but Paula Scoley just saw them as scruffy. Probably why her brothers Jordan and Russell had not given into growing one when they were on trend.

He stood up to at least six foot proffering a chubby hand, but only to Jake she noticed.

With his dark grey suit jacket off, hanging on a hook beside his desk Nicky was quite taken by his shirt. Pale blue, but the cuffs and button-down collar were denim. Unusual.

Within minutes of her and Jake Goodwin taking their comfortable deep red seats, Nicky was pleased to welcome the arrival of a choice of tea and coffee in pots, milk, cream, sugar and sweeteners plus Bourbon biscuits. Top marks.

Drinks all poured, introductory chit chat overwith and Goodwin asked this Tyson to elaborate on his phone call.

Although he had not particularly asked for it, this thick set tanned Nathan Tyson started with background, a rough history of his association with the group Rockapelt and then coupled this with his own personal achievements and life journey.

The blonde bass guitarist and singer advised the two detectives how he had been grammar school educated which he made a point of emphasizing, including the fact none of the others had. Scoley looked at him, and tried to remember how he had appeared in the picture from all those years ago Darke had downloaded and described him as the charismatic one. He'd also oddly mentioned his education. Back then very much all shaggy hair now sadly fast receding but good for him, no daft comb-over.

Tyson then trudged on to emphasize how he became the most successful of the group once they had disbanded. He began to bore the pair with talk of how he had been involved in property from back at the end of the nineties. Told them he now ran a string of four estate agents in towns around the county, and attempted to describe them as highly successful. Jake knew better in this day and age, despite an upsurge after the pandemic.

Hike in interest rates and a clamp down on mortgage issues must have made a dent.

Forty-seven year old Nathan Tyson with an expanding but not obese waistline sat with his elbows on the arms of the big navy blue executive chair. his fingertips touching. 'Sad business of course as far as Alerick is concerned, and what I have to bring to the table quite possibly has absolutely nothing whatsoever to do with your situation.'

'How did you hear, just out of interest?' Jake Goodwin wanted as background.

'Heard on the radio as it happens,' he hesitated. 'In truth my wife Monica heard it on Radio Lincolnshire I think it was.' He stopped talking to sip his coffee, annoyingly lifted a biscuit from the plate and took two bites before he went on. 'What do you know about the adverts?'

'Mr Tyson. In a situation like this, we tend to be the ones asking the questions. So might I ask the same question of you?' was Nicky Scoley quickly retrieving an awkward situation. She only knew what she had managed to glean from Wood the bit about how a song was to be used in advertising.

Tyson then explained how he, Jonnie Dumbrell and Vic Jenkins had all received letters asking for their permission to include their 1998 record in an advertising campaign for a new soft drink.

'Assume Rick received one too, but we've had no contact with him for absolutely ages, years in fact.'

'Although he lives in the county?' Tyson just simply shrugged his response with white cup in hand. 'You see the other two regularly then I take it?' Scoley probed.

'Not see so much, but we keep in touch. Christmas cards and that,' he blew out his breath. 'Little in common these days of course. Nothing changes, Jonnie lives near Nottingham, Vic's still a brickie,' and he just had to add: 'Pair of us share a pint once in a blue moon, but he's still a complete prat to be fair.'

'This Vic Jenkins you mean?'

'Course.'

'In what way?'

'Been a big mouth from day one. Remember once on our way back from a gig, the old van developed a problem,' he chuckled. 'Like the back wheel was loose. Vic the dick we call him, decided if he drove slow we'd make it home. Did we hell as like. What a plonker? Bloody wheel came rollin' past us! Then another time he got done for driving us with no insurance, then as if that wasn't enough, got done for the same damn thing next soddin' day.'

'Why did you let him drive if he'd already been done for it?' Jake Goodwin was quickly onto.

'Because of how he was and still is, always knows best. Sort who'll never listen to advice. World's best driver, you must come across the sort just full of bullshit,' Tyson sighed. 'Got banned too,' he shook his head. 'How stupid. That's Vic all over I'm afraid.'

'What about Keating-Price?' Goodwin asked.

'Nutty as a fruit cake that one.'

'In what way?'

'All this environmental business even back then,' he picked up his cup. 'You'd not get away with this in his place I bet. Tell you how much meat's in coffee or some utter garbage. Into all this green organic nonsense and houses made of straw. How many of those would I sell in a week, I ask you?' He sipped. 'As I say he was an odd one way back. Now he's just a woss...or was.'

'Climate change surely is a serious issue,' Goodwin suggested.

'Mention GM to him and he'd go ballistic, mention GM to all my friends and they'd want to know what new models they've got out,' he sniggered. 'Look, we all recycle and put our bins out, got solar panels and buy those bags for life. Of course we do. Do our bit.' He drank more coffee. 'But as for that bunch of lazy rich kids with their Extinction Rebellion nonsense. We need to open up one of the disused Army camps and lock 'em in there for six months see how they like that. And that Insulating shower; stick them somewhere too and they can glue themselves to their heart's content. To each other preferably.'

Both detectives knew they could not provide an opinion, so just let it ride.

DS Scoley was not about to reward Tyson with tales of their coffee experience with Bryony Furneaux or repeat her explanation of whys and wherefores, but woss was new to her. She was however amused by thoughts of this creature before her once being found attractive by teenage girls, writing him letters, sending dubious photos and scribbling his name on their backpacks. Less amusing was the concept of him autographing their breasts.

'Rick Howard dreamt of a world full of gender neutrals and vegan gluten-free snowflakes. You into all this vegan business?' he asked Scoley who shook her head at him sporting an insincere grin.

'We recycle, we don't use plastic carrier bags.' Nicky was well aware she and Connor eat things which could be classified as vegan. Yet had never felt the need to make an issue about it.

Scoley sat observing this eponymous hero of the band as he picked up a biscuit and held it up. 'Sorry about these,' he chuckled too much. 'All the hippie sun worshipping bilge is what broke the group up in the first place. Be mud pies in Waitrose next,' he thought was amusing. 'Sorry but all this environmental business just gets my goat. Different colour bins everywhere, some take glass, some don't. Some place takes paper but not if it's been shredded. How bloody stupid is all that nonsense?'

'How d'you...' Goodwin tried when he thought Tyson had stopped to bite his biscuit, but hadn't.

'Don't get me started on climate change,' he said with his mouth full and then took another bite and carried on pointing at Jake as if it was all his fault. 'Big wigs all spouting off and then what they do? Tossers fly off to some conference and pollute the atmosphere. Like bloody Rick charging off here there and everywhere gobbing off as if we're all idiots, in his diesel guzzler. Time they got their own house in order before we take 'em seriously.'

'How d'you mean broke the group?' DS Goodwin managed.

'Look,' he said pointing again as if we was intent on destroying his welcoming image. 'Had that COP26 climate change conference a while back. D'you know anybody who has any idea what COP actually stands for or why 26 when it was in 2021?' When neither detective reacted he went on. 'Thought not. Flew in their thousands from far and wide not to mention all the limousines,' he smiled with. 'Why should I pay good money I've worked hard for, just so a load of lazy idiots who wont get off their backsides can have their homes insulated. Eh? Answer me that.'

From his point of view Goodwin felt the whole thing was counter intuitive. Thousands of people off on a jolly for a week or more, while at the same time imploring the man in the street to make sacrifices.

'The band,' said Jake ignoring him. 'Breaking up.'

Tyson blew out a breath of exasperation. 'We're living the life, we're into sex, drugs and rock 'n' roll and we gotta dope wants to save the Western Prairie Orchid or something equally ridiculous.' He leaned forward onto his desk. 'Look, one time he came round home and me old lady offered him a fried egg sandwich, turned his bloody nose up coz it came from a chicken and it'd been cooked in bacon fat. That's the sort of pillock we were dealing with. We were Rockapelt a pop group with records out, on the road in our beat up old van, but one of us wouldn't even set foot inside a McDonalds. The same freak who upset TV people one time when he harangued backroom staff about meat paste sandwiches in the green room. We're trying to be all rock 'n' roll and make our way in the nasty music business. What we didn't need was crap like a row about meat paste!'

Tyson had not been over friendly, but not out and out hostile either, just maybe wary and certainly too talkative and on edge.

'And you've never been vegetarian?'

'Not as such, not to spout about all day long like he did. We eat salad almost non-stop in the summer months not for any religious reason or whatever but because we enjoy fruit and vegetables prob'ly everything except lettuce. We have a salad where you just chuck everything in and we probably eat a Mediterranean diet a lot of the time. Lot of the five-a-day's as easy as. But not for any silly pompous reason. It's just about taste and choice, but we don't ram it down people's throats like idiot Rick did,' he chuckled. 'People who disagree with the way we eat you can see waddling down the street any day you like, with their thighs rubbing together.'

'So Nathan, what is the situation with the song now?'

'No idea. Had my solicitor write back to them to confirm I have no objection to the recording being used. Why would I? Since then, nothing.' Scoley went to pop in a supplementary but was beaten to it. 'Had the record company on,' he took a bite of the biscuit he'd been waving about. 'Actually the American entertainment conglomerate who bought up the record label we were with back then. They were just saying they might very well re-issue the single if it all pans out.'

'Asking for your permission.'

'Don't be silly, they'll just do it. In the same way they stuck *Sheer Delight* on the B side in the States.'

'I have to tell you. Bryony Furneaux claims not to have heard from anybody.'

'Musta done.'

'Not according to her.'

'But I'd have thought as Rick wrote the damn thing he'd also have his music publisher onto him asking for permission.'

'Apparently not. You ever been to the house?' Goodwin asked.

'You mus be joking!'

'Can we be serious for a moment Nathan? How quirky was he really about all this environmental business?' Scoley asked, then set about her cooled coffee.

'Nutty as a fruit cake,' he chuckled. 'Yes we all appreciate something has to be done about the atmosphere, about climate change, icebergs melting but people like him are just...you know,' he made a face. 'Sort who should be for fracking if he'd got any sense but chances are he wasn't. All right for him he can afford the gas bills.' DS Scoley was not at all sure fracking and vegans went hand in hand. 'That sort of thing just confuses the man in the street let me tell you. Rick driving a diesel they reckon all over the country spouting his garbage is so hypocritical it's unreal. Like so much these days, so-called experts being hopelessly weird doesn't help.' He stopped to sip coffee again. 'His wife buggering off tells you what he was like. Guess even she'd had more than a gut full.'

'Do you by chance have her address?'

'Italy some place someone said, was last I've heard. Well according to Vic that is, a good year or more back.'

'Will you be upset if having the record out again doesn't come off?'

'Be the world cruise gone up the spout,' the chortle told Scoley might just be a joke from Tyson. He was never going to admit to anybody about his personal issues. His grey eyes crinkled at the sides when he grinned and she guessed his tan may well have been bought on a cruise. 'Bit of publicity never did anybody any harm, and might show my daughter how much better even people like Rockapelt were compared with the so-called bands off that X Factor nonsense and all the hard beat drops garbage.'

'Are all these on-line estate agents having an effect?' Goodwin asked to change subject.

'We're more into property lets these days, so we were hit but not as bad as some. Few folk lost their jobs and struggled with rent. Bloody lucky that Corbyn weren't in charge then or we'd all be down the river. Since then interest rates hike and difficulty with mortgages are serious issues.'

'With the song,' said Scoley to halt the political stream. 'What happens next?'

'Jonnie reckons give it a week or two and we need to start asking questions.' Tyson sniggered. 'What he means is, I'll be asking the questions.'

'Except the one who needs to give his approval for the song itself can no longer do so.'

'Be up to his woman. Jonnie's suggesting we contact the record people and the advertising lot to see what's cracking off.'

'And if it's all change?'

'They're never going to change the name of the drink, and the label'll probably still issue the record whatever.'

'Can they do that?' Jake Goodwin posed. 'Without Rick's permission as songwriter?'

'You bet your life. Just won't be on the adverts that's all.' Jake was not sure about it at all.

'The other two,' DS Scoley queried. 'Dumbrell and Jenkins, have you got their contact addresses?'

'Not on me.' Tyson realized was not enough for her, and picked up his phone. 'Address book at home prob'ly.' He then spoke on the phone. 'Chezza, can you give Monica a call for me. Tell her I need the addresses for Jonnie Dumbrell and Vic Jenkins. Soon as.'

It was time for Nathan Tyson to ramble on again about his business and Nicky wondered whether to ask about the house in the picture behind his head, but in the end decided against it. The break in conversation provided an opportunity to enjoy the coffee and a second biscuit.

Eventually the phone rang and Tyson was able to scribble down the addresses his wife was giving him and he handed a post-it note to Jake being closest to him.

'Dumbrell's in Lincoln,' he frowned as he read. 'Thought he was over Nottingham way. Well Arnold actually and Vic Jenkins's...that'll be off lower High Street. Supposed to have downsized,' said Tyson quickly. 'Silly sod.'

'How d'you mean?' blonde Scoley wanted to know.

'Got himself in deep trouble somehow, been bloody mouthing off more than like. When he needed to raise a few grand by downsizing to pay off his creditors did I see him, did I hell as like?'

'Why would you expect to see him?'

Tyson lifted his hands and spread them wide. 'It's what I do,' he said. 'Could've got him a really good deal, darn sight better than the one he got stuck with I bet. We own quite a few properties to rent, usually to students these days. But no,' he sighed. 'Still carries the grudge I guess, still thinks the world's against him.' He raised his shoulders. 'What can you do?'

'How do you mean the world's against him.'

'Rick was fit to burst with all environmental and vegetarian nonsense, Jonnie Dumbrell was too immature, too naïve by half and nowt more than a pen pusher. Vic always had this chip on his shoulder. Always thought he was something he wasn't, almost as if he'd swallowed the jealous pill. No matter how deep in the clag he was, and I've been told he's been well down in the doo-doo at times he'll not step foot in here. Listens to Radio 4 and all that guff. Bitten off his nose to spite his face all his blinking life.'

'Do you know what the trouble was?'

'Some sort of scam I guess, about all I know or all he'll admit to. Not the sort of guy to put his hands up and admit he's cocked up, come clean and let people help. The past ten or fifteen years or more there's been rumour, innuendo and half told stories about him and his missus. I've really not been interested enough to bother to find out the truth among all the tittle tattle.'

'Such as?'

'He and his missus divorced a good while back, then he wed some other tart which went pear shaped and now's back with his first missus. Not married according to the grapevine they call Facebook, just living together nowadays.' He grimaced to show he didn't think much of the idea. 'So they say.'

'And Dumbrell?'

'Jonnie's still working for the council over in Nottingham I assume, but when he found about all this business must admit he did sound a tad desperate to get his hands on a bit of cash. But then he would I s'pose.'

'Why?' she queried.

'All the business with his missus,' he saw the questioning look. 'Nicked all that cash off the old bloke.'

'What old bloke, as you put it?'

'You saying you don't know?' he frowned. 'Four or five grand, if not more.' Jake Goodwin made a mental note. 'Disabled guy. All in the papers, well *Sun* and *Star* anyway as per normal. Got done a few years back for nicking off her employer. Story went she's working as a carer for this old disabled guy over Nottingham way and nicked his cash.'

'How did she do that?' a serious Nicky Scoley asked as her mind reminded her of something she'd read somewhere, but not in a newspaper.

'Think the old boy was blind or not too good anyway. Margaret Dumbrell went to the ATM for him once a week, added a few quid each time they say. Got away with a fair amount according to the paper.'

'And now?'

'Got a year or two in nick somewhere. Think they got the money back like. And Vic,' his shoulders were raised and lowered. 'Always been a brickie.' Jake was not best pleased at the way Tyson said it. He was the successful grammar school boy, singer and estate agent and his unseemly tone suggested his former colleagues were almost from a lower caste.

'And Alerick?' Scoley questioned. 'What did he do?'

'Nothing. In his position would you?'

'In his position?'

'Married to landed gentry.'

'Are you saying he had no need to work?'

'Not in need of a regular salary, not with what she inherited.'

'Which was?' keen Scoley pressed.

'Member o'some la-di-da family, Lord and Lady goodness knows who. Inherited couple of million.' Jake noted in order to check with his mother. She'd know or at least would know of somebody who'd know the truth or something damn close to it.

'So he's always been not much more than a kept house husband?'

'What were you doing on Sunday evening Mr Tyson? And overnight as well if you'd be so kind.'

The change pulled him up short. 'Be poker.'

'Who with?'

'Once a fortnight, four of us. Chatting over a few games gave us the idea.'

'What idea?'

'Being on line estate agents.'

'You?'

'No. Three of us. Realized some folk these days are so into their phones and tablets and all that, walking into an estate agent's not what they're about. Some never go near a shop let alone a place like this. Want the news but don't buy a paper. So, we got this plan to combine the three of us into one on-line set-up.'

'These estate agents?'

'Yep'

'Rather than operate, as you are now? Goodwin checked and gestured towards those outside.

'No,' Tyson said shaking his head. 'As well as. We keep going with good money off the rentals and still sell a fair few, alongside we combine to run a localized on-line service.'

'And who would vouch for your poker game?'

'Dominic Coleridge.'

'And where would we find him?' Scoley asked although Goodwin knew the estate agent of that name was fairly close by as Tyson confirmed.

The pair finished their coffees and bade the one time shaggy haired singer good day.'

8

Heading back towards the Stonebow, Nicky stopped at the heavy glass door of an estate agent and tried to pull it open.

'What we doing now?'

'Checking his alibi. Dominic Coleridge he said, that's who this is.' Goodwin pulled the door open wide for her and they walked in. 'Dominic Coleridge, please' said DS Nicky Scoley.

'I'm sorry, but do you have an appointment?'

'I think this is my entrance fee,' the Detective Sergeant said and held up her warrant card.

To be fair it took less than a minute for this navy suited chubby faced man to waddle out to the pair of them.

'Dominic Coleridge,' he offered his hand for Goodwin to shake. 'How may I help you?'

'Just a quick one,' said Scoley cheerily. 'I'm Detective Sergeant Nicola Scoley making inquiries. Just like to know what you were doing last Saturday evening?'

Coleridge looked nonplussed for a moment. 'I'm sorry, but what does this concern?'

'Your whereabouts, please,' Goodwin paused. 'Then we'll explain.'

'Last Saturday?' he considered to give himself thinking time. 'Be poker,' he said from beneath a frown after a delay. 'Once a fortnight few of us get together. Nothing very serious you understand.'

'Who with?'

'Usual four, been going on a year or two now.'

'Thank you.' blonde attractive Scoley smiled gently to encourage him. 'Just your name has been given to us as an alibi.'

'Who by?'

'Mr Tyson,' he looked bewildered. 'Understand you're planning on being part of one of those on-line estate agents.'

'At least we he hope to,' he shrugged.

'Problem?' Goodwin asked.

'No,' he shook his head. 'Nothing serious.'

'But there's obviously an issue.'

'Liquidity. All a case of raising finance, particularly for some in these troubled times.'

On-line estate agents Jake knew had been operating successfully in the UK for years. How on earth did this bunch imagine they could begin to compete with those up and running with television advertising when the old fashioned high street shop versions with sky high commission were falling by the wayside?

'Tell me more if you will,' Scoley suggested.

He looked all about in case ears were wagging. 'Well, the way erm... she is. You must have noticed.'

'Who are we talking about?' Scoley insisted.

Coleridge sucked in as if he'd made an error of judgment. 'Monica. Monica Tyson of course.'

'Please enlightened us,' Jake suggested.

'Domineering, over spending,' he added a slight grin to his mouth then looked left and right. 'She may not be a Jones but demands she keeps up with them.'

'I've not met her.'

'You have that pleasure to come.'

'Tell me Mr Coleridge, why have you told us about her? It has nothing to do with the reason we called in,'

'Being honourable, to be honest,' he admitted and gave the impression he should have kept his mouth shut.

'Always the best policy,' Goodwin said. Somebody with principles was refreshing.

'Look,' was with his breath. 'When I was younger a good friend of mine was a witness to a bag snatch down Portland Street. He was interviewed by police and answered all their questions, but that's all he did. Truth was he knew who had done it, we'd both gone to school with him at one time.'

'But he never told police?'

'No. Just answered all their questions.'

'But didn't offer information?'

Coleridge nodded. 'Not a word. See, they never asked him if he knew the person.'

'You're offering Mrs Tyson as an extra on top of answering our questions about poker.'

He shrugged. 'About the size of it.'

'Thank you. Sorry to have disturbed you,' said Nicky Scoley handing him her card, before turning and walking to the glass door.

'Excuse me, you've not said what this is all about.'

'You're right,' said Jake and they were back on the street heading for the Stonebow. 'Not sure her spending habits have anything whatsoever to do with it, but that's one where the promise of money could very well be a motive.'

'How much she spends on shoes and handbags is hardly relevant.'

'But does that maybe suggest our man Tyson is not as well-heeled as we might think.'

'That make him a third in need of cash?' Nicky posed.

'And this Monica's a fourth.'

66

9

His team had gathered in the Incident Room as they do each and every morning and often afternoons for their briefings. All looking at their Detective Inspector for a route to travel down, for guidance and for some inspiration.

The previous evening when she and Connor sat down for their evening meal Nicky couldn't help but think about Keating-Price and what he might have sat down to.

Aloo Gobi with chickpeas or some similar vegan concoction was a possibility, she pondered. Served with a green salad no doubt which to her was the cheap and boring part of any vegetarian diet let alone vegan. To call just a few leaves and a bit of grass a salad did irk as by definition salad is a mixture of vegetables and fruit plus cheese, grains and nuts, not just a handful of odd-ball leaves plucked from anywhere some restaurants have the audacity to offer.

Nicky'd looked down at her plate of liver and onions instead of kumquats, quinoa along with an unwashed scrunched up bunch of rocket leaves.

The full team were in residence, plus two from PHU manning the hotline phones in addition to Michelle, bored by the fifteen minutes of fame cranks wasting their time. The do-gooders desperate to offer help without beginning to understand the request for info put out by the media and the one or two hoping to drop some poor innocent bloke in the clag just for a laugh.

First in as usual DI Oliver Bristow had already been through the overnights, the burglaries, nicked cars, drink drivers and all the drugged-ups from bars and clubs the cells and A&E were always stuffed full with.

Pleased about the Darke boss securing the services of Alisha, he was convinced she'd be a real positive. The twenty eight year old had suffered from racial abuse when patrolling the streets for her first few years on the force. That she had not quit, and generally never complained were the attributes Bristow had been looking for.

After what Alisha had been through, the DI knew there would be a willingness to succeed rather than face the prospect of returning to the drudgery of walking the streets of purgatory. Her finite appreciation of all things to do with social media was a real added bonus.

Time to treat the post mortem report in the particular way he'd always dealt with them down in Grantham. Read the front page carefully in particular the pathologists findings then he'd speed read through all the medical long words and finally concentrated on the conclusions.

As he frequently did almost by habit the DI perched himself on the edge of a work station with morning black coffee, the choice of psychopaths, at hand.

Jake Goodwin often wondered if he felt the need to do that to make himself feel part of the team.

'To be fair,' he said waving his tablet. 'I'm not sure if the post mortem is good news or bad.' He looked at Jake Goodwin in particular. 'Firstly might I say this is not the done and dusted version, as they tell me further tox investigations are being undertaken.' he paused for a breath wondering how many of his team would fully understand what he had to offer if he gave chapter and verse. 'Anaphylactic shock,' he said carefully instead and saw Jake's face and others peer at each other. A look of confusion had taken control. 'When your body, as this professor kindly explains. Goes into anaphylactic shock your blood pressure drops suddenly and your airways block normal breathing.' By now Jake was eager to intervene. 'This as I'm sure you all know,' was Bristow continuing. 'Can be brought about by nuts...'

'This is nuts!'

'The list,' the DI went on despite the outburst. 'However is fairly extensive...'

'That's ridiculous,' Jamie shot out. 'Had one of those before. This a copycat and some goon put nuts on that bandage or...?

'Jake,' stopped him as did his boss's look of rebuke. 'So far, and this is all we have to go on. They have no idea what the warning was all about, as all that has gone to CSI Leicester and it may then need to go down to Porton Down. The post mortem tells them and now us, why he died. It also discounted Anthrax, when before testing there were no boil-like lesions on the skin with a black centre. What we don't know as yet is what caused it.' Bristow annoyingly stopped to sip his black coffee. 'The list Jake, includes penicillin, insect stings, nuts, shellfish, milk, eggs and even latex.'

'What's any of this got to do with that thing strapped to his arm?' was Jake this time pointing to one of Connor Mitchell's photographs pinned to the murder board.

'That's what's gone to CSI.'

'Boss,' was new girl Alisha. 'Might be a stupid question but is it possible with him being a strict vegan, his body reacted badly to something normal he ate? Such as a milkshake.'

'Always possible but we'd need a pathologist to advise. Just out of interest and something we don't need in cases where the cause is never identified. This is often the case with anaphylactics, called idiopathic.' He pondered. 'Don't forget you had that woman killed by Brazil nuts a while back.'

'Somebody stuffed nuts down his gob, or cooked him an omelette. None of that explains why that thing was strapped to his arm,' was Jake once more pointing to the board.

'Enough now,' said a stern Bristow. 'That is until we hear further as we will. In the meantime we just carry on the way we are. Murder by person or persons unknown at an unknown location sometime between 01.00 and 04.00 on the Sunday.' Ideas were forever tumbling around Oliver Bristow's head, competing for space and such an occasion was no exception. 'We don't rest until we find…' glanced down at his tablet. 'Thank you lab,' he peered up at his team, then read. 'DNA has matched samples on the DNA Database following Alerick Howard Keating-Price's arrest for possession,' he was grinning. 'Of a Class B drug ten years ago.'

Despite what the forensic people would say and come up with, Oliver Bristow was never convinced forensic evidence alone was ever enough. It would help convict of course but other means were always his first priority.

Time for him to set actions for his team to add to the information they had already gained, but first an update.

Jake Goodwin reminded the entire team, as some were missing previously, by explaining how totally disinterested and uncooperative Bryony Furneaux had been. How scruffy the cottage was and why nobody could get hold of her at the actual Hall. He told all about the chat with Tyson the estate agent member of the band and his confirmed alibi.

'First up,' Bristow tapped the white board. 'Alisha. One thing were struggling with is Keating-Price's car. According to his partner, call her what you will, he had and I quote, one of those Land Rover things,' he said in a put-on voice to amuse.

'Hybrid is it nae?'

'Sorry Sandy, no,' Nicky advised. 'But to be fair she has one, but then she also serves the worst coffee known to man.'

'Recipe for murder?'

'More than likely it'll be organic.' Their DI went back to Alisha O'Neill. 'Have a word with DVLA for a car belonging to…and this is where it'll get a bit complicated and you'll need to apologize to the people down there for being so vague. Any one of Alerick Howard Keating–Price or Rick Howard or Alerick Arbiter or even Rick Arbiter he called himself sometimes and his woman Bryony Furneaux,' Inga was amused by. 'Don't worry I'll send the list across to you,' he said to stop Alisha scribbling it all down.

DS Jake Goodwin knew he'd need to be careful with providing information on the case so close to his parents' home in the village near Anwick. Do that and chances are he'd be lumbered with all the inquiries and his parents would easily become sick to death of him calling to check out all the nonsense they would no doubt be fed. Or sought out in Reg Goodwin's case.

Knew his dad would know exactly what Rick Howard drove, being the sort of guy who knew the mpg for every car everybody he knew owned or rented, and could no doubt list all the road numbers from Lincoln to Blenau Ffestiniog and would spend all day eavesdropping at the residents shop.

Unless Alisha had serious issues in her search he'd just keep mum or he'd be annoying his folk.

'Tell you where we may have a problem,' was Jake. 'Alisha, you can quote Gorgie Hall as the address, but,' he aimed at Bristow. 'What if that pig of a place we went to was the actual address? Does it really have an address? What's it called? Post Code?'

'Pig Sty?'

'Michelle,' said the DI. 'Can you take it on? Jake will explain about where they live, can you do a search, post office, land registry and all that, get a defined village address and post code.'

Nicky looked at Jake. 'Did she say Shepherds Cottage or something like that you can remember?' He just shrugged and pulled an obvious gurn.

'Start with Gorgie Hall,' said Jake. 'And work from there,' aware Michelle was not the type in need of him to keep an eye on, to chivvy her along.

'Now Alisha,' said the DI to his new detective going back to her actions list. 'When and if you get a vehicle we need to start looking at ANPR for when he was missing. But, and it's a big but, she claims not to actually know when he went out and where he went to, would you believe.'

"I'm not my partner's keeper, think it was Wilberforce did away with slaves" said Jake to amuse. 'Typical of the stupidity we had from the woman. Pick Nicky's brains for the contact she's got down in Hendon.'

'Sorry,' said Jake to Michelle. 'If all else fails, I'll ask my mother to ask the village postman what the address is.'

'Thanks Jake. Now Michelle,' was next on the DI's list. 'Team of two. You and Jamie. I want to know everything there is to know about the life history of this Rockapelt group. Jonnie Dumbrell, Vic Jenkins and our Mr Tyson. If you need music info from back then arrange to have a chat with the boss.'

'Do they have to?' Nicky moaned in fun. 'Joking apart, use him,' she said sharply. 'Please understand Michelle. He knows more about popular music than any man I know. Pick his brains.'

'Sandy,' said Bristow across to the DC before anybody could have another winge. 'Short straw this time. House-to-house are pretty much all in but there's no big housing estate, couple of hundred live in the village at most and a few others dotted about, but we also need to discover when and where he went. Pop in the village store place, even look at a few places such as Anwick, Billinghay. We need a sighting. Remember we're talking serious vegan off the telly…'

'Witha pony tail!'

Bristow smiled. 'So ignore the butcher and the chippy.' He screwed up his face. 'Unless they do veggie burgers and chips with a side salad of stinging nettles.'

A glance from Jake told Nicky this guy was mellowing. Until then it had been months of him being very studious and serious about anything and everything. Boring almost. Now they'd had a quip or two. Add that to the coffee with Nicky and they were maybe getting somewhere. Slowly.

'His laptop has gone up to the Digital Forensic guys in the Tech Crime Team and they're also looking at his phone records,' Jake advised. 'Be a while as I had to get her ladyship's number off her iPhone because she claimed she didn't know it and I had to get Keating-Price's off hers as well.'

'Sir,' a totally unnecessary subservient phrase they all knew when she was DI, Inga Larsson hated. 'Might I suggest a local Land Rover dealer would have him on their customer database?' an accent richer when the big man had a point to make.

'Thanks. Work with Alisha on it if you will and its guv if you must.'

'Nae bother,' from the Scot, Jake knew was until the next time.

'What happened to all his low carbon emissions philosophy and solar energy business? You can't get a plug-in Land Rover surely?'

'Read somewhere aboot a hybrid electric pick-up, Chevrolet I think.'

'Can't see someone like Keating-Price having a Yankee car, can you?'

'Please remember,' Jake reminded everybody. 'In the village next door to Gorgie Hall there is no CCTV. In fact something which could be a little job for somebody. Check where the nearest is and borrow the disc.'

'No pub you say?'

'Village amenities don't even consist of the usual ubiquitous pub as you say, nor a petrol station and the shop is just a small community run place.'

'I don't expect you all to suddenly become vegetarian,' said Bristow. Although Nicky suspected he was. 'Yesterday when Jake and Nicky spoke with Tyson, his view was Keating–Price as a vegan should be in favour of fracking, but I think possibly he could have been quite the opposite. Where it all gets confusing and unless any of you know different it's difficult to know who to believe.'

'Thought vegans were against fracking,' Alisha offered. 'Or is it…?'

'That surely's the problem,' said Nicky. 'Who to believe, both sides of the argument seem to create facts to suit their particular perspective and the public are confused.'

'You're right. Fracking one side says,' Bristow continued. 'Will stop us burning coal, but on the other hand they reckon it will be a threat to human life by contaminating drinking water, but the others say it's stuff and nonsense. Who drinks water straight out of the ground anyway? It will create jobs one side of the argument say, and so on.'

'Anybody any idea what carbon sequestration or air capture mean?' Michelle queried but the answer was shrugs.

'But there are so many fanatics on both sides which has to be where the problem is for us. Complete fanatics who'll stop at nothing and some of the brain dead were Coronavirus deniers, remember. Whichever side he was on and I understand there are vegans playing for both teams, could very well be the other side set out to shut him up. Stop him spouting in public because he's better known now than he ever was with Rockapelt.'

'Called deniers,' said Jamie. 'People who say global warming is nonsense. Wouldn't have the vaccine. How stupid can you be?'

'And selfish.'

'Fracking could be a real game changer, but those against moan about energy bills.'

'D'you want an ugly big rig down your street?'

'Enough now,' said the DI to bring it to hand before he finished up with two factions going toe to toe when there was work to be done.

10

Detective Sergeant Jacques Goodwin was pleased Alisha O'Neill came to him first with the Land Rover info, and he was able to keep it to himself for an hour and add bits and pieces to what she had discovered.

'Alisha has done well,' he said when it came time for some to reveal. '1983 Land Rover Defender 109 in black. 4 wheel drive, 6-cylinder diesel. We've had it put on ANPR, just have to wait now for Hendon to get back.' Jake didn't mention how he'd phoned his old man who'd had a quick scoot round the village looking for a black Land Rover and came back with zilch. Still he knew Reg would be well chuffed to be involved.

'Really good for the environment then!' Jamie Hedley chuntered.

'As I keep saying, with people like this it's always the same. A case of not as I do,' Nicky reminded.

'It's registered in the name of Rick Howard but his driving licence is in his full Alerick double-barrel one,' Alisha had been able to reveal. 'His woman Bryony Furneaux owns a fairly new white Yaris Hybrid, or assume she does as it was the only car there. Would have expected electric but no doubt she'll have some unfathomable reason why not. Both vehicles have Gorgie Hall, Anwick as the registered address. So do their driving licences and insurance according to MIDAS the Motor Insurance Database. All tickety boo.' Alisha checked her tablet. 'Last but not least DVLA still have a current driving licence for his wife. Now just waiting for ANPR to come back on where the Land Rover's been and where it might be now of course.'

'Registered to where they don't actually live of course,' grinning Jake popped in.

'Technically yes they do,' Nicky insisted. 'But practically, no way. Reason nobody can ever get hold of them of course. Just sit and fester in their…'

'Pig in a poke,' smiling Jake finished for her.

'Pig in a poke Cottage sounds good.'

'Let's look at this band, Jamie. Or should I say group to please the boss,' Oliver suggested.

'Jonnie Dumbrell rhythm guitar and youngest member. Too young we're told by the Darke boss, too naïve for the environment and unemployed when the band turned pro and went on the road. Ended up working for a local department store then the council. Doesn't work for the actual council these days. But then does anybody? He's employed by the management schemes company who deal with all the administration and he works in what they call Exchequer Services doing wages, we've learnt he deals with the hourly paid and those on zero hours. Think there may be more to come,' Jamie admitted. 'Still looking into it.'

DI Oliver Bristow pretended to scan the room and checked the door. 'Please use the boss for info on the group, we'd be fools not to as I understand his knowledge is is quite extensive. But, keep it just to the stuff we can't find out on our own accord, or he'll be camped in here.'

Michelle Cooper was next up. 'Vic Jenkins is a self-employed bricklayer living with his ex-wife off High Street. Fine, except they have two kids, a daughter in her twenties who has a little kid of her own and a son…'

'Hold on,' said Sandy. 'How d'you mean ex-wife?'

'Married, divorced and got back together but so far we can't find them being wed second time round.'

'What about a bloke for the one with the bairn or is he just shacked up there?' the Scot queried. Michelle could only shrug.

'In a house in Appleby Street?' she went on as Sandy shook his head.

'Be serious! They're two up, two down with an outside lavvy probably.'

'Mate's got one without a bathroom.'

'Two bedrooms with three adults and two kids,' Michelle carried on. 'One of which happens to be a young lad, plus the daughter's fella as well probably dossing down there more than likely?'

'Near Tealby Street?' Jake asked, and Michelle nodded.

'This Tyson we know about,' Bristow said to move it on.

'Can I just mention, he's not as successful these days as he makes out,' DS Goodwin remarked for all. 'On line estate agents are taking their toll on the whole high street shop overcharging smarmy types. Some of the nationwide chains will probably carry on doing well for a good while, but eventually like everything else it'll all be on line. But having said that most of us have only ever heard of a few of these on line companies, so being local might suit.'

'Hear some places you don't even have to go on a viewing, even. All done on line. VR apparently.'

'Being local,' said Michelle. 'They can use their own people for viewings and pricing. Better than borrowing as on line tend to do.'

'Divided loyalties.'

'Something else we need to check,' said DI Bristow. 'Tyson's alibis for Saturday evening and night,' he reminded Jake.

'All in hand,' he assured him. 'If you remember Tyson claimed he and three friends play poker every other Saturday night, take it in turns.' He glanced at DC Jamie Hedley who nodded and smiled.

'Missing two have now confirmed where they all were until about half one. Arthur Hildred and David Toogood the partners in Toogoods estate agents. Coleridge you've already checked guv.'

'Where does all this leave us?' Bristow queried in his quiet careful manner.

'Waiting for info especially ANPR on the car, phone company records for both, interviews with Dumbrell and Jenkins and odds and sods.' Jake Goodwin looked at his watch. He also had irons in the fire back in the village he hoped might come up with something positive.

'Social media being checked Alisha,' he glanced towards. 'ASBO Orford's got his boys upstairs working on a second batch of forensics results anytime and not forgetting our friend the DNA. That'll be enough to keep us off the streets.'

DI Oliver Bristow as per normal was first in next morning early despite having the furthest to travel, with the desire for progress driving him on. That and another sleepless ridden night and a morning alone with only the kitchen to chat to over his cuppa. He hoped the initial forensic report from Leicester would drop in his lap but knew that to be unlikely under the circumstances. Oliver knew they'd get the phone records off one at least and if luck was on her side for once a geeky wiz from the Tech Crime Team would come up trumps with something on Alerick's laptop.

The incident boards along one wall told a different story with scant information written on and stuck to, with Connor Mitchell's photos of the crime scene. He'd taken many from a distance, just one being Keating-Price. Body shot closer to illustrate no signs of blood, one of his bandaged arm, another two of the note attached.

One major surprise for Bristow had been the victim's mode of dress. He'd been expecting a grey benign oddball in a tweed scruffy jacket and brown corduroys, the sort likely to be completely unperturbed about his very dated image. The pony tail to his mind was not that unusual as Jake had suggested given his interests, but the clothing was most certainly not on trend.

Early days of a major crime investigation were recognized by Bristow's nose. The Incident Room simply reeked of coffee and adrenaline, and told him instantly he was in the eye of the storm. His first storm in that role.

He was in need of two things, some form of lead or breakthrough and a black no sugar start of day coffee to get his brain in sync.

The DI had logged on, turned on the photocopier and completed his normal morning checks of the overnights and then stood at his office door arms folded as the team began one by one to slowly wander in, mutter a *good morning* and switch on their IT modes.

Best he'd got so far was notification of Justin Whittaker the dapper solicitor he knew was representing the absent next-of-kin Lady Arbiter, calling at the mortuary to identify the body of one Alerick Howard Keating–Price.

Jamie who had emailed him overnight was first in, so Oliver allowed him to get settled. Time and again when he looked at him. Tall Bristow wondered whether he should work out on a regular basis in the same way bulked up and fit looking Jamie Hedley did. Both a good six foot tall, Jamie carried himself well and just seemed to ooze good health.

His mind kept taking him back to what he'd been told about Gorgie Hall and the Furneaux woman living in a dump. Oliver had a preference for plain speaking, honest, hardworking people. Had no time for airs and graces some hide behind, preferring real people who lead by example.

Furneaux's attitude stank to his mind, particularly in the way she'd virtually dismissed her partner without even a smattering of sorrow at his passing. Aware the team'd be back knocking on the woman's door before long with no holds barred this time. He'd be asking from his team what she was doing for money, if he was penny thin as Jake and Nicky claimed and with no right to any he had slithered away somewhere. Time to stop feeling sorry for her.

When Alisha O'Neil arrived for work thoughts of her father flashed across her mind when she spied the boss stood leaning against the door post to his office. Arms folded across his chest looking just like her dad in a *you're late again* mood.

Alisha could remember him striking such a pose and tapping his foot. In this case it was a simple *'Morning'* as a smile winged its way between them followed by the passing of a fiver and the young DC was back out.

Bristow knew from what he'd been briefed on by Darke how she'd come through a bad patch some years suffering untold sexist abuse when patrolling the streets. When offered the opportunity to choose a new career direction it had been her sheer determination to beat the racists which had won her this new role. Plus she was an avid social media almost addict, a phase of their operation which nowadays produced good fruit from the tree.

She'd settled in well and it appeared the others had accepted her. That morning Bristow felt Alisha seemed a little shadowed around the normally bright eyes she possessed yet were infrequently dull.

DI Oliver knew one or two of the main team still had a few partials of the previous day's actions to complete, and he could only hope the info they were waiting on just might be the key to progress. If one of the band members had been in anyway involved in what had happened to Alerick Keating–Price it made little sense to astute Bristow. None of them surely, even Nathan Tyson, would turn down the chance of a few grand and a bit of notoriety. Especially in this day and age, when almost any talentless thicko with a back to front baseball cap pretending to be a rapper can clean up for five minutes as an over-index celeb among the inane on social media.

Alisha returning with two coffees one black for the boss, one normal was the fillip he needed.

Suited, tidy Bristow perched himself on the edge of a work station, hunched forward, leant on his thighs just peering down at the grubby floor as if he was thinking of something else entirely. Then his head came up and he nodded to the dark haired lad from Gainsborough.

'Jamie?'

'Still got to check his personal situation but it looks like our Jonnie Dumbrell erstwhile rhythm guitarist's got a bit of a finance problem with his wife inside.' Jamie Hedley then peered down at his tablet to read. Oliver Bristow waited in case there was more. 'We can assume this means with only one wage he's short of money with her inside,' said the DC. 'But would that be a reason to kill Rick Howard? Surely he'd want the song reissued probably more than any of the others, it'd be in his best interest so he can have a few quid coming in.'

'Why d'he move from Arnold?'

'Think its the job. Being short of money from what I can gather wont help and he's probably bloody embarrassed.' said Hedley. 'Plus. Would you be happy with the local riff-raff shouting the odds every time they pass your gate with crap about her nicking off some disabled bloke? Some wassock stuffing yesterday's excrement through your letterbox'd be fun to deal with. Housing's cheaper here anyway, understand he only just managed on one income when she was in to start with, but now he's on his uppers and forced to downsize.'

'Imagine what trolls are doing to him on the net.'

'I was going to say,' said Alisha. 'What I've seen so far is quite mild but go back a while and it was absolutely vile.'

'Renting rates over here are far less,' said Michelle. 'He is renting I take it?'

'Yes,' said Hedley. 'There was a marker about his wife when we brought up Jonnie Bryn Dumbrell.'

'Tells us he'd certainly want Rick Howard alive and kicking if he's really hard up.'

'Be the goose who can lay the golden egg. Or was.'

'Same as Nathan Tyson, estate agent of this parish,'

Jake said. 'Big gated house out at Swinderby. Sally and I popped out to have a peek last evening. Has to be worth a good few bob. But like so many think maybe he's suffering as I said, from on-line estate agents,' said Jake Goodwin. 'Not seen pages of property in the *Lincoln Leader* for years. Plenty of new names on boards these days instead.'

This confirmed what Oliver Bristow already thought, there was no good reason for the band members to want their former member dead. Doing so would surely pull the rug from under their own feet.

A change of direction was required and he knew it would only come from evidence. Not from the door-to-doors which so far had revealed next to nothing. Folk saying Keating-Price is either a national treasure or just a plain "cranky boring old fart" in the main, was hardly evidence or a serious motive. Others as expected regarded him with some degree of fondness for his environmental work but were loath to give up their petrol cars. Or not go to Burger King.

At morning briefing the day before, Craig Darke had suggested Keating-Price dying just as the record and adverts were out, would prove far more valuable to the band. In this day and age Oliver was aware sympathy sales are as popular as bunches of flowers. Was increased sales another version of the same motive to consider?

Some locals were rightly not at all happy Keating-Price or the Rick Howard they knew him as, never took part in village life. Never showed his face at events. None of them seriously good reasons to slay him, how unintentionally it might have been.

'Nathan Tyson's been spoken to,' Oliver Bristow said to bring the attention back. 'Michelle, Jamie, your turn to complete your dossier on Dumbrell and Jenkins. Knock on their doors.' He put a hand up as an apology. 'Let's not cause either of them too much grief, don't try to catch them at work to get the tongues wagging or alert bosses looking for any excuse.'

Bristow knew they were not dealing with the small pockets of south Lincolnshire low life he'd been used to. This was the posh set at the top, with a well known environmental activist. Him along with his beautiful partner going all the way down it seemed to Dumbrell really short of the readies with a wife in nick. In between Tyson and Jenkins both with issues. A real mixed bag.

To his mind Oliver knew older folk buying property had proved beneficial and was aware some younger ones would do the very same providing they can shed the instant gratification model holding so many back. Owners including Jake's parents as a good example were out in a lovely quiet village nestled in North Kesteven, as was cocky Nathan Tyson according to Nicky. Not to mention Oliver's own mother living part of the year with him down at Great Gonerby.

To some extent it was a relief to appreciate how all this business was never going to be a case involving a whole list of good-for-nothing wretches. No scrotes of this world, no druggies or the bad and ugly was making a nice change. The stop-in-beds, benefit layabouts and scroungers, filthy dirty beggars with their mangy dogs.

Not been the first case to get off to a slow start, he thought to himself as he downed more of the warm black coffee. The second layer of forensics, histology and toxicology he'd not yet been privy to. With laptop results and the phone data all still to come he was aware how somewhere somehow among all that he'd need to spot clear pointers to set himself and the team off in the right direction.

Nathan tried hard not to show how down he was in the office when the lads were discussing football. Rot had set in before the World Cup. With Liverpool losing to the bottom of the table club when he had a wad on them to win.

11

DCs Michelle Cooper and Jamie Hedley might as well have turned up with blues and twos and the big red key, for all the appreciation they received by just knocking on Dumbrell's front door like polite insurance salesmen.

Jamie had at one time acted as her bodyguard soon after she returned to work after suffering a hell of a beating from some boozed-up scrote, now sharing a dank cell some place.

A crumbling post-war terraced pebble-dash council-house in a previous life, in serious need of a freshening up north of the cathedral and castle. Not to mention the tatty wooden window frames with peeling white paint.

The moment they introduced themselves the tubby fella in a scruffy seasons old Norwich City shirt, grey jogging bottoms and dirty feet in flip-flops who answered the door, looked at big Jamie as if he were the devil incarnate.

'Here we bloody go for crissakes!' he moaned. 'You lot got nothin' better t'do? Aint there any old ladies what needs help crossin' some bloody road, son? What about knobs on their phones driving eh? How many o'them you pulled up today?' he almost spat out his breath. 'Take that as a bugger all then. Jeez,' he sighed loudly. 'And I pays yous bloody wages!'

'Might we come in?' Jamie Hedley suggested very calmly. 'Better for all concerned if we don't do this in full view of the world and his wife.'

'Not here I'm not.'

'Why?' abrasive big Hedley asked.

'Not done sonny, never grass t'cops. Not startin' now as like. No bloody way.'

'We're not asking you to grass anybody up, we're here on a quite different matter entirely.'

'Go on,' Dumbrell sighed with a look of complete disinterest but remained arms folded, legs crossed at the ankle so any puff of wind would blow him over.

'What's crackin' off Jonnie?' and suddenly there were two when this scrawny man in a black vest with shaved head and a few days beard growth, appeared behind Dumbrell.

'We're here to interview Mr Dumbrell, sir,' Hedley emphasized. 'And you are?'

'Who's asking,' made him very dubious.

'This is a private matter sir,' said Hedley. 'So, if you wouldn't mind.'

'Anythin' you gotta say you can say in front o'him,' Dumbrell insisted.

'With due respect,' said the DC. 'It's very doubtful if he would be able to answer any of our questions. This is not quiz night down the pub.'

'Can't you buggers just leave us alone? You got yer pound o'bloody flesh. Like a dog wi'a bloody bone you lot, gets on me bloody wick all this shit.'

'Mr Dumbrell,' said Michelle Cooper to him slowly. 'We can do this the easy way. You can stop swearing, kindly invite us in, make us a cup of tea, offer us a biscuit and we can have a nice quiet chat or…'

'Tell you what,' said beefy Hedley pulling his phone from his pocket. 'I'll just call up a van get 'em to swing round here with blues and twos. Wake your nosy neighbours up, give them something to have a gawp at eh? How d'ya fancy it?' He turned slightly away. 'Control, this is DC Hedley could do with a wagon up here…'

'Piss off!'

'Or,' said Cooper. 'You can join us at the station but I must warn you the tea there's not up to much and we don't have biscuits. Either way we'll be interviewing you *today*.'

'There's bloody shite going on all over this place and what you lot doin' about it eh?' this thin unshaven man asked. 'All these bloody kids shootin' up wiv all that drug stuff down the underpass. Students given everything and as appreciation gets pissed up every night an' kip all day. Right mess this place innit, and all your sort can bloody do is make folks life a bloody misery. Just tell 'em to sling their hook Jonnie.'

Jamie Hedley casually produced handcuffs. 'The choice is yours Mr Dumbrell,' had an effect. The older one of the two looked left and right out the green door and down the street, then just stepped aside and shrugged to the one in a dirty vest. DC Hedley stopped his pretence, closed and pocketed his phone.

'Alerick Keating–Price,' said Cooper once they were inside. 'What can you tell us about him?'

'Rick Howard yous mean?' Dumbrell responded from a care worn brown chair in the small living room. Hedley will admit he knows little or nothing about interior design. What he does know is, if you plan to put garish metallic wallpaper on just one wall then choose the right one. The purple flowers sprang off the mottled silver in a cascade of horror.

'Yes. What can you tell us about him?'

'Apart from the fact the bastard's dead you mean?' Dumbrell said with a chuckle.

'Why did you say that?'

'Coz he is.'

'No,' said swarthy Hedley. 'Why didn't you like him?'

'Cocked it all up, the shit bag.' He looked all around at the room. 'Ask yersen why bastards what did it same time as us, aint living like this?'

'You think you should have done better?'

'Course,' he insisted. 'You think Dire Straits are dossin' like I am in a bloody dump like this? I should bloody coco.'

'In what way did he cock it up?'

The room was tidy enough – not good enough though for Cooper's mum – and from what they could sense at least there'd not be an overflowing bin in the kitchen, a pile of dirty crockery and nappies on a radiator.

'Wrong bloody songs, too soddin' fast. Jenkins's a knob and Rick, what can you say 'bout him?' He just let his head swing from side to side. 'Chuffin' hell.'

'What's the situation,' Hedley said quieter, 'with the song for the drink?'

'God knows,' he shrugged. 'I said bring it on. Nathan reckons he's said yes. Don't know 'bout Vic but he'll be in if he's got any bloody sense.'

'Where were you on Saturday night?' Harsh Hedley threw down to him.

'This Saturday?'

'Gone.'

'Be at home here like.'

'Any chance you can prove it?' and in an instant Dumbrell looked sheepish and embarrassed.

'Me missus is in Peterborough, bet you knows already,' he said with his head down. 'Visit booked for two, they'll have me on CCTV I guess.'

'Saturday?'

'No Sunday,' he said as his head came up.

'We're here about Keating-Price,' Cooper assured him. 'Just need an alibi for Saturday.'

'We's all here,' and he was back looking down at the scruffy carpet. Dumbrell blew out a breath of frustration. 'Danny!' he shouted and they waited for the long streak of nothing to appear back. 'Where was we Sat'day night?'

'Round here, why?'

'Your daughter?' Hedley asked. 'What about her?'

'Sara!' was next to be shouted. 'You made the tea yet?' he asked when this natural redhead poked her head round the door. All pulled back severely with a big plait swinging behind her.

'You're fine,' said Cooper. 'We need to be off in a minute. Just need to confirm where you were last Saturday night, Sunday morning.'

'Here, why?' this Sara asked back.

'Not trying to be awkward but, can you prove it?'

'Wanna ask the kids?'

'That won't be necessary.'

'Watched TV like we do. Best night Sat'de.' Michelle Cooper could imagine this bunch all sat down to watch one of those dreadful talent shows for the totally untalented with a cold shabby over-priced pizza delivered to the door by a bloke with a big bag on a bike.

'It's just that your dad once knew Mr Keating-Price as Rick Howard and you probably know he has been found dead. Just a case of eliminating people.'

'And you think?' she almost shouted.

'Not at all lass,' said Dumbrell.

'We're eliminating people,' Cooper went on. 'Who might for some reason have wanted him dead and I'm sorry to say this, but. People he was once in a band with might just have an axe to grind, be interested in his demise. See where we're at?'

'What about any o'them loony folk he mixes with? You tried any of them?' the thin one chucked in.

'And you are?' Hedley asked, with notebook in hand.

'Mullery. Danny Mullery why?'

'If you were all here together, we can eliminate you all from our inquiries,' Jamie looked at the redhead. 'And you are?'

'Sara Dumbrell, sweetheart.'

'Fine,' said Hedley. 'Wasn't too painful now was it? It's not just a case of searching out the guilty it's also a case of checking the innocent.'

'Remember now,' said this Sara. 'We watched Gogglebox and stuff on tele an' 'ad takeaway.'

'From where?' Cooper asked giving herself a tick in their box of bad taste.

This scarily dressed female just gawped at at the DC. 'You mean…Deliveroo?'

'Absolutely fine,' said Hedley as he moved away. 'If you remember anything you think might be of interest to us,' he said down and handed Jonnie Dumbrell his card. 'Let us know.'

'We will need to check for DNA,' said Cooper by now stood next to this Sara at the door out to the hall. 'Perhaps you'd arrange to call at the station. Just take a few minutes.'

'Not sure I got time, what with…'

'Oh but you will Mr Dumbrell,' was the blunt Jamie Hedley towering over him, in a manner everybody in MIT all knew so well.

'But what if…'

'What if nothing. You will.' He moved in closer. 'Tomorrow,' then withdrew a pace. 'This is to eliminate you,' said big Jamie just as Dumbrell in his yellow football shirt with food dribbled down the front, went to protest. 'As you can imagine the forensic guys have found a lot of DNA and we need to eliminate people', he lied they had no serious DNA results as yet apart from the victim.

'We'll see ourselves out.'

12

Vic Jenkins in a terraced house in Appleby Street in the south end of the city was more welcoming by far, but then he didn't have a wife languishing in jail in the way Dumbrell was quite obviously thoroughly ashamed of.

The hall carpet had a hardly discernible pattern but at least it all looked fairly clean. Not at all posh and modern without the IKEA look as far as Jamie Hedley could see, but fine all the same. If you like the cheap flat pack chipboard look, it was just about acceptable.

They were offered a cup of tea, both were pleased to accept and Cooper noted there was not even a Kit Kat.

'What can you tell us about Alerick Keating–Price?' Jamie Hedley started with.

'What's to tell?' said Vic. 'Pain in the arse back then and from what I hear nothing's changed. Bloody loony made us look a bunch of pricks back in our heyday, like.'

'What do you mean by that?' Jamie continued. Fascinated as he was by Jenkins with his head shaved like a fourteen year old close to the sides with one of those quiffs like a hot dog perched on his bonce.

'All this environment business he's always spouting about. Like one of them politicians who can only talk about the ins and outs o'politics, while everyday life just passes them by, seems to me. What the hell does he know about anythin', about getting up and going to work, putting in a hard day's graft for next to nowt. Never seem him looking fer the next job scraping money together for a damn holiday. Sits there in his f...lipping ivory tower just soundin' off about climate change nonsense and some other rubbish. Sorry pal, just bloody need a decent summer despite the shit he comes out with.'

Jamie Hedley understood bricklayers are on a good wack these days, due to a skills shortage brought about by all the turning sour Brexit business.

'When did you last speak to him?' The DC had yet to try the tea. It looked too weak for him, but needs must to show willing.

'Crissakes!' he scoffed louder than was at all necessary. 'Like, last century I reckon,' he blew out his breath.

'Any reason why?'

'Why what?'

'Why you have no contact with Keating-Price?' Hedley asked.

'Why d'you think?' He tossed back loudly. 'Hardly move in the same crowd d'we? All his pontificating bunch of loonies in their sandals, carrying pissing placards protesting about this that an' t'other gluein' themselves to the bloody M25 and all that other shit. Not seen him to speak to for bloody ages. Heard him on radio spouting time enough, but n'er to speak to.'

'What about Dumbrell and Tyson?'

'Them neither. Prats.' Jenkins tossed back. 'D'you reckon all this business'll scupper the advert?'

'We've no idea, sir.' He could just make out a female voice in the kitchen.

'All I bloody need. Government shower going on about building more affordable homes, but never get off their backside and do anything 'bout it. Four days this month I've sat on me arse here twiddling me thumbs, I could be building them places what folks need.'

'Have you been in…?'

'Bet bloody Howard's never done a day's proper graft in his life. Strummed a guitar, wrote a song or two, since then…' he raised both hands. 'What's he ever done, I mean really done about the environment? Actually got off his arse and got his hands dirty. He ever cleaned a beach some place? Yeh right,' he chuckled and shook his head. 'You'd not see blokes like him living off his wife's millions litter picking on South Common that's for bloody sure.'

Michelle Cooper knew from Alisha's research how Keating-Price had been done a time or two for causing damage to GM crops. Might not be actual work but at least he was willing to some extent to put himself in the thick of it.

'As I was saying, have…?'

'What's all this rubbish about the green belt, cockeyed bloody fools like Howard saying soon all the fields'll be concrete? What utter tosh I ask you? Get them houses built and stop all these bloody landlords filching joe public and getting away with bloody rotten places for folk to doss down. You wanna see some o'them. All wet rot, dry rot, right bloody mess and no mistake, son.'

'Mr Jenkins,' was louder from Hedley. 'Have you been in touch with any of the other members of Rockapelt?'

'No. Why should I?' Jenkins snorted. 'Can't be doing with their sort.'

'Their sort?' Cooper slipped in. The best thing about the tea was, it was warm.

'Apart from that goon Howard, we've got Tyson thinks he's the bloody bee's knees and Jonnie married some daft bitch got hersen in the clag,' he chuckled. 'What can you say 'bout a bunch o'tossers like them?'

'We'd prefer if you did say.'

'All in the papers innit. Maggie the silly cow nicked savings off some old disabled bloke. Got all she deserved, her. I'da sent her down for more, what's the bettin' she'll be out in no time. All tagged up and that.' He let his head shake. 'How in God's name did I ever get involved in a bloody shower like them? Tell you what,' he went on. 'He's a prize prat now, but if it weren't for me and Nathan with all our beat and bass they'dve been nothing. Nothing at all matey.'

'Can I ask? Where were you last Saturday night?'

'Where?' he repeated. 'Had a bevvy or two down the Old Crown, got me usual kebab on way home. Just the usual pretty much.'

'Any witnesses?'

'What? You want names and addresses of folk in t'Crown?'

'Just who went with you or who was here when you got home will do for starters.'

'Carole me partner went wi' me. Janice were here, had a friend round…can't remember the name now, and o'course there's our lad Jay and Lucy the little'un,' was what had Hedley assumed. It was good to receive confirmation of what he'd been able to ascertain already but even so he jotted down the names. 'That's L-W-S-I,' Jenkins insisted.

'What is?'

'Lwsi.' Jamie Hedley crossed out the name Lucy but left it still readable and wrote in what he'd been told. 'It's Welsh.'

What was wrong Jamie asked himself with giving your child a name they can live with? One you don't need to spell or make an excuse for every time for seventy years.

They'd been quickly ushered into the 'front room' as Jenkins had described it and not seen anybody else since they arrived although there was a background noise of talking from time to time. Except for the busty hippy woman with fair hair, black roots and too much glossy lipstick they took to be his ex-wife now partner who'd delivered the teas in mugs, all different patterns, shapes and sizes.

'We'll need DNA I'm afraid,' said Cooper. 'Need to eliminate you from our inquiries.'

'You serious?'

'Very,' the Detective Constable assured him. 'Does Janice have a partner?'

'Not really.'

'What d'ya mean. Not really?'

'High days and holidays if she's unlucky.'

'A name would be quite useful,' said Cooper sarcastically.

'Tommy Reynolds,' triggered a familiarity gene in Hedley's brain. He just looked at Jenkins who took time to realize they wanted more. He pulled himself to his feet and wandered out. Both detectives gestured to each other about the tidy state of the place and both took drinks of their teas to show willing. Short stocky Vic Jenkins returned with an address scribbled in blue felt tip onto the back of an old envelope which he handed down to Cooper.

'Thanks,' she said getting to her feet as Hedley joined his colleague. 'Don't forget, you, your partner and your daughter need to pop in the station to give us a swipe of DNA. Take just a few minutes. Give us a call first though.'

'And this Tommy too, please.'

His phone rang and DI Oliver Bristow in response to the call left his poky office, strolled through the Incident Room, along the corridor and down the wide stairs. The front desk team of civilians had a solicitor he knew fairly well wanting to speak to him urgently.

At the bottom he pushed through the double doors and it was exactly who and what he expected. The too good looking, smartly dressed Justin Whittaker from the strangely named Shaidy and Day solicitors in town; everybody he knew left out the 'and'. There he was, stood there as ruggedly handsome to anybody's eyes as ever.

'Detective Inspector,' he said sincerely the moment he spied and to his mind a bit formal the DI considered. What had happened to his normal "Oliver"

'I'm good, and you?'

'Fair to middling,' he responded. 'Heard on the grapevine you'd taken over from Larsson. How's it going?'

'Fine so far. Thank you.'

'Here on another matter just thought I'd better mention,' and hesitated as if he were making a point to a Magistrate. 'Ms Furneaux. Not sure who it was got their knickers in a twist so to speak, but somebody from here has asked for her to provide a buccal swab. Be one of your young DCs I guess.'

'And?'

'Sorry old boy. We're not talking dregs here, dear me no. This is not the bottom of the barrel as we both know all too well, just thought I'd pass it by you personally. Get this silliness knocked on the head sharpish. There'll be no swab, but then I'm sure you already realize. Just get it sorted for me please, if you wouldn't mind.'

'Your connection Justin?'

'Representing her in this matter, that's all. Local knowledge shall we say, is always of great benefit.'

'She your client?'

'Not as such, no.'

'Sorry?' he perceived was not at all the attitude he was expecting.

Oliver Bristow much admired the way Whittaker was as eloquent as he was in court. He would never describe him as smooth although some women tended to swoon. Charming very much so and certainly ruggedly handsome and even his eyebrows appeared proud.

'I would have thought it was obvious. Just one of your juniors allowing their enthusiasm to run away with them, no doubt. Happens.'

Bristow always had two questions about Whittaker. Why was he one of those people who appeared to have everything he could wish for in life, yet had not attained the one thing people say he hankered for the most?

'But if she's not your client...'

'I'm quite sure somebody of your ability can get along quite nicely with this little matter,' extended his act of superiority. 'Without the need to ask Bryony Furneaux to suffer the ignominy of the pantomime reserved for criminals.'

'Swabbing the inside of her mouth Justin is hardly a hardship. For us it's to do with elimination as you know only too well.'

'Not at all sure your higher authority will side with you, my good man,' he smiled a disarming smile.

'What are you suggesting?'

'Word here, word there in the clubhouse or wherever when our Jackson Moore happens to bump into your Chief Constable socially. As I'm sure he does.'

Probably at the Masons but that's for me to know. 'How dare you.'

Whittaker grinned and tapped the side of his nose. 'Jackson's wife and Allan Townend's lady belong to the same book club I understand. And you're the new boy on the block.'

'Do you by any chance know of the whereabouts of Katherine Arbiter?'

'Lady Arbiter I think you mean,' was so wrapped up in British pomp it was laughable.

'Whatever. Her husband is dead and obviously we quite rightly need to speak with her.'

'Somewhere abroad.'

'But aren't you her solicitor?'

'I'm sorry, but my expenses don't run to trips abroad and certainly not to sunnier climes.' A pause. 'If that's all, I'll leave it with you,' he said smiling again. 'Just sort it, there's a good man. Chin-chin,' he added as he turned and walked off briskly to the door.

A very annoyed Bristow wandered off to the Duty Sergeant to ascertain condescending Whittaker's reason for being there, then trudged back upstairs to his office.

He normally had trouble with the slime bag brigade some solicitors tend to employ, but surely Justin was one of the good guys he'd got on well with, what on earth was that all about?

'Guess what Andy Fleming downstairs just told me?' he said to Jake Goodwin when he returned from his meet. 'Justin Whittaker was in earlier acting for Liam Spruell.'

'Be serious! If I'm not very much mistaken Spruell is a repeat offender. Thought he'd just take whichever duty dog happens to be passing. What use is a tasty lawyer like Whittaker when all they'll get is no comment from the brain dead?'

'And another community order I bet.'

Oliver Bristow threw a breezy smile before he slumped down behind his desk to ponder what had happened.

'Cheeky sod,' he said to himself sat at his desk in the cramped office. Why he queried did he allow the likes of Whittaker to get to him? Whittaker is just the bee's knees among the women, damn good solicitor, sharp as a button and film star gorgeous. The sort who makes the likes of George Clooney and over-inked Beckham some still drool over, look less than average. Absolutely charming was Justin, great manners, real gentleman, but then now and again by reputation tended to pull a stroke. First time he'd done it to him.

Oliver Bristow had been reminded about Justin Whittaker more than once. How self-righteous Shaidy Days have five partners, but if Whittaker's ambition in life is to join them or so he understood he'd need to move on. Been told by Darke he has a weak spot. Apparently the partners are all from supercilious bespoke country land-owning families and most are not from thereabouts. As good as he is, Oliver understood this Justin had been brought up on what used to be called a council estate. Old man was permanently out of work and his mother somebody once told him, had two jobs, one cleaning floors and took in washing to support her son. What had he got to be so snooty about?

The DI knew he'd been at Oxford and was pretty much the best criminal lawyer he had ever known, but was still a square peg in a round hole in Shaidy's eyes.

His train of thought was disturbed by the arrival during his absence of the Tech Crime Team's laptop results for Keating–Price. They'd found no porn or any record of him having visited even smutty sites in his browsing history. He was either quite happy with Bryony or he'd somehow erased it all, but Bristow realized the Tech Crime Team would know if he had.

The business downstairs still rankled. It had all been unlike the Justin Whittaker he knew, who he'd never actually had legal battles and good banter in court with. Bristow and his colleagues down in Grantham had enjoyed a degree of appreciation of the ability he obviously held and had always admired his good grace and sharp mind.

Was this the Justin he knew or was he being used by his toffee nosed hierarchy? Had he been put up to it he wondered, and was his assumption of a young naive DC being behind the swab idea what he really thought? As he sat there, elbows on his desk, chin resting in cupped hands he had to consider the smart-suited one had possibly been carrying out somebody else's dirty work for sychophants. Maybe, just maybe this was Whittaker having a dig at his new position running MIT.

He was an elegant man despite his attitude earlier, and he knew there were smart-alec lawyers about. Those who will move heaven and earth to discover some technical loophole to allow their client no matter how scurrilous to scarper free from court. Nobody he knew had never had Justin down for such antics.

13

Incident Boards were at last starting to come alive with all the basic Post Mortem info included. With GHB dispersing within 6 hours they could not confirm the use of the colourless date rape drug that would have rendered the band member immobile within fifteen minutes. There were early Digital Forensic indicators and the names Cooper and Hedley had returned with.

They were now checking through the alibis given to them by former band members Dumbrell and Jenkins. Oliver Bristow in his office had already heard Jamie moaning about Pizza Dough they'd been put onto by Deliveroo not opening until 11am and the pub manager being out at the wholesalers.

To make the whole band members' scenario a great deal clearer one of the civilian women had created a whole Rockapelt section with information on all three of the band members. No guesses from where she got all that. Plus they now had extra names Tommy (Thomas Patrick) Reynolds and a Danny (Daniel) George Mullery.

Bristow had Alisha head down running the two names through social media and undergoing basic database checks.

Sub sections on the boards indicated news about Dumbrell's wife's sojourn in HMP. The wife, ex-wife, partner saga involving Carole Jenkins their children and this Reynolds.

Concerned Oliver Bristow would never admit to his MIT crew how the case without major forensics was heading down one little alley in double quick time. Had they just lost their way, had the wheels come off or more disturbing had there never been any wheels on this case in the first place? Had they built a soap box cart but nobody had come up with a couple of decent old pram wheels or in this case the reasoning behind that bandage and that warning sign?

On a wild goose chase with just the three middle-aged band members in the frame with no means of making their journey to the finish. If alibis for all three stood up, where would they be then?

Whoever it was had to be taken off the streets.

Why was it he so often asked himself, in cases such as these very few appear to live normal lives? One had married and divorced a woman who was now his partner, another had his wife in prison. That Bryony woman was not married and chose to live in a hovel. Why was nobody boringly normal?

On the board Nathan Tyson only had his wife's name Monica listed against him as DS Goodwin planned to call on him later to add bits and pieces of background.

One interesting development to lift Bristow's spirits was the rap sheet for this Reynolds, somebody the PHU (Prisoner Handling Unit) downstairs were very familiar with apparently which Alisha had cottoned onto. A list as long as your arm with the latest being four months inside at the start of last year plus a fine and a driving ban for cloning number plates he stuck on a Toyota Carolla he'd nicked when going equipped for burglary. Plus inevitably as his sort do, no insurance.

Danny Mullery who Cooper and Hedley had come across living with Jonnie Dumbrell's daughter had been quite the opposite. No record at all on PNC got him a black tick on the board.

Hand in the air, Alisha was full of enthusiasm 'This is odd, guv,' she called out 'There's no Keating-Price or any combination of his name on the 2011 or 2021 census.'

The DI whistled. 'Interesting, well done. Why'd he want to be hidden from view I wonder?'

'Isn't that typical of him?' Jake offered. 'To a certain extent he's not living in the same world as the rest of us. Anyway, bit too late now to prosecute.'

Nathan Tyson must have seen the familiar look of DS Jacques 'Jake' Goodwin walking along Corporation Street from his glass walled office, to be at the door hand extended the moment Goodwin spotted him.

Empty coffee cup on his desk was not good news, and as it proved when there was no hint of refreshments.

'Did your DNA thingy first thing if that's what you're here for, matey,' was Tyson before Goodwin had even managed to sit down.

'Yes, thanks a lot. Forensics are dribbling in now, so any we can eliminate make life so much easier. First today, can we just fill in a few names? Yours obviously, your wife Monica we have.' He looked at no-neck Tyson. 'Children?'

'Frazer up at Durham, Sonia taking A Levels this year,' Jake noted. 'Any reason you need to know?' They were another drain on his dwindling financial resources he'd have to cut back on somehow without the missus knowing.

'Just completes the picture, boss likes things neat and tidy. Makes the job easier having everybody in little packages. You, Monica, Frazer and Sonia, your alibi, DNA swab done plus bits and pieces of information. Lot of boxes we can tick,' he smiled.

'Those who don't confirm to your box ticking are then for the high jump I take it?'

Every time anybody told Jake what their children were doing, the phraseology they used annoyed him for no particular reason, but just did. "Up at Durham" was a case in point. Yes, from there in Silver Street, Lincoln not far from the ancient Stonebow, Durham was indeed *up*. What was not so easy to accept was "up at Southampton" or "up at Bristol" and all the rest down south who are never "up" no matter if you get a first in Geography or not. Do Scots living in Aberdeen come out with stupidity like "up at Exeter" about their precocious daughter studying Peace and Social Conflict.

'Pretty much. I'm here in the main to talk about the group today. Tell me about them.'

Tyson popped out a breath. 'What's to tell? I was always a bit of an outsider. Think Jenkins held it against me. I was in another group before Rockapelt and reckon that didn't suit. Their old bass player'd had enough of Jenkins, spouting about this that and the other all day long, I found out later. How the group'd be nothing without him, how he was driving us on, best sticks man on earth.' Cocksure Tyson snorted. 'Yeh?' and chuckled. 'He dealt with all the bookings initially and made a right mess apparently. But of course it was never his fault.'

'Alerick Keating-Price? How about him?'

'Just thought of something. One time near the end had an audition for a bloody big club in Rome, and idiot face Jenkins insisted we try to mimic groups out the charts. Like we're not the Barron Knights! Dumbrell's scared of his own shadow, and idiot features Keating-Price or Howard or whatever he is this week, couldn't give a sod as long as the club had a policy of environmental values or some other hogwash. We were crap, in fact we were worse than that. Rome here we come? You must be joking! Finished up doing a tacky gig somewhere like Romford instead.'

'Alerick Keating-Price?' Jake had not forgotten.

'Just away with the fairies most o'the time him. Should have been born earlier and gone off with all the flower power business in the sixties. All the free love smoking weed in pipes, barefoot and all the Maharishi Yoga nonsense. Last I heard be back a bit now he was into one of these environmental charities. Can't remember the name of them now some light of the life or whatever. All new age somehow connected with gypsies.' He stopped to chuckle. 'Tramps and Thieves.'

'Sorry?'

'Song title, Gypsies, Tramps and Thieves.' He grimaced to stop Jake going on. 'Bet you're not allowed to say that with all the political correct crap. What's the betting Cher's song has been banned by the BBC eh? Another poor bugger missing out on royalties.'

'Crunch question,' said Jake to move him away from the nostalgia he didn't fully understand. Tyson's phone had not rung once and although out of the corner of his eye he could see the female out the front on the phone she didn't look at all stretched. Could be she was ordering a to-go coffee to be delivered, to remind him he'd not been offered one.

'Hear the silly sod spouting on local radio. Can't be doing with it. Extinction Rebellion? Have people seriously not got anything better to do? Like fund raising for cancer? Could do with a bloody rebellion to get rid o' some of them wasters.'

'Crunch question,' Jake tried again.. 'Why d'you think anybody would want Keating-Price dead?'

'Search me.'

'You have no idea. Yet you're very critical.'

Tyson shook his head just above steepled fingers. 'He could bore for England. Maybe somebody just got pissed off with all this climate change garbage. One sort of plastic in here, another in there, paper in one bin, cardboard in this nonsense when we all know they bung it all in together. Talk about mummy state,' he added shaking his head.

'But hardly worth topping somebody for d'you think?'

'Hardly. Pain in the butt, remembering to take a carrier bag to the shops, so how come you can still buy job lots of 200 plastic ones on line? But kill some silly sod like Howard for it? No chance, gotta be pickled if you do.'

'Tell me about her ladyship. Katherine Arbiter.'

'Every now and again you come across the odd-couple. Folk you know should never ever be together. Seems no rhyme or reason for them ever being more than nodding acquaintances.' He shrugged. 'She's a good few years younger. Met in that commune place and maybe she was the Vestal virgin. What d'yer reckon eh?'

'They married?' Jake knew the answer to.

'Could be I suppose, her family'd probably insist I reckon. Their sort'd want things done properly. Or what they think is. He'd had no experience of girls like the rest of us had, so she'd not know any better.'

'Talking of family, what do you know about them?'

'Look. She cleared off so they coupla years back, but,' he said holding up a hand. 'Never been into all that Twitter and WhatsApp stuff and nonsense. Not into all this celebrity garbage so when she cleared off I'd not know what was cracking off. Must be what a good year or more since I heard she'd gone.'

'She's been gone seventeen, eighteen months or thereabouts, apparently.'

'Didn't know any of that till...forget now, could 'ave been Monica. Reckoned somebody'd seen her out some place having coffee.'

'Eighteen months ago?'

'Maybe a year or so, more could be.' he grimaced. 'Sunning herself in Italy some place. Family'd lived out in that damn big house for like,' he lifted his broad shoulders. 'Centuries so they say. Think her mother was last to go. All in the papers a while back.'

'Is Katherine the last of the line do you know?'

'Honestly? I haven't a clue. Never coming in here looking for a three-bed bungalow is she?' he thought was amusing.

'Any more news on the drinks advert?'

Tyson smiled and chuckled. 'You looking for a motive, that'll be a good one. Probably good job he is dead. If he hadn't pulled his finger out and said yes there's one or two'd be after him let me tell you.'

'Such as who?'

'Not me,' he shrugged and blew out a puffed breath. 'I've done well, business is still doing okay despite all that pandemic business,' he lied. 'But gotta move with the times. In business you can't stand still of course. Working on a link with a few folk about going on line. Offer the best of both worlds, on line, in shop, on the net, on the high street,' he hesitated for a moment then gestured with his head out towards his staff beavering away or at least looking as though they were. 'Between you and me,' he said and winked. Jake Goodwin was waiting. 'Dumbrell's missus in a bit of trouble according to the paper, so if it's a no go he'll not be bloody happy for sure. And big mouth Jenkins?' He chuckled and let his head rock from side to side. 'Anything's possible with a dickhead like him. Been told booze and too much wacky baccy just might be where his problems lie.'

'Two with money issues you reckon?'

'And some,' he snorted. No chance the others were up shit creek like he was. 'Bit of a bastard all this eh? One too young, one away with the vegan fairies and the third one always unwilling to take advice and to a degree arrogant, and what good has that all done him?'

'You're not very enamoured with Jenkins I take it?'

'Always had this inane sense of self-worth. Worthless is a better description.'

'A Danny Mullery and Tommy Reynolds,' said the DS from his notes. 'They mean anything to you.'

Tyson just made a face and pouted. 'Nah,' he shook his head. 'Nothing. Should they?'

'Just names we've come across. One is known to us.' Jake pushed himself to his feet. 'Think that'll be about it for now. Thank you. If you hear any more about the song or anything comes to mind, give me a bell, please' Jake said and handed the former bass player a card.

Nathan just sat there engrossed in his own morass of life. Why'd he ever got personally involved with that Finnish lad Lukas wanting to buy an apartment, apart from the fact his old man was rich? At least he knew he had not as yet been totally swallowed up by a mountain of debt like Jussi Lahti had done.

Been with him three times he could vividly recall to that flashy Casino place in Nottingham in his Bentley. Stood there behind Jussi watching this little white ball skittling around all the time aware his new friend was praying and hoping it would drop conveniently into one of his lucky numbers.

Nathan back then could never understand the point of betting good money on something over which he had absolutely no control whatsoever.

He'd been with Jussi for the last time when he'd lost a pretty packet but fortunately not the time when his house of cards finally all came tumbling down.

He'd be the first to admit he tended to throw too much the bookies way from time to time. But never ever had he been like Jussi with a serious pile of mounting debts back then he'd no inkling ever existed. Why didn't the bloody fool stay at home with his gorgeous wife rather than watching that stupid ceramic ball, which for some inexplicable reason time and again would drop perfectly, only to plop out again with a cackle of *'Fooled yer'*?

He'd long ago settled on football as his weekly indulgence. Horses he knew nothing about and would only take a punt on the Derby, Cheltenham and the Grand National maybe but even that was risky. Maybe a bit too heavy last year though. All to his mind very much in the same stable as that stupid little ball bouncing about.

At least with the football he knew one from another among teams and players. Studied form, knew who were good home and away, read about injured players who they bought and sold, could name the best managers, who were at the top and those under threat of relegation from day one.

That was until some goon introduced VAR.

Before scooting back to Lincoln Central Jake Goodwin decided to do two things: check up on the mystic Tyson had mentioned and get a good coffee. Down the High Street into his coffee shop of choice. Americano with an extra shot he'd not tell Sally about and soon had his phone out while the coffee cooled. Unsure of the actual spelling he was forced to make a guess on Google, and in the end came up with Maharishi Mehesh Yogi and transcendental meditation. Had to be the guy Tyson had mentioned. Not important, but at least it gave Jake more infill about this increasingly weird Keating-Price. Far more interesting had been Lady Arbiter coming back from...Italy according to Tyson, but somebody'd said Greece.

Sat there with his good Costa coffee just scanning around to see who was about Jake got to thinking about the Italy business. Time to have a Border Force check of her passport movements. Then there was the three remaining band members to think about.

Nathan Tyson was undoubtedly the better off of the trio, and was sensible looking at an on-line business. Seemed to Jake such a move was at least a good decade late but keep it local it could possibly do well. Knew he'd have all the income from lettings and property management to keep him going in the meantime, but some of the on-line businesses were well established.

Dumbrell's wife was in nick and from what Michelle and Jamie reckoned the place was fairly scruffy and they'd also discovered he was still renting when he should be close to paying off his mortgage. Struggling to keep the family together on just his poor basic wage possibly.

Then Jenkins, who according to Tyson was just a complete arse and from what Jamie'd said, could be quite objectionable. As a bricklayer he shouldn't have money problems, providing the snorting powder suggestion wasn't true. Two in the frame he surmised, sat there happy with his thoughts, supping.

14

With a paper mountain on his desk Oliver Bristow knew he had to clear as soon as, it was not necessary for him to digest every iota of his team's work. When both DC Jamie Hedley and chestnut haired Michelle Cooper both shrugged on their jackets and headed out, pocketing phones as they did so, he guessed there had to be an alibi issue somewhere.

DC Alisha O'Neill he knew with assistance from experienced Nicky, was running through a DVLA list she'd printed off. It listed all the black 1983 Land Rover Defenders in the county. In Lincolnshire such a vehicle was always going to be a darn sight more likely than you'd find in say Birkenhead, with all the yellerbelly farmer boys and their kids lording it about.

Even so he'd been surprised when Alisha waved a long list at him. Owner details plus vehicle registration number and vehicle specification. Once done the DI knew he may have to ask Nicky to assist her young DC with authority when the need arose to get onto Hendon for their ANPR tracking data.

Michelle and Jamie soon returned from their sojourn to the Old Crown pub, the takeaway and the local bookies.

'We nipped to the pub and the one star takeaway place and as we were nearby had a sniff round the bookies near his place,' they admitted to those in the Incident Room, with the boss all ears in his office.

'Good news for him. The pizza place,' said Jamie. 'Confirm they ordered,' he stopped to snigger. 'Ready for this? One Pepperoni Lovers which is Pepperoni, Mushrooms and Jalapenos,' he read from his notebook still smiling. 'Plus a Super Piggynormous. Pepperoni, Salami, Garlic, Sausage and Spicy Beef on the Saturday evening.'

'Ye gods what in…?'

'But,' said grinning Michelle to interrupt. 'We have no way of knowing if Jenkins himself was at home when it was delivered, but at least we know the pizza alibi he offered is true.'

Nicky Scoley didn't imagine Piggynormous was ever likely to be what Keating–Price enjoyed for his evening meal. She'd read recently about sweet potato, chickpea and cauliflower curry she assumed was eaten with bog standard rice. She'd long given up on blogs by seriously underweight stick thin women talking about zoats she discovered is a combination of zucchini and oats.

'And two lots of potato wedges,' Jamie finished with. 'Old Crown was a bag of worms. All the usual anti-cop saga about having no idea who was in on a busy Saturday night. Claims his CCTV is not working, not wanting to upset his customers by grassing them up and I quote, 'to the pigs.'

'Nice,' was Jake. 'Old Crown d'you say?' to which Jamie nodded. Jake knew in this day and age from their stats it is quite often only dopes who frequent certain down market pubs on a regular basis. Maybe a word with some of the eager cops downstairs might not go amiss.

Jake was listening and working at the same time. He'd brought up a crime mapping programme on his PC and was just going through the process with one ear on the room.

'We visited the bookie on High Street nearest to where Jenkins lives just on the off chance,' Jamie Hedley went on. 'All he'd say was some nonsense about company policy and data protection. Reckoned he daren't risk talk about individual customers but got the feeling he knew who we were talking about.'

'Could just be company policy, to be fair,' Nicky Scoley suggested.

'No details,' said Jamie. 'But the manager said we should be able to work it out for ourselves.'

'Interesting.'

'Need to ascertain which other pub he frequents, as they're still open down that way.'

DI Bristow knew despite the fact Jenkins and Dumbrells were along with Tyson, the only likely suspects they had in the weak frame. He realized there was little point in bringing them in with all the hassle it would no doubt involve. Just because a couple of alibis were being awkward or stupid or both.

He was also aware there was little point in asking Dumbrell about the programme he said he'd watched on telly. These days even to cover himself he could easy have recorded or watched it on Catch Up or was having a quick gander right at that minute.

'If he bets on line how will we know?' Alisha queried. 'Adverts on all the time, telling people to bet on some amazing things. Took me ages to fathom what an acca was.'

Oliver Bristow in shirt sleeves at his office door. 'Tech Crime Team can pick up emails and run a print out of websites he visits easy enough. Need his phone. Having a list of numbers from the phone company is one thing, but reading the texts is a better bet. Remember Hari Mistry that hacker come computer analyst upstairs can unpick phones in no time. Could also do with his laptop or whatever for Dexter,' The DI shrugged. 'Might be worth a try.'

'You think he'll have such a thing?' Jamie sniggered his query. 'Didn't look the sort to me.'

'Phone you mean?'

'No,' was unnecessarily moody. 'Tablet, laptop.'

'Want me to see if I can get a wee something?' Sandy offered. 'In the morning how about I charm yon lassie to hand over something when she comes back from the school run,' produced a few chuckles. 'Say her dad promised, and as I'm passing...'

'Take it easy though,' was cautious Bristow. 'Might have to go down the warrant route. Need his bank account the economic lads are after too, but it just might be a long shot, so we can see what the score is with any debts.'

'He'll have his phone with him surely.'

'Could see if super nerd ASBO in the Tech Crime Team can get what we want by underhand snooping.'

'You mean hacking?'

'Does it for a living seems to me.'

Newish boy on the block Bristow gave Jake a quick look to say he wasn't at all sure what the Tech Crime Team did was always above board and within the law. 'Try the daughter first,' he said and gave Sandy a look. 'Any warnings bells, just pull out. Don't want complaints, not with the media waiting with baited breath already crawling all over this. Not to mention Lady whatsit in the background and her solicitor friend trying to pull strings.' Bristow grimaced at the thought of Justin's attitude. 'Here's a thought. Is that Furneaux female the same as the band members? Says she has no contact. Maybe doesn't know them personally. Think all she said was it was all in the past, all another world back then...'

'Before she was old enough to understand?'

'But the truth is she knows full well what's been going on?'

'Always possible Jenkins's debts if he has any, have gone beyond not having any spare cash, or possibly its just a case of not budgeting properly. One we spoke to wouldn't go into details and came up with all nausea about data protection of clients' rubbish.'

'And if he's not admitting he has a problem even to himself?' Jamie slipped in. 'Just has a permanent chip on his shoulder seems to me. Not accepting the situ for gamblers is always an issue. Probably spending his time hoping against hope for the big win to clear all his debts.'

'As they do.'

'And the song's his last throw of the dice.'

'Remember,' said Bristow. 'This is from Tyson's perspective. He says Jenkins's short of cash, which he probably is compared with him.'

'If he's seriously in trouble he'll be absolutely banking on the advert. And if by chance he's a gambler, you can bet he'll put money on it going to number one as well,' made a few smile.

'In the meantime Sandy,' said the DI. 'If you want the job of top snoop until we need ASBO, you could get onto Dumbrell's employer for his details? Bank account is probably enough, be easy to get his salary, rent and stuff from it. Need to see how close to the wind that one's sailing as well.'

The Scot's response was a nodded 'Aye'.

'What about Tyson?' Jake asked. 'I hope we're not assuming he's clean?'

'Think money issues we can discount,' said Bristow scratching his beard. 'Reckon the song to him is more about bragging rights and keeping his wife in the state to which she has become accustomed.'.

'Have we done backgrounds on his poker mates?' Jake queried and Michelle shook her head. 'Would you do it next for me, while I check a few folk about this on line estate agency thing he reckons he's going into.'

'Well done,' was heartfelt from Bristow to chunky Sandy MacLachlan as he plonked a Dell laptop down onto the Detective Inspector's desk with a mobile perched on the top.

'Nae problem. What you're after?' he grinned with lashings of self-satisfaction.

'These Jenkins's?' his gushing query was answered by a nodded grin.

'Och aye.'

'I won't ask,' said Bristow shaking his head and wondering to himself with a degree of concern.

'Only worry guv, the daughter was a bit over co-operative, almost as if she was too keen to help.'

'Any reason why?'

'No idea, but it was all very much along the lines of concerned member of the public doing everything she can to help us with our inquiries. With a proviso.' Bristow with fingers steepled sat back and waited. 'Laptop has to be back with her before four. Before Jenkins gets home.'

'So she is working against him. Just doesn't want to get into a load of bother with him when he gets home I should imagine.' The DI screwed up his face. 'Interesting.' He lifted the Android. 'And this?' he queried.

The grin returned on MacLachlan's good face. 'Old trick guv, always the best. I called him down off the scaffold at the estate over in Washingborough and chatted to him. Jamie called him on his phone with a wrong number for me. "Nice phone Vic, mind if I have a look…" Works every time.'

'He not protest then?'

'Of course.'

'Had a whole load of guff about how he couldn't operate without his phone. When I've done a wee bit of bricklaying in me back garden I've never used a phone,' MacLachlan chortled. 'Want me to pop these up to ASBO?'

'Phone to Hari if you would,' Oliver Bristow answered. 'Well done. Make sure you get the laptop back in time for her.'

'After the ridiculous school run business. Dumbrell's bank this after,' said Sandy as he picked up the laptop. 'Made an appointment.'

Well satisfied Bristow sat back in his black chair and drank the cold remnants of his black coffee.

He smiled to himself. The CSI rules on computers he knew would not apply in this case. First thing they ever do is photograph a PC or laptop in situ, take pics from all angles, show all devices plugged in and if possible what was showing on the screen at the time. No plugs, no devices and it had been shut down. Oliver felt a tinge of excitement start to take over the space previously occupied by the sense of impending boredom he loathed.

Phones were easy for the team. First thing is to remove the SIM card to stop the owner destroying evidence remotely.

This was suddenly a bit too easy with things slotting into place. Back now to waiting for the Digital Forensic guys in the Tech Crime Team to wade their way through Jenkins's technology. Then there'll be Dumbrell's bank account with an indication of salary, direct debits including rent and overall a general picture of his financial status.

As Forensics reported more DNA results it reminded Bristow about the missing stuff. The bad news Darke had called him about. Porton Down were now involved and he knew that could take days if not weeks.

All three band members had come back negative along with Carole and Janice Jenkins and Tommy Reynolds who was immediately linked on the database to his PNC profile as expected. Sara Dumbrell and Danny Mullery were two more negatives unfortunately. Same went for Nathan Tyson and he'd not bothered to take his wife with him for some reason.

Probably not the sort of things she'd want to dirty her hands with. Hardly a conversation piece over cocktails for the ladies who lunch

Missing however was the one they needed if they were ever to find who had left a meagre amount of forensics on the body. Last but no least problem for the DI, was how he would deal with it.

Bull by the horns time and he walked along to the Darke ivory tower and a chat.

'We have one missing one,' he admitted after telling him about the DNA negatives. He took a deep breath. 'This Bryony Furneaux woman,' made the boss grimace.

'Take it you don't like her?' Bristow looked at him enquiringly. 'Calling her that Furneaux woman.'

'Sorry but this is a murder inquiry and it's her partner who just happens to be dead. I'd expect her DNA to be on him or at least on his clothes. According to forensics there are two main samples and several lessers. One hers maybe, but how will we ever know which is hers and which isn't and who the other one belongs to if we can't eliminate her for starters?'

Darke's mouth moved peculiarly as he obviously considered the problem he now faced. 'Justin Whittaker was serious you say?' Bristow nodded. 'Can we take this very gently?' he asked speaking sympathetically. 'Say, take maybe Nicky with you rather than somebody with size tens clomping all over her carpets.' He sucked in a breath and grimaced. 'Not wed I know, but how about treating her like a widow?'

Oliver Bristow spluttered and chuckled. 'Carpets?' he said. 'Be serious, boss.' He appeared perplexed. 'Cold stone floor they tell me. It appears to be a run down old stone cottage. Jake imagines was once home to pigs of the bacon variety. Hob nailed boots'd not leave a mark.'

'And I'll tell the Chief, forewarned is forearmed. Be best eh?'

One thing Oliver Bristow hated was bad news the moment he stepped foot in the place. He'd always loathed starting work on the wrong foot. A mind wanting to succeed, full of plans and ideas all suddenly kicked into touch. Walking through reception was the worst. Some copper catching his eye and spouting the gloom before he'd had his coffee almost as if they took great pleasure in the act. Second pet hate was receiving word to destroy his evening. He was quite sure there must be a hidden camera to spy on him at home just as he sat down to relax. If there really was he was in serious trouble except the whole house had been swept. Right out of the blue, phone call. Crap news.

That morning it had been Andy Fleming the Duty Sergeant who had told him why Justin Whittaker had been in the building when he'd asked to speak to him about her ladyship.

'You heard?' had an ominous charge to it. DI Bristow, bag over his shoulder probably showed his feelings through his face but made no real gesture. 'Liam Spruell got off on a technicality. Magistrates Court,' and as he went to ask the obvious supplementary question his hand went up with a supercilious grin. 'Hoped he'd go down,' Andy blew out a breath with spittle. 'Did he buggery. Little sod had that Whittaker up there proud as a peacock giving it law of the land chapter and verse so they say.'

'Has to be the reason he was here the other day. To make a big issue of a nasty little sod like him who nicks pool cars for the druggies.'

'Seemed a bit odd at the time.'

'Odd?' was louder. 'It's more than bloody odd!' Oliver tapped Andy Fleming on his shoulder. 'Thanks for making my day,' he grinned, turned and walked to the stairs.

DS Jake Goodwin was the recipient of his mood when being second to arrive reached the confines of the Major Incident Team.

'Just been told about Liam Spruell who Whittaker was here to see the other day, getting off,' he said to his second in command before he'd thought about slipping his grey jacket off.

'Hang on a minute that was a bit quick.' he shot back. 'Since when did CPS work at such a pace when the queue's a mile long?'

'Exactly what I thought,' Bristow smiled a disarming smile. 'Just out of interest, and I know it's nothing to do with us but I'm curious. See what you can find out. I'm assuming of course Andy Fleming's not got his wires crossed.'

The feeling this was not going to be a good day increased in ferocity when once he'd downloaded all the overnights, had a quick spin down his emails, even before he'd grabbed a mug of coffee from the canteen, who should appear but DSup Craig Darke.

Nice guy, fine person to have as his boss. Certainly a giant step up from some he'd worked with. With his reputation flying ahead of him and one he'd come across a few times previously. A good looking man is Darke, doted on by his attractive lovely wife the notoriously successful banking executive who works from home with just a solitary weekly first class trip down to the smoke. Father of one pretty little daughter and successful copper.

Downside was him having accepted promotion in the full knowledge it would have little to do with catching crims. He must have known he'd spend his life knee deep in paperwork or bored to tears with seminars and meetings with the 'partners' they all talk about he had yet to see sight of.

'Morning Oliver,' he said brightly at his door.

The DI didn't exactly ignore him but looked past out to the team and gestured to Michelle to get three coffees.

'Good morning, sir.'

'This song and the advert,' Darke said as he just plonked himself down and crossed his legs.

'Of course,' Bristow responded as he lowered himself. 'Any news?'

'Made useful contacts with the record company, the music publisher and would you believe a bunch of very quirky folk at the advertising people. Shock to them let me tell you, about him popping his clogs.'

'What do you mean?'

'Nobody's had the decency to tell them.'

'But...he's been all over the news!'

He chuckled. 'Can't imagine their sort mess about with the simple things in life. Agree with you, just what I thought when they said. Trouble is one I spoke with sounded about thirteen. Sometimes see these adverts on the telly and I can never fathom what they are advertising. Now I've spoken to one or two of their people I know why. Different world let me tell you.' Oliver sat forward and rested his forearms on the arms of his black chair. 'Once upon a time I was told in the world of advertising they never employ anybody over the age of thirty. Because older people never have good modern ideas. Yeh right, as they say, or zop on as one of their goons said to me yesterday.'

Oliver Bristow was in no mood to ask. 'What's the situation?' he did query however.

'Advertising people have had letters of acceptance from,' he pulled a mini tablet from his pocket Oliver had never seen before. 'Vic Jenkins, Nathan Tyson and Jonnie Dumbrell, so it means at the very least the record will be re-released because they'll take a majority verdict. Nothing I'm afraid from Keating-Price.'

'They've been in touch though.'

'Apparently. This bit of a kid told me he took some finding but in the end they went through one of these strange environmental groups he was all wrapped up in, made contact through them.'

'And?'

'Reluctant. In fact this goon calling himself Dex, which I assume is twitter speak for Derek,' he twittered. 'Who insisted he Zoom me, I ask you,' Darke just shook his head. 'Initially he appeared very reluctant. Wouldn't leave his phone number or anything. Said he'd think about it.' Darke grimaced. 'Told me the idiot had a bit of a rant about commercialization and how producing the record would likely harm the environment and a load of other nonsense. Told him he'd need to speak to people about the likely impact it would all have. How many CO2 emissions manufacturing it would cause. This Dex even asked me if he carried his own soapbox round with him.'

There was then a lengthy explanation of how he'd got in touch with all these people and how odd some of them were, particularly those working in advertising.

'That where it is, now he's dead?' the DI was in need of clarification once he finished. 'I take it you don't Zoom or Skype?' he had to ask. 'And if he wouldn't leave his number how were they to get in touch?'

'Don't be silly,' Darke chuckled. 'Had to get the Tech Crime Team to organize it all, for me. They do it all the time of course,' Oliver had to assume he was now talking about Zoom.

'And Keating-Price's phone number?' Oliver asked to remind. 'But he didn't have his phone, we've not found it. Or at least nobody from CSI have said anything. Could very well be messages on there.'

'All these advertising fruit cakes had was this enviro place number where they had to leave calls for him'

'This some sort of defence mechanism?' the DI pondered. 'Stop the cranks getting to him maybe. All the bad lads off Twitter having to leave messages sounds like a good idea.'

'Until you have to listen to the playback.'

'What if they won't now go with a majority verdict. Our guru could have died for nothing.'

'Not so sure about that,' Darke assured him. 'Alerick alone wrote the song, so it should really be his sole decision, but those I've spoken to are after money.'

'Which they'll not get now.'

'Think there's too much riding on it. Listening to them, more than likely they'll go with it and if somebody like the Furneaux woman sues it'll create a lot of extra publicity and you know what they say about bad news.' The dark boss hesitated. 'But if he left a will.'

'Is it possible?' he was asked.

'Of course,' he assured. 'Just like leaving your gold watch to your grandson you can leave the publishing rights and the subsequent income to someone in your will, like you can anything.'

'And if he hasn't left a will?' Oliver just put up a hand to stop the boss for a moment. 'His girlfriend told Jake and Nicky he owned nothing,' he hesitated.

'What about his Stratocaster?' the DI frowned. 'His guitar,' Darke explained. 'Must be worth a few bob by now.'

Oliver Bristow was pleased to see Michelle heading their way with the coffees. Last thing he wanted was for the conversation to end and have him hanging about waiting for drinks to arrive.

'You're not going to enjoy this,' Bristow told Jake leaning against the doorpost to his office ten minutes after a refreshed Darke had headed off. 'We need to go back to Gorgie Hall.'

Biting back a sigh, the DS said 'Go on.'

'Jenkins, Dumbrell and Tyson have all agreed for the record to be released and for it to be included in the advert and all the rest of it.'

'As they would,'

'But and this is a big but…these advertising people made contact with Keating-Price, but he said he'd think about it.'

'As he would.'

'Worried about the effect on the environment.'

'With a download,' he really laughed. 'Chances are he didn't know what they were talking about.' Jake chuckled more. 'Bet he imagined the old days with black vinyl discs being churned out in their thousands if not more.' He looked at his boss with a degree of exasperation. 'Gorgie Hall?'

'Did she mention the song last time?'

'We never brought the matter up. Only the group, deliberately. And when we mentioned the PI she never asked about him.'

'Has she made contact?'

'Not according to the Darke boss,' Jake chuckled at. 'What's up?' Bristow asked.

'Nicky Scoley came out with *the Darke boss* once upon a time, now it's a vital part of everyday talk and even you're using it.'

'Until he hears one of us say it. Sounds like something out of Star Wars. Hidden behind the new galaxy a trillion miles away emerged a creature. It was the Darke boss.' Amused all who heard the DI.

'Jenkins, Dumbrell and Tyson saying yes will get two of them out of the clag, but our Alerick says hang on there a minute. What about the environment as if we're planning to open a mine to dig for coal to fuel a big factory to churn out goodness knows what into the atmosphere and flood the county with smog like China do.'

'You know what it sounds like?'

'Motive.' Jake grinned. 'When we going?'

'Hope you don't mind. Thought I'd take Nicky.'

'Good news?' Jake asked.

'Such as?'

'Her ladyship. Keep being told she's trotted off to Italy sometime back.' Jake smiled. 'Guess what? She hasn't even got a passport. Got onto Border Force to see exactly when and where and up that pops.'

'What the hell's going on?'

'You tell me.'

15

It was Detective Inspector Oliver Bristow driving his Shadow Grey Renault Clio Hybrid, through the gates, between beech and sycamore into darkness beneath the gigantic oak trees across acres of land and about to head up the incline to the front of the big house sat on a rise. Just about as far as he got.

Perched on high in front of the huge house was one Iris Blue Morgan forcing the DI to slow to as halt.

'Bugger! Just got to be Whittaker, last person we need,' he said as he began to reverse rather than risk turning in front of the building and quietly drove backwards all the way carefully through the trees and down to the road in. 'Now what?'

'Back to Central and call it a day?'

'He'll be very pricey, so time will be of the essence, think we'll give him half an hour.'

'He always make house calls do we know?' made Bristow snigger. 'One possibility is coffee at the garden centre in Anwick. What think you?' Nicky Scoley suggested. Either that or nip to Jake's parents on the cadge.

'Point the way.'

It was getting on for fifty minutes by the time they'd enjoyed coffees and returned to the entrance to Gorgie Hall. Slowly and carefully and with an excuse in mind if they bumped into smart boy, Oliver Bristow drove up to the Hall. Morgan gone, no sight or sound of anyone.

This time the Detective Sergeant knew not to bother with knocking on the big oak door, and once they had alighted from the car trooped off around the right hand side of the huge home for her eventually to knock on the scruffy door of the old cottage and the pair of them waited.

'No to coffee,' Nicky whispered just before the door opened and there stood the stunning Bryony Furneaux dressed in what looked to her like the same clothes when they'd met previously, but different colours, and this time with her carefully crafted streaked blonde hair tied back.

They went through the introductions less formally than before The pair removed their shoes out of courtesy not out of necessity. Turned down the offered tea or coffee and took seats around the wooden kitchen table once more.

Once all the chit chat had ceased it was DI Bristow to venture forth with their reasons for calling.

'You haven't been to give us a DNA sample as yet.'

'I'm sorry, but my solicitor said it really isn't necessary. Appreciate it is part of your procedure, but says it's aimed at the less worthy shall we say.'

'Probably true,' Bristow responded as he ignored the phrase. 'Just makes our life somewhat more difficult when we come across DNA which could well be yours, we could so easily spend many hours searching high and low for a match.'

'Have you?'

'Yes, more than one sample as it happens.'

'When I was here before,' said DS Scoley as the pair had arranged during the journey. 'You didn't mention the advertising and use of Alerick's song.'

'Was it relevant?'

'Not necessarily, but it is certainly an interesting aspect to the situation.'

'In what way? I'm sorry dear, but I'm not following your drift.'

'What if your Alerick told somebody he would not agree to the song being used which would affect the other party financially?'

'He never mentioned anything about it,' she said shaking her head slightly with disinterest and pouted. 'Why would he?'

'What were your thoughts?'

'How do you mean?'

'Was Alerick happy to go ahead with his song appearing as part of an advertising campaign for a soft drink?'

Whereas Nicky Scoley is blonde, strikingly attractive and strongly built, this Bryony woman was paler, slimmer and bustier.

'Shouldn't imagine so. No certainly not.'

'And why is that?' Bristow joined in.

'I would have thought it was very obvious,' was as sharp as Scoley had experienced, almost as if this woman had suddenly come alive. 'We all need to consider the very serious environmental issues involved. Just take a moment to think about the business of just producing all those bottles for a start, not to mention the drink itself made in huge factories and the affect not only on this environment but in all the countries where they no doubt plan to make it. Countries I might add already struggling to cope with the desperate need for low carbon technologies to combat climate change.' Bristow went to speak but was beaten to it. 'We are so fortunate in that we have people who care, every day combing the beaches to collect rubbish thrown into the sea or overboard from these huge ships. Do we really want to add more ghastly plastic bottles to do so much damage and create havoc among our wildlife when we can so easily avoid it?' she asked. 'Do we?' was up a notch.

'So you think it would be a no?'

Scoley loved it when people think they're superior to her and she knew it was exactly when they let their guard down thus not feeling threatened, to hand her the advantage.

'Go down to the sea and you can hardly see the water for the rubbish people just toss on the beach.'

'But, if people buy this new drink instead of those already on the market. I don't see people drinking double the amount.' Scoley suggested.

'Think about it sensibly, based purely on CO2 emissions, what do you think?'

'But surely if the manufacturer's decide to go off on another tack they'll simply give the drink another name and still produce millions of bottles of the stuff,' had no effect on Furneaux sat there in a very passive mode.

'You'll not agree to this drink marketing campaign then?' Oliver Bristow asked.

'Not necessarily,' surprised the pair of them. 'I'm sure Alerick would have been dead set against it, such were his concerns for the long term future of our planet and the principles everybody so admires.'

'What about the other members of the group?' Bristow asked softly and watched her face. Scoley was annoyed by her use of everybody.

'Forgive me but I don't believe they wrote the song,' she sniggered in a derisory manner.

'No. But if the record is to be included there will be money to be made, and I understand the record is more than likely to be re-issued whatever happens.'

'Money?' she almost shouted, 'Is that all the world's interested in? Damn money!' she looked horrified. 'Do we really have to go through such silly nonsense all over again, just for grubby money?' was asked by a young woman Nicky Scoley wanted to give a mouthful to.

According to what Alisha had so far managed to piece together her billionaire father was the senior partner in a major Hedge Fund and despite relentless searching she had so far not established any way this young madam was likely to earn money, except from the bank of daddy. It was almost as if this was a different person from previously.

'You're probably unaware, but we understand at least two members of the group are not in good positions financially.'

'And you think it's my fault?' was sharp. 'Like these appeals you get asking people to text a word to somewhere to somehow send five pounds to pay for new wellington boots or a scarf to hide their faces in some war torn ramshackle hell hole. Always worded as if it's our fault.'

'In the case of Rockapelt…'

'Then a while ago the high rate of income tax was rightly done away with, and sniveling morons became upset. What on earth had it to do with them?'

'As I was saying. In the case of Rockapelt,' said Bristow, to annoy Scoley about to give her a gob full. 'This might be their one chance of making a few pounds and having their fifteen minutes of fame.'

'Oh dear me no,' the woman looked distressed at the thought of it. 'Not all this celebrity tripe, please no. Just stop it now if you will. I want nothing to do with any of it, thank you very much.' She shuddered. 'All this business is so distasteful. Just horrid, vulgar as are the people involved.'

'But you wouldn't be involved,' said Nicky, trying desperately hard not to be rude to this bitch of the first order. 'Only the three band members, who've not had the privileged life some have had. From what I understand had the people involved in managing and marketing the band back in the nineties got their act together, they may well have had their fame and fortune then. As a result none of this would be necessary.'

'I wouldn't know who to contact anyway,' was her new contrite excuse.

'We have sources who can provide the information and I do believe the record can be re-issued on a majority verdict they call it, where three of the four members are in agreement. So, the record will be out whether you want it or not and whether we like it or not bearing in mind what happened to Alerick.'

'Social media will pick up on the song not being in the advert, and some geek in his bedroom no doubt will add his own soundtrack after downloading the record.'

'And he'll make a good bob or two as well.'

Bryony Furneaux looked completely perplexed as if it was all in a foreign language and silence took over. Nicky Scoley wanted to ask why she felt it good for her to be all over social media yet three others should not.

'Social media and blogging in particular are such big things these days Bryony,' said Oliver Bristow with an easy tone. 'Seems as though there is no power to stop all this silliness. It's the way young people are. Making worthless people a short lived form of being known beyond our imagination. Next week some other trifling soul.'

'Think it will happen whatever,' Scoley slipped in. 'Publishers will want their slice of the cake for sure.'

'Know it will. And with the Alerick connection many will make the most of.'

'I was planning to take advice,' Furneaux said suddenly.

'Whittaker?'

'Look. I don't begin to understand all this internet business, but then I don't come into contact with it to any extent. Yes, he's been able to offer advice.'

Scoley was staggered to hear that from somebody constantly splashed across the social media nasty version of news.

'He your solicitor?'

'No. My family always use Barristers' chambers in Chancery Lane,' was her bigging it up. 'But as Kate's lawyer he has local knowledge. Daddy put me onto him.'

Although this was the only room she had visited Scoley could certainly see no outward displays of wealth she had to give the woman credit for. In addition she didn't appear to be seemingly preoccupied by what other people might think as so many do these days. No phone visible, no gadgets or devices plugged in as is normal in most households. She smiled thinly, but not a real smile of genuine warmth and Nicky wondered if she was capable of such a thing.

'Can we pass on a message to the other group members?'

'As I said, I'll take advice.' She glanced at her man's watch. 'Was there anything else?'

Bristow sucked in a breath. 'DNA swab?' was gentle.

'Do I really have to?' she sighed.

'We can do it right here and now,' from Scoley caught her by surprise.

'What was that all about?' Oliver Bristow gasped when they were well out of earshot walking back towards the big house. 'One minute she's very anti playing the climate change card, then before you can turn round she's talking about taking advice.'

'And claiming she knows nothing about social media, when she's been all over it for ages and been trending every day since he died. With millions of followers.'

'With daddy's money and living that sort of life in the full knowledge she has millions to fall back on when she's tired of it.'

'No guesses who she'll be seeking advice from?'

'But he's just been here. Did she really mean, I've taken advice?'

'From low life Liam Spruell's legal eagle?' Nicky Scoley chuckled as the pair strode on together.

'I'd have thought she'd make a bigger effort when Justin was calling.'

'Cost a pretty penny that get-up like she wore before, just slightly different. Doing it for show is my guess,' said the DS. 'Good bone structure.'

'Someone like her with that body and looks could take her pick. So why Keating-Price?'

'This her doing the young rich woman's environmental bit like so many of these protesters get up to for a year or so? Second time I've visited, and it seems to me it's a case of what we haven't been asked. When can I bury him, when will you release the body, any closer to a suspect?'

'How about, how did he die and what about where or when?'

'No. Nothing.'

'But the moment we mention the environment she's up and at us, like a rat up a drainpipe.'

'Don't think we'd better build Rockapelt's hopes up, do you?'

'Just a thought. D'you think the group might reform if the record does well?'

'Why not. Stones are a lot older than them, and there's not much competition these days, except those who were around at the same time. Today's music scene produces nothing at all to write home about.'

'You sound like…'

'The Darke boss,' made them both laugh.

'Trouble is of course, he's absolutely right.'

DI Bristow suddenly announced: 'This week's number one, Rockapelt with *Sheer Delight*.'

'Do they still do it I wonder, run down the charts?'

'Feel so sorry for the kids these days, all the stuff they miss out on.'

'But they're much better off. They've got TikTok and YouTube. Likes. Over priced phones they drop down the toilet, selfies, porn and bullying instead, remember.'

'Of course, how silly of me.'

16

When they got back to Lincoln Central, Oliver Bristow was initially not at all sure whether the news greeting him was good or bad.

ASBO (Adrian Simon Bruce Orford} had asked to see him up in his Tech Crime Team conclave part of the DCI Luke Stevens' empire as soon as. His techy-geeks had been working on mobile phone numbers, checking phone mast data, call logs from service providers and Keating-Price's laptop they'd picked up from Bryony Furneaux.

First, although not entirely necessary, Bristow felt it was the right thing to bring the Darke boss up to date. He explained how Furneaux had agreed to a Buccal swab, and Nicky Scoley had carried it out, rather than expect the woman to traipse up to Lincoln for a five minute episode.

Adrian (ASBO) he of the darkside skills was certainly an odd bod compared with Craig Darke. A geek of the first order, drank hot water and lived with an aunt, but astoundingly clever at the same time with a remarkably inquisitive mind.

'Alerick Keating-Price we've dubbed plain Price to keep it simple,' he opened with. 'There's still the subject of a number of issues we're still ploughing our way through basically, because there is so much dross we're wading knee deep in.'

Oliver so wanted to make a quip about Basmati Price rather than plain Price, but knew it would be lost on Adrian. 'You mean environmental?' he went for instead.

'From what the boys reckon he's taken on the whole battle to reverse climate change, as a result we're finding it difficult to see anything not that way inclined.' Bristow had got used to him not talking directly to people. Adrian spoke to him but his gaze never left the screen. 'Have a list of email addresses on Vic Jenkins's phone with some very interesting people,' and as he spoke a list appeared. It was obvious to even Bristow what he had done. The list he had pulled off the laptop was on the left hand side of the screen with an overlay taking up most of the other side giving details including, names, addresses, phone numbers.

'Well blow me!' the DI exclaimed. 'Look, Jenkins's been in touch with Keating-Price.'

'Seventeen emails, and a lot of them refer to phone conversations and texts we guess have gone back and forth between them. More than once Jenkins's texts say things like "I'll text you," but he never appears to.'

Still gazing at the screen Bristow saw the names Jonnie Dumbrell and Carole Jenkins and in recent days one from Bryony Furneaux. 'We desperately need Price's phone,' he said.

'Phones.'

Even when Bristow turned her head swiftly to look at Adrian he didn't flinch. 'What d'you mean phones?'

'Be a burner. Probably got an off the peg pay-as-you-go from somewhere like Hemswell market as well as the main phone.' For once his head turned away from gazing at the screen for him to smile at Oliver. 'Frankie reckons it's probably one his blonde piece doesn't know about.'

'Be serious!' Oliver gasped but knew of course he was always very serious. 'We got Price's phone number off his partner's phone, we've not actually come across the actual mobile itself. You saying he's got another one she doesn't know about?' received a nodded reply. 'You must have it wrong. He's a bad coffee drinking environmentalist not some kid with a phone in each hand, any passing slime bag can snatch.'

'What they all say,' left Oliver Bristow momentarily speechless.

'No Nathan Tyson I notice.'

'Not so far.' Adrian's head turned slightly. 'Get Price's phones for me and we should have his full story and maybe a few more surprises. Then add Dumbrell to the mix.'

ASBO Adrian had never been able to fathom why some selfish people were anti wind farms and solar fields. But then he'd never been able to get his head round any reason for refusing a Covid jab. Had the public simply been confused by all the mumbo jumbo? To his mind, the global warning and climate change wording had gone stale with the public losing interest.

With supercilious nerds like Keating-Price chuntering on incessantly about net zero and climate justice, it might as well be in Latin for all most people understood. Add that to the need for people to calculate their Carbon Footprint and talk of the earth absorbing solar energy and they've switched to Netflix.

Back downstairs the DI revealed what Adrian Orford had told him about Keating-Price and Jenkins's call log records, including the fact they were now more than ever in need of Keating-Price's missing phone.

'We've got the number but Adrian's been calling it on a regular basis. So all we have to go on are the phone company's records of the numbers he called and the closest mast. Hari's onto all that.'

'We are having to assume Keating-Price and Jenkins have been in contact,' Nicky slipped in. 'Guess Keating-Price was saying no way and then Jenkins's wife….Carole gets involved.'

'And gives him a mouthful over the phone, is my guess.'

'About the strength of it I would think.'

'So,' said Jake, with his hands clasped behind his head. 'Are you saying there are phone calls from Carole Jenkins to Keating-Price's second phone they've not gone through yet?' Oliver Bristow nodded and smiled. 'Any others calling his number?'

'Not any Adrian's got to so far. Remember the phone company's not in any hurry and we're not the only team ASBO's dealing with.'

'Nobody like his partner? Perhaps I'm being naive,' said Jake. 'But are we thinking a second phone is seriously something Furneaux knows nothing about?' Oliver nodded again as he smiled. 'We think this means some sort of tryst between Mrs Jenkins and Keating-Price.'

'Always possible.'

'Don't be ridiculous! If they did boring in the Olympics he'd be among the medals. No. No way.'

'How long before they come up with Carole Jenkins's calls?'

'Remember,' said Nicky. 'They're more interested in folk on the dark net. When I first got up there the talk was all about the impenetrable anonymity of TOP and the repugnant trade going on. I walked in the other day when they're discussing things like downloading encryption software vulnerability and expect them to be keen as mustard about idle chit chat between members of Rockapelt,' said Nicky. 'We need Dumbrell's phone and Tyson's as well, by the way.'

'Think that one might be easier said than done. He'll not fall for the three card trick with his phone.'

'You're looking at him in particular,' Oliver Bristow told Jake. He walked back to his office but stopped at the door. 'By the way, who is somebody Adrian called Frankie?'

'Frank Frankowski,' Sandy responded immediately. 'An anglicized Pole, the one with an earring like a polo mint.' He saw the look on the boss's face. 'Called him Frankie to make him sound more British,' just made the DI sigh. 'No idea what his real name is.'

'Michelle,' he ushered the DC to him. 'A word if you will.' Oliver Bristow returned to his big black chair as the policewoman walked in.

'Yes boss.' Michelle having endured the assault a few years previous had grown her hair long at the time to hide the effects. Recently encouraged by her partner Matthew she had reduced the length of her locks now the scars had faded.

'Need you to do a complete open source search on this Carole Jenkins woman. Sit down,' he told her, and waited. 'From the simple PNC and database checks to a link through to DVLA and most importantly, births and marriages. Carole Jenkins married Vic Jenkins we assume in Lincoln probably after the band split up at the end of the nineties. They then divorced so we're told and are now back living together in....Appleby Street. When they divorced what we don't know is, did she revert to her maiden name or keep Jenkins? If she did, is Jenkins her real name now or just one she uses for convenience?' Bristow sat there while young Michelle scribbled it all down on her pad, then looked up. 'Got it?'

'Yes...boss. Think so.'

'Now family. There's Janice we assume was born when they were married first time and then a youngster Jay who must be a product of the present liaison. Janice by the way has a daughter Lucy, but spelt...'

'Saw it.'

'Less said the better about that,' Oliver grimaced at the thought. 'We seem to think this Janice might work evenings once the parents are home to look after the little one. Probably a pub or burger joint, KFC or whatever. Okay?' the reply was nodded and the DI was left alone to ponder the situation.

'Just Eat or Deliveroo if she's gorra bike.'

'Good thinking.'

Not exactly idling away his time, but Oliver Bristow brought up Liam Spruell on the PNC database just to become au fait with why it was supercilious Justin Whittaker had become involved with such a scurrilous waste of space.

Perverting the course of justice by producing a false insurance document. Oliver had to read it twice. Was such silliness any good reason for Whittaker to get involved with him? He then casually brought up what he could find on Justin Whittaker himself. First class honours degree at West London, but nowhere could he spot a word about his humble social housing start in life, but it went from him being down there to him being an associate solicitor.

Had he re-written his Wikipedia entry, and if so, why?

Whittaker had to be in his mid-thirties with that well groomed thick hair, in a sharp but nowhere near ridiculous style. Eyes always bright and wide and to some extent Oliver to a degree was jealous of the look Whittaker often carried so well.

Time to look at Shaidy Days themselves and he started by looking into how the law firm's business had been incorporated. Started by a Martin Frank Day back in the early 1920s, and now all the full-equity partners were he guessed those who know who they are. As far as he could gather, none of those were dragged up in a council house as Whittaker had been, and educated at what was then Yarborough High School.

Two had been to private schools from the age of about 3, one went onto an international Baccalaureate and then the University of Law. He was Alwyn Hunter son of a farmer and horse breeder from the hunting and racing fraternity who had probably left with his LLB (Hons). That made Hunter a good few years older than him.

Interestingly, Hunter was a full-equity partner with Shaidy Days. Yet Justin was still only a salaried associate solicitor with little or no say.

With all his team busy beavering away, Oliver Bristow decided to do a spot of delving himself and headed off down to talk to the Custody team.

According to Sergeant Bobby Compton the appearance of Justin Whittaker to represent Liam Spruell had been noted in the log, but a cryptic note left by the duty team at the time to the effect somebody of his rank representing low life on a half-baked something and nothing charge was worthy of note.

According to Bobby, serious assault, major fraud, child cruelty, murder and at least serious heavy involvement in shipping or dealing in Class A drugs would be the minimum the Shaidy Day's lawyer all decked out in his Savile Row suits would show his face for.

Back up in his office with the door open, Oliver Bristow was enjoying a coffee he'd fetched himself from the canteen, sat there pondering the whys and wherefores of Justin Whittaker and his cronies when his thoughts were disturbed.

'Penny for them.' Oliver peered up to see pale green shirt-sleeved Jake Goodwin stood there in the doorway and beckoned him in.

'Just been thinking about Justin Whittaker again representing idiot Liam Spruell, for...' and he looked at his notes scribbled on a pad. 'Perverting the course of justice by coming up with a false insurance document?'

'Be serious. Spruell?'

'Traffic lads stopped Spruell, when he'd come up with no insurance on an ANPR information marker. Then when he produced it at the desk to stop being charged, turned out later to be false.'

'What is going on?' Jake asked. 'Not the first time Whittaker has got some nasty off on a technicality. PHU were telling me when I mentioned how we'd heard about him and Spruell, appears one of the Interceptors recently made an error in their roadside procedure and the owner of a vehicle they knew full well had been nicked suddenly remembered he'd loaned it to the skank.' Oliver sat there shaking his head.

'And you?'

'Estate agents and poker,' Jake said as he slid onto one of the chairs across from the DI. 'All three who play poker with Tyson happen to be estate agents. Makes sense I s'pose, except. Would you be pally-pally with people and then in competition with them next day? Been going on for a good year or two, regular get-together apparently.'

'Be his alibi cut and dried then,' he sagged with and sighed.

'Yes probably, but the aside is interesting. Rumour has it these are the ones thinking of setting up the on-line business.'

'How d'you know?'

'Sources,' was smiled to Oliver. 'Sally's Matron up at the County was married to a guy in IT and his brother worked for an estate agent in town. Talk one day about them looking to move, brought up the subject naturally of good and bad estate agents and in particular those on-line these days. Estate agent insider information from this IT guy to Sally's matron came a story about three getting together on line. Nathan Tyson, Arthur Hildred and David Toogood both from Toogoods plus Dominic Coleridge. All estate agents.'

'They're seriously about this localized on-line version you think?'

'From what my snout understands it's a four way split with each throwing in a property to set it all up.' Oliver whistled. 'One snag...one very interesting snag.'

'Hang on a sec,' stopped him. 'What d'you mean all four are throwing in a property? His DI asked. 'Go on.'

'Rumour has it,' Jake put his hands up. 'Don't take this as gospel please, but apparently so rumour has it, Arthur Hildred and our friend Tyson are struggling to come up with their share of the money,' Jake nodded when he saw the look on his bosses face. 'Spot on. Sounds as though our Vic Jenkins is desperate to raise the necessary to deal with debts and lo and behold so is Nathan Tyson who dare not miss out on this new venture. Only need to find our Jonnie Dumbrell also has a problem and is desperate for...'

'Motive. For any one or any combination of the three.'

'He must have surely. His wife's inside remember,' boss Oliver Bristow reminded him. 'They all need money and the song on the advert will give them what they want.' The DI just sat back. 'Well, would you believe it,' he grinned. 'Even flash git Tyson can't come up with the readies.'

'He could sell that bloody big house for starters.'

'Seriously. With a wife like he's got? You need to read her Facebook page sometime Alisha's keeping an eye on. Talk about ladies who lunch,' he smiled. 'Narcissistic with constant talk about me, me, me. What I've got, what I'm gonna get and where I'm going. Sounds like Boris Johnson.'

128

'All three have motive you think?'

'I think,' said the smiling Detective Inspector. 'They have a sure fire reason to want it in the advert. Get back onto your contact. Where do these properties come from they're throwing into the pot?'

'Will do,' Jake said and got to his feet.

'Here's a question. Which one do we think could have been responsible for that message on Keating-Price's body?'

'Could easy be all three?' he left the DI with and was back to his work.

'That means,' Oliver called after him. 'The group reformed for one last performance,' made Jake spin back toward him.

'Seriously?'

'In a cabbage field rather than the Marquee Club.'

17

The news to land on Oliver Bristow's desk just before he left MIT for the day had done him a world of good. Young Michelle was looking into Carole Jenkins, doing a complete open source check through all the agencies she could lay her hands on and had come up with a few early snippets.

He knew Michelle would never mention it, but it now seemed possible being attacked on a doorstep by that foreign nutter he'd heard all about down in Grantham, had in effect done the young woman a power of good. Put her on light duties for a while according to her record but in a position where she was able to take on an historical cold case she had apparently handled with great aplomb.

From that she'd gone on to meet a really good man by sheer chance and now she was settled at work and at home.

Oliver was hopeful previous traumas would have the same effect on Alisha. Nicky Scoley had told him about racist abuse on the streets of Lincoln from the local riff-raff when in uniform as a PC had he guessed, made her stronger and more determined to succeed. So far, so good.

What Michelle had discovered was more of her great work. Vic and Carole Jenkins had married at St Katherine's Church back in February 1998. Janice Marie Jenkins had been born at Lincoln County Hospital on 5th December the following year and one Alerick Keating-Price had staggeringly been recorded on the birth certificate as the father. No record anywhere so far of this Carole and main man Alerick actually having any kind of lasting relationship whatsoever. A nation's favourite enviro freak going into what could well have been a one-night stand, was new.

This had reminded Oliver of the young DC a few years earlier who had sex in a ladies toilet with a bloke she hardly knew at her hen party a week before her wedding. The baby arrived and the whole world assumed including her husband it had been a honeymoon baby. Wrong.

Had it happened with Carole Jenkins, had she got herself pregnant by Keating-Price around the time of her wedding to Jenkins and passed the child off as his? If that was not the case why on earth would she have Keating-Price on the birth certificate?

DC Michelle Cooper had discovered Jay Leo Jenkins had both Vic and Carole listed as his parents. To add to the family spice this Lwsi just happened to be the daughter of Janice Marie as they expected but somebody named Jeffrey Pinner had been listed as the father. Not Tommy Reynolds the local skag who Michelle herself and muscular Jamie Hedley had come across at the half decent family home.

They'd checked Pinner on PNC and he was a no show. What a tangled web some people force themselves to weave to have dropped in his lap out of the blue. Little wonder his mind was elsewhere when the DI sat alone at home pondering.

Oliver Bristow was thoroughly enjoying his Indian meal courtesy of Just Eat with a glass of their own wine. He was asking himself what picture the nineties paint like the sixties always create one being full of flower power and free love and stuff. Full of drugs more like he decided when he stopped eating to think. Quick Google on his tablet and he was reminded of Tamagotchi, Hubble telescope, Berlin Wall from his early days he'd no recollection of. Decade of things getting bigger including debt he read on. They'd had to suffer the Spice Girls and wondered what the Darke boss made of them.

Before long he was back to the tedium and loneliness of his life away from work. Breaking up with Eloise had been the only option with her old man being a top cop in the Met. Apart from him he dare not risk her. If anything happened to his great love he'd never be able to live with himself.

A double-edged sword had come in overnight to annoy Bristow once he was back seated behind his desk, black coffee to hand and the overnights checked for the detritus others would be lumbered with.

Secret e-mail from CSI Leicester, with an attached toxicology report confirmed by the Professor who Jake had dealt with at the crime scene. All with a codicil explanation and request from Porton Down as an attachment.

This was sit back, sup and read time, with the door closed. In fact to make absolutely sure he fully understood what was being said and being asked of him and the team, he read it twice.

Just a cheery if slightly sarcastic 'Morning' to two late arrivals and he was heading for Darke before he was summoned, with him on the distribution list of copies.

Half an hour he spent discussing the matter with the boss and from there headed upstairs to the dapper DCI Luke Stevens who added his own contribution to the plan he and the boss had formulated. On his way between the two he sent Jake Goodwin a text suggesting everybody remains in the Incident Room and get themselves refreshments in time for his return.

Printed email to hand, another coffee he'd grabbed on the way back and DI Oliver Bristow sat at an empty work station desk Jamie Hedley pulled into place for him.

'First things first,' he said to his team. 'Good morning, or perhaps I should say good and bad morning. Sandy,' he spoke to. 'I've closed the door and perhaps you'd ensure nobody enters during this discussion. At last we have the toxicology report concerning the demise of Alerick Keating-Price. Having said that we also have explicit instructions we are to carry out in conjunction with our CSI Team and Health and Safety.' He stopped to take the first sip of his fresh black coffee.

'Please listen to what I have to say very carefully because the content of this,' he waved the email, 'You will find is more than a little unusual and somewhat peculiar, and speaking to both the Darke boss and Luke Stevens it may well be a unique murder.' Bristow hesitated deliberately. 'Alerick was poisoned. Not by arsenic, drain cleaner, wild mushrooms or anything of that nature. He was poisoned with snake venom.'

'You're….joking,' was just the start of exclaimed chatter, so Oliver sipped more coffee until the time was right.

'I'm sure I don't need to warn you,' said a serious DI. 'But whoever is responsible for this is extremely dangerous. In truth the toxicology report actually states a specific snake. He was actually killed by what is known as...a Russell's viper,' he read.

'Take it they're very poisonous.'

'I've already had it pointed out to me Nicky, by the one wearing a Tyrwhitt pale blue shirt and expensive brogues. Snakes are venomous not poisonous, but we digress.' Boss Oliver pointed to the murder board. 'Connor's photo we've all got very used to is the way the venom was delivered. As we can see there looks to be some sort of padding in the crook of his arm. At least we got that right. That part of his arm was scraped with something, and they suggest something of the nature of a sharpened table fork and the skin was scraped away,' made a few grimace. 'The padding was doused in this Russell's viper's venom laid onto the exposed area and because it's so deadly the arm was then bandaged and the warning sign added.'

'Wearing PPE,' said Jake recalling his experience in the field with the pathologists all dressed up.

'Where's the Russell business come into it?'

'Named after the guy who discovered them I should imagine. Something to Google, but just says here one of the most venomous snakes in India. Earth coloured so difficult to spot and kills hundreds each year.'

'Not good if you've got bare feet.'

'You saying this could be unique?' Michelle at the back asked as others couldn't help but chunter and voice opinions.

'Think Stevens and Darke are Googling it as we speak, but.' He pointed at them. 'This is secret and I mean government secret. This gets out and we'll have absolute panic on our hands.' He took a good drink. 'Its possible the venom container and Porton Down are suggesting a metal vial, could so easily still be on that field and that means those cabbages,' he again pointed at the photos. 'Could well be contaminated.'

'Shit sake!' and 'bloody hell!' were the least of the remarks.

'What happens now?'

'Some of the work has been done for us including using the facilities provided by the Forensic Investigation Bureau and the reason there's been a delay. Plus they all had to tread very carefully around that stuff. CSI Leicester have already established the bandage was basic Boots Cotton Crepe bandage more than long enough to wind around the arm a few times,' back to reading. 'Hydrocolloid Wound Dressing Pad a sterile and waterproof adhesive pad it says here, but available everywhere and the grey Duct Tape can be got from almost anywhere apparently places like B&Q, Screwfix and all sorts, although Leicester are still working on it. They checked for trace evidence on the adhesive side of the tape. Nothing.' He stopped again to down coffee.

'When I left,' said Jake. 'Shona and her CSI lads were just starting on the deposition site.'

'There is as you know only too well Jake, a priority to get DNA from the body. Which because of the warning sign, harvesting was not possible on site.'

'Shona find anything by any chance?'

'Cabbage plants,' lightened the mood.

'Seriously though,' Oliver went on. 'They've been carrying out exhaustive analytical techniques we've probably never come across before. Anything they did find is not on the National Database and no forensics they are able to attribute to anybody. DNA from his clothing is most likely from that Furneaux woman and people he mixed with that evening.'

'What d'they want us tae do?' Scot Sandy MacLachlan asked with an air of enthusiasm.

'So pleased you asked that,' Oliver smiled with. 'How d'you fancy a couple of days out in the fresh air? And you can take that smile off your face Jake. I want the pair of you back at Slindon Farm at the very least by about one thirty, but,' he said with his voice raised slightly. 'This snake business took resources and was organized. This was never some scroat fed up with Keating-Price ignoring his complaints about his garden full of refuse bins with the council not emptying because he stuck a bottle in with the cardboard. This is seriously serious.'

'Oh,' his DS gasped eyes closed. 'Not that Herring again. He'll go bloody barmy'

'This morning he will have been visited by specialists from Health and Safety. They are in the process of organizing two teams and more if they can get them, of local metal detectorists to scour that entire field for the metal vial.'

'Seems a wee bit over the top,' Sandy suggested. 'But then would you wanna stuff a plastic bottle in your pocket with that in it?'

'They suggest,' Oliver came back with. 'That's the very reason it's still there. Trodden into the ground is one line they're going down.'

'How long'll that take?' Jake queried.

'Two days max they suggest. More uniforms are being sent there right now to keep the whole area safe and free from the media and social media turnips. If the metal detector people come across anything it will be these Health and Safety specialists who will check it out and if need be, dig it up.'

'In PPE.'

'Of course. Now Jamie and Michelle,' he turned to. 'While all this is going on I'd like you to carry on down the road we've all been on for the past few days. Seems extremely unlikely but we do have to consider somebody we've already spoken to carried this out.'

'What?' Nicky shot out with a breath. 'A goon like that Jenkins?'

'I can't imagine people like this group shower would have the wherewithal to do something as dangerous and complex as this. But it would be amiss of us if we stopped looking. After all, do any of them keep snakes for example?'

'D'they think Keating-Price was beaten up so they could add the poison?' Nicky posed.

'Seem to think he was unconscious, be chloroform or somesuch. Oh, by the way there was no blood except that area on his arm, where incidentally veins are close to the skin like when you have blood taken. Now.' Oliver paused. 'One more snippet. Initially they found a bruise and what looked like two injection marks in his arm. Part of the delay, they've been doing exhaustive tests searching for whatever was injected.' He stopped and shook his head. 'Professional or what? They've decided it was not in going, this was blood being taken.'

'We talking nurse maybe, or a doctor?' Oliver shrugged at.

'Alisha,' he moved onto. 'Your main aim is to keep right up to date with every social media site known to man. Just in case some troll in the village gets to know what's going on. Nicky, you and I will need to take on some of the interviews while everybody else is preoccupied. Stevens will be sending a couple of extras down, more if needed and I've suggested to him our old friend Tigger Woods from Intelligence Gathering could prove useful for one and maybe Sam Howard if he's available.'

DS Jake Goodwin in good time with Sandy MacLachlan in tow set off for Anwick and purposely the small village next door where his parents lived. Boss Bristow had emphasized a reminder for the pair to keep receipts for every penny they spend as he knew they'd need food and drink at the very least for a couple of days almost in the middle of nowhere.

Jake knew they'd need something for their refs. Best bet was his mother. He'd phoned ahead and when they arrived at their home his mother had sent Reg Goodwin into Ruskington for supplies and had made a batch of ham sandwiches, bought cereal bars, a muffin each and two flasks she'd fill for them.

It was agreed if they were in need of more, a phone call would have Goodwin heading for the turning into Herring's farm where his old man could meet him.

Jake knew his dad was far from happy to be told under no circumstances was he to attempt to reach the farm itself.

When they eventually got to the field after a cuppa and a slice of Dundee Cake with his parents, they were ushered by uniforms to take the gravel drive right through the farm and to the top end of the cabbage field.

They were both pleased to see the normally uniformed coppers were all in plain clothes and in unmarked cars. The kitted out HSE team vans were also without any obvious markings.

They were first introduced to Alan Lomas the Health and Safety Specialist Manager and their Regional Manager Stuart Hopwell. They were instructing the five members of a local treasure hunting team on the process they were to adhere to.

Jake had not seen sight or sound of David Herring but he was mentioned by Alan Lomas in his briefing to the detectorists to do their very best not to trample on the cabbage plants.

The five were instructed to start from the gate it was assumed the killer or killers had arrived and left by, and to make their way slowly across the big field. The crime scene still roped off at least three quarters of the way across. Thoroughness was instilled into the five rather than any need for speed.

Stuart Hopwell explained once they'd started their metal detectors up, how the day before two suitably dressed skilled members of HSE with metal detectors had already done the same to the crime scene itself. He also explained how arrangements had been made with David Herring to share any remuneration gathered from their finds with the five now slowly progressing across the big field.

They'd been told to use a toilet in one of the barns and to all take breaks at the same time, once Hopwell's men had placed progress markers.

18

He'd had to wait a good twenty four hours to satisfy Carole Jenkins, but the opportunity was now available for DI Bristow to hopefully fill in all the cracks in the Jenkins family history. Providing the woman actually turned up of course.

This Jenkins woman had refused to meet Nicky Scoley at home on her day off. Was adamant her daughter should not become involved once she understood the Detective Inspector wanted to chat seriously about her relationships, her husband and her children.

Oliver Bristow had a speed read down Jake's latest report on his screen about progress at the farm, made a quick scribbled note of actions he required for Nicky Scoley to now take the reins with the change in emphasis.

Time for Michelle Cooper and Jamie to meet Carole Jenkins rather than him. Those dropping by for their lunchtime caffeine 'to go' were never interested in who just might happen to be in a coffee house. Those with more style preferring to sup from a proper cup were it always appeared concerned only about their phones and tablets. Than what the three in the corner were doing together and chatting about.

They initially discussed as they waited for Carole Jenkins, about the good weather and the ongoing business of the council looking to protect farmland from the introduction of solar panels. During an energy crisis they both wondered how anybody could come to such a conclusion. Attractive wind farms which give life to desperately uninviting areas was another subject they had to leave when she appeared.

Latte was as strong as Michelle fancied at that time, having had a tea with her toast and Marmite breakfast and another when the boss was telling them the amazing news. Detective Constable Jamie Hedley some had cheekily described as her support worker, had an Americano but this Carole Jenkins went for a pot of tea.

Chestnut haired Michelle judged by Jenkins's dark roots her untidy brassy blonde hair had been bleached and all scouped up onto her head. No make-up save for bright garish scarlet lipstick; set against a pasty face it was just too much. Michelle decided she'd be one of those who didn't feel dressed without her lippy.

Her clothing attire was never Michelle's choice. A multi brown check shirt under denim dungarees and seriously out of place high heels.

Carole Jenkins looked on edge and troubled in their presence as Michelle Cooper gave her a smile in an attempt to relax and encourage. She quickly decided she was strangely uncomfortable in the environment. Perhaps this woman was a coffee refusenick she'd heard about? People who for some reason abjectly refuse to give in to coffee culture, who still favour cheap-jack or bog standard filter coffee you still can find in some supermarket cafes or as in her case go for weak tea.

Just maybe she lacked experience of the social reaction and interaction coffee brings. She'd certainly not feel comfortable with former boss's old friends back home in Sweden with their regular order of fika – coffee, cake and chats.

A bit like folk her dad had told her about. Those who always order fish and chips wherever they go. Or go for a big Mac they can easy stuff down. Something they know how to eat, something not likely to show up their lack of good table manners. A dish they know will at the very most only require the use of a knife and fork or grubby mits. No protocols about sipping soup or how to tackle a lobster. Had to be the reason burgers were so popular, but how on earth do people open their mouths wide enough to scoff such tawdry offerings had always amazed her.

The seats were adequate, not hard backed as some places go in for so as not to encourage you to stay. *Sup up and go* was how a friend described some of these places she normally steered clear of. Ominously trying hard to be environmentally friendly was a somewhat strange place for Jenkins to choose under the circumstances. Maybe it had been somewhere of that genre where she and Keating-Price had met for their lovers trysts.

The news about the snake venom had certainly been a real shocker, and Michelle was pleased as a result of the news to be able to take on some of the boss's work. Rather that, than being stuck out in a field like Jake and Sandy, or poor Alisha desk bound and staring at a screen for hours on end.

'Anyway,' said Jenkins with no come back. 'What's this all about? He aint done it.'

Time to move on. 'How did you and Vic meet?' was Cooper's opening salvo.

'Through the band, duck.' Jamie noted her short sharp response and the use of band rather than group, as they would have been in those days.

'Did you go about with them all?'

'Pretty much.' Cooper had her down as a groupie. 'Sorta gang of us, wiv a couple more.'

'And Katherine Arbiter?'

'God no,' was sharp and chuckled. 'She's well after. Think dozy Alerick knew her years before any o'us got to hear.'

'After the group folded?'

'Pretty much.' Carole Jenkins lifted her cup and held it in the fingers of both hand. 'What's she all about? Tryin' to be something he's not Vic reckons?' Jenkins put the cup down without even a sip.

'Surely she is though,' said Cooper appearing to confuse the woman.

'She *is* a lady,' Jamie added to clarify but it seemed to fall on deaf ears when there was a cursory shrug.

'What about you and Alerick?' Michelle knew she had to move this on or they'd be there all day.

'Sort of,' she used her one shoulder shrug again, to hide the truth.

'If it's not too rude a question. Were you and Alerick lovers?' although she doubted whether love actually came into it.

'If yer like,' was sighed.

'You had Janice.' Cooper perceived the look slide cross Carole's face as if suddenly her secret was out.

'Not a bloody crime is it?' was feisty.

'Certainly not.' Cooper took her time to sup a little more of her warm Latte. 'We just need to establish the situation as it was back then, which I'm sure you will appreciate is our need. I just feel it's far better to get the real facts rather than listen to people telling us stories, some of which more than likely wouldn't be true.'

'Oh bugger it,' Carole said almost to herself. 'Look, tell you what. Between you and me like, I panicked and course that shit Alerick wanted nothing to do wiv me being up the duff. By then o' course he's well into all the nonsense he's a bit doolally about. Thinking back now being stuck with him'd be a bloody nightmare to be honest. Bet that silly sod'd be more interested in some vegan nettle he plucked from a field nonsense than buying his own daughter a bag o'chips.'

'Did he not support her?'

Carole Jenkins looked to her right, as if checking there was nobody trying to listen in or who might spot her. 'Only much later on when I threatened to tell that Kate woman when they got hitched, did he bother to cough up a few quid,' was interesting.

'Might I ask, why is Alerick's name on her birth certificate and not your husband's?'

Jenkins grimaced as if she couldn't fathom the reasoning. 'He was her dad.'

'What did Vic think about it?'

'He's her proper dad,' she blew out a breath of frustration. 'Yous a bit outta date missus. S'not who had sex what makes him her dad, it's who brings her up and that. Bloody heck we've moved on from all that.'

'Vic thought he was her father I assume?' Michelle Cooper leaning forward inquired softly.

'If yer like.'

'But eventually you got back with Vic?'

Jenkins closed her eyes to collect her thoughts. 'Yeh, s'pose so,' she sighed. 'Be all this damn song business coming up again what's done it. Last thing I bloody need.'

'Are you married?' Hedley asked just in case there'd been something untoward going on they knew nothing about.

'What? Go through all that again? No bloody chance.'

'But you've been together a while now and you've got…' just momentarily Alisha forgot the name. 'Jay,' she suddenly recalled. 'Can't be all bad.'

'Me?' she chuckled and pointed at her own chest. 'I'm just daft as a brush eh?' Cooper thought she was suggesting it was a mistake. 'He's not a bad bloke really, better'an the veggy man, we call him.' She chuckled. 'Like mother like daughter, all in the genes and that I s'pose,' confused Michelle and a look at Jamie showed he was equally at a loss.

'Sorry?'

'Janice,' she said as if it explained everything. 'Got herself done up by soppy Jeff Pinner. Like mother, like daughter right?' Cooper went to speak but was beaten to it. 'Not a bad lad, usedta cough up a bit o'cash regular like, so all credit to him.'

'He still supports Janice?'

'No chance,' she shot in quickly. 'Put a stop to all that when Tommy comes on the scene. He don't want some bloke poking his hooter in and can yer blame him? Next he'd think he'd got free licence and all that. Bloody hell no.' Supporting his daughter to Michelle could hardly be construed as poking his nose in.

Reynolds was like a bad penny forever turning up for one illegal misdemeanor or another. He'd never be a good role model for the kid with the oddly spelled name which Michelle was struggling to recall.

'Does Janice know who her father is?' Cooper tried next.

'Don't talk wet,' she scoffed at. *The sin punishes itself* came to Michelle's mind as something her mother used to say.

'Does she know her father's dead?'

'Not her father, it were Vic what brought her up.'

'Yes fine, but he is her biological father.'

'And?'

'We've been told Vic likes a bit of a flutter,' DC Cooper suggested looking for a subject transfer.

'All the rage innit? Bet on any damn thing these days, you can get odds for second in the Boat Race they reckon,' she laughed at herself. 'Some you win, some you lose' was not exactly the picture Jamie Hedley had established about any gambling issues.

'Has Vic ever run up any big debts with his gambling do you know?' was Jamie Hedley attempting to establish their relationship.

'Few quid here and there that's all,' she shrugged. 'Does a sweepstake with mates at work if he's on a big site. Grand National that sorta stuff. His money, so he can do what 'e likes wiv it, but its just a few quid.' told Hedley they kept their money separate, probably the reason why one of them had not wanted to re-marry he guessed. He probably paid the rent and utility bills, she paid for the food and all that business like some 'partners' tend to. Until it's all too late o'course as so many discover to their cost.

'The Saturday night Sunday morning when Keating-Price was murdered, you were both in the pub, then went home with a take-away. Correct?' Cooper knew the belligerent landlord would not or could not confirm acting on some perverse loyalty to his regulars. Admitted when pushed he'd said how Vic Jenkins had been in the Old Crown at some time but claimed he was unsure exactly when.

'Yeh. S'what yer do.'

'And he never went out again?' When Carole didn't respond Goodwin spied an opportunity and took a chance. 'Where'd he go?' and saw the bottle blonde swallow.

'Dunno,' she grimaced and shrugged again. 'Down south somewhere maybe.' The cabbage patch as Jake jokingly called it was *down south* from where they were sat off Tritton Road in the city.

'You mus have some idea.'

'What if he did go out?' she allowed her head to wobble and left her mouth open. 'So what?'

'We need to establish exactly what…'

'Don't talk wet!' was harsh.

'Carole, we need to…'

'Don't you Carole me, pet!'

'Carole,' Cooper tormented as a policewoman. 'We need to establish where people were when Alerick was attacked, if for no other reason than to eliminate them from our inquiries.'

'Can't get him for one thing, likes of you lot'll stuff him for some'at else eh? Typical bloody cops aint yer,' and her arms were folded tight into her adequate chest and Jamie feared they were at an end.

'Look,' said Michelle Cooper resorting to calm. 'Unless he was up to some really serious unlawful business I'm really not interested I've got more important things to deal with than a bit of messing about,' well not at that juncture anyway. 'I'm sorry but I don't deal with scrags shoplifting or brain dead not wearing their seat belts. Both of you need to establish his innocence.' They had to wait. Jenkins drank a few sips of her weak tea and Cooper wished they'd got a biscuit each.

'Betting?' Hedley popped in.

'At that time of night? What sort of betting he'd do at night?'

'Foreign football maybe. All sorts in the Far East.'

'Dogs,' she admitted quietly after a pause and Michelle watched the woman bite her bottom lip.

'Greyhounds you mean?' Jamie Hedley slipped in. If there were any local it'd be the first he'd heard of it. Maybe Skeggy, but then in this day and age could be greyhounds in Adelaide or Singapore. 'Where?'

'Dunno.'

'Doncaster's possible,' Cooper advised.

A huge sigh of acceptance came before the admission. 'Look duck, he's only trying to get a big win,' Jenkins said as she sat forward. Her voice had become more strident as if she had forgotten they were in a public place or didn't give a toss. 'Things'd not been going too well lately. Rent's gone up, big gas bill,' Jenkins shook her head. 'Said when he's straight that'll be it. No more like.'

How many times did gamblers wives hear such empty promises?

'And did he?'

'What d'you think?' was sharp and quite loud and fully expected.

'This a gambling debt?'

'Not I knows of. Times was real hard in that pandemic, lost his job for a good few months. Self employed so none of that furlong business.' She sighed and grimaced. 'Payday Loan,' said as if she had to give in, answered the question.

'Tell me about these dogs.'

She blew out the next breath. 'Dog fighting,' she admitted to stun both coppers. 'Goes on a lot, loadsa people do it, nothing special. Way to fund the loan, like.'

'Sorry Carole, but I'll need details.'

'No chance duck. He'd bloody kill me.'

'We need to establish he was where he says he was, and with whom.'

'Went with Tommy. Lost five hundred odd, how much more d'you need to know for crissakes? Bloody sick of it, me.'

'Your Vic lost five hundred pounds on dog fighting?' was gasped more than spoken.

'No bloody chance! Idiot Tommy did,' in an instant Carole Jenkins was on her feet, pushed the chair back noisily with her calves. 'Woulda thought you'd got betta things to do,' and strode off pushing past customers with trays carrying drinks, and out.

'Went well,' grinning Jamie quipped and grinned.

'But at least it's a more likely alibi d'you think?' Michelle asked then drank down the remainder of her coffee. 'Than just down the pub.'

'You're probably right. Need to speak with the rural guys see what dog fighting, we assume it was, went on.'

'Thought she was talking greyhound racing. I'm sat here racking my brains for a dog track.'

'Pay day loan eh? Well, well, well.'

Nothing and nobody untoward Michelle spied as she scanned down the coffee shop. Two women, legs crossed stood waiting for the barista to complete their choices caught her eye for she always questioned some women's stance and the sanity of those who these days still only wear high heels.

'At least they won't have to get a divorce!'

'What a waste of a decent cup of tea.'

'She hardly touched it? Sort of half-hearted sip.'

'Same again?'

'Why not?'

'Anything with it?'

'Get thee behind me Satan.'

19

Back at Lincoln Central, Michelle and Jamie's news of what they had managed to squeeze out of Jenkins naturally included her mention of dog fighting. DI Bristow rattled off a quick message to the rural team asking for any information on illegal dog fighting in the county over that weekend, and called Jake Goodwin down at Slindon Farm to link a discovery he'd made of CCTV in the small village, with his news.

He told his DS about Carole Jenkins's admission concerning leaving the pub on the Saturday night, Vic Jenkins and this Tommy Reynolds having gone off 'down south' to bet on what appeared to be unlawful dog fighting.

Bristow remembered what one of his old Grantham nick colleagues had said once. "Gambling is a drug and going to the dogs is a fix."

'This CCTV in a house you say?'

'Nothing else so far. Early days with this metal detecting, so I left Sandy who's more interested than me and visited my parents so my old man could steer me round the village away from the main street through. There's no petrol station of course, the little local shop run by volunteers I knew about doesn't have cameras. When I mentioned the lack of, my old man pointed out one of the people who've recently had a fine old house done up, with cameras fitted.'

The house was solidly built but Jake guessed it was a facade. All the guts he guessed would have been removed along with partition walls to create the open plan some still crave. How long before a new walls are erected he wondered, to make it more like a home than a barn.

'They show the road?'

'Not been in to see them on screen you understand. Just walked past a couple of times. One looks as though it films right across the front of the house and the other is on the garage roof and points down the drive and out to the road. With any luck it'll show what's passing.'

A double garage he'd noticed had been tacked onto the eastern end with large front garden's manicured lawn to a new front wall made to look old.

'You thinking Jenkins?'

'Why would he go there for dog fighting?'

'Not in the village. Dad'd be gagging to tell me the moment anybody mentioned anything like it and no mistake.'

Jake could never fathom why people who desire old property don't actually buy one and if they do, then have to modernize the layout inside to whatever formula daytime television tells them is all the rage that particular year.

'Might be worth a punt though.'

'Jenkins's car?'

'Either that or Tommy Reynolds.'

Jake chuckled. 'We'll have it on ANPR you can bet your life, probably got a marker on it too, but guv,' he sighed. 'Do we really imagine a couple of scum bags like those two could organize snake venom and all that must have entailed?'

'You're probably right, but we have to cover all possibilities, every avenue. Can you go for the disc, as you're related to a local?'

Jake smiled at his DI's suggestion.

'We got both their reg numbers?'

'Pretty sure we have. Anyway we know where Jenkins's working out at Washingborough, and Roads Policing guys'll probably know Reynolds' off by heart.'

'Of course we may be way off beam with all this, be just our luck he took the main road to wherever the poor bloody dogs were.'

'But as the road with the CCTV leads round to the Hall, you never know who we might capture if it's not him.'

'Jamie appearing to have got to the bottom of Reynolds' gambling debts, was another update from Oliver. 'Just been reading about it among the shower of stuff queueing up. Two bookies in town have banned him, had a couple of county court judgments against him a year or more ago and so far Jamie estimates he's at least three or four grand in debt not including all the on-line people and there's hundreds of them. Done the main ones like Bet365, Ladbrokes, Corals and so on. Some of course are asking for court orders.'

'No wonder he's desperate for a win somewhere, somehow. What about Casinos on line, Roulette, Blackjack and Poker?' Jake moved onto, as he spotted one of the detectorists signalling about a possible find. 'Better go. Might have a find.'

'That the first?'

'No. Just a couple of screws, a bolt and bits and pieces probably off one of his old tractors so far,' said a beleaguered Jake Goodwin.

'You say Sandy's taken an interest?'

'Yeh,' lacked enthusiasm. 'They can detect metal of course but according to him the machines this lot are using can tell what the metal might be. Gold of course, these chaps are hoping for, but the bigger the metal object the deeper the detector will go. He reckons they can find stuff a good few inches down. Got a useful way as well when they get a reading, as it looks as though they have now. When the Health and Safety bods start probing and digging, the machine tells them whether what they're after is still underground or in the soil they've dug up.'

'Better let you get on. Keep in touch,' Oliver then walked to his open door and Jamie. 'Casinos worth a look?'

'Got them on my list, but not started but I think they'll have picked up on the court cases, and I guess the big boys will have too.'

'They'd check his credit score.'

'Just out of interest. You ever done that guv?' he asked the boss.

'No.'

'Know anybody who has?'

'No.'

The Detective Inspector then told Jamie, Michelle, Nicky and Alisha if she was listening, about Jake coming up with CCTV.

'He get this from his dad?'

'Think he has to tread very carefully with him particularly under the new circumstances. According to what he's said in the past I reckon given half a chance Reg Goodwin'd buy a balaclava and start sneaking round in the dark and set himself up as a vigilante with the old guy next door!'

'Carole Jenkins's attitude is odd,' Michelle moved back to. 'Well to me it is. She can't see a problem in having Keating-Price on the birth certificate. Gave me a load of guff about Vic being her proper dad because he brought her up.'

'Adultery seems to be a given these days for some.'

The boss then told the four a story he'd once been told about a young PC who'd been duped in a similar fashion. 'Could be the same scenario. They knew each other through the group, Alerick was at the hen party, one thing led to another and whoops!'

'Not her was it?'

'Who?'

'Carole Jenkins.'

'Did for Alerick?' Jamie nodded.

'Not her DNA remember. She'd need help and claims she was at home with the daughter, and what would she use for transport?' The DI chortled. 'I've not met her but by what you say, can you see her dealing with snake venom that'll kill her in minutes?

'Yeah. Fair enough.'

When he thought carefully about the possibility of ex-drummer Vic Jenkins and his possible motive for killing Alerick, the thought began to mentally create a list for Oliver. Sex, money and refusal were his headlines at the time. First was of course aligned to his wife's infidelity with Keating-Price, which quite possibly still aggravated the bricklayer deeply. As a macho male with all the man-up nonsense his pride would have been seriously dented. Money was certainly what he owed and quite possibly there was more, maybe even family and friends, and last but not least was refusal. The environmental stranglehold which simply prevented Vic's former band colleague to just be more positive about *Sheer Delight*.

All it would have taken was, for Alerick just once in his life to put human beings he knew first. Before some obscure plant in what even to him must be a far flung tropical rain forest.

Was it possible taking out a Pay Day Loan had put Vic at the end of his tether and on the way home his anger and frustration about his woman's past sex life got the better of him. His role as a mere brickie plus his debt forced him in the end to take a detour round to Gorgie Hall?

When his brain produced the image of a Russell's viper snake he'd found on Wikipaedia, with an aversion to snakes he knew not to go there.

20

With police work dealing with major crime there are often snippets of information which appear not to be pertinent at the time, but then later slot nicely into use. DI Oliver Bristow could always remember what had been explained to him at one time.

Major Crime Groups tend to stop communicating with others involved in their racket, close to the time of the event. He knew he was in need of ASBO and his darkside skills to go back a while and see who all these band people were talking to a year ago or more.

In the same way by sheer chance some criminals bring their downfall upon themselves, so too did luck play a part. Downstairs he had been discussing another unrelated matter with the duty Custody Sergeant big bulky Bobby Compton, when long time legal associate Veronica Smallwood happened to be passing by with a client.

They agreed it was time to meet up for coffee and Bristow said he'd call her later to arrange.

DC Jamie Hedley had scoured the world of localized and on-line gambling involving bricklayer Jenkins, really as a case of crossing all the Ts. It appeared he was simply living beyond his means with the debt tagged on, things were bad enough without resorting to backing horses. The DI listened to his report and Jenkins remained seriously enough in the clag to put him back in the frame, were it not for the circumstances surrounding Keating-Price's death message.

In truth he had never physically removed his name from the boards just slipped him to the outer perimeter.

That was conveniently where inquiries came up against a brick wall. No matter how hard they tried they could not get anybody to admit there had even been dog fighting down south of the county or even into Cambridgeshire that Saturday night, let alone confirm that Vic Jenkins and his sidekick had actually been there.

Even the rural guys admitted it was an event they knew nothing about. Hare coursing was still sadly happening but not dogs.

Bristow just added LIE? in red against mention of dog fighting underneath sidelined Jenkins on the main board.

Major inquiries were always like a roller coaster going up and down, good news and bad news following in order, after every climb a drop to the bottom again.

One of ASBO's minions young hacker supreme Hari Mistry the Computer Analysis Team's Digital Forensic Analyst, appeared at Bristow's door with a print out of Lady Arbiter's phone records.

'Nicky!' he called out almost instantly as he scanned down the colour-coordinated highlights. 'Madam Arbiter's phone records,' he told the butterscotch blonde when she appeared. 'Look at these,' he said as Nicky walked round the side of the boss's desk to peer down at what he was pointing at. 'Her ladyship made all these calls to our friend Justin Whittaker on his mobile.' Bristow pointed to the blue lines and then to a handwritten key at the bottom explaining what each fluorescent colour represented. 'Sixteen months ago!' he said excitedly.

'But didn't you…?'

'Yes,' Bristow responded with an assumption instantly. 'According to the Poldark look-alike he claimed he's not her solicitor.'

'But only two if you notice,' said intrigued Nicky. 'To him actually at Shaidy Days, or at least I'm guessing by the days and times.'

'And,' Bristow casually flipped over the three sheets. 'In that five day period she only made two to Alerick. So, she did come back.'

'We we're told she was in Italy. But these are not from there obviously. So where?'

'Alisha!' was the boss shouting. 'Here if you will,' and the dusky DC headed his way. 'Drop everything you're doing and go through the murder book. Somebody somewhere was reported as saying they'd seen Katherine Arbiter somewhere local a good while after we're told she went to live in Italy. Need a name.'

Nicky sucked in a breath noisily as Alisha headed back to her laptop. 'Don't see any to his second mobile.'

'Interesting,' said Oliver all perked up and full of new found enthusiasm after another boring evening at home alone. 'What's the betting she doesn't know about it? Her ladyship doesn't know he had another phone.'

'The lives people lead,' Nicky said with a sigh as she plonked herself down on one of the chairs facing the boss. A phrase she used so often in her work.

'Tell me about it,' the DI sniggered sat with his fingers steepled a habit he'd always had. 'Every day I think to myself, do people really live like that? Are we the odd ones?'

'Can you ever imagine,' Nicky asked. 'Any circumstance where you'd have a mobile phone you bought off some skurk in a pub?'

'Skurk?'

'Sorry guv bit of a throwback,' she grinned. 'Swedish word.'

'If you had a couple of million would you live in such a crummy place and be in a relationship with an oddball conservation nerd like him?'

'Rather than Whittaker say.'

'Some of these others are short of money so they'd struggle to change their lives, but not her.'

'Michelle was telling me Jenkins's place is a bit cheap and cheerful and so they say is Jonnie Dumbrell's…' She caught the look on her boss's face and stopped.

'But if you like, they have excuses. Overspending on Sky, phone, drugs and take-aways and all the rest of the now generation nonsense. Plus Nathan Tyson desperate to join in the new business online. Desperate for every penny and our third with one income living on the breadline with a wife inside. What excuse has her ladyship got compared with those three?' Oliver looked down at his to do list. 'Have you read the report on Keating-Price's laptop?' he queried.

'Just going through it for what it's worth when you shouted,' Nicky commented. 'They reckon it's just full of environmental stuff. No social media at all, no football, not even him having a peep at himself on BBC News.'

'And no porn, thank the lord, or child abuse photos to muddy the waters for a change.'

'Hardly drugs, sex and rock 'n' roll this lot are they?'

'You don't think.' her DI hesitated. 'Maybe her ladyship was in conversation with Whittaker on the quiet about breaking free of Keating-Price?'

'Always possible. Why else would she have need to be in touch with him back then? Anyway, he might have the likes of Spruell in tow but surely he can't be down so low in their pecking order he's now doing common divorce.'

'I'm meeting Veronica Smallwood for coffee, she of the nose in every pie, see what I can find out.'

Next up was DC Ian 'Tigger' Woods borrowed for the duration with an insight into the finances of Jonnie Bryn Dumbrell for all to listen in to.

'His take home pay,' he said at Oliver Bristow's door so the whole team could heart. 'Works out around two grand a month. From that, first lump out is six fifty for rent, hundred and a bit Council Tax pays his gas and electric direct debit, another big wack. Finance on his car wipes another ninety off the total and then there's a legal bill he's paying.'

'For his wife?'

'Assume so.'

'Go on,' Bristow sighed from his office. 'How much?'

'Five hundred.'

'Up a gum tree,' Jamie popped up with.

Oliver's phone rang. 'Odds and sods leave him with three or four hundred a month, less than a hundred a week,' said Nicky. 'That's for food and your normal everyday odds and sods like toilet rolls, lottery, petrol, washing up liquid.'

'No big loan like Jenkins, but life's got to be pretty grim.'

'Living hand to mouth pretty much.'

'Do we assume the daughter and her bloke contribute?' Michelle asked.

'Something else to assume,' said Jamie. 'He's another with a motive, if it were not for that damn snake.'

'List is kinda creeping up.'

'That's what snakes do!'

'This is interesting,' came the boss's voice from inside his squat office. 'According to the Hari upstairs, Dexter's discovered there are no phone calls from Nathan Tyson to our Alerick's phone or vice versa.' He reached the door with his phone in hand.

'Not for a year or more, but they're now checking how far back the last was.'

'He's not as desperate as the other two though is he?'

There was always something dogged and determined about Oliver Bristow. As ever his target was to identify the right suspect despite all the issues, and proceed along with a watertight case.

Probably down to his upbringing but he always retained a duty of care to the victim. Even an odd one like Keating-Price. Also to the family he'd as yet seen nothing of, and not forgetting in this case the small close knit village community, they all had a strong link to.

Veronica Smallwood was, as a good friend of Bristow had once remarked, predictably unpredictable. Always designer glasses, this season they were bright blue frames and her thick brunette hair was as always at work, pulled back tight to make her appear more studious.

She had always been let down by her teeth. She was all gums on display whenever she opened her mouth as if her top lip was somehow dragged up above them. Her usual strawberry lipstick had been replaced by maroon with matching nails. At the Café Nero chosen Oliver knew because it was plumb opposite the Magistrates Court and for no other reason. Plus the predictable unpredictable continued when she chose a Caramel Macchiato. Always an odd ball drink to show off, but you'd never guess which one was in favour.

The Darke boss was always willing to explain to all and sundry about coffees if you ask, but Oliver already knew it was basically an espresso and steamed milk with he assumed some caramel syrup just plopped on top for no good reason other than upping the price.

They went through all the latest news about her daughter and husband, about how well they were both doing, as if she was ever likely to admit the kid was as dim as they come, and he was having an affair with their Syrian asylum seeking cleaner?

Not wishing to be outdone Bristow made a great deal of his talk about the increasing expansion of his mother's vineyard in Alsace, and promised her a bottle or two of the new red.

'Justin,' Bristow said quietly. 'What's the news on him?'

'Whittaker?'

153

'Yes.'

'In what way?'

'Taking on a few ropey clients I hear. Not good for his image I should imagine.'

'We all have to do so from time to time.'

'Liam Spruell?'

'I thought you were going to say Roger the dodger Hawkes.'

Bristow chuckled. 'He'll never make partner surely by listing the unwashed as clients.'

'Between the devil and the deep blue sea,' said Vron, as most people called her. Just the utter silliness to exasperate Bristow. Why not come out and say whatever it is, why go through the question and part answer sequence?

'Devil and the deep blue sea? What's that all about?'

'Don't you know?' was also laborious. 'Stay with the champion breeds as we call them, or slide down and be a partner shall we say, among the lesser mortals.' Oliver noted there was no suggestion of where she stood in the pecking order. 'Day to day Liam Spruell is never a good career move.'

'How will having the dregs of society as clients help him?'

'Money.'

Here she went again. 'What about money?'

'They need it.'

'Be serious.'

'True as I'm sitting here,' in her navy blue hand-made costume.

'You saying?' Oliver Bristow dropped his voice. 'They're in trouble?' was close to a whisper.

'Not exactly in trouble, but they've always had need for run-of-the-mill stuff behind the scenes. The client culture of rich landowners they brag about are never busy enough to keep them in the luxury some of them have become accustomed to. Company cars always Range Rovers, Jaguars, top of the range of course.'

'And Justin being only an associate solicitor has to take his turn dealing with…'

'The likes of Hawkes, Spruell and a bottom of the pile nonce such as the likes of Clive Lander is never a good daily dose.' Sat beside Oliver she turned her head. 'What's your interest, or is it hush hush?' Veronica had to ask, then sipped this macchiato.

Bristow explained briefly about how Whittaker had given him short shrift about Bryony Furneaux and the DNA swab.

'You mean Alerick's er, how shall I put this?' she smiled. 'Woman?' she grimaced. 'To be kind.'

'That's the puzzle. When I inquired at the desk why he was at our place, it was then I was told about Liam Spruell.'

'Bear in mind since Edmund Goddard retired they've not had top notch practice specialization in criminal law, perhaps they're lining him up for something but I doubt it.' Vron took another few sips while she pondered. 'When he had a go about this Furneaux female did you get the feeling she was actually his client?'

'Very much so.'

Veronica chuckled. 'Two hardly go together easily in the same bed, looking after that fancy piece's interests and major scrotes like Spruell and Lander.' She buried her face in her drink.

'Exactly my feelings. I'm not one for idle gossip as you know, but he's not married,' he paused momentarily. 'Is there an issue?'

'Gay?' was chuckled, so silly did it appear.

'Not thinking that actually,' Bristow had to admit. 'Wondered more along the lines of a secret wife, who lives away, divorced maybe...'

'Would you put up with it?' Veronica asked abruptly. 'His career means everything to him. Burden he never carries well, being dragged up on a council estate. Yarborough School as it was then, is hardly the epitome of all things top notch.'

'Council house not Charterhouse.'

'Our guess is the reason he's stayed with Shaidy, is he's absolutely determined to make it with them. Obsessed with being in the Man U first team squad rather than the successful top striker for Rotherham.'

'And it affects his relationships?'

'Very much so. I know at least three who've tried and failed miserably.'

'Is he in the Masons do we know, or anything similar maybe?' Bristow could now surmise how in truth he was all window dressing.

'Masons?' Veronica Smallwood repeated. 'As in Freemasons you mean?' Bristow nodded. 'Would image such an olden days sort of thing is more the world of Shaidy and Day. Mixing with people they consider important. All the mystery and bizarre rituals. Cannot imagine they'd want Justin as a member of their flock, except maybe in order to treat him like a lapdog.'

'Not something you're enamoured with, then?'

'Don't believe in secret societies. Think Alwyn Hunter was the head honcho a year or two ago.' It was interesting how Veronica knew such things about people like Hunter. 'All wheeling and dealing behind closed doors hidden behind a cloak of symbolism.'

'A bit odd don't you think? Justin handling Arbiter's business, then when she clears off and he takes on her substitute.'

'No,' was sharp. 'Jackson Moore senior partner looked after Katherine. I mean,' Vron chortled then sipped her drink. 'Lady Arbiter going with the council house boy, absolutely no way.'

'But I thought?'

'Lap dog. Did all the running about, bits and pieces drove out to her probably with papers to sign, but anything seriously legal Jackson was her man. No doubt about that.'

'Would he know where she is?' Bristow probed.

'Probably but chances are he'd never tell you. Client confidentiality and all that.'

'Somebody somewhere in our inquries suggested she may have been seen in the past eighteen months.' Bristow sat back with his drink in hand to await the oracle's insider information.

'Bit of a rumour I'm afraid. Crossed my path too. One woman reckoned she'd spotted her twice but nothing's ever been confirmed. Mistaken identity I should imagine. Italy apparently, living the high life with some debonair smooth Italian romeo no doubt. Drinking those silly little cups of coffee.'

'Greek islands have also been mentioned,' although he knew going anywhere abroad was impossible unless it was done illegally.

'News to me.'

'If you hear anything let me know. We really need to talk to her about Alerick. All the next of kin business.' Bristow just looked all around for big ears. 'Always possible she nipped back to see...Jackson Moore.'

'More than likely. Still a funny business, just up and left. Media made a bit of a fuss at the time and she's being mentioned again now of course.' She glanced at her gold watch. 'Time and tide,' she said as she got to her feet, bent down to drink more and with a wave of the hand was gone across to the Court.

A thought to ponder as he watched Vron crossing the busy High Street, had been Keating-Price's relationship with Furneaux. He was so Oliver understood, a nice man. According to those who knew him. Away from all his campaigning obsession he surmised he would be lonely and grateful for a younger woman's attention. Well away from all Climate Change issues, was he a simple boring Billy-No-Mates?

As an alternative was this femme fatale looking for a lonely man she could snare. Not to provide as a rich, very rich man could. But gaining in notoriety instead. A form of online celebrity to attract the paparazzi with the intention to bolster her investment status as a top influencer of the susceptible.

21

As luck would have it there had been just a few of what the CSI geeks call *alien substances* or many DNA samples in evidence at the body site. Without CCTV in a field, DI Bristow was really no further forward.

Linking what CSI had to say with what he had learnt from the PM, it was now pretty obvious Keating-Price had most probably been delivered to the field already dead.

Worrying though, was to realize the perpetrators had avoided leaving suspicious samples, DNA or fingerprints and all this meant it could very well be the work of those he really had no wish to chase after.

Were they really looking for a seriously experienced hit man or somebody else? A rogue copper maybe, CSI operative or forensic scientist were always possibilities. Every one of them he knew would be seriously forensic aware.

Oliver Bristow slumped back in his chair, as he frequently did when considering issues. Then his mind added doctor to the list of possibilities.

Sat there in silence he wanted to blame somebody. The internet would do for now, providing as they do, all the pathological information known to man. Just ripe for the world's saddos to slave over and scoop up anytime sat alone in their tawdry bedrooms.

As he went to turn off his PC, *pathologist* was added to the list by his over-active brain.

He chuckled to himself at the thought of the lovely Dr Bronagh O'Carroll getting so uptight about what Keating-Price had spouted about the carbon footprint from her holiday in Mauritius on local radio, she'd felt the need to put an end to all his silliness.

His perverse brain turned full circle for a moment or two and made him wonder if the validity was because of even more austerity cuts this was a way to reduce the expenditure post virus by allocating dual roles to people.

He sat there pondering the amusing thought of charming pathologist, wife and mother Bronagh killing people then carrying out the post mortem.

In the same way a bunch of complete nutters had suggested that Covid pandemic was a scheme to reduce the world's population, nothing more. Their reasoning was based on the fact China started it and they have the biggest problem.

Time to return to reality.

'We need to start rattling a few cages,' he said to surprise everybody beavering away out in the Incident Room.

What he'd just announced elicited many a wary look from those assembled at their various stations around the room.

'Who you got in mind?' Nicky Scoley asked with an air of concern as she peered up.

'How about we start with Jenkins?' he saw his DS frown. 'He's in a debt for his Payday Loan and Keating-Price had the means to an end. Or at least the makings of a big hole in what he owed. I guess when Price said no way he'd not be a happy bunny, and unfortunately for Keating, the drummer boy had Tommy Reynolds as an in-house sidekick.'

'Now?'

'Yes,' he responded instantly. 'Why not? Pulling him off the building site'll upset him which is how we want him. Weather's nice for a day or two so he can catch up when we're done.'

'Jamie,' was all Oliver had to say as the big man slowly scrambled to his feet.

'Your wish is our command,' he said to the boss.

'Can we?' he asked Michelle 'Carry out a background check on Tommy Reynolds, please?'

As he shouldered into his jacket Jamie Hedley provided information new to his DI. 'After Michelle and I spoke to Jenkins, I did a check. He's been up to all sorts. Latest was something about being done on suspicion of conspiracy to cause actual bodily harm. Been bailed pending further inquiries I think.'

'Interesting,' Bristow responded.

'Apparently boss,' piped up Alisha. 'He was goading drunks into assaulting others.'

'Very nice. Just the sort we're looking for.' As was the way in a flash Oliver had changed subject. 'Tell you what Nicky, how about you go along with Jamie for a bit of fresh air. We need a CSI check on his car. Body in the boot. I'll phone Shona Tate to warn her what's coming her way,' she said as he turned to take the few steps to his office but then spun back. 'Just out of interest, was it Keating-Price who once said the only way Earth will survive is for all humans to be wiped out?'

No words were spoken among the troops, but there was a whole range of odd looks and grimaces.

22

DI Oliver Bristow got word of the arrival of one Victor Jenkins, but left him in the interview room to stew for a while with just a young PC for company, long enough for worry to have an effect on his mental state.

'Not saying nothin' wivout me lawyer.' Why the DI asked himself yet again, do we allow America to dominate us? Why is it all lawyers now, and why did we have to change from SOCO to CSI, trousers to pants, hello to hideous hi, criminals to crims, cinema to movies? He didn't know, but was sure that utterly ridiculous wow nonsense just had to come from across the pond too.

'This is just a chat Mr Jenkins. We're not recording and the video's off. Have you ever helped the police with their inquiries before?'

'Mebbe. Who's asking?'

'I am, Mr Jenkins, watch my lips,' Blunt Oliver Bristow opened the file in front of him with 'Jenkins' printed clearly at the top in black permanent marker. It was all show he'd done many times before, put a suspect ill at ease unaware most of the sheets were blank. To concentrate his mind, for him to wonder what all the papers inside were all about. What did they know? What had they dug up? Bristow pretended to read then closed the file and rested his coupled hands on the top. 'Tell me about your recent contact with Alerick Keating-Price if you will.'

'What's t'tell?' His big calloused hands were still dirty from a morning's work.

'You told my officers you'd had no contact with him in recent times' He slowly opened the file again to annoy and to bring his doubts back to mind. This time Bristow flicked over three or four sheets and pulled out a clutch of ten held together with a blue paperclip he then spun the batch round in order for Jenkins to read. He pointed to the yellow highlighted number at the top. 'This your number?'

'What if it is?' he scoffed.

Bristow sighed obviously. 'We know it is. This list was produced for us by your phone company.' With more than a little help from in-house hacker Hari Mistry.

'And?' He was slumped down in his seat with his chubby arms across his belly, hands linked at the fingers.

'Why did you lie?'

'Who said I did?'

'I just have,' Bristow pointed then to the first line the Digital geeks upstairs had highlighted in pink. 'Whose number?' he asked bluntly.

'How should I know?'

'Call phone numbers at random. That what you do? Make obscene calls to women? Perhaps I should get one of my sexual offence officer colleagues in to investigate you.' Jenkins went to speak but was too slow. 'These are numbers you have called Alerick Keating-Price on.'

He was still trying to get the words out about obscene calls. 'Prove it,' was all he managed in the end and another loud scoffing chuckle was becoming tedious.

'We don't need to, it's a fact of life we can present as evidence to any jury.' The last word just happens to be one of those to put the shits up the likes of him. 'You called it and only one person has access,' he said and stabbed in with his thin finger.

'Oh yeh.'

'Keating-Price's number not the local take-away or a taxi.'

'Huh,' he scoffed. 'Where yous wrong fella so there.' There it was again.

'How d'you make that out?'

'Because I know his number starts 777, dunno rest of it like.'

'Somebody who has no contact with him but just happens to know his number off by heart,' Bristow mused. 'Interesting,' he chuckled to add to his annoyance. 'His environment number does start with sevens.' Oliver Bristow stabbed at four 7777 numbers highlighted in blue. 'Here, here, here, here.' Had he been one of the dumbasses some of the PHU teams have to deal with on a regular basis he'd not have batted an eyelid.

To his credit Vic Jenkins was making a good attempt to appear casual and without a care in the world, but his face just wasn't up to it. 'Eight there are,' said Bristow and tapped the pink highlighted numbers all the way down the first two pages. 'These are all from you to Alerick Keating-Price on his personal phone.'

'So what?' he sighed, as she looked down at the sheets. 'How much longer this going on? Knows yer can't keep me here for bloody ever.'

'Is that right?' he responded without lifting his gaze.

'I knows me rights let me tell yer, mister.'

For some unaccountable reason Bristow pictured this Jenkins as he imagined he had once been. Sat perched on one of those little round padded topped stools on a screw thread. He imagined his big podgy hands feverishly racing around the kit, snare below his stomach he'd hardly see if he tried it now, toms, hi-hat as he worked the bass drum pedal nineteen to the dozen. Thigh muscles all turned to fat he guessed would these days ache so quickly were he to try to return to what he'd done in his stick thin youth.

'Go on,' said DS Scoley. 'Tell me what your rights are.'

'You can only keep me here for a certain 'mount of time, everybody knows that. Don't you?' he threw at the DI. 'Aint you done the course yet?' he chuckled at then he was leaning forward as if about to be privy to a morsel of good old fashioned gossip.

'You think?'

'I know,' he sniggered.

'Sorry to disappoint you old son,' and his look said he was. 'But we can keep you here as long as we damn well like.'

'Just cack!' He grinned nervously. 'You gotta let me go after a while, like what I've seen on tele and that.'

'You're not on the bloody telly!'

The Detective Inspector sat there looking at Jenkins. Boss Darke had told him and the team the thing sat across from the pair of them in the old worn navy blue shirt had once been a fair rock drummer. Played major venues home and abroad, made records and appeared on TV. Darke to be fair had suggested he wasn't exactly top drawer, but at least he was better than the monotony of a drum machine.

Bristow just couldn't for the life of him imagine it in his current surroundings.

'Fair enough,' said Nicky Scoley as boss Bristow took a back seat. A controlled silence is she knew all important when interviewing and he'd be worried by the DI being quiet. 'Then when you get out in the car park we'll turn you round and bring you back in for more questions,' the DS lied. 'We can keep on doing it in shifts, there's enough of us and as long as no particular retained term lasts more than twenty four hours,' she just made up on the spot. 'Probably long enough for you to lose your job,' she exaggerated very seriously, though chuckling inside.

'No you can't. I'm self-employed anyway it's a contract set-up.'

'Fair enough,' said Scoley sat there arms folded to stop him gazing at her chest. 'We'll arrest you instead, more questions for twenty four hours, then we'll charge you and bring you up before a magistrate in a couple of days and get you remanded.' Blonde Scoley leant forward. 'Pop goes your contract,' the DS said and laughed in his face.

'You wouldn't bloody dare!'

'Try me,' he said as he unfolded his arms to sit up, shuffle forward on his chair and look down at a slumped tubby Jenkins.

DI Oliver had no reason to suspect Nicky was violent, nor did he seek to force such elements from others yet he knew her calm attitude hid a hard edge you'd not want to savour. If it happened to Jenkins he'd not enjoy the experience he knew, for absolute sure.

'What d'ya wanna know like?'

Bristow looked up without making it obvious. It was running true to form. A couple of veiled threats as is often the way, hurried the interview along. 'Oh, well done,' Bristow enthused and smiled. 'Joined the ranks of the sensible have we?' Bumptious people like Jenkins could never admit it, but deep inside he was shit scared of what might happen. Visions of being strip searched by some big hairy goon giggling and insulting him as he did so, in some God awful decrepit Victorian prison would be scuttling across his mind.

'Tell me about last Saturday evening, Saturday night, after the pub.'

'Awright,' he admitted as he linked the fingers of both hands together on top of his head. 'So I went t'see him.'

'Him being?'

'Alerick. Mr fruit and nut case. What sorta bollocks is that for a name eh? he grinned. 'Taken enough crap off him one way or t'other.' Scoley had adopted an interested expression and sat forward to encourage the tubby.

'Why d'you talk about him in such glowing terms? Keating-Price is well respected in environmental circles.'

'They're all the bloody same that lot. Lads at work call 'em echoes, coz they just keep repeating the same old bollocks. Like them bloody MPs. Don't have a clue what's it like in the real world. Anyway, why they all lawyers?'

'Think the work of lawyers and other professionals fits in nicely with the hours in Parliament.'

'Why d'you say that?' Jenkins threw at Scoley. 'Why'd you call people like them professionals? I'm bloody professional I gets paid, bloke who digs graves is too and me bin man. Here's me bloody working all hours, actually building homes for folk, people off the streets like what can live in somewhere decent and all prats like him can do is criticize. Told me few weeks back I was insignificant, as if.' He took a breath. 'Said I live a meaningless life, just coz I'm always hoping for a decent summer for a change.' He blew out his breath. 'That's from some idiot with a poofter's pony tail who's no more use than a chocolate fireguard.' He shook his head.

'This at his home where you called?' Scoley asked in the knowledge he'd just admitted how they'd been in touch.

'Weren't in were he?'

'You were on your own I take it?'

Jenkins hesitated momentarily. 'Nah.'

'Who with?' DI Bristow had to ask rather than being told straight out.

'Tommy,' he said sheepishly. 'Tommy Reynolds,' he grunted as if they'd have no idea who he was.

'P'raps you didn't knock hard enough,' Scoley suggested.

'Bloody did.'

'Big Door eh?'

'Bloody massive. You seen it?' Scoley nodded.

'Did you ever have a DNA check done?' she casually queried. The curved ball would hopefully disarm and with luck tickle the bails off.

'I thought…' the furrows in his brow were deep.

'You thought what?' Scoley asked calmly.

'Nothin.' They had to wait a few seconds for him to unravel his brain. 'Yeh I did. Came in t'other day…what was it you call it?'

'No,' Scoley made into a long word. 'Not you. We're talking about Janice.'

'Do what?' he grimaced and kept his mouth partially open.

Bristow was sat there enjoying the exchange between this idiot and a woman, and the way he kept looking at the DI for help said Jenkins was not happy dealing with a female. Certainly not as good as her.

'Did you ever have a DNA check done to see who Janice's father was?'

Another time delay. 'Too much water under bridge now, duck.' Nicky Scoley knew not to speak immediately, and was proved right. 'Thought you wanted to know…'

'Know what Vic?'

His next breath was a long drag in and then released in a rush. 'Mebbe about me and him.'

'You and Alerick?' she asked. 'Sorry, but we already know all about the pair of you, don't you worry your little head about that,' Blonde attractive Scoley smiled at him to increasingly annoy.

Jenkins looked straight at her, flicked his eyes across to Bristow asking to be rescued and then back. 'What d'yer mean?'

'You're up the Swanee with a debt you can't cope with and guess what? Your old mucker Alerick had the means to end the misery or at least pay off a big chunk. But he'd not play ball would he?' Scoley guessed and as she spoke Jenkins's head had started to gradually sink lower. This was not the belligerent individual who had started off with attitude.

'Bout what?' he mumbled.

'Him and your Carole.'

'Jus' wanna know 'bout him and the song.'

'What about baby Janice?'

'Bloody fruitcake!' he said hands flat on the table peering down at it. 'Googled some weird group what he's with, turned out he'd been over in Macclesfield. Some'at to do with… a Solar Radiation Bounce-back lecture,' and Bristow wondered what it all meant and how on earth did this dope know about such things?

'You know about all this stuff then?' inquisitive Bristow knew he may be proved wrong but guessed by the look of him, he was on about Alerick and his ecology rants going back decades.

'Climate change and all the gubbins?' Scoley posed, as her boss shuffled his way through papers in the file.

'Jus,' he blew out a breath. 'Don't have a clue, but stuff kinda sticks in me mind. What the hell's it gotta do wiv anything?'

'You have no interest in the environment and climate change I take it?' the DI posed.

'Too much stuff and nonsense. Not about to move to a forest, buy a coat made o'leaves and live off pine cones and stinging nettle chips am I as like,' he grinned at. 'Got told some time back how he'd talked a year or two back about how a dinosaur had become a vegetarian.'

'Dinosaur?' Nicky chuckled in disbelief.

'Said, so I'm told. This thing living millions o'years ago originally had teeth. Some bloke reckoned over the years teeth no longer developed and from being a meat eater he became vegetarian.'

Nicky Scoley had to accept what she was being told was indeed serious, but even so was willing to consider Jenkins had got it all wrong and it was a long way from reality. 'Take it his woman was not in at the Hall when you called?'

'No,' he responded. 'No lights on was a clue, s'pose.'

'Perhaps she went with him.'

'Doubt it.'

'Why?' Scoley asked as Bristow began to read.

'She's not into it all like he is. Not been a kranky died in the wool veggie for ages they say. Before she buggered off out of it.'

'Have you not ever wanted to know if you're Janice's real father?' The switch worked so well it was written all over this dum dum's face. Curved ball, googlies he was all at sea or in Test Match parlance beaten all ends up. The reference about her ladyship not being vegan remained.

'What you on about?' he gasped and grimaced.

'You ever had a DNA check done?'

'What the fuck for?'

'To see if you're her father.'

'Who? My Janice? Course I am yer silly sod.'

'But,' said Scoley very calmly. 'Are you? Are you absolutely sure?' she said slowly and deliberately.

'We was together and that.'

'In the commune?'

'Well, yeh.'

'And your mate Alerick. Where was he?'

167

'Sorta down the road, seeing this piece in a bit of a gypsy encampment place.'

'We talking about Lady Arbiter?'

'Bit afore her.'

'And Alerick never came visiting.'

'Mighta done, few times like,' Jenkins looked at Bristow still pretending to read papers in the file, then back to Scoley. 'Whas this all about?'

'Just trying to piece the relationships together.'

'She said kid was mine,' he muttered after a few moments and shrugged as he did so. 'Treated her like mine,' was quite soft as if he was thinking it all through in his mind as he spoke. 'Coulda bin,' he hesitated. 'Truth is coulda bin anyone's, to be fair.'

'How it was down there was it?' The DI grinned slightly to add to his emphasis.

'And the rest.'

Oliver Bristow had found what he was looking for. Yes according to his Enviro Focus website, Alerick Keating-Price had indeed been giving a lecture on the Benefits of Solar Radiation Bounce-back, but that was on the Friday.

'After you found Alerick was out,' said the DI as he closed the file. 'What did you do then?'

It was make your mind up time again for podgy Vic Jenkins sat there with his eyes closed. Which box would he choose? Drop himself in it or end up in a bloody dank cell.

'Went to the dogs.'

'How about if you give me a dogs contact Vic?' Scoley asked softly. 'What sort of dogs?' Not something she'd ever been involved with. Hare coursing for a few weeks was her best rural attribute.

'What's it matter?'

'So we can verify what you're saying.' Just in case he was reluctant Oliver Bristow had the get out of jail key in more ways than one.

'Then we can let you get back to work.'

'Down south someplace,' he rushed out once freedom was mentioned. 'But, what about me car?'

'Lads'll give you a lift back to Washingborough and we'll let you know when you can collect it.'

'S'pose it'll have to do,' he sighed.' It was all he was going to get and he knew it.

'Did you win on the dogs by the way?' the blonde DS casually queried.

'Did I hell as like.'

'The name?' Bristow reminded him. 'Location would be useful, and by the way,' he added with a grin before Jenkins had chance to answer. 'We have you on CCTV near to Gorgie Hall.' They both saw the look on his face. 'Just thought you'd like to know. You and Tommy,' he prayed. He was given no time to consider what he was being told. 'Betting you do sometimes,' said Bristow with another change. 'Just the bookies is it or d'you do it on line?'

'Don't talk wet,' he chuckled. 'What and all the lads taking the piss like. Yeh right.'

'Why would they do that?'

'Me there at work thumbing one of them smart phone thingys,' he chuckled.

'You not got a mobile?' Bristow knew the answer to.

'Yeh, what me missus makes me have.'

'But you don't use it.'

'Only if she sends one of them, er…'

'Texts?'

'Aye.'

'What type?'

'BT pay as you go, think.'

'Be useful for betting these days you know, for the football and all that as well as the horses.'

'Can you see me,' Jenkins said splaying his hands. 'With big babies like these,' he said to show off his big fat fingers. 'Be a bloody laughing stock what say you?'

'Time you were getting back to work,' said Bristow glancing at his watch. 'Once you give us the name and place.'

169

23

DI Oliver Bristow wondered how long it would be before thoughts of Eloise did not pop into his mind the moment he relaxed.

Missed her so much still, but knew in his heart of hearts her old man was right. He was well aware how she could so easily have been used as a pawn to get at him, to draw him out. Had that come to fruition he'd never be able to forgive himself, or worse he'd be in no position to even think.

He still wondered if Eric Hawkridge had done that to protect himself as much as his daughter, such was his reputation.

With everything going on he was pleased the media uproar for information was being dealt with elsewhere. He was fed up with reading and hearing on the radio how Keating-Price was according to the posh papers a visionary environmentalist. The red tops just stuck with him being the nations favourite and how he'd been taken to their hearts. One of the Sunday papers running a double-page spread added pressure.

To his mind it is often the case it is these so-called blue-eyed boys and girls given such an accolade the public in truth in general don't give a fig for. Some in the past had of course turned out to be paedos.

Without all that to concern him he was back up the A1, back to Lincoln Central and MIT.

'Jenkins and his mate more than likely went to the big house just like we did. But of course nobody was there,' he started with. 'Then being desperate he went off to chuck even more cash on the fire of stupidity. This time on dog fighting.' Bristow tapped the note he'd made of the dog organizer. 'Rural lads'll find this name useful.'

'Jenkins went to have it out with Alerick…?'

'Except the poor sod could already have been a goner by then.'

Even if he had his suspicions, Bristow knew as they'd not found a shred of evidence against anybody in particular. Not even a glimmer of hope upon which they just might be able to tag a DNA sample to. If they had one.

'We've only got numbers off the phone he says he never uses.'

'Another phone?'

'Could be. But we know how hard it is to track down a burner.' The DI screwed his eyes shut. 'Need a warrant to give his place the once over.'

'Dumbrell next you think?' Nicky wanted to know.

'Not his fault his wife's inside,' Bristow reminded his colleague. 'Kinda feel sorry for the guy.'

'But he's still desperate for money just like Jenkins.'

'We'll wait and see if anything comes from Jenkins's car and see what else we get from ASBO and his merry bunch.'

'According to him, there was that suggestion her ladyship had not been a vegetarian for ages. Sound right to you?' Nicky checked.

'Drink drivers say they've only had a pint when they're breathalysed. People lie all the time, and when the cat's away…'

'And he was away a lot.'

'Exactly.'

Although it appeared far from it at times, DI Oliver Bristow had to remind himself now and again how Operation Oldfield was still very much an active investigation.

Out of nowhere there'd be a spike in activity then quickly defused or set aside. One such annoying case had been overnight notification of Keating-Price's Land Rover having popped up on ANPR on three cameras on Lincoln by-pass from the south going north from Damons up to Carholme roundabout, uphill and under the Burton Road flyover, then nothing. Miles and miles away from where Keating-Price lived.

Nothing before, nothing since.

Almost as if somebody was playing catch-us-if-you-can by swopping plates or had reason to move it despite the risk. To a safe house maybe, to a valeter to be cleaned inside and out or was it now being resprayed, used as a pool car, a company car, or more than likely stripped and sold for spares? Bad company's car to do with as they think fit unaware it had a priority stop marker.

'How would you get a Land Rover or anything come to that from somewhere near Anwick to Lincoln by-pass without being picked up on ANPR?' he'd thrown at the team to ponder.

Back had come a whole range of ways from keeping to the back roads, from low-loaders, to a tow, a trailer with the vehicle covered with a tarpaulin, to false plates.

'You spot a black Land Rover Defender and note the number. Go to some back street garage and get spurious number plates to match. Why do we allow it?' was the boss. 'Plates on a Volvo in front of you read BDT. What's that mean? Brain dead turnip or Bloody Dick Turpin? Never seen the point. KWZ on mine is also anonymous.'

'And have DVLA miss out on millions in income?' Jamie piped up.

'Because some people are so wrapped up in their own importance they think a daft plate gives them some sort of prestige. Why are we as a country so damn good at so many important issues,' Bristow droned on. 'Yet make yourselves look childish with all this sort of nonsense?'

His own circumstances meant he had a serious need to be and remain anonymous. OKB on his Renault Hybrid would have been the height of stupidity.

'I've never fathomed it either, boss,' DS Scoley admitted, but knew nobody would ever dare to suggest the system be changed. 'It's all just utter twaddle. Why would I ever want my name on my car, so any scrote in a car park who thinks I'm a total knob, can scratch down the sides for a laugh?'

'Why not put a strip on your windscreen saying I'm a pillock? It'd be cheaper.' was Michelle's contribution.

'My old man remembers when bozos did that too. Maureen and Mervyn on the windscreen.'

'Way of the world. Some dickhead decided to put his name and his bint's name on the windscreen and before you can turn round every wassock was doing it.'

Jamie Hedley kept his head down. His dad in days gone by before he's moved out, had paid a silly sum for the registration number HED. Not something he wished to admit in this company.

'What about saving a fortune on traffic officers time?' was aimed at Jamie. 'DVLA can make it up by selling the actual number plates and nobody else. Job for you Jamie,' worried the

DC momentarily. 'Need registration numbers of every black Defender in the county and put them to the ANPR boys.' He nodded. 'Let's see if one of them has been trundling up the by-pass.' Bristow must have recognized his look. 'In case somebody has changed plates. Are there two running about with the same number? Find an AKP and we're halfway home.'

Back in his office he didn't swear when he read an email from the force's Senior Crime Scene Manager Shona Tate, who had arranged for Forensic Scene Examiners to check Jenkins's car. Scruffy, dirty and a bit of a tip inside as people's cars often are, but forensically 'clean'. She did add as an aside a slight smell of cannabis, but none actually discovered. He thanked her very sincerely for all her hard work.

Another waste of time.

24

With the Incident Room fairly quiet, all waiting for news from Jake and Sandy, Oliver Bristow had taken up a seat out there in order to face all three of the major incident boards. The third of which was all part of his particular process he could not see totally from his pokey office in the corner.

Each person they had made contact with was listed down the left hand side. Across the top were the various categories: Name, Links, Alias, Alibi, Prints, DNA, Means, Opportunity, Motive and Yes/No. A non-techy tickbox giant spreadsheet the guys upstairs would laugh at.

Plenty of blue ticks, a few green crosses and red question marks. In some squares there were notes such as the figure '12' in the Link box against No 5 Jonnie Dumbrell related to No 12 Sara Dumbrell his daughter to indicate a link.

Lady Katherine Arbiter had more red marks than anybody. Number 2, then her name in the second column. 1 to link her to Alerick at the top of the board. Red question obviously for motive, and for alibi and fingerprint.

What if he played hardball Oliver wondered and not for the first time sat there on the end of a desk considering his next move? Smooth as silk Justin Whittaker would no doubt have something to say, but it was a murder inquiry so he had all the cards stacked in his favour. Bristow guessed, or rather hoped Craig Darke would support him if he insisted on taking Furneaux's fingerprints. But and it was a big one, would he be there for him if it was decided to go the whole hog with CSI giving her ladyship's scruffy cottage a good going over? What Nicky Scoley had once said about her mum had reminded him of his own, by giving something a good bottoming.

Good to know his own was safe and sound in France, but at times at his empty place on winter nights living a boring life alone got to him.

What about the big cheese Chief Constable? Would Allen Townend cowtow to pressure from on high and put his relationship with Shaidy Days, the dinner party, barbecue set and self above his major murder squad?

DS Scoley wanted to continue scouring down the print-out from the DNA database but knew when Bristow spoke you pay attention which appeared imminent. Some of those from PHU appeared unable to sense his mood and perhaps as a Detective Sergeant she was meant to put them straight.

Bristow caught Tigger's eye. 'How does her ladyship finance herself day to day?' he asked. 'Once left a couple of million, but keeping such a big place going must still cost a fair bit, even though she's not there.'

'Two million in stocks and shares,' Tigger announced.

'How does Furneaux finance herself?' Oliver asked. 'Because I can't imagine being just the girlfriend she'd not pay for the upkeep although I understand she can afford it or at least her old man can. And according to her, Keating-Price didn't go in for money.' Oliver continued. 'Council Tax just goes up and up the bigger the place you own? What about energy bills these days, they'll be a fair wack?'

'If she pays at all,' made him look across at DS Scoley.

'How do you mean?' he enquired.

'We reckon Gorgie Hall's empty, right?' Nicky checked, and Tigger nodded.

'Assume it is.'

'In her case she has several options. If when Alerick was alive they could easily put him down as a student, because he had no job. As a student he'd not have to pay, as a lone occupier that'll be another chunk off her bill. If they claim the cottage as a holiday home knocks, if my memory serves me right, fifty per cent off. If the big house is kept empty then no fuel bills and they can't be that much for the hovel she lives in.' Nicky smiled. 'Reckon the legal eagle of hers could get her living tax free. She could be claiming the hall is derelict in which case you pay no tax and she could also be registered as unemployed. What's the betting she pays nothing.'

'Where d'you get that from?' their DI boss wanted to know.

175

'My past catching up with me. Rogue down in Cambridge up to all sorts, and chatting with Tigger,' she smiled glancing across at.

'Wind turbine remember,' Bristow slipped in. 'Wood burner and she's got plenty of trees.'

'Chopping them down's a disaster environmentally surely.'

'Not as I do, as I say comes to mind yet again.'

'I could live on a couple of million,' Jamie offered.

'Would you want to live like she does?'

'On second thoughts,' Nicky smiled.

'Just looking at the board,' said the DI. 'Bits and pieces still missing but the big empty column is her ladyship.'

'We're not seriously looking at her?'

'Want me to have a look to see if she has any pecuniary difficulties?' Nicky queried.

'See what a Cambridge education does for you,' Oliver Bristow quipped.

'Got contacts who can strip her down to the basics,' Nicky admitted, having spent a good few months seconded to Cambridgeshire Police at one time.

'Please,' said the boss.

'The gardener and the cleaner? I take is one for me?' Jamie queried.

'Best if you deal with the village.'

'Except it's not where they live. Been wondering if it just might be deliberate. Employing people who are not part of the local populace, so there's no poke your nose chitter chatter in the pub.'

'No pub,' Tigger reminded.

'Where'd they live, do we know?'

'Think Ruskington, but I'll check.'

'Pubs there.'

'Just one gardener we've been told,' Bristow mused.

'Gang mowers must do the majority, he probably just tends the borders around the hall, think there might be a veg patch some place he looks after.'

'How about an eco nutter who doesn't like gardening?'

'Cleaner. What about her?'

'His wife? I'll find out.'

'Bet Jake's dad knows.'

'How well d'you know this Justin Whittaker?' DS Scoley asked those gathered a good hour later.

'Quite well. Why?' the boss responded. 'Come across him a good few times in Grantham. Not pals or anything like that.'

'Her father Lord whatsit, left Lady Katherine Arbiter £2.34 million, and there'd be death duties, which could take a good 40% away at a stroke, but if you have a good lawyer...'

'Sounds Shaidy!'

'Is this why Whittaker is her solicitor, because he's too clever by half?'

'No he's not,' Nicky told them. 'Senior partner Jackson Moore is her solicitor so I'm told. Whittaker although you'd not know by looking at him's just the lacky doing all the running about.'

'What's a criminal lawyer doing messing about with bits and pieces? Wouldn't a solicitor's clerk deal with that sort of thing?'

'There's more,' said Nicky. 'The whole place is actually owned by an off-shore company and as far as contacts of mine in the Economic Crime Team can make out so far, it's on their books as derelict property valued at just two hundred thousand.'

'Don't be daft,' said Tigger. 'Got to be Grade 1 listed.'

'Means there'd be no inheritance tax,' said Nicky Scoley brightly.

'Who decides what property is worth?'

'Normally the price it's sold for when the person dies.'

'Have to get a valuer in.'

'My guess is Lady Arbiter sold it to this off-shore business cut price to avoid inheritance before she buggered off. Now he pays or rather did, no rent,' Scoley continued. 'If he also paid no council tax, and if the power is supplied by wind turbine and wood as you suspect, he and the girlfriend lived for next to nothing.'

'Way of avoiding paying tax I seem to remember,' Tigger Woods offered. 'Case a year or two back where papers were released about the rich and famous and rather than buying a property and paying taxes, somebody bought the company that owned it, and saved a small fortune.'

'Thank you, information gathering,' was Bristow's quip about his day to day job.

'Bill and Rhona Gutteridge are the gardener and cleaner,' Jamie joined in.

'In which case what does madam Furneaux do all day?'

'Picks bloody mushrooms,' Michelle popped in.

'Did Whittaker bend my ear just because he happened to be the one passing by? Was he told by Jackson Moore as he was calling in to have a word?

Bristow knew the likelihood was there'd be hidden accounts in British Virgin or somewhere which he'd heard called offshore shelters and the chances were the real owners would not be the ones registered as the chances are it'll be just a shell company. 'I'll ask the boss,' he told them. 'His wife remember is a financial guru down in the city, I'm sure she'll know what that's all about.'

'Why were they so bothered about her having her cheek wiped?'

'Likely she thought it was all beneath her,' said the DI.

'My guess is it would be somebody at Shaidy and Day toadying up to her or rather her father the billionaire hedge fund manager. He'd be the one who thought it beneath her. We could have easy sent someone out to her all along rather than expecting her to come all this way for just a couple of minutes.'

'Still doesn't tick the rest of the boxes.'

'Is all this fiddling with council tax and inheritance part of Alerick's green credentials?'

25

The basic Major Incident Team were at the point where there was nobody on the list remaining to be interviewed and there had been no news of DNA on the body they could link to anybody they were aware of.

The Rockapelt members certainly had issues of one sort or another, but they were all of a personal nature and simply involved finance or a lack of it.

Jake Goodwin had messaged the boss the previous evening with regard to a short interview he'd had with Bill and Rhona Gutteridge. By chance he and Sandy had spotted them leaving the Hall.

According to him, a company from Sleaford handled the mowing of the acres and acres of the estate and where necessary once or twice a year dealt with the trees and major bushes. Jake had made a note of who the old gardener said they were.

Gutteridge had explained to Jake how his work concerned the grassed areas very close to the hall, the flower beds and a large vegetable patch and greenhouse at the rear of the cottage. Through his work it meant Keating-Price was self-sufficient in virtually all foodstuffs he grew for them.

That revelation amused Bristow having seen Furneaux all dressed up in her gardening clothing which was as he suspected at the time just all pretence.

Rhona Gutteridge had happily explained how her job was a two day a week task of cleaning, dusting and hoovering all aspects of the cottage, upstairs and downstairs. Was responsible for doing all the washing and ironing which she had to take home. The pair cleaned the windows inside once a week and explained how her husband dealt with them outside and took on any minor maintenance issues in the cottage.

'If Gutteridge is growing all the veg, I once again have to ask. What on earth was her ladyship and now Furneaux doing all day?'

Oliver Bristow looked at his gathered throng the majority of whom had worked for MIT for a good time. Nothing untoward, no stale beer, no fags these days of course, but it was all far less delicate than when he'd first worked down south for the Met. A whiff of perfume often lingered even without the presence of females in the room, as if they had each left a calling card.

When the door to the Incident Room opened and Craig Darke appeared, Oliver took it this was to be when those extras he had borrowed, would be packing their bags.

'Surprise, surprise,' he said with a grin as he walked into his office. 'Advertising bods confirm its all go and I've also spoken with the music publisher just now and they confirm the drink is set for launch in time for Christmas.'

'How come?'

'Keating-Price's solicitor has emailed his acceptance of all the terms and conditions.'

'But he's dead,' Bristow gasped hand to mouth.

'Not if he signed before his demise.'

'According to those I've just spoken to they've received a letter of acceptance from Shaidy and Day signed by Alwyn Hunter.'

'Aaah,' Bristow released. Both were with Shaidy and Day with her represented by Jackson Moore. He pulled a face. 'Conflict of interest?'

'Not unless they were against each other.'

The DI was more than surprised he didn't mention coffee and a free biscuit, and without further ado Darke just trotted off back to his ivory tower down the corridor.

Bristow was just thinking it was about time for a coffee to go with his lunch. That day Honey Roast Ham and Salad Baguette with a Jam Doughnut. Stopping off at Greggs at Moto Services was something he did now and again rather than make his own. His phone rang.

'Oliver Bristow,' he said stood by his desk.

'Morning guv. You sitting down?'

'Why do I need to?'

'We've got another body,' Jake said gravely.

'Shit!' Oliver gasped loud enough for everybody out in the Incident Room to hear. 'Where we talking?'

'In the field…'

'What?…'

'Listen,' Jake's voice insisted. 'The cabbages are planted by a machine they hire in, done in very straight rows up and down the field all done with GPS. Every now and again because the field's not perfectly square, at the sides there's small run-off areas where the machine can't adjust its position for and has no cabbages. The metal detector guys finished the bulk of it all this morning. They've just gone over these small areas and across not far from the entrance gate up pops a signal. So far they've found a ring, couple of coins to please old Herring and bits and pieces. This one signalled as metal and when the Forensic Archeologist uncovered it, she came across human bones and it looks close to being a skeleton. Thinking is this is a deposition site.'

'How much do we know about it?' he was asked.

'It still needs to be properly excavated and we've got experts on their way, together with that Urquhart the professor heading here when he's finished a PM, just in case.'

'Anything we can do to help?'

'Not really. I'll keep you up to date with events here but at the moment we're just stood here looking at another taped off crime scene. This'll all take a good while, pop down and have a look see if you fancy it.'

'No you're alright. How's the farmer taking it?' Bristow enquired as another non-appearance rankled with Jake.

'Think he's got over the grumpy stage with all this going on,' he responded rather than mention the reluctance again. 'Probably the centre of attention spouting down the pub every night. Trouble is, he's now got boring and droning on about using a John Deere tractor, I think it was. Using an automatic planter and that's the reason they're all in straight rows. Not chucked in by skallywags from Romania.'

'Thanks Jake,' Oliver said and then walked out into the main room. 'D'you get that? Another body in the field,' anything more he planned to add was lost in the reaction. 'Skeleton but no further details as yet, so chances are that'll take some time. Detectorists picked up on jewellery I imagine.'

'Jake and Sandy were hoping to get back today,' sighed Nicky. 'Told me last night they were almost done.'

'One has to assume there's no message with this one and they'll get it removed. But if there is...who knows?' Bristow blew out a tired breath. 'Time for lunch.'

Nicky Scoley was first up after the short break and Bristow had returned from bringing the Darke boss up to date with what had been discovered down at Slindon Farm.

'Gorgie Hall and the estate were sold by Nathan Tyson.' Oliver Bristow sat back in his chair, eyes closed with hands on top of his head.

'You're joking!' made him sit up. 'D'you hear that everybody?' he called out. 'Our bloody friend Tyson sold Gorgie Hall.' Oliver then looked out at Nicky smiling. 'You sure?'

His DS nodded firmly. 'But,' Scoley popped in. 'He put it on his website only and for a very short period according to my friend Dexter upstairs.'

'How on earth …?'

'Learnt about a special fraud link on POLKA, the on-line knowledge area.'

When Darke had moved DC Nicky Scoley as she was then, down to Cambridge for experience she had been sorely missed in MIT. Now they were privy to the benefits of her short term move. The knowledge and understanding she had gained with another force were proving invaluable.

'Why the...?' Bristow blew out a breath of sheer frustration. 'You got anything on right now?' he asked. When the response was negative it was jackets on and down to the car park.

When they'd entered the estate agent the pair faced the same scenario as Nicky had encountered before.

This time the subject of their attention was not expecting them and brushing the staff aside they walked into the glass walled office where a shocked Nathan Tyson was sat.

For a second Nicky had the feeling he was about to protest but then thought better of it. His look told her he was not a happy bunny for sure. This time no coffee or biscuits were offered and he appeared more than a trifle flustered.

'We understand,' said Scoley without introducing her boss. 'You sold Gorgie Hall. Yet if my memory serves me right you told me previously how you'd had nothing whatsoever to do with Lady Arbiter and had not spoken with Alerick for ages.'

'I beg your pardon,' he shot back with his forearms leant on the desk as the pair plonked themselves down on the red chairs uninvited. 'I think you'll find if you care to check. I said Alerick is somebody I've had no dealings with.'

'You don't deny selling Gorgie Hall.'

'No why should I? Its public knowledge,' he sniggered. 'Land Registry, you'll find under gov.uk.'

'For how long?' she threw at him. Ignoring his sarcasm.

'How long what?' he smirked.

'How long was it advertised on your website?'

'How should I know' he chortled.

'Was it in the *Lincoln Leader*?' he just pouted and shook his head. 'Are you saying you've had nothing to do with Alerick?'

'I am.'

'What about Katherine Arbiter?'

'Not her either. Never met the woman, well at least I'm not aware I have. Not since the nineties anyway.'

'So. How come you were chosen to sell the estate and by who?' Scoley demanded.

'You'd better ask them. Shaidy and Day.'

'Anybody in particular?'

Tyson shrugged. 'Some woman, bit of a fancy piece with a funny accent. Norfolk I reckon.,' he said. 'You really want to know?' he asked.

'Of course.'

DI Oliver Bristow and DS Nicky Scoley sat side by side in silence when Nathan Tyson heaved himself to his feet and wandered off to talk to one of the two young men outside. He then stood back arms folded as the taller of the two out there brought something up on his PC.

'Hilary Oldale,' was all Tyson said when he walked back in, closed the glass door and returned to his perch.

'May I ask,' Bristow queried as Nicky Scoley scribbled down the name he had given. 'Why you didn't think to provide this information before?'

'You didn't ask for it.'

'Did you not think as we are carrying out a murder inquiry we might just welcome such information? Their home being sold to an off-shore company.'

'I'm not a mind reader,' he sighed. 'You appeared only interested in the song and how we were struggling to get permission. You asked the questions and I answered them. Not my fault you cocked up fella.'

'We, now is it? You spoken with the others about this?' Scoley joined in.

'About what?'

'The estate being sold,' was Bristow.

'Why should I? None of their damn business.'

'You just didn't think we'd be interesting in such a major development or tip the wink to the others hoping against hope the advert comes off?'

'What's it to them?'

'They are as interested as you are. They've got serious needs like you have with the on-line business you're desperate for funds for.'

'What's that got to do with anything?'

'It's a reason why you want this to go through. From our perspective it's a motive,' said Scoley.

'Part three of what we're looking for,' said DI Bristow with the hint of a grin Tyson couldn't help but notice. 'It's what we call MOM. Means, Opportunity and Motive. You're big enough and ugly enough to give somebody a good smacking which to us means means, and you've given us your motive with the on-line business.' Tyson grimaced at the remark.

'Just opportunity left,' said Scoley. 'DNA and we can easy mark your card with all three.' Tyson appeared desperate to respond as his forehead glistened but it was all coming at him too fast.

'For instance,' said Bristow. 'Were you really playing poker? Can the partners in this on-line scheme be trusted to tell the truth? Would they fancy us bashing their doors down in your name?'

'What the hell are you on about?' was almost him pleading for peace.

'We're on about…murder Mr Tyson,' was louder Bristow pointing at him.

'How dare you?' he shot out in his increasing unease.

'We dare,' said Scoley as she deliberately crossed her legs and hitched her skirt up to show more thigh.

'You can't just come in here, I mean…' he was lost in his own confusion. Which one to look at, what to respond to, and those great legs.

'Tell me all about it, and I mean *all*,' Bristow who had yet to be introduced, said sitting forward, looking right at the bull necked tub sat at his desk. 'And coffee wouldn't go amiss too.'

Had Tyson been in control he'd most probably told them to get lost. Instead in desperate need of respite from the torment he got up with the hint of a stumble and went off to organize coffee.

'Thank you,' said Bristow calmly when he returned. 'How about you go through it all for us, and this time perhaps you'd be kind enough to start with what contact you've had with Keating-Price since your days with Rockapelt.'

Nathan just sat there in his big chair sick to the stomach about what else this devious copper and his woman might know. Where'd he appeared from? Wasn't there some foreign bitch running the show?

Lack of funds had seen him go back to some of his old tricks. Rather than persuading potential buyers to fork out £240,000 rather than £230,000 he'd have done in the good times. Now he'd do his best to snatch the hand off a £230,000 offer to get his fees banked in quick time.

Big worry was, could he afford to play strictly by the rules and still come up with the cash?

26

Only two of the regular members of MIT were in situ, along with Tigger Woods and Sam Howard the pair they'd borrowed. Oliver Bristow pulled out a spare chair and sat in front.

'Yes, Nathan Tyson did sell Gorgie Hall and the estate,' he announced as an opener, then sat there shaking his head in exasperation. 'But, it was Shaidy Days who requested they act as estate agents, and it was a Hilary Oldale one of their conveyancing women who handled it all.' Bristow hesitated. 'Interesting fact is, it was Katherine Arbiter who signed the paperwork to sell the place to this company who now own it.' He glanced at Michelle Cooper sat at her desk at the far end of the room.

'Got to be about somewhere. Surely local enough to deal with paperwork. But not local enough to be recognised.'

'Hang on,' said Tigger. 'What's to stop this all being the crack I mentioned, about people buying a property from a company rather than the owners and saving on Stamp Duty. She buy the company maybe?'

'Next bit of useful info,' said Bristow looking down at his tablet. 'We don't think our Alerick Keating–Price knew anything about it,' caused a few murmurs around the room. 'No reason why he should legally of course because it's her property handed down through the family, it was left to her and anyway he'd not dirty his hands buying and selling property or anything of that nature. Dear me no.'

'Think I'd be a bit peeved if my partner sold our home without as much as a by your leave.'

'Perhaps she told him it was none of his business. Or having buggered off she could do what she liked.'

'Could be he was just not interested. Remember, he sounds as weird as heck, boss.'

'Got rid of the property we've established somehow, some way,' said blonde Nicky. 'Having said that we're still waiting for

Dexter to come up with information about the company who bought it,' she aimed at Tigger.

'Why she sell it, when its a family heirloom and why are they not divorced when she's up to things like that?'

'And allowing him to live there.'

'Bad PR. Just imagine what the *Sun* would make of her kicking their favourite environmental guru out of house and home.'

'Good motive. Get rid of him and sell the lot.'

'Obvious to me,' said Oliver ignoring that suggestion. 'From what little we've seen, it appears all run down but there's the big hall just imagine how many rooms, all those acres and acres of land, the outbuildings, old stables. Cottage would make a good holiday let. Got to be worth a couple of million at the very least, maybe a lot more.' He looked at Nicky sipping a welcome coffee. 'Just think how many affordable properties some clever dick could build there.'

'Suit you,' Jamie told Michelle. 'But you'd have to contend with Jake's dad as a neighbour.'

Michelle Cooper's partner Matthew was an architect who also bought old properties with his father to refurbish and sell on.

'Think Matt would be more interested in the old cottage from what you say, than the huge mansion. Not quite at the development of estates stage yet.'

Her couple of years down in Cambridge had changed Nicky Scoley's outlook on policing. To a certain extent she followed laid down procedures, but never to the level Jake Goodwin insisted upon, even if you expel his authoritarian exterior.

She'd worked with Serious Crime Analysis for six months. Murder, serial murder, abduction, and some awful scenes but never a case of snake venom.

'Got to say,' said Bristow, sat with his legs crossed stroking his beard. 'When we spoke with Furneaux she had a strange attitude to things like relationships. For starters she claimed she had no idea where Keating-Price was when he was murdered. Said they didn't live a life like that when couples know what each other are doing, where they're going, what they're up to. Wonder how long she'll be allowed to stay put?'

'Did Tyson know its full steam ahead with the drink advert?'

'Yes he'd been told,' the DI responded. 'Not sure he said who it was told him,' and he looked at Nicky who shrugged and shook her head. 'But he knew and we guess the other two do as well.'

'So Jenkins'll have good news when his lender bashes in his door.'

'Payout'll takes ages though.'

'We suspected all along this has been about the advert? Alerick didn't want to know, the other three needed money, with one a darn site more desperate than the others. Maybe he was getting his own back on them for events in their past.'

'Now it's been sorted, it's all sweetness and light.'

'Why sell the Hall for a pittance?'

'Been thinking about that,' said Tigger back to his Stamp Duty scam. 'What if like I suggested before, she set up an off shore company to buy the place at a knockdown price. Would that mean when she dies there'll be no capital gains tax and all that business. Right now no Council Tax to pay. She another rich bugger fiddling their tax? After all she doesn't need the cash.'

Sessions like these are something Bristow supports. Allowing his team of experienced coppers some more than him he would admit, to voice ideas and opinions in what was in effect an intelligence review.

'Here's a question,' Nicky suggested. 'Why did Shaidy Days choose Tyson of all people, or didn't they know he was connected to Rockapelt?'

'Wasn't advertised very long,' said Tigger. 'Means that was just to make it all appear legit.'

'Surely the moment they told Katherine about Nathan Tyson handling the sale, she'd say something about the group. Know it's all a long time ago, but had to ring a bell surely.'

'Or just like Alerick, living on another planet, she didn't actually want to know. Couldn't care less who the estate agent was.'

'Anybody else we need to look at?' was his next question as Bristow saw Craig Darke approach the door. 'Morning, sir,' he said over the gathered throng.

'Maurice Sohn. What do we know about him?' Darke asked as he walked to the front.

'Who?' was what the DI returned with a frown but it could have been any one of the team asking the very same thing.

'Sohn. S-O-H-N, their manager,' said Darke with this amused superiority face on him.

'Go on,' the DI suggested with a sigh, knowing he was going to no matter what.

'Been doing a bit of delving, asked a few people in the business. Sohn is the guy who discovered *Rockapelt,* the one they owe everything to in fact. Without him they'd never have got past little church halls.'

'And he is what?'

'Think the word they use now is entrepreneur. Rock bands is just one string to his bow, or was. Not been in the business actively so to speak for donkey's ages my contacts think.'

'If it's not a stupid question,' Nicky offered. 'We've spent a lot of time on this case discussing what people gain by Keating-Price being dead. What does this…Sohn gain?'

'Money.' They all waited. 'Here's how it works,' and they all new the boss was in his element, on his pet subject. 'Our Maurice Sohn sets up a music publishing company, but he knows nothing about the business. Therefore he goes into partnership with one of the major players on a fifty-fifty deal. The big boys do all the hard graft, all the actual publishing rights bit and he supplies the songs written by his artistes. Money for nothing.'

'Still?' Scoley asked.

'Certainly. Takes people like this Rockapelt into a studio he hires for an hour or two and they run through any songs they've written, put each on a demo CD and these they give to the publisher. The chances are his management contract with the group ran out decades ago, so there'd be no big fat twenty five per cent cheque coming his way these days. Except,' he hesitated to highlight. 'He still owns fifty per cent of the music publishing. He personally owns it. Him and him alone.'

'Another one to add to the list,' said a grinning Bristow.

'He gets fifty percent of the publisher's income from a song Keating-Price or Rick Howard as it says on the label, wrote,' the Darke boss said carefully for clarity.

'And what's the betting he pays them a measly amount?'

'You saying sir, he could get more out of this than the likes of Jenkins, Tyson and Dumbrell.'

'Most probably, and depending how his original management contract was constructed despite what I've said. It's entirely possible he could still take a slice of what the others earn from the record release.'

'With our Keating-Price out of the way he's laughing all the way to the bank. Thirsty business all this,' said Darke.

'Mmm' Bristow mouthed to Scoley and flicked his eyes to glance at the ceiling. 'And then there were four,' before Nicky motioned to Alisha to get a coffee for the great man.

'Another little piggy going to market then.'

'Sir,' said Nicky. 'Is there any chance you could track down this Sohn character or give us a few pointers if you want us to do it?'

'And your reasoning?'

'We're not at all keen on coincidences. What odds are there of two quite separate killings of two unrelated people happen to be found in one cabbage patch?'

Darke went to speak 'And your...' he was beaten to it.

'Jake's got that other body. Keating-Price is dead, and if it's Sohn lying in that cabbage field...'

'I'm with you. Good thinking. Why yes certainly, I'll sort it.'

27

DI Oliver Bristow had no need to keep reminding himself of the absence of form or pattern of thought. Data, interviews. DNA, evidence, bloods and still no defining feature. Just three lousy old pop music people and an old music publisher in the weak frame for murder.

Group members he said to himself remembering how adamant Craig Darke had always been about the word in his attempt to keep them at arms length from *boy bands*. A form he constantly reminded everybody had not to his mind been, ever.

"A band has instruments," he would tell anyone willing to listen, and Bristow knew he was absolutely right. Duos, trios, quartets, choirs and the boy band description are for people who simply can't play or don't.

'Sometimes think we'd be better off waiting,' said tall Bristow sat at his desk with Nicky stood arms folded in front of him once the Darke boss had finished his coffee and wandered off. 'Looks as though we've got to go back to Jenkins again. Carole Jenkins said he claims he leaves his phone in his lunch box. Turns out according to Jamie that Tommy Reynolds could well have opened accounts in Vic Jenkins's name and reason why there's little or nothing on his phone. He doesn't use his own.'

'Why the bookies clammed up when they heard the name but never saw the face.'

'Waiting to see how much Reynolds account owes,' Bristow motioned for Nicky to close the door and waited until she had done so. 'Now Jamie's taken it upon himself to take another look at Carole Jenkins's laptop. Reckons Reynolds might well have done the same with her. Used her laptop to place bets in her name.'

Nicky whistled. 'Nice bit of fraud me thinks.'

'Good reason for another chat?'

'And people wonder why some folks' relationships go for a ball of chalk.' Nicky stopped when his phone rang, and watched the expression on his face as he made scribbled notes on his yellow pad.

'Was it you said Dial M for motive?' he asked as he put his phone down. 'Got another one,' the DI sighed deeply and allowed her head to shake. 'That was Nathan Tyson apologizing. He forgot to mention one of his on-line cohorts has been approached by a property development company looking for an estate agency to handle the sale of luxury apartments. Guess where?'

'What?' she gasped. 'In the state that place is in?'

The boss hesitated as he glanced down at his notes. 'You're right. Gorgie Hall,' made Nicky just shake her head. 'Coleridges' have had initial discussions so he reckons, and are planning to bid for the work.'

'He just forgot?' sounded incredulous.

'Let's be kind for once and say this is new and he's decided to play the good guy,' he smiled with. 'If they get it, by then the business may well be handled by the new on-line company. With the advert getting the thumbs up, our man Tyson'll have the money to join the board.'

'Sounds like a win win. D'we know who the developers are, or can I guess? The ones who bought the place for next to nothing?'

Oliver Bristow nodded and smiled. 'Didn't actually say. Eighteen luxury apartments, according to him.'

'Worth a few bob, and a good few million if they develop the whole site.'

When his phone rang again it was Jake they were expecting good news from.

'We'll be finished today. Just waiting on Urquhart now but there's no message this time. Nothing suspicious except what looks to me like blunt force trauma to the skull. Says he wants it taken up to Lincoln, for the PM, so you can take it from there.'

'Thanks Jake, you'll be glad to get away.'

'Other reason for calling. Every time my old dad spots an old Land Rover within ten miles I get a call. Latest is about a bloody Morgan,' Goodwin sighed. 'Not to do with the case, but the old lad's a bit of a petrol head. Had an old Morris Minor Estate for a good ten years in his garage he's doing up, or says he is. Sort I'm afraid who when he sees something out of the ordinary goes on and on about it. Last night he was bending my ear about a Morgan.'

'Interesting. Justin Whittaker's got a Morgan.'

'Thought he had,' he shot back. 'Been trying to be kind, but without going into detail I'm struggling to get my dad to understand you'd struggle to get Keating–Price's body in a Morgan unless you put him in the passenger seat. If we were looking for a bog standard Focus or a Honda Estate he'd not be interested. Gets all overcome with emotion when he spots something like a Jensen. Like he's playing I-Spy,' he chuckled. 'Spotted a red E-type, saw a souped up Wood and Pickett Mini Cooper one time, now this blue Morgan.'

'Could have worse hobbies.' Bristow gestured to Nicky.

'I blame Clarkson.'

'Thanks for that Jake, no rush in the morning understand?'

'Thanks guv.'

'Anything yet on the Land Rover?' he asked Nicky stood at the door.

She shook her head. 'Been thinking,' she said. 'Had a case down near Cambridge when I first went there with a missing van. Worked out in the end, what they'd done was to switch plates. Nicking top of the range motorbikes, you know the sort, do nought to hundred in half a second. Van they transported them in just vanished off the face of the earth, except later it was spotted twice on the A428 I think it was. After,' she shrugged. 'Nothing. In the end it was discovered by sheer chance at the back of a workshop the CSI had been through twice before. Nicked the bikes and took them to an old industrial site using all the back roads with no cameras and on false plates. Month or so later when CSI had done their best and the case was heading for the back burner, out popped the van with the same false plates, passed two cameras to ping the ANPR, then back it went into hiding.'

'Where CSI had already been,' said her boss nodding his head. Oliver Bristow sipped his black coffee. 'How'd they know which van?'

'They struck lucky. Eye witnesses. One a girl out riding her horse early on the Sunday morning trotted down this bridlepath and saw a big Yamaha being loaded. Then a jogger training for London caught sight of one. In both cases they were transferring the bikes to a bigger van.'

'And you think?'

'Somebody nicked a Land Rover, added false plates, did for Keating–Price then hid it away. Wait a while before bringing it out again. Jamie's still on it. Been spotted twice but that's all. If nothing else it's a way to move it across the county.'

'We've been to Gorgie Hall. If that Land Rover was parked round the back we'd never have seen it. Think there were what looked like old stables too.'

'Interesting, but that's as far as we seem to get. Jake's just been on, finishing up in a while and the skeleton's coming up here for the PM. Tomorrow with any luck depending what the waiting list is like.'

'You doing it?'

'Not sure I'll bother if its just bones.'

Next up was good news in more ways than one. An email from the Darke boss about this Maurice Sohn. He'd spoken with the fella's PA who informed him he was currently in the Maldives. He'd got PHU to run a quick check with the Border Agency and they'd come back with confirmation of a Maurice and Gracia Sohn departing Heathrow for the Maldives where the PA had said he owned a holiday complex on Vakarufalhi Island, more than a week ago. According to the great man this Sohn divides his time between his holiday resort, New York and Soho Square in London.

The further good news was, by sending text he knew Darke would not be popping by for coffee and biscuits again any time soon. With any luck he'd be off glad-handing the blue rinse brigade again.

There was bad news, but for this was also one for Jamie to make him re-think the allocation. Bristow off-loaded the Land Rover job to Alisha O'Neill to give her a change of scene and gave Jamie the task of re-checking Jenkins's phone records the Tech Crime Team had obtained. This time solely for betting calls, and cross referencing any with the numbers they had for betting companies and local shops in particular. Either his woman was wrong or he was telling lies. One or the other.

28

Rather in the same way tunes sometimes stay in your mind all day he knew were called earworms, by the time he got home to Great Gonerby, Oliver Bristow was fed up with his brain reminding him of every little aspect of the Leon Phipps case he'd been involved in at one time.

During his time in Croydon before joining the Met for that one fateful operation, he had been very much involved in the arrest of the man responsible for three hideous rapes.

Almost as a last resort when all their inquiries took them nowhere his then boss had suggested they create a list. Everybody and anybody they had come into contact with during their investigations no matter how trivial their part might appear.

All he could remember now was a way to ensure they'd not missed a vital clue. They'd been back through all the evidence and statements time and again, but this was focused on individuals.

It had been exhaustive just compiling the list as so many of the people they eventually included for all intents and purposes had been little more than strangers in the night.

Two of the rape victims had said the man who attacked them viciously as well as sexually had been East European by his accent, the third said she thought he was Slovak although Bristow had never worked out how she could tell the difference.

What his boss had asked, was for everybody to do complete source searches through every database they could lay their hands on. From HOLMES2 ([Home Office Large Major Enquiry System] PNC, PND [Police National Database] and the DNA database all the way through DVLA, banks, credit cards and in a few cases Wikipedia, Facebook and a whole host of particular internet sites.

Leon Phipps had been discounted fairly quickly because he spoke perfect English and claimed to have been born and brought up in Middlesex.

Reality was, which these tedious and time consuming searches revealed, he was an inconsequential bit player in the investigation. In truth he had actually been born in Warsaw to a father who worked for the diplomatic corps in the British Embassy at the time.

Leon Phipps had dual Polish and British nationality and having lived there until the age of six could speak fluent perfect Polish. His UK passport issued in the Embassy in Warsaw actually had London as his birthplace.

A reference to his father working for the Foreign Office. Something his gaffer at the time felt was a civil service scam of some sort he'd threatened to investigate but never had.

Phipps had been in a nearby pub in town and witnesses had spotted him leaving around the time the second victim young Susan Knapp happened to be walking past heading for the taxi rank she never reached.

Reason this rapist from his past was on Bristow's mind that evening was news from one of his old colleagues about Leon Phipps having been released.

Twelve years he had got for the vicious rapes which they all felt should have been a lot more and the justice system had decided to release him after eight years and five months.

Him being back on the streets occupied his mind all evening, Surely to god this'll not be another out for revenge his worry pill asked as he watched telly with mind elsewhere. At the same time Oliver was reminded of all the tedious work he and his mates had put into bringing one guilty person to justice.

Next morning he was furious and thoughts of Leon Phipps had been quickly blown away by the barrage he received when curtly summoned to the office of Detective Superintendent Craig Darke.

His brusque command had him forewarned, but nowhere near ready from the onslaught when Bristow found the Assistant Chief Constable Dylan Whatmore stood erect in Darke's office, complete with full best uniform.

Bristow was sure he'd not worn it for his benefit, but at least he wasn't sporting his medals.

'What did Justin Whittaker tell you about Ms Bryony Furneaux?' was loud but not shouted. 'And the Detective Superintendent?' he gestured at.

'He said tread carefully, for some reason.'

'There you go,' his voice raised a notch, shook his head and sighed obviously. 'How come it's not obvious to you? I've had her solicitor on to me already this morning, while I was having my damn breakfast. Jackson Moore phoned me at home, and you can imagine what he's had to say.' Bristow stood to attention facing such a barrage for the first time in his career had to be very careful what he said so as not to provoke either of these two further. Realized there was no point in trying to reason with the Irish Watmore when he had the bit between his teeth.

'We asked her if we could do a swab while we were there to save her coming up here for it, we were....'

'Why?'

'In order to eliminate her from our inquiries.' This was most certainly the naughty chair although as yet he'd not been offered a seat.

'Don't be ridiculous! Have you forgotten who she is?'

Bristow knew better than to provoke the beast. 'Alerick Keating-Price's, partner, girlfriend, not really sure. One or the other,' was maybe a bit too sarcastic.

'She not mean anything to you?' Before Bristow could react stood there hands clenched tightly by his side Dylan Watmore went on pointing at him. 'Ms Furneaux is a member of one of this country's most respected families and as you say the partner of a gentleman this nation have taken to their hearts. A man standing up for the future of this country if not the world. I appreciate they are not quite what you're used to from where you've appeared, but you need to understand this is a critical part of why this is Great Britain. Why such a small island always has and always will be a major forefront nation in this big wide world. Countries ten times, a hundred times bigger than us are nothing, have achieved nothing compared with us. And why?' The tirade went on. 'Because we have an establishment behind us to guide us through. People who know right from wrong, people who know how to behave. People like Lady Arbiter, Alerick Keating-Price and Ms Furneaux are the absolute backbone upon which this great nation was built.' As Bristow went so speak Watmore just waved him away. 'Just get out before I say something I'll regret,' as the Detective Inspector turned quickly he left with words of advice. 'We've been good enough to take you in. We're doing our best to

197

protect you. You are here earning a good salary, enjoying a fine life all thanks to good people like those you're doing your level best to undermine.'

'Inspector,' Darke said as he reached the door. 'Did it not occur to you Ms Furneaux had just lost her partner?' At that point he couldn't get away fast enough but he stopped him from moving an inch. 'Might I remind you Inspector, we don't have the budget to start poking into trivial unimportant matters we already know will draw a blank. Seems to me more than anything else in this case in particular you lack respect for authority. Might I remind you of the need to keep your head down?'

Was there any point in answering? Oliver told himself sternly not to rise to it, not give either of them the satisfaction.

'Remember Detective Inspector any silly business you were involved in down south is irrelevant up here.'

Detective Inspector Oliver Bristow left Darke's office without another word, even though a book's worth were on the tip of his tongue, and he closed the door firmly behind him. No slamming his door, no show of annoyance or immaturity, no sign of temper contrary to what was building up inside.

As he'd walked away back to his den Oliver wondered how people like Darke and the other senior officers dealt with such an enigmatic man on a regular basis.

Where had such a maelstrom come from he wanted to know. Sat there in his pokey little office in his big black chair daring not to show his feelings to any of his team. Had it really just happened? Had the tirade already been shouted at Craig Darke while he was eating his corn flakes? Such an intelligent man like Darke couldn't possibly believe in such insufferable rot in this day and age, surely. Had he just been tarred with the Met's current bad image?

Oliver Bristow because of his strict upbringing and background had never considered himself better than anyone else, or ever thought anyone better. Those few minutes with the top man said their attitudes were not aligned. As far as the DI is concerned we are all cast from the same mould.

To Oliver a person's real value to society is in herself or himself not monetary which can be and so often is fraudulently gained or worse, stolen from the poor. He was always reminded that the rich and powerful man with everything will die, just as the humble man with nothing will.

Perhaps Darke believed in such outdated shit, maybe the matter had never raised its head before, as he sat there trying hard to think back to any previous episodes to do with the overblown self-righteous sorts in society. He'd certainly thought more of him than to react to such self-important silliness. Wasn't it part of his management role in life to defend his staff? Had, he wondered looking out at his team, Inga Larsson ever suffered in that way? Next time he bumped into her, he'd check.

As far as he understood Shaidy Days were Katherine Arbiter's solicitors. Why was they then representing Furneaux, her partner's new woman? Conflict of interest came to mind.

Right there and then all he wanted to do was go home or at least call France and have a chat. To the one he knew would support him wholeheartedly.

In the end before anybody came being nosey as to why he was just sat there, Oliver decided it was best to keep himself busy. Keep a distance from Darke and certainly the pernicious Furneaux bitch and Moore's lapdog.

Bristow knew he'd not bump into Dylan Watmore. His sort was only ever seen on high days and holidays or heard spouting to the media and glad handing an assortment of misanthropes.

With his basic team looking on, DI Bristow went off to the store room and returned wheeling in a fresh incident board

He wondered just how long it would be before MIT were handed an all seeing all dancing glass incident board. One of those you simply touch with your fingertip and a rogue's life history is there in an instant as they used in the Met. Complete with his mug shot, previous record, DNA profile and fingerprints. While he waited for never-never land he'd have to make do with the pinboard, but at least he was thankful to have colour co-ordinated pins at his disposal. Luxury indeed.

Apart from anything else, he always puts the victim's family through PNC first. Just in case somebody somewhere, a third cousin twice removed happens to be an old lag currently on day release having done time for GBH. Sort of thing the media would clutch in their grubby paws and drive the PR team mad with.

In this case, all they had so far was icon Alerick Keating-Price, and this partner female. Best they'd managed to find so far had been his parents having been killed in a motorway accident in Belgium seven years ago and as an only child now, his sister having been still born. Oliver doubted whether Furneaux had any more knowledge or even cared even if he had spoken about his other relatives.

They understood the victim, but what they didn't understand was why.

Nobody is unimportant, nobody, Bristow told himself as he began to write the basics on the fresh board. Including about the skeleton and the gold medallion to trigger the detectorist on Slindon Farm. Once the meagre facts were jotted down he turned his attention back to the main boards.

The rag bag of different people produced interesting results. The landlord of the Old Crown came up as being done for receiving and for handling stolen goods in the past. Oliver wondered if the brewery were aware of. Three had been done for speeding and two for shoplifting including Jenkins's ex-wife and now partner.

The Watmore episode still rankled. He had been talking about the smarmy so-called ruling classes, the very sort people his mother has always seen as one of English nation's negative aspects to life.

Detective Superintendent Craig Darke was nowhere to be seen all day, unsurprisingly. Be mooching elsewhere cadging free coffee is how Sandy'd put it eloquently.

29

Jake Goodwin was down at the front desk handing over his weekly dues for the Lotto syndicate when his Detective Inspector strode in the front door.

'Morning,' said Bristow and walked to the stairs.

'Morning,' said a surprised Goodwin.

'He always use the front door?' Jake asked of civilian Joe Riches once Bristow was gone..

'Think must be having his car serviced.'

'How d'you make that out?' Jake queried.

'Pulled up outside, when he got out his passenger took over and drove away.'

'Fair enough,' said an unconvinced Jake, paid up and headed for MIT.

It was as if the whole team were just biding their time, waiting for the post mortem on the skeletal remains found close to the cabbages.

DC Jamie Hedley was one who was still working hard double-checking some of the work he had already dealt with, and looking at situations from a different perspective. Not bothering with the well-known and already thoroughly investigated, but chose a couple of people the boss'd not mentioned of late.

The owner of Pizza Dough and Justin Whittaker were two with names on the board but little else.

'Did you know he's divorced?' Jamie suddenly asked at the DI's door.

'Who we talking about?'

'Whittaker. Got a brother who's a successful accountant. And,' he hesitated. 'Done for a spot of criminal damage when he was at uni in West London.'

'Justin Whittaker?' he had to ask. 'How?' was a grimaced question. 'You absolutely sure about that?'

'Drunk in a pub with a load of other students. Done for smashing up a couple of chairs. Not much more than a slap on the wrist or so it seems.'

'And we wonder why he's still only an associate,' Bristow said smiling. 'The wonderful establishment got him,' and he laughed partially to relieve the tension he'd suffered since his telling off. 'Bad enough being dragged up in a council house. Good stuff Jamie.'

Oliver was back to another period of contemplation and he guessed somebody had surmised all was not well when Nicky Scoley walked in with a coffee from the canteen, a crumbly oaty biscuit and a smile.

Council house, no private education, rough and tumble in a seedy pub. The DI wonderd to himself how Whittaker had managed to make it to Shaidy Days at all. Surely this was never them joining in with the diversity spread. One ethnic minority, one gay, one blackfishing, one one parent, one council house kid?

'Just a sec,' Bristow said phone to ear, as he gestured for his DS to sit down. He'd tried to phone Veronica Smallwood but in the end had to wait for her to call back and she'd done so.

'Just a quickie,' he told the solicitor to stop her asking for another call back. 'You didn't tell me Whittaker's divorced and…'

'Didn't know he'd been married.'

'Or the fact he has a brother.'

'Oliver. If you really want to know much more about him, best person is Colin Hislop. I'll give you his number. Hates his guts for stealing his fiancée and then dumping her. Plus he's ex-Shaidy and Days, now with Hartbrown Denby.'

'How interesting,' he grinned at Nicky sat across her desk sipping coffee. 'Thanks.'

The quick chat with Veronica had reminded him of something.

'What about our Alerick belonging to a Masonic Lodge?' Bristow queried of his DS.

'Can't imagine him at a Ladies Night in sandals and black socks tucking into a medium rare, chatting endlessly about income tax fiddles, can you?'

'Guess you're right.'

'He'd got no money, so what good would he be to such dosh obsessed folk?' Scoley offered. 'They'd be looking at how much they can make out of fracking, not trying to stop it.'

'Fair enough. Just a thought.'

His call to Colin Hislop was short and sweet and Oliver Bristow guessed from what he said he was unwilling to talk over the phone in the office, so they arranged for a meet the following evening.

Rather than go all the way home he stayed in the office, got himself a bite to eat and ventured into Lincoln city centre to a fairly new wine bar or at least one he'd not been to before.

Hislop was not there when he arrived and when he did appear fifteen minutes late apologizing as he did so, it was Bristow who bought him a glass of Chablis and then moved away so the pair could talk one to one.

He was close to six foot tall of slim build with his hair having departed his head some time ago, except for a well groomed wavy lump running around the back. His rimless glasses were perched on the end of his long nose.

Bristow told him about the issue concerning Bryony Furneaux and the DNA swab, leaving out the subsequent bollocking he'd got from Whatmore who'd he'd not seen since, let alone spoken to.

Colin Hislop put down his glass. 'Sibling rivalry,' he said when Oliver Bristow had expected him to reveal what had happened to his girlfriend. 'Two brothers. Simon is about eighteen months older than Justin and the story is their father encouraged the rivalry. Reading between the lines I believe Justin was adopted and the conflict was built up to help him drag himself out of the environment in which he had been born. Some ridiculous psychotherapy twaddle about making him fight for everything in life. At one time somebody said his birth father was alcoholic but I don't know how true that is. He did well. Simon was head boy at school but Justin despite such a bad start in life made prefect. Story of his life.'

'What is?' Oliver asked then supped from his glass.

'Second best. How life has always been for Justin, but then it frequently is, when part of a blended family of course. One went into accountancy, the other into law. Simon is happily married with a couple of kids apparently and is a partner with top accountants Rodgers and Hawksworth in Leicester.'

'Ah.'

'You know all about Lady Arbiter?'

'Not exactly.' Oliver waited for him to sip his wine again, but he could see a glint in his eyes.

'Alerick Keating–Price was an absolute pain in the arse if I'm perfectly honest,' he said very quietly. 'We represented him when I was with Shaidy on one of his GM foods campaigns, but because as he tediously says he's working on behalf of us all, he thought we should act on his behalf free and for nothing. In the same way he gives of his time to the universe without charge.' Hislop sat back grinning and shaking his head.

'So, they got rid?' Bristow said as he chuckled.

A shake of the head was the answer. 'He was just as soft as tripe, I'm sorry to say. But powers that be kept hold for the good PR. Could still be with them.'

'And Lady Arbiter?'

Colin Hislop sat back and looked around the bar carefully, even standing up momentarily to peer into two alcoves.

'Please don't include my name if you want to use this at any time, but I was told in strictest confidence some time ago when they were both clients and caused a few issues before he got on his high horse.' He hesitated. 'She was turfed out by her family,' he sucked in a breath before blowing it out obviously and sipping more Chablis and licking his thin lips. 'Went away somewhere to get rid.'

'Pregnant you mean?' Oliver so wanted to laugh out loud as the words of Dylan Watmore came to mind. *People who know right from wrong, people who know how to behave.*

'Something amuse you?'

'No, sorry. Carry on.'

'Any use to you?' Colin shrugged his query and it was obvious he knew something had cheered Bristow.

'Do we know who?'

'Got her pregnant you mean?'

'Well, yes.'

'Getting on for twenty years ago or more,' he sniggered. 'Phew,' he breathed out. 'Sorry, got to be well before even my time.'

'Keating–Price's?' Oliver threw into the mix.' You think?'

'No idea.'

'How come she was left a load in her mother's will if she was thrown out?'

'Understand. Well, according to the story,' he clarified. 'It was her father who kicked her out, the old don't darken my door again routine, all about the good name of the Arbiters and the usual old school nonsense.'

'The establishment?' was there again.

'Probably. Well,' he pulled a face. 'You know what they're like.'

'So the mother must have kept in touch somehow.'

'Guess so.'

'What has all this got to do with Justin Whittaker?'

'Think Shaidy Days wanted to keep her on board for prestige which tends to be their watchword, but knew of their reputation so they gave her to Justin for any day to day business. Meant they had her ladyship on board they could boast about, but'd not get their own hands dirty individually.'

'Why he resolutely defends her,' Colin nodded and smiled. 'Thinks if he does well by her he might…'

'Get the partnership he craves to keep up with Simon?' Colin sipped his wine again twice as Bristow just sat there shaking his head slowly. 'Even down, so I'm told to both owning a Morgan,' he chuckled, 'But as ever Simon's got a brand new one apparently but Justin rattles around in one which has to be fifteen years old if not more,' he sat there glass in hand smiling.

In the end Oliver Bristow hadn't the heart to ask Colin Hislop about the loss of his woman. However chatting with someone who to his mind had good reason to do the dirty on a rival solicitor had proved fruitful. Fresh their-ears-only gossip for the Incident Room in the morning this most certainly was.

An offer of a couple of bottles of a French red as a thank you Colin accepted eagerly, with Bristow for safety reasons not explaining where it would come from. He already knew Justin drove around in a Morgan. The remainder had been a real insight into the fancy dan and her ladyship.

30

.Nicky Scoley a *Who Do We Think We Are?* avid viewer began to tediously quote intensely about the Earl of Gorgie. About him being created in 1514 for the politician Heneage Arbiter the great-grandson of Elizabeth Heneage, first Countess of Broadbridge. It was DI Oliver Bristow who found it difficult to retain interest.

In the end without delving right through the family history she had graciously concluded how Katherine Edith Penelope Arbiter the present Lady was the sole child of Lord Gregory St John Arbiter and there was as far as she could gather no reference whatsoever anywhere to a child of hers being likely to lay claim to money or title.

Bristow being unaware of Nicky's interest in geneology was expecting to hear what his DS had discovered in her own time at home. In particular, any secrets she had uncovered about the illegitimate birth.

What he had not expected first thing was an email from the Tech Crime Team regarding Vic Jenkins's phone numbers.

It appeared he was defrauding one major bookmakers by running an account under a false name and using an email address the geeks upstairs as yet knew nothing about.

Source of the email according to the geeks was untraceable. Anonymous Hotmail account could have come from anyone home or abroad. Sent on a time delay ages previously, would likely as not hinder their research.

What was more surprising to Bristow was being told about him taking out a swingers membership on line using his smart phone.

Not something he could keep to himself.

Morning briefing and having gone through the actions for the day and an early brief from Alisha still ploughing her way through websites and social media, Oliver made his announcement aware of the likely reaction.

'Interesting information from the Tech Crime Team,' he said in a subdued tone as if it was likely to be of little interest. 'There's only one bookmaker Jenkins's using on his smart phone, and what he's doing is fraud and they tell me the company have been advised already by DCI Stevens crew upstairs. He has opened an account in a woman's name from an email address they've never come across before. Being a bit of a...' he looked towards the door. 'Thicko, he's used the same password as he uses on the phone we knew about. Password,' he said smiling. 'His password for both phones is all lower case password. In the top ten most popular,' brought smiles and whispered comments.

'Better than 12345.'

'Only just. But,' the DI said to bring them back. 'He's also got an account on a swingers' website.'

The Detective Inspector just stood there as the remarks flooded out and he was particularly amused by the looks on the faces of Nicky, Michelle and Alisha aware their sentiments were exactly the same.

'You can't imagine anybody would be so bloody hard up,' Nicky gushed. 'Crissakes no ! If he had any taste he'd not go on it. Dear oh dear,' she said with her eyes firmly shut. 'Just imagine having somebody like him watching.'

'That's the trouble,' said Alisha. 'I am! Yuk!'

'But,' and Bristow paused. 'Was that what he and Reynolds were doing when he claimed to be going to the fighting dogs? Spying on folk? His woman's not bothered about fighting dogs but what's the guessing she'd be less impressed with swingers.'

It was two hours later before DC Jamie Hedley was in a position to announce his findings about the likely scenario concerning the commune where they understood Keating-Price and Arbiter first came across each other.

Jake Goodwin back in the fold was quick to mention gossip from the village and suggested Keating-Price had probably first met Katherine when he visited Gorgie Hall to spout when she was in her teens. He suggested the commune came later.

In the same way Nicky Scoley had been searching at home in the evenings for the Arbiter family tree. Jamie had been alone in his flat, when not meeting the new woman in his life, tracking down these hippy types. Putting his career ahead of more wasted hours in a bar infested with students spending their grants.

'Without obtaining absolute confirmation from anybody who was there at the time, it appears likely we're talking about Xendon. This is a hippy type gathering of like-minded people who now live in integrated buildings called Isosys with central courtyards,' had them all listening intently. 'From what I can gather it is to some extent like they have abroad in places, with the whole family living together almost as a family commune in amongst the brotherhood.'

'Do we know where?' Bristow questioned.

'One in a wood in Norfolk, another up in Cumbria some place and the one I concentrated on is in Wiltshire.'

'Anything else?'

'Their homes are designed,' he went on. 'To allow in little light in summer but maximum light in winter in order, along with everything else in their lives for it all to remain constant.'

'Save on power and with high bills they could be the winners.'

'Not something new boss,' said Alisha suddenly. 'Read about this someplace else in other religions. I hear tell in Egypt they build another floor or top of their house for the next generation, so they say.'

'Lots of love,' Jamie continued. 'Together of course with peace, and they truly believe despite all the atrocities in the world we are all slowly and surely coming round to their way of thinking.'

'Energy bills'll see to that.'

'Peace and love, tell that to the Taliban.'

'They say Xendon in the end'll succeed and rule the world.' Then big Sandy bowed his head. 'And we will all,' he said very slowly as if talking to a child. 'Live wi' peace and harmony,' made him sound like a Church of Scotland vicar with his intonation.

'There's plenty of other nutters thinking that way too don't forget!'

'Closest place of any size,' Jamie added. 'Is Malmesbury.'

'D'you hear Alisha?'

'Yes,' came a voice from behind her monitor. 'Got it from Jamie earlier, working on it already.'

'They believe in both the existence of a god and a devil and the power of curse,' big Jamie chuckled to himself. 'Curses they can both bestow upon us all, believe it or not.'

'No,' somebody added.

'They live and work in total harmony with their environment,' he continued. 'These days of course very much into solar power for lighting and heating and wind power particularly for cooking although just eating god's food is their preferred option.'

'Alerick would have been very much at home there then.'

'Maybe where all his nonsense started. What gave him the idea.'

'Thanks Jamie. Good job. Gives us something to go on.' Oliver Bristow brought it to an end before a few of the team lost the will to live.

Within fifteen minutes Alisha O'Neill was at his door and she by then had the information the boss was looking for when she walked in sat down and crossed her legs.

'William Franklyn Arbiter born 14th August 2001. Mother Katherine Arbiter on the birth certificate with the address as Xendon, Five Oaks, Wiltshire.' She looked up. 'No father registered.'

'Bastard!'

'But there's more. Means he's into his twenties now, and his mother maybe early forties,' made the DI whistle. 'But so far I've found absolutely nobody with the name anywhere.'

'No wonder she got kicked out, she'd likely still be in her teens back then. Kid could easy have been adopted,' Bristow thought out loud.

'And not to mention the father being in serious trouble.'

'No records in Wiltshire,' dusky brunette Alisha responded. 'But what if she just gave him away to another pair of childless hippies down there? Weren't they into such nasty habits, ignoring procedure and the law?'

'The more I think about this the more I'm liking it. Let's say he finds out who his mother is, bearing in mind he has the right these days. Turns up at Gorgie Hall, falls out with our Alerick.If it's the first he's heard of her having a son, things could have become extremely nasty.'

'Or on the quiet Katherine and this William actually get on well, but when Alerick turns up after one of his spouting tours finds he's down the pecking order. One day this newcomer will be lord of the manor and he never will be. Alerick in the meantime had always expected to inherit and then hand it all over lock stock and barrel to the vegan brigade. Readies in hand to get homes insulated or pay for the glue they can stick themselves to the road with. I digress,' Alisha sniggered. 'There's a big fall out and this son of hers along with a couple of mates sort him out.'

Bristow was smiling as he got to his feet. 'Reason you can't find him's because maybe he's living with his mother and that's why she cleared off.'

'Good thinking. Could very well be.'

'Might be pushing it a bit, but let's see what the team think of our theories. Well done, good work.'

The DI was just thinking he should pass on his new reveal to the boss when he walked into the office.

'Thanks Alisha,' he said as the DC squeezed past Darke. 'You go first,' he insisted to the Detective Superintendent stood there and he closed the door as if another big row was on his to do list, again.

'This is all about limiting damage to a family of good bloodstock,' sounded as if he was talking about racehorses. 'You have an excellent reputation, don't cast it asunder.'

'I'm not planning to,' Bristow responded in readiness for what he considered was likely to come next.

'Might I remind you, the interviews with Bryony Furneaux were only meant to be cursory. Us flying the flag of intent.' Oliver still could not fathom why he was so damn bothered about who her father was. Surely in his position and more so in the case of the Assistant Chief Constable they still recognized how major violent crimes are in the end down to family members, partners, lovers or spouses. She was certainly more than one of those.

Then as he sat down his brain reminded of something that had come to mind in bed. Was this woman's father somebody Darke's wife Jillie had dealings with as a top notch Financial Consultant in the city?

'Understand the body or rather the skeleton is at the County mortuary.' Oliver nodded. They were both aware there was no necessity to get in touch with Durham University, the UK Centre for Anatomy and Human Identification. They'd identify bones as being human or from an animal. In this case a whole skeleton told them both the emailing of photographs would not be necessary. 'Your news?' Darke asked.

Oliver Bristow knew he would not get the hang of all this toadying with people. He'd not come across it personally down in the Met although there were all sorts going on down there, good and bad all the time. Coming from common stock but even so never been brought up as a boot-licker and was not about to start now.

'A William Franklyn Arbiter, we have reason to believe is the son, the next Lord Arbiter.'

'Really?' produced a frowned grimace almost as if Darke disliked the news and was struggling to believe.

'Katherine Edith Penelope Arbiter is listed on the birth record as the mother, but no father listed and so far no record of this William being adopted.'

'Where was this?'

'Wiltshire.'

'What a pity,' Darke mused. 'Don't think I know anybody down that way.' Oliver Bristow when speaking to Inga Larsson had been told with due respect Craig Darke could be a help rather than a hindrance most of the time.

'Think we've found the commune too.'

'You have been busy,' he said but his disinterest was obvious.

'Thank you.' There was little point in explaining he had hardly lifted a finger. 'Could be the next Lord Arbiter murdered his mother's partner.'

'Steady on there…'

'Please boss,' he hurried out and shook his head. 'There's no easy way to say this. The child was born out of wedlock and as far as we have been able to ascertain Alerick was not the father. If the son's involved, then we'll…'

'I was only going to say,' was stern suddenly. 'Go easy on it all. There are those in this land of ours who consider it not appropriate we should treat everybody as equals. All this levelling up business is nothing to do with it. I know of people who would just sweep all this under the carpet and you'd be left with a cold case which would never be allowed to see the light of day ever again. I'm sure with your time in the Met you've come across many similar attitudes, particularly with the race card. Just bear it all in mind as you progress and let all this be a lesson to you.

There are I'm sorry to say, people who are above the law. Kid gloves have to be the order of the day, always. Trust me. Treat them with the respect they deserve.' *Demand* Bristow so wanted to say but kept his mouth firmly shut.

'Just out of interest, your drummer friend Vic Jenkins has more than one phone. DCI Stevens is after him for fraud – placing bets under a false name from a false address and goodness knows what else, plus,' he chuckled. 'He's got an account we believe with a swingers' website. All about...'

'I know what they are,' he assured the smiling DI.

'Already up to his neck in debt and gets involved in...' he grimaced his disapproval.

'Married isn't he?' Darke posed.

'Was. Twice but just lives with his first wife now,' made Darke grimace. Time to take a chance with him. 'Been wondering about having a quiet word with our friend Whittaker about the baby Arbiter appears to have given birth to.'

Darke sucked in his breath. 'And if he speed dials the Chief Constable, we could both be for the high jump and I'm not ready to retire.'

'If only we could knock on her door, and hey lady what's to tell about the bastard son of yours?' even Craig Darke had to chuckle at.

'Trouble is of course way back in history a large number of children were illegitimate, so the chances are the perfect stock she purports to come from are not as good as she makes out.' He'd changed his tune all of a sudden.

'You're probably right,' Bristow admitted. 'Doubtful if Whittaker knows anything about her past history, understand he's got lumbered with dealing with bits and pieces for the pair of them because Alerick was an absolute pain in the butt.' He paused. 'Guessing here, but it could be Alerick expected them to do it all for free. As some sort of environmental gesture.'

'Strange how quite often people's public image belies what they're really like. All this child abuse business is tragic for the victims of course, but it's the fact how often it involves people so greatly admired by the public. There's certainly a great many people who think Keating–Price was the best thing since sliced bread.'

'Not at all from what I've been told.'

'Please remember,' was suddenly back to serious. 'The names Arbiter and Furneaux can curry significant favour in this county and you seriously need to bear that in mind at all times as you progress.'

Oliver Bristow could hear his father now. Suggesting the country was and always had been class-ridden. Feudal no less with everyone reminded constantly of their place.

31

After a short period of contemplation and reflection about the half-hearted change in attitude from the boss, Oliver Bristow instituted the team action to find William Franklyn Arbiter. More for his peace of mind than anything else. Out in the big wide world probably among a bunch of nomadic hippies living in old broken down buses or wigwams and grubby campervans with flat tyres and no MOT, had once been a lonely abandoned young boy. Oliver Bristow was determined to discover what happened to the lad.

When he thought about the possible scenario all those years later it appeared to him to contain all the necessary ingredients for one of those old fashioned cosy novels they sell cheap at airports.

In the intervening time Jake had received a phone call from his mother who had been asking around the village as casually as she could, about life at the time when Katherine Arbiter was very likely to have been told not to darken the Gorgie Hall door again.

The locals were always too devoured by what others think. Overly concerned by what would be the outside world's opinion. Superciliously worried they may not be drinking coffee in the right place today, and ludicrously what type.

Small tightly-knit village communities always worried Jake. To a greater or lesser degree there was always to some extent a dictatorial state among a few of the citizens. Over the years he'd heard lurid tales of the ignorant bombastic nature of some his old man couldn't abide. Often new to the village, living in second homes, and only there half the time.

In one case a few years back he'd heard about an elderly pensioner in the over-rated swanky Cotswolds being mercilessly harangued about the colour of his car. In the end the old fella had been forced by some pompous residents in this scruffy, rag, tag and bobtail village to change his pride and joy.

If any of their neighbours contemplated trying anything like that on Reg his dad, Jake knew they'd very soon get their head in their hands to play with.

Jake had not heard of anything as nasty as the disgusting treatment of pensioners happening locally. However, he had picked up aspects of a local attitude from odd questions his mother would pose out of the blue.

What are Shiitake mushrooms, what are Mangosteens and had he ever had a Macchiato? Be things she'd heard them chatting about in the resident-run shop as Mrs Goodwin bought her washing-up liquid, half a dozen free range eggs and *Daily Mail*.

There was absolutely no doubt Jake's parents mixed with generous kind folk, but a few of the 'those who know who they are' dying breed are still alive and well and living in the small village unfortunately. The ones he'd heard about who still insist on toilet rolls and sanitary towels being hidden in brown paper bags before being handed over.

'Just imagine,' his mother had suggested. 'The utter shame and stigma around here about being pregnant out of wedlock,' she found amusing in today's society.

To be fair, his mother had arranged for Jake to call on a Brenda Little who had lived in the village virtually all her life and could recall most of the major events in the small locale.

As he was explaining all this to his boss and he'd agreed he could make the visit that afternoon, suddenly Darke was back.

'Big mistake,' said Darke to worry Bristow once the three were settled down. 'Allan Townend is offering free rein. Pull out all the stops in your search for this…William Arbiter,' he read from notes. 'Continue to investigate his mother the chief suggests.'

'What the...?' a flabbergasted DI slipped out with his breath. What on earth was going on now? How'd the Chief Constable get involved, as if he didn't know. Truth was he didn't know.

'Big mistake,' said Darke again. 'Abandoning a child the way it seems she obviously did, simply to protect her family name and goodness knows what else. To a born again Christian like our main man that's an absolute no no, particularly as we hear so much these days about child abuse. Just do it, and you have his backing I can assure you. Play it all strictly by the holy book of course and you'll be fine.'

'Seriously?' Bristow asked, keeping a smart quip about changing his tune to himself. Lincoln County had not suffered the amount of bad press foisted onto the Met by their own officers, but he guessed this was still all about good local PR.

'Take me through the group and where we are with them? Group members, then Private Detective, then who we left with? We have DNA samples linked to nobody so…'

Bristow's hand had gone up. Not an opportunity to be missed. 'DNA from Furneaux helped us discount her remember.'

'So be it,' was nothing like an apology. 'If you like, the group can be forgotten, and what does it leave us with?'

Piece by piece the DI went through the main participants for their boss as a reminder although he always copied him into all the reports.

'Who are we left with once we've dealt with that bunch?'

'Lady Arbiter who's goodness knows where, and her son we have nothing on.'

'What's the motive? At least with the group members they all need the money from the drink advertising. If Keating–Price hadn't been murdered would he have agreed to the advertising do we think?'

'An illegitimate son turning up out of the blue after all these years, looking for his inheritance Keating-Price was banking on coming his way from his missus.' Jake slipped in.

'And passing it onto a climate change cohort when we could do with another decent summer.'

'Wrong way round. Alerick killing her son makes more sense,' Craig Darke suggested.

'Arbiter's a millionairess,' Bristow reminded. 'But perhaps any row as Jake suggests, had nothing to do with the song or the money.'

'Who else have we got, when the likely lads have all got alibis?' Darke posed.

'Of sorts. They're the ones with any sort of record. One of the hangers on has a few minor indiscretions for things like possessing dope and one offence of shop-lifting an Xbox, or tried to.'

'True but no DNA, no spit and sawdust from them anywhere on the cadaver.' Darke pushed himself to his feet. 'Leave it with you,' and off he strolled again.

Jake sighed and shook his head.

'What in God's name was all that about?'

'Inga used to reckon he gets easily bored pen pushing.'

'At least he wasn't after another coffee.'

'Car alright?' Jake asked.

'Sorry?'

'Saw you being dropped off.'

'No, no. Nothing like that. Now, where were we?''

'Yes?' was an abrupt reaction to a call on his mobile, but one you sometimes hear folk utter.

'Sorry to phone you at home, boss,' was Jake Goodwin. 'Decided it's best to give you a chance to think on what I've found out.'

'Hold on a sec Jake,' Oliver Bristow said as he walked into his kitchen, pulled out a carver chair and plonked himself down. 'Carry on, I'm sitting comfortably, you can begin,' he smiled to himself at.

'Spoke this afternoon to Brenda Little down in the village. Interesting conversation, could have done with it a week or more ago. Back at the time we're talking about, the Hall was still in full use and from time to time they held big functions there. Summer balls, big Bonfire Nights and the like and guests stayed over most weekends. Anyway this Brenda used to do a bit of waitressing at most of these big functions to earn a bit of cash-in-hand pin money. She remembers Katherine back then of course and has a quite vivid recollection of when she went away.'

'To have the baby?'

'Yes. Except Brenda had no idea why at the time. In fact this afternoon was the first time she's heard mention of such a thing. Story put around to cover her disappearance at the time was about young Katherine undertaking some flamboyant long term residential cordon bleu cookery course, but Brenda had no idea where.' Jake took a breath. 'Ready for this? According to Brenda and I quote as close as I can remember. "Of course there was that darkie living in the village around the time," just came out of nowhere.'

'What? What she…?' the DI stumbled out. 'Oh my God.'

'Said, from the moment Katherine suddenly disappeared off to the commune or this cookery place she reckons the 'darkie' was never seen again.'

'You mean coloured? Black?' Oliver gasped.

'Way she described him, I'm afraid. She is eighty six for goodness sake and not into all the woke business. Mention LGBT to her and she probably thinks it's another train company taking over from LNER. In his late twenties, thirties at the very most she reckoned, but then said they all look the same,' he chuckled. 'Brenda described him as not being one of those "really dark ones" and, "like some places have got a lot of these days, not round these parts thank goodness," quote, unquote.'

'Lady Arbiter's heir to the title is black!' Oliver almost shouted 'These days of course there'd be some making sure he'd inherit the title, and not only because he's illegitimate.'

'According to Brenda, but please remember she didn't say he was the father of the child, just he was about at the time. But in her opinion as soon as Katherine went off to the commune or whatever, he disappeared too. She did add however there were rumours around at the time about having some sort of secret lovers tryst. Wasn't just this Brenda. She told my mum one woman she thought might know more unfortunately died of Covid more than a couple of years ago.'

'That's a bugger!'

'Please bear in mind Brenda has not lived through the permanent need for integration. Doubt living out there in such a small locality she even realizes in some areas we now live in a multi-cultural society. White, heterosexual country folk with ruddy faces is what she's been brought up with and of course who she mixes with day to day. My mother even said when I checked with her, there might be an Asian woman living in a cottage at the far end. Rest are white, British, Anglo-Saxon middle class yellerbellies through and through. No turbans, no rap, no dreadlocks, no hijabs anywhere near there remember.'

'Be why she was sent away to have the baby. Guess the family must have realized from what had been going on or maybe she even admitted who the father was.'

'And why he's not on the birth certificate.'

'Just a thought. This reeks of that business with the Royal Family and that Meghan woman saying the likely colour of her son was discussed. You can just imagine exactly the same conversation up at Gorgie Hall.'

'Doing the family tree is no longer an option then! Been thinking,' said Jake. 'Gives us a good reason to speak to Whittaker maybe?'

'In what way?'

'We could play the doing our best to protect Katherine line, tell him how all this information has come to our attention. Make it a bit of a chat rather than any sort of formal interview.'

'His place or ours?

'Use a conference room, tea and cakes.'

'And who might they be for?' he teased.

'By the way. Basic PM's online all about your skeleton,' Bristow said as he walked through to the lounge and his laptop. 'Blunt force trauma, year or so ago or thereabouts. Tox has all gone to Leicester because of the state of Alerick, and they've sent off for her dental records.'

'Her?'

'Oh sorry. Yes a woman. They've got small scraps of hair, skin and clothing that've survived. Load of medical jargon but that's about it from our perspective.'

'Not embalmed then,' said Jake. 'Bodies last longer if they have been.'

'Not exactly back to square one but again not a great deal to go on.'

32

DI Oliver Bristow was at work at his usual early time on the Monday morning aware they had so far not managed to locate this William, or if they had nobody had taken it upon themselves to bother him at home.

'You look a bit rough,' he told Jake sat head in hands peering at his monitor as if he had suddenly forgotten the password he uses every day, as happens.

'Rhubarb wine,' he admitted. 'Spent yesterday back with my parents after spoiling last weekend for them.' He peered up at his boss. 'Rhubarb wine my old man said was just right for drinking.'

'Say no more,' Oliver chuckled. 'Bring you a coffee?'

'Any news on our William Arbiter?' Jake asked as he dragged himself to his feet. 'Surprised we found any with his moniker.'

'I'll get the coffees, you take a pill,' and the DI was off.

Jake was worried he'd become obsessed by Bristow. Talking it over with Sally she had suggested he have a word with Nicky. Had she been spiked by the same oddities? Never attending a crime scene, no mention of family, of hobbies or what he does for a weekend. Sally had suggested he was just ambitious. A new DI feeling his way with a point to prove. Was that any reason to limit his link with his team? Didn't he want them on side? All anybody knew was, he lived in Long Bennington outside Grantham. His mother owned a vineyard in France and he'd given people a bottle for their birthday and at Christmas. All the usual chatter he excluded himself from. Now out of the blue getting coffees for the first time since his arrival.

'Sandy's got it down to three,' Jake said as his DI slipped an orange mug onto his work station.

Bristow was not at all sure his deputy was firing on all cylinders even by the time they got to the morning briefing despite his black coffee.

The short sharp morning briefing itself was all about this William Franklyn Arbiter. About a black man seen around the village close to Gorgie Hall back at the end of the nineties. Plus the meeting he'd arranged at the end of the day with handsome as handsome be, Justin Whittaker.

As a start of a new week, although they'd all been at work on Saturday, had not gone well. DC Sandy MacLachlan with the help of Alisha and Jamie was still struggling with the William Arbiter name having cut it down from five, were all far too old or in one case far too young.

Bristow had busied himself setting up the small conference room with a coffee machine, milk, cream, sugar, sweetener, glasses of water and a selection of biscuits for the arrival of Justin Whittaker from Shaidy and Day. Plan was for a cosy chat whereas their visitor would more than likely report back with talk of a breakout networking session or some such silliness.

When shown up to where Oliver Bristow was waiting with Jake Goodwin by a young PC, his greeting was more as he would expect rather than the last time they had met each other downstairs.

He at least had no need to suffer the mwah mwah kissing fresh air silliness he thought the virus had done away with. Now knowing he had been divorced did give a greater insight into the not so perfect. The Whittaker persona possibly was purely a veil to hide a vulnerable man he'd not even considered before.

After the initial chit-chat and pouring of coffees, Bristow got onto subject quickly.

'Our inquiries into the family background regarding the murder of Alerick Keating-Price lead us to believe Lady Katherine Arbiter has a son.' His training could sense the effect in his eyes as he struggled to give away as little as possible. 'In fact our information from reliable sources is, she went away to have the child.' Out of wedlock would have been a nice touch he refrained from.

'Is she a suspect?' Whittaker shot back. 'Because if not I have to ask why on earth do you need to probe into her personal life in such a manner?'

'Who would benefit from inheritance?' said Jake Goodwin. 'For starters.'

'I'm sorry Sergeant, but in case it has passed you by, Lady Arbiter and Alerick Keating-Price were not in any form of legal relationship.'

'He was her partner.'

'Exactly, which is the basis for nothing, in law. Something the unwashed and unemployed seem so unwilling to understand.'

'She may have left her worldly goods to him and he could leave them to anybody he liked,' was Bristow. 'When we set out on this journey we had no idea what we would find.'

'Or discover she gave the baby away.'

'You have no proof,' was sharp and just as Bristow sipping water had experienced watching him in court. 'I sincerely hope,' well groomed Whittaker went on. 'This will not be leaked out to become public knowledge. In fact I will be looking at an injunction to stop all this nonsense.'

Bristow knew exactly where that had come from.

'Difficult when it's already in the public domain,' said Goodwin who lifted his cup to drink coffee.

'How do you mean sergeant?' There he was using his rank to put him fairly and squarely in his box.

'I know a woman who knew Katherine Arbiter when…'

'Lady Arbiter, please.'

'Who knew her when she was young and went away to have the baby. She volunteered to us what was at the time common knowledge around the village.'

'What about the people who may well have legally or illegally adopted the child? Or wasn't adopted and went into care.'

'What proof do you have either way?' Whittaker pounced on. 'Sounds to me as though you are really floundering with all this total nonsense.'

'I'm sorry Justin,' said Bristow. 'But if he was adopted, you should know they have rights too. It may on the other hand have all been illegal but they brought him up.'

'Not if they adopted the child illegally. If there was no adoption, then there is no claim it would be treated as if nothing had happened.'

'If it is illegal, then might I suggest your Katherine Arbiter could be in serious trouble?'

'Gives us another case to investigate,' Goodwin smiled which Whittaker spotted.

'I take it you know where? Where all this nothing took place?' he grinned.

'Wiltshire, in fact a place called Five Oaks in Wiltshire.'

'Justin,' said Bristow before he could react. 'Might I suggest you persuade your Katherine to come clean? Tell us the full story about who, what and where in order we may locate William Franklyn Arbiter born 14th August 2001 he read from his tablet on the table.

'You've not persuaded me why you need to go down this route, surely this is all to do with a blasted song, and the mess those three from a band have got themselves into. As I understand.'

'Think you mean group.' Whittaker grimaced and sighed at Bristow's accurate retort. He'd latched onto Justin's last remark which must have come from Arbiter.

'Mess?' chirped up Goodwin. 'Being an estate agent a mess now is it?'

'Hardly something to boast about I shouldn't imagine. After all the public having so little regard for them.'

'Perhaps I'll tell him what you've said.'

'Please yourself.'

'Think on,' Oliver Bristow said. 'If Katherine comes clean, we can locate the next Lord Arbiter and see what he has to say for himself.'

'Which is what exactly?' Justin asked and drank a good amount of coffee and wiped his lips with his red handkerchief.

'Where was he on the Saturday night when Alerick was murdered? How well did he know the man? Does he just happen to be an environmental sympathizer or quite the opposite? Perhaps he avidly supports GM crops some say will feed the world or goes on and on like Alerick did about what he describes as the utter desecration of the Green Belt.'

'And if Lady Katherine decides not to cooperate?'

'Then we will carry on searching for him. In fact we've already made a start and by the time we return to the office we may well have video of him or a picture on Facebook.'

'Hook or by crook we will find this William, have no fear of that with the resources available to us. But what I will say is,' Jake Goodwin said to Whittaker firmly. 'It will be far less embarrassing for her if we can work together than if the team have to go around asking all and sundry all over Britain if they've ever met Lady Katherine Arbiter's bastard kid.'

'More coffee, Justin?'

223

Whittaker blew out a breath and sat back. 'Please.' The look the DI received from his DS was pleasing. 'So tell me, what you want to know exactly?'

'As much information as possible about her son William,' said Bristow as he poured coffee into a fresh clean cup. 'Has she had recent contact and if so, when and where. Plus background information. He'll be in his twenties now. Is he an unemployed waste of space addict living on the streets or has he attained a first class honours degree in Psychology, in Law or maybe drives a van for Tesco?'

'Thank you,' said courteous Whittaker when Bristow placed the cup of black coffee in front of him, and followed it with the plate of assorted biscuits.

'You met him?'

'Who?' Whittaker asked with the cup halfway to his mouth.

'William.'

'You're the first to mention him.'

'How much do you know about the song?' Jake asked to just make a switch.

'Understand it has all been agreed by all parties First trench of adverts due out pre-Christmas is my understanding.'

Bristow nodded. 'Good. What about the Hall?' he frowned at his question. 'Katherine has sold it we understand. Any idea what she plans?' Oliver noted how he had forgotten to add cream.

'Your grapevine got a fault?' he chortled.

'No. Just heard somewhere down the line, wondered what the plan was,' he lied.

'Luxury apartments.'

'Sounds good.'

'Put my folks' bungalow value up,' Jake Goodwin chipped in with.

'Your parents?' Whittaker queried, then began to drink his fresh coffee.

'Live in the village,' which the solicitor never remarked upon. 'They're Arbiter's close neighbours.'

'What about your brother?' Bristow dared. 'How is he getting on these days?' caught Justin Whittaker by complete surprise.

Er...fine. Yes, doing fine. Thank you.'

'Still down in Leicester?'

'Er…yes,' made his brow furrow.

'Good, good.'

'Anything else?' Whittaker asked before he attacked his coffee again.

'Think that's about it,' he looked at Jake. 'You?'

'Fine thank you.'

'No nothing more from me Justin, thank you. Appreciate your time with us.' He looked seriously at the solicitor. 'Let's get all this out of the way so we can get on and bring this to conclusion without being sidetracked.'

'Been good,' Justin said as he rose to his feet with plenty of coffee in his cup.

'Just one thing,' said the DI as it came to mind. 'Have you ever come across an organisation called Ecouk?' he then spelt it in case his pronunciation had not been correct.

'Something in the back of my mind says I've heard of them. In what context?'

'Just something somebody said,' he shrugged. 'Just wondered.'

'So many of these ragtag websites on line, that's the trouble these days. Thank you again Inspector, Sergeant.'

'He's a bloody charmer,' said Jake upon returning to the conference room after seeing Whittaker out of the building. 'Why is it some people have to have everything?' he said as he poured more coffee into his cup. 'Good enough to go to university, great talker, tall, dark, bloody handsome, clever. When some of us struggle along with not very much going for us.'

'Didn't suit somebody.' Jake looked at his boss. 'Divorced.'

'Of course,' and he smiled with that boost to his ego. 'Word has it he's got a chip on his shoulder,' said Bristow as he nibbled a biscuit. 'Driven on so I'm told by jealousy. Jealous of his elder brother, a full partner for a firm of accountants down in Leicester I think it is.'

'Just because he's a partner?'

'Apparently. What he's striving for all the time? He regards as some sort of status.'

'No, no,' said Jake shaking his head. 'Not with Shaidy Days, far too proletariat for them. Not want a Comprehensive School pleb's name on their headed paper. No way.' He drank coffee from the cup held in both hands. 'And to think it's not long ago this country was run by people with that sort of attitude.'

'Talking of the aristocracy,' said Oliver. 'How about bees knees Justin and our Katherine?'

'In what way?'

'Anyway you like, but have we considered away from the solicitor client association?'

'You mean?' Jake frowned.

'Why not?'

'With his looks he could have anybody.'

'Point one, she has position. Point two she has money. Point three her partner just happens to be dead. How convenient eh?'

'Sorry,' Jake shook his head. 'Don't see it.'

'Because she makes no effort?'

'Maybe and too old I guess.'

The DI just glanced at the door. 'What if when he calls she has full make-up, silk underwear, stockings, high heels...' Oliver stopped when Jake chuckled.

'Be serious.'

'I am. What if that's Justin's predilection, what if that's his turn on, floats his boat.'

'And she satisfied that desire and his ex-wife was all missionary and really didn't want to know?'

Oliver Bristow turned his head towards the door again, leant forward to lower his voice. 'And satisfies her desires at the same time. Pictures I've seen of her in all her glad rags year or two back, she's got a good head of hair, excellent bone structure. Face is a bit weathered but she's slim,' he shrugged. 'Could be fairly good. Something to think about.' He stretched his arms above his head, making his intertwined fingers crack. 'Back to it,' said the Detective Inspector downing the dregs of his coffee and dragged himself to his feet.

'People are murdered by family or friends and reasons why include money of course which she has. Sex naturally we've now covered. Revenge maybe,' Jake pulled a face. 'Plus the need to cover up facts and information such as a black son and more we've not discovered.'

'Most people saw Keating–Price as just a nutty conservationist spouting to joe public who just want a holiday to top up their tan or an excuse to get the barbie out.'

Back in the Incident Room DS Nicky Scoley was waiting for the pair of them.

'Your Ecouk bunch were way off the mark. On the day in question none of the three on their list had any chance of even seeing Keating–Price let alone do him any harm.'

Bristow sat behind his desk hands on head, sighed with thanks.

'Tamara Nelson was too busy to talk to me but her PA advised she had spent the weekend in Paris doing a spot of retail therapy. If we need confirmation he did at least say she flew British Airways so we can check. Even gave me the flight number.'

'PA?'

'She's a Senior Operating Officer for a major energy conglomerate. Sounded as though low life like me are not on her radar.'

'And she's going to give Keating–Price a good bashing is she? I don't think so.' Bristow sighed again. 'Go on.'

Nicky looked down. 'Lewis Benson. Had his kids for the day on Saturday, then went out for a meal in the evening. Dean Pattinson is some sort of union big wig also in the energy business. His excuse was he was watching his son play rugby in Wales.' Nicky looked up at the boss. 'Want me to go on?'

'What was that all about?'

'Did they think we'd just take a team with a big red key and knock their doors down, cause absolute mayhem just for a laugh.'

'It's not as if these are just a lowlife bunch with records as long as your arm.' her DI stopped when Nicky smiled.

'Pattinson was done for breach of the peace few years ago Caused trouble on some march in Birmingham.'

'Like a lot of union people do, I would suggest.'

'D'we need more?'

'Sorry, but we've got better things to do with our time.' Bristow drank the half cup of coffee he'd brought with him. 'Wasting police time comes to mind. Anti-frackers for good reason seems to me. They're just in competition.'

'Maybe we should take the big red key to the knob who told Nicky they were worth looking into.'

'Tempting. Very tempting.'

33

Jake Goodwin planned to return to his work station, check his emails, any incident report logs and then get on with his action tasks for the remainder of the day.

Oliver Bristow beckoning him over to his office the moment he sat down, putting paid to all his plans.

'Tell Jake,' said a self-satisfied shirt sleeved DI sat behind his desk with his customary steepled hands the moment he joined him along with Jamie Hedley.

'William Franklyn Arbiter proved very simple in the end with a little help from my friends upstairs with their newfangled aka app, it turns out...'

'Hold on there a second,' said Goodwin to stop him. 'Aka app?'

'Also Known As app,' Jamie advised slower. 'Changed his name by deed poll or I'm guessing his parents in inverted commas did, from William Franklyn Arbiter to William Lord.'

'Lord!' Bristow exclaimed loudly. 'How ridiculous is that?'

'Sounds good,' Jake laughed. 'He could finish up as Lord Lord!'

'I thought it was too stupid for words,' said Hedley, 'but I've been thinking about it. How about if the people who adopted him or took him off Arbiter's hands were actually named Lord. Plenty of people named Lord about. Make life easier, less questions asked when he went to school. Mr and Mrs Lord and their son William.

'Unfortunate clash but there must be loads of Charles King's. There's Robbie Earle played for Wimbledon I think it was.'

'Every day that passes,' Nicky slid in. 'I'm pleased I did my family tree when I did. At least on my dad's side it was Scoley begat Scoley begat Scoley. Nobody did anything ridiculous like they do now. Teenage girls changing their name to some nonsense off the internet because they're not their father's chattel. Then some divorced women want to rid themselves of their married moniker but going back to their maiden name according to some, is considered emotionally regressive. Miss Black, becomes Mrs Green and ends up as Ms Brown. Don't fancy trying to track that in a hundred years. I reckon Lord Willam Lord will be fine bearing all the other utter stupidity you read about.'

'These days some guys take their wives names to add to the mix.'

'Wait a minute, said Oliver. 'If it was all done officially when he was just a kid, surely they'd need Katherine Arbiter's co-operation as his blood relative.' He shook his head. 'What's the betting she knows he's now William Lord? Anything else?' he asked.

'According to PNC, he got a year for ABH for his part in a pub brawl in Cirencester.'

'ABH?' Jake shot out as the DI went back to a smirk. 'Like the sound of him being handy with his fists.'

'Under the name William Lord?'

'Yes. That's the final link we came across when he had to give previous names.'

'Where is he now, do we know?'

Jamie Hedley chuckled to himself then waited. 'Grimsby.'

'Interesting. Long way from Wiltshire though.'

'Made more sense when we were looking at somebody like Jenkins being responsible,' Bristow mused. 'He's in debt and the chances are Keating-Price wasn't going to play ball with the song and put money his way, but his partner's secret son? Whole different ball game.'

'If he's upset about her dumping him on this Lord couple when he was a kid, why take it out on Keating-Price? If anybody you'd think he'd take it out on her.'

'And Keating-Price has no money so hardly a motive if he's hard up. Be a waste of time threatening him if he didn't cough.'

'How long's he been out did you say?' Inga asked Jamie.

'Year and a bit. Did seven months.'

'Not a case of coming out of nick and getting his own back then.'

Half an hour later on his own in his office running down the emails to read, to leave for now, to forward, to reply to, to delete, Oliver's phone rang.

'Detective Inspector Bristow.'

'Dominic Coolridge here.'

'Hello Mr Coolridge.'

'Dominic, please.'

'How may I help you…Dominic?'

'The business with Nathan Tyson,' he said. 'Afraid I asked him what it was all about and he explained about the unfortunate Keating–Price. Hope I haven't done something wrong, but…'

Bristow wanted him to get on with it. 'How would it involve us Mr…sorry, Dominic?'

'Just wondered…how shall I put this? Read all about that nasty business in the *Leader* of course. Didn't realize Nathan knew him at all. But he was telling me about this drinks advert and the record.' He chuckled slightly. 'Reason I'm phoning, don't know if it's relevant but we're planning to go into business with Nathan and a couple of other people in the industry with an on-line localized hybrid website.'

'We had heard.'

'You see,' he hesitated. 'He appears to be struggling to get the money together for the set-up. We'd hoped to get it up and running by now, but Nathan and one of the other guys just seem to us to be stalling. We think it's probably over finance. Could be wrong of course. Does all the business with Keating–Price have anything to do with money? Or lack of it rather.'

'I have no idea, but it could be he's waiting for income from the advertising people which he plans to use for your business deal.'

'How long do you imagine?'

'Could be ages. Keating–Price being alive or dead will hardly speed up such people.'

'It's just that we assumed it was…his wife holding the purse strings being the issue, until he told us about all this business.'

'Are you saying his wife might not be supporting your venture?' Bristow posed.

'Not as such, but she does tend to have…what shall I say? Other priorities.'

'Which are?'

'Have you been to the house?'

'No I'm sorry I haven't had the pleasure.'

'Probably shouldn't be saying this but…as you're the Police. Gated community, five bedrooms just for the two of them, three quarters of an acre, separate granny annexe, and all the decking he installed last year along with one of those huge hot tub things, and a barbecue right adjacent to it. All burger and bubbles is how my brother describes it all. Almost as if there's a permanent list of must haves.'

230

Was this jealousy Bristow asked himself, hoping he'd get to the point? 'Not sure how this would interest us with regard to our investigations concerning Keating–Price?'

'It's what she wants next which is of concern.'

'Which is?'

'A motorhome.'

'And your concern is he might well buy the motorhome his wife wants, rather than invest in your on-line estate agency business?'

What on earth did he think that had to do with them? Sort of social media tittle tattle many go in for on their phones.

'Why now all of a sudden, when this business has all blown up?' he asked. 'One day this Keating–Price's death was on the radio and next time I spoke with Nathan he was saying how he'd been taken to look at a hundred odd grand motorhome. Just seemed a tad suspicious.'

'Think this all sounds like an issue you'll need to deal with rather than us.'

'Any idea how much he'll get from this advert business?'

'I'm sorry…Dominic. I have absolutely no idea.'

'Don't you think it's a bit odd? What about if he gets more money now because Keating–Price conveniently is out of the way?' Worth thinking about.

'Surely he will have left everything to Lady Arbiter.'

'Can it be done?'

'Do what?'

'Leave something like future royalties from a song to somebody? Doesn't make sense to me, means you're leaving nothing just a vain hope for the future. Like me leaving income from a house I've not sold to my nephew.'

'Yes you can. Absolutely you can.' Bristow assured him.

'Oh right,' sounded as though he'd burst his balloon. 'You sure?'

'Yes, we've had it all checked. We have a music expert on board,' Bristow grinned to himself as he pictured Darke being as proud as a peacock.

'Fair enough,' sounded disgruntled.

34

According to PNC this William Lord had not offended again and to his credit had behaved himself right until the whole sentence was fully spent. Or he hadn't been caught. His mug shot did however confirm just what had been suggested, William Lord was indeed coloured.

He was living in a flat in Needles House on the Nunsthorpe Estate known locally as the Nunnery in Grimsby with an eighteen year old Rosie Luxford. At the age of fifteen she'd been caught shoplifting and been given a juvenile conviction along with a friend. Humberside Police were not aware of anything since nicking twenty quid's worth of cheap tatt jewellery whilst still at school.

Bristow doubted whether this pair were quite the perfect couple Katherine Arbiter would have in mind for the next generation to proudly carry on the centuries old aristocratic family line.

Needles House was just a bland twelve storey oblong block on its own, built fifty odd years ago when the powers that be had to go skywards rather than out onto the precious green fields, folk get so uptight about keeping for themselves.

These places the team all knew are in the vast majority of cases never as bad as some people seem to think. Often given a bad name by smug folk who have never bothered to visit.

There'll be people living in them quite happily, and thankful all over the country aspiring to something better. Grateful they at least for the time being have a roof over their heads, and not sleeping in the underpass or in a bus shelter under cardboard with all the real skanks of this world.

When the DI got the message he was hoping for, it was full steam ahead with a number of his plans which as a direct result saw Jake Goodwin and 'Tigger' Woods packed off up to Grimsby once Craig Darke had a quick word with his counterpart in Humberside Police.

Fifth floor by lift brought the two detectives to a corridor with the left hand side open to the elements. Not at all bad. No graffiti, no old bikes or prams, virtually no litter save for the odd fag end and no overflowing bins littering the space downstairs.

The view of the Nunnery in fact was quite decent from that height and Jamie knew from the top floor it was likely to be a view out to sea. If this was pretty much crime free, it'd be a fair place to live and no mistake.

Jake Goodwin knocked on the pale blue door at number 25. In order not to cause alarm he used his insurance man's rat-ta-ta using the alloy silver knocker. The door opened on the chain after a few seconds and stood there peeping out was a female.

'William Lord?'

She nodded and bit her lip. 'Yeh Billy.'

'Lincoln County Police,' said Goodwin offering his warrant card. 'Need a chat with him, can we come in?'

'Oh, my days,' she gasped and left her mouth open.

At least Tigger realized she'd not scarper out the back as people often do, leap over the wall and hot foot it down the warren of cut through alleyways such places often invest in. If she tried it five floors up there'd be no chat. The female closed the door, slid the chain out, pulled the door open wide and stood back to let the detectives enter.

'Is he at home?' Goodwin asked down to the female in the main living room.

'No...sorry...why?'

'Any idea where...Billy is?' Jake Goodwin asked as he looked around. This was fine. The flat was at least clean, neat and tidy and not the dumping ground he'd come across when some folk open their doors.

'Working.'

'And you are?'

'Rosie Luxford.'

'What does he do?' Nothing posh or pretentious about this place, save for the giant TV screen slammed on one wall to dominate the room. Less and less people some claim are watching television preferring laptops, tablets and their phone. Yet more and more were buying bigger, and to their mind better.

'He's a delivery driver,' there was a not unpleasant slight northern burr to her voice. 'Drives round, dropping off internet

233

stuff, parcel and that mostly, like they do.' A photo of their target subject was in a white frame on a shelf along with one of the pair of them, to confirm accuracy and his colour.

'Where's he deliver?' DC Tigger Woods posed.

'Doncaster,' said Rose. 'Well, south side mostly for Fasters.'

'What time d'you expect him home?' Goodwin asked.

'Sevenish.'

'Long day,' Woods offered.

'Some are quite a bit less than a quid a drop like, means he works long hours. Has to.'

'And you?' was a query from chunky Tigger Woods. She was small and neat with a pasty face with her hair cut far too short to enhance femininity to his mind.

'Work in a coffee house, mornings all week.'

'Enjoy it?' Goodwin wanted to know.

'Yeh good. Trouble is dead easy to drink too much caffeine, then I can't sleep.' She took a breath, then, 'Look. We're not on benefits you know or anything like that. We're not scroungers like some people think.'

'We didn't say you were.'

It most certainly was not a moth eaten flea bag of a flat. All likely IKEA flat pack was how Jake saw it.

'What is it you want Billy for?' she asked later than they'd expected. 'Not been in an accident has he?' she asked wringing her hands as she did so.

Goodwin shook his head to reassure her. 'Need him to help with our inquiries.'

'You local?'

'Lincoln County,' he admitted and she nodded. 'Thanks,' he said and moved to leave, but she was off the mark and at the front door first. They both thanked her and wandered back along the passage.

Oliver Bristow back at Lincoln Central received a text from Ian 'Tigger' Woods. They planned to stay in the area and talk to Billy Lord at his depot in Doncaster when he returned from his last drop later.

At the depot in Doncaster in front of his line manager William 'Billy' Lord explained exactly where he was when Alerick Keating-Price had died. He was with his partner spending the

234

whole weekend with her family. After work Friday late, through to Sunday evening they'd both been in Huddersfield from where Rosie had originated, helping her brother celebrate his 21st birthday. Held in a room at their local pub they named if DC Woods wished to check and offered fifty witnesses.

Once that was done and dusted, Tigger was not finished and asked William about his relationship with his mother. According to him he'd driven down to Gorgie Hall. There without giving his identity away spoke to a gardener handyman who called his wife who Goodwin and Woods reckoned by the description had to be Mrs Gutteridge the cleaner. She explained how Keating-Price was away and Lady Arbiter was as far as she knew, living in Italy.

He'd report back to Bristow but Tigger Woods could not imagine for one minute the genuine guy he'd spoken with would have the know how to organize killing anybody with snake venom.

35

Straight after the row with the Assistant Chief Constable, DI Bristow had become so down in the dumps with the case he kept wondering whether or not it was time to give it up as a bad job and once again make a fundamental change. Head off to France, to the vineyard in the sunshine. Put all his troubles behind him and become free again. Or as free as he was ever likely to be

Somebody was on the ball next morning even before he'd managed to grab his first strong coffee when a Priority message popped up on his monitor.

It was one of those moments when he had to mentally question the validity of what he was reading. Then to break his intense concentration the phone rang.

'Oliver Bristow,' he said slightly too abruptly with his single-mindedness on the news before him.

'Hi. Vron here.'

'Hi.'

'Not really sure I should be calling, but erm...look, last Saturday me and Rick went to a barbecue Leah Boakye and her fella put on. You know what she's like. Enough food to feed an army, bar in the summer house, hot tub and all that business.' Oliver had no idea what she was talking about and wanted to scream *get on with it!* as he scanned down the vital report. He had no idea who this Leah was.

'Carry on.'

'So. Friend of yours was there drinking too much and mouthing off.' There was a pause and Oliver was not in the mood for a guessing game. 'Can I ask. Have you had a bollocking?'

'What?' he gasped back.

'Our mutual friend reckons he taught you a lesson. Said and I sort of quote, got that new Mr Plod sorted, be gone back to Thatcherland in no time. Teach him to mess with me.'

'How many guesses?' Oliver asked turning away from his monitor for a moment.

'You had trouble?'

'Not really. No. Just came in being all high and mighty.'

'You're not in trouble then?'

'Not that I'm aware.' Or was this more bad news he was having handed down to him? 'Angry yes.' *Spitting blood at one time certainly and now hearing this, worried sick.*

'According to him he put you in your place. Gotta say Johnnie Pugh and a couple of others put a stop to him making malicious remarks about you and your mother's crap wine.'

'Interesting,' it was a lot more than that but his feelings had to remain his own. Stay in control. 'Look Vron, I'm up to my ears in stuff right now. Can I come back to you, have a chat, meet for coffee and you can fill me in?'

'Yeh right. Thought you have a right to know being in the same business sort of. From my point of view told me why his wife probably buggered off,' she chuckled

Time somehow to clear his head, go for a spot of fresh air and think. Dispirited Oliver shut down his laptop, grabbed his jacket, told the team he was off and to be ready for morning briefing, headed outdoors for a walk around.

On his return to the Incident Room via the canteen he was surprised not to see Craig Darke waiting for him with bad news such was his mood.

Half drunk mug of black coffee he pushed aside, a livid Oliver Bristow propped himself up on the edge of an empty desk. Maybe just maybe heading for Alsace was closer than he'd expected.

'Operation Oldfield dragging its feet has as you know a second body. Talk was of asking the system for another old copper's name to tag onto the skeleton. Not any more.' as he so often tended towards Bristow annoyingly sipped his coffee to gain their attention. 'Dental records have come back. To tell us the cadaver skeleton is...Lady Katherine Arbiter.'

He just perched there on the corner of the desk sipping coffee until the gasps of reaction had almost subsided.

'Dental records d'you say?' Nicky checked.

'Only way, seeing as we have no DNA. They've got it now from small samples of flesh just about surviving apparently.'

'Why both of 'em for God's sake?' was Jake.

'What the fuck's going on?'

'Good question. What that means is, we need to move away from Alerick for now and concentrate on her.' He checked his tablet. 'A gold "There's No Planet B" medallion round her neck is a sort of confirmation. '

Nicky was used to the boffins being busy, but what she walked into upstairs was something different. Somebody had been hacking into major companies particularly in London and Birmingham causing attack alerts to come alive. Several forces were hunting down a hacker. Hari and Dexter were knee deep in the search they been asked to join by the Met and West Midlands when Lincolnshire suddenly popped up as a location.

A character calling himself TricTok used other aliases on chat channels and some required passwords to delay the forensic guys heads down burrowing.

Their major problem so Nicky understood was this TricTok never logged in directly. Instead using a secure virtual private network.

Time for Nicky to leave them to it and her request with ASBO.

Tigger Woods had been tasked with making contact with William Lord in person, to perceive his reaction to the news about his mother. Alisha O'Neill was still checking all the social media sites awaiting reaction to the news when released.

Craig Darke never did appear but he phoned down and summoned Bristow to his office.

Oliver's mouth was dry stood there looking down.

'It has been decided we will be releasing the way in which Alerick Keating-Price died. We're lifting the blanket ban,' he said slowly and carefully. 'Reasoning behind it is it might be beneficial to retain the news about Lady Arbiter. Holding onto info on two murders is fraught with danger especially with the media sniffing around.'

'You're probably right.'

'I appreciate the idea was to keep mum about those aspects because it meant only us and the killer are aware of the detail, but this has to be the right move under the new circumstances.'

'Any idea when?'

'Today, so I understand. Think even you'd agree despite all your hard work, the Keating-Price murder has stalled somewhat and releasing info particularly about the snake venom and the warning notice will gain fresh coverage.'

'Front page,' said Oliver starting to relax. 'Snake venom, danger sign and the national treasure all wrapped up together, what more could the media ask for?'

'Be just our luck there's an earthquake in Hampstead to get us spiked.'

'They still do that?'

'Just press delete I guess.'

'With any luck this'll trigger something with somebody. We cannot afford to have the pair of them unsolved.'

On his return to the Tech Crime Team late in the day, Nicky discovered this TricTok was just having a laugh. Causing untold mischief by hacking into important sites to cause alarm, simply because he could and to illustrate the vulnerability of these so-called secure set-ups.

He'd stolen nothing as it turned out and Nicky wondered why somebody that good had no job in the industry, rather being sat alone in his bedroom bored to tears causing havoc.

Two days were spent handling the deluge of concerned folk withing to help, including the sort of dopes who put up their hands up to every crime known to man. Getting through those with concerns about the local pet shop and talk of neighbours housing snakes at home became more than tedious.

Once again Oliver Bristow was pleased his circumstances meant it would be others dealing with the clamouring media bent on digging for dirt. Thoughts of sitting up there at a press conference, cameras clicking and dealing with some of the daftest questions journalists rely upon, filled him with horror. Front page news he dare not be and a photo could easy mean a death sentence.

These cases would be even worse and he understood Craig Darke would be assisted by DCI Luke Stevens formerly from the Met. Pleased no doubt to be away from that environment these days.

36

Detective Inspector Oliver Bristow having confided in DS Nicky Scoley had decided it would be best policy to use a friendly approach for delving inside the mind of a possible killer. In the hope somehow when he felt more relaxed he just might admit to something in a weak moment.

The system more and more these days is for Sergeants and Constables to carry out such interviews at least down in PHU they did. This was up a big notch, these were murders, his baby, his first big ones the media were desperate for. What drove him on each day but with caution.

To bend towards that premise, he'd chosen Nicola Scoley as a companion having confided in her. Two birds to catch a worm.

Oliver had managed to grab use of one of the half decent interview rooms rather than one of those used frequented to ease confessions out of drugged-up scumbag contenders for a pillock of the year competition.

He was ready for a lengthy interrogation which he knew lay ahead. Be another late shift and guessed he'd be too late to finish off the cheesy chicken remnants before settling down to watch football or some obscure sport on BT.

Due to the nature of what he planned he'd not gone through the normal arrival procedure. None of the business of being booked in by the Custody Sergeant, fingerprints, photograph, a written description of tattoos and scars and DNA swab taken.

With no duty advocate sat beside him the questions and answers followed along a natural progression he'd been through time and again. Bristow had a blue folder in front of him full of evidence data, and Scoley had a remarkably similar brown folder detailing everything they expected he had been involved in most provided by hot water drinking ASBO and his team of geeks.

The interview Room 3 could at times feel quite claustrophobic with even three people in there with featureless cream walls and the dull grey lifeless floor tiles which all somehow made the aura more and more despairing for the accused, the longer such nerve wracking events went on.

Plus point was it was more depressing for the interviewee who would sometimes quickly hanker after an easier cell away from the glare of constant bombardment of questions and the sarcasm such interviews tend to abound with.

This case was different, the subject had experience.

'I take it you know why you're here?' DI Bristow started after the opening rigmarole of introductions without switching on tape or video.

'Guess so.'

'As you are more than familiar with the process you'll realize this is to a degree a casual chat. No tape, no video and no accompanying solicitor. I do have to warn you however if you admit something here today relevant to the case we're inquiring about I have my assistant as witness. Do you understand?'

'What do you think?' was surly.

Bristow spied the look in his eyes. 'As you know we're looking at the untimely death of a man well established and well known in conservation and environment protection circles and beyond.'

'We talking stone circles?' was accompanied by a half snort, half chuckle as if he wanted to congratulate himself.

The DI ignored him. 'That he was killed by snake venom has been confirmed by the Home Office Pathologist, CSI Leicester and Porton Down,' he tapped his folder as he saw a degree of concern. 'Then transported to a field where his body was just dumped. He'd been lying down or sitting for some time according to lividity.'

'This is all good stuff. Liking it so far, tell me more,' Whittaker falsely enthused. 'Good fairy story, little kids'd love it. You make this up yourself or have you read it somewhere in one of your kid's books?'

'We are also investigating the death of his partner Katherine Arbiter, who was actually discovered in the same field.'

There was just the slightest hint of delay before, 'Bully for you.'

Bristow ignored him. 'We have uncovered your DNA on his clothing and in the very vehicle used to transport his body,' he lied.

'Getting more exciting by the minute.' As if his remark had been clever a hint of a smile flitted across his face. 'This my DNA you don't have is it?' he chuckled.

Bristow opened his blue folder and pulled out a sheet of paper. 'Let me take you back a while. Remember The Station House pub in Ealing?' brought a look of surprise to the solicitor's eyes. 'You were lucky being a student, as they were probably used to a bit of boisterous antics and lucky for you, you don't have a criminal record. Having said that. Can you recall how you reacted say to those who arrested you or the Desk Sergeant?'

'Yeh, like it was yesterday?'

'I'm guessing here Justin,' stern Bristow continued. 'But experience tells me you were swabbed for DNA on your arrival, but when you loud mouthed one of the coppers and started acting up with all the I know the law crap, somehow they forgot to delete your DNA from the records.' The DI smiled at him. 'Only guessing of course. So what was it you were saying about us not having your DNA?' He was back to his folder. 'We also have O positive blood found in the vehicle. Alerick was O positive.'

'Which Inspector, half the nation has running round inside them,' said Justin Whittaker doing his very best to retain his composure. 'Think you'll need to do better than that,' he smirked.

'48% of people actually,' Scoley reacted.

'Guess it's a few people,' the solicitor popped in. 'If you're planning to go through all twenty million one by one.' Inga ignored again. 'Better get a move on if you are. Not got all day you know.'

This is not the Magistrates Court,' said the Detective Inspector. 'There's nobody to impress here,' he added. *This is not a tatty barbecue where you can mouth off either.* He turned his head to ask Scoley: 'Are you?'

'No.'

'What was your problem with Keating–Price?' Bristow asked Whittaker. 'We are willing to admit at this stage as yet we don't know exactly why he had to be murdered, we know how and we certainly believe you know something about it.'

'Really?'

'In fact a great deal.'

'How ridiculous. I wasn't anywhere near Gorgie Hall then.'

'How d'you know where and what time? I've not said.'

'Very good,' was accompanied by a sneer as his breath snorted out.

Oliver Bristow had read somewhere or heard at conference how what criminals say provides him or her with a justification for the action taken.

'And?'

'Been on the news for all the world to see.'

'I missed it,' Bristow told him. 'Please remind me.'

'Said Sunday morning. Reckon I saw it on *Look North* Sunday evening.'

'Very good,' blonde Nicky Scoley smiled as if congratulating him. 'Except,' she said before he could respond. 'There's no *Look North* at weekends.'

'Well, whatever.'

'Sorry, whatever's not on either,' she chuckled. 'Bit of a bugger eh? Keating–Price picked the wrong day to die. How silly of him.'

'Very funny,' was sneered.

'Can I offer a piece of advice? This,' said Bristow. 'Is not going to get any easier from here on. A major mistake and we've hardly started and you've got hours and hours of this to look forward to.'

'Thanks.'

'You're very quiet, any reason?' he probed to take him off subject.

'Not enough room for both of us, with you trying to put words in my mouth, it's a bit full.'

Deflecting questions was one of the annoying aspects of initial interviews.

'We have ideas of course about what happened some of which you may tell us are spot on. On the other hand we could quite easily be way off beam. Here's your chance to tell us your version, what actually happened from your perspective?'

'This is just pure speculation.' To be fair, he looked less attractive than Nicky Scoley had seen him previously.

'You seem to be forgetting the DNA and fingerprinting in places you say you were never at.' Bristow knew they'd not even found the old Land Rover. Did his silence on that subject suggest he knew they hadn't?

'Not enough by a long chalk,' the lawyer in him responded. 'That it?' He moved to get up. Bristow was surprised he'd not walked out before. He'd not been arrested or charged, simply going through the helping police with their inquiries business and could leave at any time. When he dragged his chair back as he got to his feet, the sound setting Scoley's teeth on edge, she decided was deliberate. How many times had she been in there over the years with the lower echelons of society?

'If you knew what we now know, you'd know it is certainly more than enough,' Scoley suggested. Her boss beside her watched carefully for a reaction but there was none as he lowered himself back down.

Was the death of Alerick the work of someone with high-order thinking skills or simply a matter of fact he'd had to deal with when he rode up to help the damsel in distress?

'Tell us, just out of interest' said the DI immediately. 'What exactly you were doing around midnight on the day Keating-Price died.'

'You talking 'bout a minute before midnight or a minute after midnight? Does make a difference you see when you think about it. Wouldn't want you to fall between two stools and cock this all up with wrong dates. Be a good laugh of course, getting it all thrown out of court.'

'Saturday night into Sunday morning.'

'Now let me see,' was his sarcasm. The pair waited for the slightly amusing yet annoying charade of a fingertip to lips and his eyes scouring all around. 'Do you know, I'll have to ask permission from the gorgeous woman I was with. To simply blurt out her name in public as I'm sure you appreciate, is not good manners,' he aimed at Scoley.

'Borrow my phone,' said Bristow and whipped it from his suit jacket pocket. 'Call her now.' The DI sensed the hint of victory in his hidden expression. A sign on his supreme arrogance being as proud as Punch about what he'd achieved. Any empathy will he knew tend to be for himself not for Alerick.

'And have you finish up with my woman's private number on your phone. What d'you take me for?' he chuckled and looked at his watch. 'I have appointments if we're finished here.'

'Don't let us stop you,' Scoley just beat her DI to it.

'Now if you've got the time I'd like to move onto Katherine Arbiter, late of this parish.' Bristow hesitated to await a remark about her being a Lady. 'When was the last time you saw her?'

'How absolutely fascinating all this is. Next you'll be telling me you plan to buy the Rockapelt record. Sorry download. Do quite a bit of walking. Tend to do my best thinking at night going for a stroll, you really should try it. Frees up the thought process which I'm sure you would need with your sort of job. Been told by all and sundry how exercise is a necessary evil.' He shrugged obviously. 'May not quite be marathon running but it's what I do.'

'Katherine Arbiter?' he posed.

'Just after the pandemic, got to be.'

'Why?'

'I'm her lawyer.'

'Please,' Bristow made into a long word. 'This is not a barbecue you don't have to impress us. I'm sure you meant to say Jackson Moore is her solicitor.'

'What?' was all he managed to gasp.

'Justin,' he said gently direct to his face. 'You don't have to play the cards you're dealt in life. You could easily have chosen a different path. As the song goes, know when to fold 'em, know when to walk away.'

'Why the fuck should I? Why's it always me? What is it they say? Coming second is the first bloody loser, right? Why do I have to work with a sag bag of bloody half-baked lawyers, foisting all the saddos of this crap world on me?' He sighed deeply. 'It's either the bunch of snobby tossers or bloody pimps, and degenerates. Get all the shit jobs people only pay fucking peanuts for?'

'Can we return to Crete for a moment or two, please?' Bristow suggested in an annoyingly calm manner '2021 when all the holiday places had been opened up and the airlines cocked it all up,' Bristow read from his file again aware the pathologist's best guess for time of death was a year ago. 'And the last time you visited her was in fact when you flew from East Midlands to Heraklion by Jet 2 in December of the previous year. For Christmas.'

'Guess these regular holidays were, sun, sea, sand and…' she hesitated longer than need be. 'Her ladyship,' Scoley popped in for fun.

'How dare you?' he almost shouted.

'We dare Justin,' was up a notch with the increasingly confident DI pointing at him. 'Because your nasty misogynistic attitude has been brought to our attention along with a degree of racist spouting heard by many decent friends of mine, some in your profession. All of which we will hold onto until we have an opportunity to talk to Alwyn or Jackson about it.'

'Can't be doing with all this,' was admitted suddenly, but no real surprise to the pair of detectives.

'Thank you Justin for taking the time to answer a few of our questions,' Bristow said as Whittaker got to his feet. He knew with the solicitor not disputing the trip abroad at that time was him on holiday alone was helping to establish they could now look seriously at conspiracy to murder. 'I'm sure you know your way out.'

'Well done,' said Nicky after a few minutes. Now she could see why he'd taken over from Inga.

'No. Thank you,' the DI slipped back. 'Getting the Border Force data means I can claim it was a pucker interview which he didn't deny and daren't complain about. Thanks.'

'Has to remain a person of interest surely.'

'Why not refute visiting somebody abroad on holiday when they have no passport?' Oliver almost asked himself.

'Why is it always just Italy?' Nicky queried. 'No town or city from anybody so far. Remember Jake checked around the village. All his parents knew was when she disappeared somebody'd said Italy. His dad would certainly know if anybody.'

'And what about him and snake venom? Educated, intelligent enough...what d'you reckon?'

Nicky sucked her breath in noisily. 'Not sure unless he paid someone,' she shrugged. 'Damn sure the sort of scrotes he deals with'd not be up to it.'

'You're probably right. Think I'll give somebody the little job of having a look at what's going on behind him. At least he didn't smell of booze.'

'Want me to?' Nicky asked.

'Would you? I've got a couple of contacts in his line of business. One guy had his girlfriend enticed away by Justin and he then dumped her. Pretty obvious to me he knows he's going nowhere with Shaidy Days. That was almost a cry for help seemed to me.' He shook his head. 'Never thought I'd see him like that.'

'D'you think we've done him a bit of a favour? Given him something to think about? Pointed him in the right direction.'

'If he does nothing else he needs to get away from that awful bunch.'

37

Mid morning next day, when the two Detective Sergeants emerged from behind their monitors and walked into his small office they gave Oliver Bristow the distinct impression of it being some sort of protest movement. Without the mandatory misspelt banners or glueing themselves to the floor.

'A word please, boss,' was DS Nicola Scoley first in, to which the DI nodded his reply, harbouring a degree of scepticism and look of curiosity.

'Just that,' said Jake. 'We appear to have missed out somehow down the line.'

'Coffee?' Nicky asked and gestured back out into the Incident Room. Someone had sent to the canteen for two big black jugs of coffee, white mugs for three along with milk and a bowl of biscuits.

They waited for the DI to push himself to his feet and wander out and join them.

'Where is everybody?' Bristow asked. 'Or shouldn't I ask?'

'Taking a break guv,' was Jake.

Likely story he sighed to himself.

'Question one,' was the senior of the two. 'Where did we get Whittaker's DNA from, and how long have we had it?' Jake queried as they all sat down.

'Not that long,' Bristow replied straining hard to keep a straight face.

'And it was obtained from where exactly?' a frowning Jake wanted to know. 'You've not been running your fingers through his hair and pulling lumps out, surely to God.'

'Look Jake,' he reacted as Nicky poured coffee. 'Nicky already knows, but I had a nasty bollocking off Dylan Whatmore about asking Furneaux for a DNA swab. With that hanging over me and a bit of a spat with Justin he had to be on the list. Sorry, but he was more likely a candidate than the three from the group,' Nicky Scoley pushed a coffee in his direction. 'Those three silly buggers are never going to concoct a deadly snake poisoning, let alone carry it out.'

'Biscuit? Or is that a silly question?'

Bristow grinned and took a digestive. 'Remember when he called in for coffee and I served water with it?' he asked the pair as seriously as he could manage.

'When we told him about this William Lord?'

'Exactly.'

'And you served water with the coffee,' Jake confirmed. 'And I wondered what was cracking off…'

'Which is what some poncey folk do,' said the DI then stopped to add a tiny dash of milk to his coffee. Nicky poured two more as she battled with thoughts of Whittaker in her mind, sat across from her that afternoon. 'Provide a glass of cold water with coffee. Said by some to be the way to drink coffee by cleaning you palate first.'

'Boss who's a bit of a coffee connoisseur,' said the blonde. 'Says to him it's just an amusing hip trendy thing to do, and not to be taken seriously. He reckons it's an Italian quirk like brown shoes with a dark suit, I see people like Stevens doing. Except very few do,' said Nicky. 'Well not in Starbucks as far as I can see and anyway they always get it all arse about face.'

'Sorry,' said Jake. 'Now you've lost me .'

'Some people, especially in Italy tend to provide water when they serve some coffees,' Nicky explained. 'Idea is you are supposed to drink the water to clean your mouth out before you taste their coffee.'

'Except the ignorant of this world drink the coffee, then drink the water,' said a chuckling Jake.

'But nobody does it with tea or hot chocolate.'

'Which tells the host or the barista, you hate their coffee and are trying to wash the taste away.'

'Like you wish you could do when you visit Bryony Furneaux and drink her rubbish,' Nicky smirked.

'I provided water for Justin Whittaker,' Bristow then admitted and shrugged slightly.

'And not because it's what he does.'

'Not exactly,' the Inspector said as the smile began to light his bearded face. 'He drank the water, and after he'd gone I just popped his glass into an evidence bag for forensics to check for DNA, along with his cup as reserve just in case.'

'Hang on, hang on,' said an amazed Nicky. 'That's just the sort of thing they do in cheap movies.'

'I was right though wasn't I?'

'But why? What did you know?' Jake pressed.

'I didn't actually know anything. It was just when I asked everybody to write on the incident board the names of every single person we had come across, and I was stood there looking down the list as you were all beavering away chasing their records, I realized there was someone else.'

'Whittaker?' Jake asked before the other two could say the same thing.

'He'd been to see me about daring to ask Furneaux for her DNA and I got a telling off from the Assistant Chief Constable and the Darke boss for having the temerity to want such a thing from a lady in her position.'

'Why did it ring a bell?'

'It didn't. I was still bristling underneath about being pulled up for it while I was scanning down the list, and had him going round in my head just seemed right. I'd told you all to put absolutely everybody on the list no matter how inconsequential you thought they were. Whittaker was certainly that. Thought I'd add his name, then realized if I did people like you two in particular would ask questions and I'd probably then have to admit to the team including half of PHU I'd been given a right bollocking. So I just put his name to one side.' He sighed. 'Thought I'd keep it up my sleeve and use it one day down the line to get my own back about something in court.'

'But?'

'Did a DNA database check just in case. Told about him getting into a ruck down in Ealing in his student days. Decided he'd not remember if his DNA was taken and if it was it'd be destroyed later.' He looked at Nicky cup in both hands sipping coffee. 'Just tossed in the name of a pub down there if you remember, and he didn't query it,' he shrugged.

'And the DNA now?'

'No match with the bits and pieces on Alerick and obviously not with Katherine.'

'Water with coffee from the canteen? You're joking. Can just see them coming up with that.'

'And what some would have to say.'

'You may not have noticed but I deliberately drank my water immediately, then sipped and sipped again,' their DI told them. 'Guess being the sort he is, he stupidly thought it must be the done thing around these parts and did the same.' He sighed again and Jake chuckled.

'Daft sort of thing idiots do all the time. Sally reckons some silly woman somewhere mistakenly tucked the front of her top in her skirt and in no time they're all doing it.'

'If I'm perfectly honest to start with, I'd have wanted to be able to put a big black cross against his DNA. Take him out of the equation. When he came onto me downstairs I carried that around for a day then when Watmore got all supercilious, decided tackling Justin was easier of the two.'

Nicky Scoley knew enough about the processes to be aware how Forensics would target ten parts. Ten specific parts within the DNA known as short tandem repeats. She knew if the CSI techies in the lab got a match on all ten of the points the chances are the odds of it not being the same person is one in more than a billion.

Nicky Scoley had listened to the boss intently with very little interruption. The sheer audacity had amazed her.

'How about I pay for these coffees?' Bristow suggested.

'Our treat,' said Nicky.

'Another thing,' he continued. 'Find a person's weak link was something I once was told at a conference, and with Whittaker of course he will just do anything to get topside of his brother.' He hesitated. 'Anything so far?' he asked Nicky.

'That Colin Hislop was really useful. Think he's got a real downer on Justin. Called me back with loads of info on the high flying brother.'

'My guess is Justin is too popular, too trendy for Colin and being good at his job I bet he investigated the whole family.'

'Desperate to be a partner at Shaidy Days we saw evidence of yesterday with that outburst. My guess is when none of their top bods wanted to have to deal with Alerick Keating–Price because he was a pain in the backside, Justin saw his chance. He decided taking on life as Alerick's gofer for Shaidy Days could, if he gained her ladyship's confidence get her to bring influence to bear on the partners, which could ultimately bring about what he desired.'

'Question,' was Jake. 'Did you already have Whittaker's mobile number?'

'No,' Bristow responded. 'Phoned Veronica Smallwood from Paxman and Shooter on some pretext and she gave it to me.'

'This is ridiculous,' said Jake. 'Whittaker?' he almost shouted. 'You name me one crime behavioural profiler who'd have come up with him.' The DS pulled a face. 'And we're no further forward with Italy.'

'I've been wondering about the pair of them,' said a grinning Nicky Scoley. 'The lady and the handsome one. Holiday in Crete we know had no connection to her. Yet if you remember he denied sun, sand, sea and sex but not that he'd never been with her.'

'Think you may well be right,' their boss commented cup in hand then hesitated. 'How about he's the same as everybody else and thought she'd gone to Italy?'

'Maybe she told him she was heading for Italy and scooted off to Skye, the Isle of Man or wherever, for some reason.'

'But then out the blue up pops Billy Lord.'

'Alerick has a one track mind,' Oliver suggested. 'Got no time for anything but his environment stuff, but suddenly he somehow discovers his partner for all those years has kept the existence of her son a secret from him. Don't care who you are, that'd not sit well.'

'Ever get the feeling all this climate change stuff over time had made Keating–Price all very moralistic. Back in his rock 'n' roll days he'd not have been that bothered maybe?'

'Her son is too brown to have just got a tan in Tenerife and her handsome boyfriend makes Alerick look like...the missing link.'

'You think maybe he was racist or was it all about somebody nodding him the wink about her being unfaithful.'

'Make him look a real pillock not knowing somebody else had been sniffing around her,' was how Nicky thought. 'Then out of the blue the son maybe turns up making demands to make matters worse.'

'What'd intensify things even more,' said the DI. 'Would be if he finds out she's not as vegan as he thinks she is. Didn't somebody somewhere say she wasn't as Vegan as was being made out? Alerick's off to the Cotswolds or somewhere to bore people to death and while the cat's away she's off out for a good rare steak or a Chinese with Whittaker.'

'Eating in places Keating-Price would never go near, and anyway people'd just think it was solicitor and client and if word got to Shaidy Days, they'd just think he was doing a damn fine job.'

'After we had a word with him yesterday I went on line last night,' said Nicky. 'Discovered Justin could easy fly to Crete on Friday evening and fly back on Sunday night. Sorry but flights are as they say, cheap as chips.' Nicky smiled at.

'Unfortunately none of this brings us any closer to Alerick's demise. Lady Katherine was already dead we now know. None of the DNA we discovered belonged to Justin and anyway he has an alibi. Band...sorry group members are not up to it are they? Could've smashed his head in maybe, but never handle rare snake poison.'

'Thanks for that boss,' said Jake as he got to his feet, drank down the last of his coffee, poured another and walked off to his station with it.

'Justin?' said Oliver Bristow as he too got to his feet. 'Hows about? He wanted something more permanent than a night or two with Katherine when Alerick was out spouting, to guarantee his future with Shaidy Days and she said no.'

'Onto it now.'

'And. Were Shaidy Days totally unaware being in the cabbage field she could no longer be their client.'

'They also thought she was in Italy. Just popped back to sign paperwork.'

'But being the way they are still listed her. Viscount this, Major General somebody and Lady Katherine.'

38

Everybody in the team were heads down working to clear the backlog of suggestions flooding in from the public about their hero being killed by snake poison.

The clamour for a while was so intense DCI Stevens drafted in three extra bodies to help sort the tedious from the totally ridiculous, seeking fifteen minutes of fame. Sorting the good from the bad and the fringe element of just maybe possible down to the regular six in the MIT Incident Room. Plus the add ons.

Only six because the seventh was making great strides towards establishing the background for Justin Whittaker and what Colin Hislop had admitted about a permanent rift with his brother.

Next up was a call to Leicestershire Police and when DS Nicky Scoley mentioned the name Keating-Price they knew what she was on with. Almost as if they were all ultra environmentalists from Alerick's close knit crew they promised an exhaustive search on her behalf.

Within two hours she had names she could take upstairs for young Digital Forensic Analyst Dexter Hopwood to undertake his search criteria. Nicky wished she had access to all his apps and processes when she was researching her family tree a few years back. With what he had at his disposal she'd have found those lost relatives in no time.

Manna from the geeks heaven after an hour. Parents Andrew and Patricia Bennet who had a son Simon now an accountant, just as Colin Hislop had said, assured Nicky she was on the right path. Then divorce from Andrew before Patricia remarried and adopted two more children: a Justin and a Kacey.

Investigation into both was to a geek like Dexter fairly simple process with Justin being a solicitor associated with a high profile practice in Lincoln and more than she had expected, this Dr Kacey Whittaker.

Simon Bennet, Justin's step-brother had been confirmed by Leicestershire as a partner in a major firm of accountants in the city. By a process baffling to Nicky sat beside him, Dexter had discovered an Oncology Consultant Dr Kacey Whittaker living with her partner Georgie Conley.

Taking notes of her progress back downstairs to the boss. The butterscotch blonde had immediately been spun round and virtually marched out of his office into the Incident Room and made to stand in front of the murder boards. Bristow pointed to the name of a woman.

'And?' Nicky asked.

'India Balouchi an environmental scientist with a PhD from Nottingham Trent has been onto us.' Oliver Bristow hesitated. 'Can I just say she's one of these over-emotional types who when Michelle spoke to her claimed she'd not stopped crying since the news of Keating-Price's death was announced. Read about how he was killed and now having pulled herself together gave us a call. But, saying that, she claims she knows of a woman she was at Nottingham Trent with her a decade ago or more, who is a Herpetologist with a BSc in Zoology, with guess what?' Nicky was given no chance to guess. 'A particular interest in....reptiles, snakes.'

'Wow!' was all Nicky managed before he went on.

'Apparently this Georgie Conley woman has written scientific papers on using snake venom to treat major illnesses. Now. There may be nothing in it, but this Balouchi woman has promised to email info across to Michelle later today. D'you want to know what she?' was a tease. 'According to this India Balouchi, the Conley woman is obsessed with being able to...' he grinned and chuckled. 'Watch somebody die from a snake bite.'

'Shit!'

'Not exactly my wording,' said grinning Bristow. 'She's sending stuff over, but as you can imagine out in the wilds of Borneo or some place if somebody gets bitten by a snake and dies, often the victims are on their own or even if others are, they're just the locals. She's been trying to discover a way of being there or at least having the death filmed of what actually happens during the short period between bite and death. All scientists have it as little more than hearsay from anybody who've witnessed it. None with any medical or dare I say it, zoological background of course.'

Nicky Scoley just stood there shaking her head.

'Hey,' was Jake. 'That's gotta be why blood was withdrawn if you remember. Twice in fact to use in the research.'

'Just to give you some idea. A bite from some venemous snakes can almost be painless to begin with,' Bristow read from his tablet. 'Next is abnormal blood clotting and bleeding which when severe leads to hemorrhage or kidney failure. Can take half an hour to die, and chances are she was stood there videoing.'

'You're...bloody joking!'

'How many Herpetologist's are there likely to be called Conley. I for one have never met one as far as I know,' Jake offered.

'Musta been late last year,' said a grimacing Nicky suddenly. 'Read somewhere about a woman out east swallowed whole by a python. Natives killed it and there she was inside.'

Bristow grimaced and blew out a breath at the very thought of it. 'Reason why this Balouchi got in touch? According to Michelle,' he continued with. 'She's in her own words, an ultra environmentalist, but. Doesn't believe all these climate change protesters are going about things the right way. Reckons they're probably doing serious harm in forcing the public to turn off. The public according to Balouchi have to be as useful as government. They she quite rightly says, are the ones with enough votes.'

'Bit of an Alerick clone by the sound of it,' said Jake behind them. 'A close disciple and been to countless lectures he's given. Heard what happened to her favourite celebrity and reckons it just clicked.'

'Or at least somebody with the know-how which has always been the issue.'

'And,' said Nicky. 'This Conley just happens to be Whittaker's sister's partner. Two adopted kids do they become brother and sister or is that just what they're generally known as?' remained an unanswered query.

'This venom business is why we dismissed the group members and local villagers.'

'Be why this India Balouchi woman came running. Somebody's killed her hero.'

'Don't begin to understand,' said Jake after a few minutes reflection. 'What use snake bite knowledge would be. Surely in countries where these snakes are rife they'll not have an antidote pack pinned to every tree.'

'Or be able give the whole population a jab.'

'Or slice open a python and cut you free.'

'Bit like spending billions sending a rocket into space,' Jamie suggested. 'Just to take photos of Venus. Question I frequently ask is, what for?'

'What on earth is Whittaker's reasoning? Why would he want to be accused of complicity in an attempt to please his sort of step-sister?'

'Is something like the desire for the Nobel Prize for Medicine worth a life?'

'Surely there are dozens of awards worldwide probably for things such as outstanding work and research into international health or whatever.'

'We come to work every day,' said Oliver calmly. 'With no prior knowledge of the events likely to unfold before us. Deadly snake bite in a cabbage patch just beggars belief. Whatever happened to beating your partner's brains out when tea's not ready?'

'Now the media wont know which way to turn with all this. Do they go with Billy Lord's life story or will they be full of every snake joke known to man?'

'Snake jokes are fangtastic!'

Smiling DI shook his head. 'I asked for that.' he admitted. 'When the morning paper slithers across out breakfast table,' even he had to grin with. Oliver put a hand up to stop a deluge. 'Justin's got to be back in the frame that's for sure. Otherwise how would this Conley woman know about Alerick apart from his public image to choose him as the victim she's been desperate to film.'

'Maybe like Justin trying to get promotion she's another desperate one after a new job or an award.'

'Has to be aiding and abetting at the very least, and some nark inside will snitch on what he gets up to for a few quid. *Star* and *Sun* will be waiting outside the gates the day he's released.'

'That's his Shaidy Days gone. Plus any hope of equalling his step-brother's achievement.'

'Lady turns back on black son,' Nicky announced like the town crier. 'So much good stuff here it'll keep the press going for weeks.'

'Better than wall to wall politics.'

'Publicity about all this business linked to Rockapelt will give drink sales a boost.'

'Didn't think of that. Be both the drink and the single.'

'On line business will now be all sorted for Tyson I should imagine. Providing he can stop his wife wanting a motorhome and goodness knows what else,' said Bristow. 'Guess Dumbrell will be happier now, just has to bide his time and wait for his stupid wife to get out.'

'But what about our friend Vic Jenkins?' Nicky smiled smugly.

'Think she may well kick him into touch again,' the DI said. 'If he continues to just throw more money after bad.'

'His problem will be having to wait for the money to come through. Remember most of what those three are due will come from the adverts, and I have no idea how long before they pay out.'

'Record royalties and song writing will be months, that's for sure.'

'What's the betting they bring a CD out after Christmas?'

'Good punt for Jenkins.'

'Excuse me,' was Oliver Bristow. 'Providing it is her,' he put his hand up to a very full room. 'Could just be a coincidence but...'

'You know what we think of coincidences.'

'But having said that,' he went on. 'Whats the odds on two snake venom enthusiasts with the same name?'

Next morning bright and early the room was full once more, all eagerly awaiting on Michelle checking her emails.

'Here we are,' she said as if it had just arrived, but had already read the email more than once.

Hi Detective

Hope this will be of some use.

As I explained, I was at Nottingham Trent at the same time as Georgina Conley. As I do with one or two others I knew back then, I tend to keep an eye on what they're now up to.

I must admit I have for the most part avoided face-to-face contact with the majority of my peers, since we were at uni together. I'm pleased with my life progress, but Georgina has certainly gone up in the world. She writes a regular quite extensive blog and I've copied a couple to you.

This is a quick fire precis of what they contain. Georgie Conley is Assistant Medical Director at Collyer's Bioscience Clinic where the Brit-Irish Research Council are funding her major project on stem cell research for the National Oncology Institute. During the research process she developed the fact certain animals do not get cancer. Elephants are one of those but mammals such as Naked Mole Rats never develop cancer, all to do with a Polymer and a particular gene.

How is the absence of cancer possibly linked to snake venom which will kill? According to one of her blogs, one channel she went down was the question: Could a venom cell serve numerous functions in different parts of the body? This has led her to concentrate on the toxicological classification of poisons, the mode of actions of their venom, symptoms and treatments and the detection in biological systems. Only Snakes in captivity tend to get cancer and this is all part of her research.

Having said all that and you can of course read a great deal more, even since her days at uni Georgina has for some reason always been obsessed with the human body's reaction to the venom of a killer snake as I mentioned.

I do believe somebody somewhere has also linked snake venom as a way of holding back the worst elements of Covid 19, but I may be mistaken.

There can't be that many people who have studied snake venom as much as her together with a possible cure for some cancers, and me telling you this could well stop her heading for the heights career.

If I can be of any further assistance or put you in touch with others, please let me know.

Regards

Ms India Balouchi PhD (Hons)

39

Detective Inspector Oliver Bristow, newish head of the Major Incident Team couldn't stop thinking about Justin Paul Whittaker LLB (Hons) and how he just didn't appear so attractive to the women in his team all of a sudden. Gone were the finely tailored suit and the handmade shoes, replaced by a navy sweat shirt, jeans and Adidas trainers.

Almost overnight he had turned from somebody many admire for his attractiveness, elegant posture, good manners and sincere attitude to have become just another person of lesser note.

It had been an interesting start to the day courtesy of Jake who had spoken to him privately about his set-to with big cheese Dylan Whatmore. Something in the back of his mind told Jake there was a word for his kind he'd researched

'Known around these parts as a quockerwodger,' amused and confused the DI at first. Some local phrases were sometimes difficult to understand, but this one was on another level. 'That's an old fashioned word for somebody acting on the instructions of an influential third party, usually titled or monied,' had cheered him no end.

He'd given him a sad smile when they met, and before the interview with Justin Whittaker had really begun it was just an everyday conversation between two associates. Friends chatting amicably was an example of the way in which this man even in such trying circumstances conducted himself.

As Bristow looked at him across the table during interview, he had appeared one way or another to have somehow become smaller both physically and in mental approach but he guessed give him a few months before he is due to stand trial and some prosecution legal eagle will find him more than a handful in the County Court.

Bristow had expected a real fight in interview, but he was experienced enough to know he'd not drag him in with little hope of success, aware he held the cachet of authority hand. Vital words like Deoxyribonucleic Acid (DNA) he could no doubt spell without any form of prompt. His experience of the justice system would have told him which way the wind was blowing. He'd just lost the will to fight a battle experience told him he should never have got within fifty miles of, and could never win even with one or two dibbos on the jury as there often are.

His stance, his general appearance were all aspects of the man Bristow recognized from the time or two their working lives had crossed in the past. What Whittaker had no notion of back then of course was all the taunting and a degree of bullying in his teens, which as he sat there had held him in good stead.

What had driven him on Bristow wondered? Had it been his life long ambition or did he have real feelings for her ladyship. If the latter why then was he now dabbling with Furneaux?

From what he knew about him already, he'd probably spent his entire life being disappointed. He could just imagine Whittaker biking home from school with an A- for Mathematics, only to be told Simon had an A+ for Woodwork.

Whittaker would be mindful of the part he had played and aware enough about the law to be familiar with a lesser charge than the one facing his sort of half sister's lesbian partner. One thing he must now know was his insatiable desire to beat his brother, which had in one foul swoop become forever unachievable.

Bearded Bristow guessed the nasty self-important masters of their outdated attitudes prevalent in Shaidy and Day would now be full of themselves for very wisely not having made him a partner.

At dinner parties they'd no doubt scurrilously brag all the time from the artichoke crostini starter right to the brandy about having seen through him, how they'd quickly recognized a bad penny. Boast to all and sundry about how they had used his brain to their own ends, had done their very best in their quest to give the underprivileged in society a helping hand and some outdated self-righteous garbage about how status will always out.

The DI knew if the worst comes to the worst he'd be heading for a spell in prison to offer advice on his wing no doubt to a whole range of ne'er do wells. At least then he would be free of the likes of those who had forced Justin to become desperate in his search for a platform of recognition.

Chances were unless he and the judge had previous courtroom run-ins, he'd get a year or two for aiding and abetting together with the inevitable Law Society ban.

Knew he would survive. His brain was too sharp not to. Being a practicing solicitor was now quite out of the question, but there are organizations willing to invest in such a good sharp legally qualified and astute brain out in the dirty world of commerce. A world where profit is the mainstay driving force and in the most part not which school you went to or the club you roll your trouser leg up in.

It would never be a shock should he in the end choose to represent himself in court. Be his last opportunity to experience his oratory gift Bristow had so admired and been jealous of.

Throughout the whole interview Whittaker had remained courteous and composed. Most people sat where he was, struggle to cope and jiggling their legs whilst doing their best to survive the next wave. Not Justin. Years of being in that environment gave him the training and experience he was making the most of.

He'd said at one point how he had spent his entire working life trying to save people, often from themselves. From situations in which they had no connection to, or control of.

'I retain that desire even now despite my own position defending my sister, who had no knowledge of any of what you have been suggesting.' He'd turned to his left, leaned in and spoke to the microphone. 'Dr Kacey Whittaker was never connected to any of my actions. I personally made a point of not involving her. Someone of her stature is needed in this world and I am doing my best to represent her now in a truthful manner.'

At odd times it had been almost as if he'd lost concentration, had drifted away to somewhere or someone else. Not thinking about the questions or his answers. Desperate for it all to be over and vividly aware of what lay in store for him.

Bristow knew Justin's rugged good looks may well have worked against him. He'd no doubt demand the great vivacious so-called beauties of this world. Not the good intelligent handsome women. To Justin the woman he was seen with in Crete, the one he bedded would always need to be a real statement to flaunt.

His problem had always been how many perceptive women would want to live in the shadow of and compete with him. The 'look at me' beauties so many men drool over desire nothing more than the waters of jealousy to flow their way rather in his direction.

Now sat in his office SIO Bristow knew the news of the arrests would have been listened to by all and sundry over their breakfast and in the car on the way to work or on that dangerous school-run. One such listener so it appeared had been Colin Hislop he'd spoken to about Justin.

'Was planning to call you anyway,' he said on the phone. 'Now I hear on the radio he's been charged so you're probably not interested in what I was going to offer.'

'Please go ahead,' Bristow encouraged. 'We will be putting together evidence with the CPS for some time as you can imagine.'

'Not exactly evidence as such.'

'Help me paint a picture I'm sure.' Added to which he was nosey.

'Haven't told anybody I've been talking to you,' he offered. 'But I spoke to someone yesterday who had snippets of information, I'd not come across before. Just happened to mention Justin Whittaker and it all came rolling out.'

'Please carry on Colin, unless you'd prefer to call in later.'

'No I'm fine thanks,' he said. 'Busy day coming up.' The DI had to wait. 'You know the business with the cars? He and his brother Simon both drive Morgans, well there's more to it than that so I understand. Goes back a long way to something in their teens so I've been told, to do with what they planned to do when they made a lot of money, like kids do. Apparently there was some sort of bet about getting a Morgan.'

'Any idea why one of those specifically?'

'Sorry no,' he said and Bristow perceived a noisy take in of breath. 'Seems it was Justin who bought a second-hand one first, but as they don't have anything to do with each other there had been no chance to show it off to his brother. Next time they did meet was at some family do a few months later, and bookish Simon turned up in a brand new car.'

'A Morgan?'

'Exactly. But,' he hesitated. 'According to what you'd call a snout, I'm reliably told their father tipped Simon off.'

'You're joking. A parent doing the dirty?'

'Seems that way,' Colin admitted. 'But it wasn't as it seemed. Simon had only hired his but won the bet for just driving it to family lunch at some swanky hotel. Never actually owned a Morgan.'

'And those awful parents were in on it.'

'So I'm given to understand.'

'What on earth's wrong with them? We talking child abuse?'

'Wouldn't go that far exactly, but you hear a lot of people referring to child one and child two to signify levels of social order. Not abuse as such, but probably a form of mental cruelty, and we know how big an issue mental health is to some these days.'

'I know some couples still socialize after they're divorced, but planning against him is just bizarre.'

'Remember. Justin is not the father's son, yet he retains a form of control.'

Oliver Bristow had read how quite often when people have been badly treated by parent as he obviously had, experts are often of the opinion they would have stood a better chance in life had they been adopted. In this case he was adopted, as was his sister.

'And last but not least, Justin's wife,' Bristow wanted to hear about her but had to keep mum about what he knew. 'She had an affair,' said Colin when Oliver was hoping for something really juicy.

He refrained from suggesting whoever it was had to be something pretty special for her to put her marriage to Justin in jeopardy. 'Go on,' he sighed.

'She had a fleeting affair, with Justin's brother.'

'You're kidding me!' he gasped.

'Thought it'd amuse you,' said Colin. 'See what more I can come up with. Busy day, meeting a client in ten minutes, have to rush.'

'Thanks Colin. Thank you,' Oliver said in return as he struggled with what he had been told.

He just sat there on his own in his office thinking about him. An overwhelming desire to do better than his dominating elder brother. The ambition gene driving Justin on to prove himself superior in every single thing he did.

Did it never occur to somebody as intelligent as Justin how measuring himself against others is futile, especially when the competition is being backed by his own parents? What on earth was wrong with his awful mother?

He looked at his watch. In just a few hours the poor man would be stood in the Magistrates Court down the High Street. Something his brother had never done or was never likely to do. In a strange way that was a feather in his cap.

His phone rang.

'Detective Inspector Bristow.'

'Hmm don't know if I'm talking to the right person, but…' was a hesitant woman's voice. 'Been listening about that environmental man on the radio and...'

'How can I help?' Bristow asked when the sentence stopped.

'See. I'm Monica Tyson,' rang a bell. 'And I think there's something you should know.' Immediately he was listening and waving for Jake to join him.

'And what would that be madam?'

'So, my husband used to know him, this…'

'Keating-Price.' That had to be Humberside and more than likely Hull speak.

'Yeh that's the one and...I was having lunch this week with a very good friend of mine and she asked me if I'd enjoyed my meal with my husband the day it turns out the poor man was killed.'

'How does this concern us?' he asked as Jake sat down opposite. 'Mrs Tyson,' he added deliberately to shock his DS.

'We didn't go for a meal. In fact we've not been out for at least a month. Truth is I was on my own at home and Nathan went to play his bloody poker.'

'Rather than taking you for the meal.'

'According to Amanda Coleridge he'd told her husband at the last minute, he'd have to dip out the regular poker for once, because it was the anniversary of when Nathan and I met, and we were planning a slap up meal at Winteringham Fields. Used to go there regular if we could get a table, but we've not been for ages.'

Bristow recognized the Michelin Star name dropping. 'Do you happen to know what he did instead?' the DI asked as calmly as he could and looked intently at his number two.

'Know the silly sod came in quite a bit later than he normally would if he had been playing poker and went straight in the shower.'

'Did you by any chance know Alerick Keating-Price?'

'That bastard husband of mine did,' made Bristow stare at Jake with his mouth open. 'Hates his guts, got money coming to him so they say.'

'You need the money I take it?'

'See. Been after a motorhome for bloody ages and last week the sod just told me we suddenly can't afford it for crissakes. Guess what that bastard of a husband's done now?' There was no time to think let alone guess. 'Fraser's been on the phone this morning in a right proper state, twenty years old and crying his bloody eyes out. Says his old man called him first thing to say he can't afford to subsidise his uni rent any longer,' and Bristow sensed the sniffles meant the woman was crying. 'Poor kid'll be humiliated. What a shit bag!'

'I'm sorry to hear that, but I'm sure things are not as bad as they seem.'

'Oh bugger off!' was almost screamed down the phone 'What'll I say to my friends, you tell me that eh?...oh for God's sake...pissin' Amanda'll be on next asking why we're not joining them with that website thingy. Then'll be the Hildred bitch and how do I explain about that bloody band thing? Be in the *Leader* this week you bet and bloody cameras parked on our lawn. It's a soddin' nightmare. How do I explain all that to people I know, you tell me that. Well I'm not. Off to stay with me friends and he can sort this mess out on his fucking' own. Me mum always said he was a shyster but did I listen to her, did I buggery? Sorry, gotta go.'

'Mrs....' Bristow almost screamed when the line went dead. 'Wow! That was very ladylike,' he grinned with. Hands on head as he looked at Jake. 'You're *never* going to believe this.'

After he'd gone through the conversation as best he could, his senior DS had thoughts of his own. 'We need to get that court order to find out what actually happened with Arbiter's money. If she did sell the big house, why was Keating-Price still living in it, or at least...' he stopped when he saw his boss smiling. 'You mean?'

'Why not?' he said leaning forward as if not wishing anybody else to hear her crazy theory even with the door closed. 'How about Whittaker with the brother he never speaks to but is an accountant got access to, or given access to her money and layered it across a whole host of accounts in all sorts of rum places. Then when it all came back as a whole...'

'As they do.'

'It slotted very nicely into a bogus company the pair of them had set up?'

'Does a bit of time and at worst comes out with access to. How much?'

'How many lies and tall stories have we been trying to puzzle out?' Oliver slid out as he went to get to his feet.

'Wait a sec,' was said slowly. 'Hear me out. Whittaker and this sort of brother Simon coalesce the scheme. Provide Georgie Conley with the snake opportunity she's dreamed of. Get rid of Keating-Price to ensure he can never make any sort of claim on the estate he planned to give to his vegan mates. They've got the keys to and bingo they've got a tidy pile.'

'You putting that to the CPS?' Oliver laughed. 'Rather you than me.'

41

Late November

'Well, what do you think?' DCI Inga Larsson asked Nicky Scoley as she sipped from her glass.

'Different, and there's...' she licked her lips. 'An after taste, but it grows on you. Bit like some mild curries tend to, just slowly creeps up.'

'Good thing if you're driving and if what they say about the low sugar content is right, got to be a winner if only for those very reasons.'

The bar they'd chosen was inviting. Inga had guessed right. Down by the Brayford across from where she'd once lived. At that time of day as she expected, the place proved to be fairly quiet.

Nicky licked her pink lips more. 'Afterburn certainly lasts, that's the best thing for me. Can't see it knocking Coke and Pepsi sales once the rush is over, but some of the others are likely to suffer.'

'Everybody's talking about it.'

'You don't say,' she chuckled. 'Advert's been on so many times some of the people trying hard to flog their Christmas stuff must be facing a real uphill struggle to get their message over.' Nicky sipped more of the Sheer Delight.

'Being teetotal they say is the new black,' Inga sniggered. 'And this fits the bill, it's new, sharp and the after taste as you say is so unusual.' She put down her glass. 'Silly really. The song, or this,' she said lifting the glass back up momentarily. 'Had nothing to do with what happened to poor Alerick.'

Inga had always used fika – chat, coffee and cake she'd brought with her from Sweden, as restful occasions. Usually at times of greater stress. This fika was unusual in that there was no coffee and cake and it was post case but pre-trial.

Since her promotion and move to be the force lead on rape and serious sexual offences with the Sexual Safeguarding Unit, she had remained in contact socially with one or to of her old team. Nicola Scoley in particular. This was one of their catch-ups.

So far on this occasion Larsson had concentrated on the drink. Previously she'd told Nicky about a case she was working on involving a woman born into the Children of God cult where abuse is normal enough for a manual to have been created on how to abuse kids.

A teenage girl had managed to escape the clutches of the cult only to have been tracked down by one of the leaders and raped. Inga was at that time dealing not only with the actual sexual assault case, but also investigating the cult's wider involvement across the county.

'Wonder how much Rockapelt will get out of it in the end?' the Swede wondered out loud.

'Record's doing well I hear,' Nicky grimaced. 'Well downloads actually, which I know the Darke boss will tell you it's nowhere near the same thing.'

'But these days of course it's no longer a proper top twenty like it should be, with all this download and streaming business.'

'Be like vinyl,' said Inga. 'Making a serious come back when they realize there's a lack of quality missing in their lives.'

'Thumbing for the next album track, lose their phone down the loo, and ping there goes what they call music.'

'To coin a phrase! Just the same as, *"had me phone snatched, lost me photos."* How often d'you hear that one? *"Got me pin numbers on there!"* and on and on.'

'Traffic lads tell me more and more numpties are dealing with car insurance on their phones. Scroll past an email, insurance cancelled and they're buggered.' She took a sip. 'This has gotta be worth a few bob to the Rockapelt three,' Nicky tapped her glass with her nail.

'See that Home From Home is up and running, and doing well without Tyson the singer.'

'From what I've been told,' said Inga. 'In retrospect, obsession has always been a thread right through the whole case. Start with Tyson's wife, obsessed about all the nonsense she gathered around her. That big place of theirs out at Swinderby was big enough for three families, but you can't brag on WhatsApp with photos of your squalid four bedroom bungalow if its not in the on-trend pretentious area to live,' she chuckled.

'That Alerick of course was obsessed, and Jake was telling me to such an extent he made his partner live in some awful cottage place, spent day after day out and about spouting to the faithful. Expected her constantly to eat crap food and absolutely refused to have a family for environmental reasons. And, although we'll never really know, allow her to have contact with the son she did have.'

'And his latest love served the worst coffee known to man, I had to suffer half a tin mug of. Be some Eco bilge no doubt.'

It was often during fika chats where Inga could test her ideas about a case she was involved in. This time it was the big MIT case. She knew from back working together if Jake or Nicky knew she was way off track one or other of them would soon let her know. Or on the other hand give her the green light assurance her channel was one worth pursuing.

The DI sipped more to relish the taste. 'Still cannot believe somebody as intelligent as Justin would even consider getting involved.'

'Our guess is having an Honourable Lady as a partner and his sister's wife recognized for all her cancer research, has to be what he assumed Shaidy would be after.'

'Understand it was a case of her clearing off from controlling Keating-Price and when she hot-footed it down to Bournemouth living under an assumed name that was one route to partnership gone.'

'Wonder if Justin thought he'd been dumped?'

'Sort of cleared off without saying goodbye from what we've been able to gather,' said Nicky. 'One aspect we're still trying to unravel is the suggestion of her moving to Italy we heard from several people. When he queried it, Justin told Oliver his expenses didn't run to trips abroad, but that had to be a charade. He must have known she was still in the UK.'

'Why pretend?'

'No idea. What had she to hide apart from keeping out the way of Alerick, her son and keeping her relationship with Justin a secret? With her dead, maybe we'll never know, but could come out in court.

'Who killed her do we know?' Inga whispered.

'All theory at present. When she returned to sort out the sale of the house she somehow fell foul of Alerick and his strict veganite brigade rules. Exposing him as a fraud maybe over something she knew is one idea. Could well have always conned him into believing she was on side with all his quirky ideas.'

'And he knew she could bring him down.'

Nicky stopped for another drink. 'Plus of course how many so-called enviro folk have got their grubby mits in the Keating-Price till? Money talks.'

'The nation's favourite was totally absorbed in the environment. Be a bit like Alec Jeffreys who developed DNA profiling was.'

'And he did for her?'

'Somehow we reckon he worked out she was no longer totally vegan, probably had restaurant apps on her phone although that was buried with her and turned out to be useless. Maybe a friend said he'd spotted her with a rare steak when he was off out and spewing to the converted.'

'But you have no actual evidence?'

'I'm sorry but who else is there? They're both dead so where do you go with it? She wasn't the one who annoyed some people enough for her to be bumped off and it looks as though Justin saw her as a box ticker on his insatiable ladder climbing.'

'See your problem.'

'I'm dealing more and more with rape of transexuals,' Inga admitted. 'Rape of trans men to women are favourite and a virgin gets you douze point,' even she had to grin with. 'When I worked with all this nearly a decade ago there was none. Now its the new sport. At least with Alerick it was better him being the way he was than being a sexual predator as some of the nations favourites have turned out in the past.'

'He'd have been apoplectic if he'd been told about her flying off to Europe.'

'Would have destroyed his image, and what had he got besides? How would he have dealt with the media when an expose hit the papers about her air miles, eating habits, leather shoes and so on? Be totally humiliated. Never met him, but from what I've heard he'd never cope.'

'Can you imagine the constant rows about her carbon footprint?'

'Whatever that means.'

'Make a change for me from frequent adultery, coersive behaviour and a good old smacking.'

'If they separated he'd lose access to her funds. Unaware as Oliver was telling me, she'd already sold the old house,' Nicky mused. 'Took a while to discover what happened to that Furneaux female. Back in the land of mummy and daddy we understand and blogging daily they say. Ejected from the scruffy cottage by Shaidy and Day dealing with the estate.'

'She'll pop up on Twitter no doubt when this has all died down. Probably be blogging for all she's worth when it all comes to court.'

'Living off the bank of Daddy.'

'Be like those celebrities flying thousands of miles to go to some Eco meeting. She was doing it for herself and for her father who I'm guessing brags on endlessly about how much his darling daughter is doing for the environment, while he sits on his backside.'

'I know she wasn't in the public eye so to speak,' said Nicky. 'But our Katherine Arbiter'd be like all the celebrities who live a lie for ages and ages. Chances are when she saw sense and came back to sort out her financial matters Alerick knew his days of fame and notoriety would be gone if the world ever found out.' Maybe he discovered things while she'd been gone and had to put an end to it.'

Inga took another sip. 'Especially if she was planning to sell her story.'

'Without this environment business what would he do? He's not qualified in anything and she owned their home for what it's worth.'

'Moment you start to unlock this climate change business you get all this utter nonsense and another obsession by rich kids and maiden aunts.'

'Sensible ideas like blocking roads to stop fire, police and ambulances trying to rescue people and upsetting half the nation they need on their side,' Nicky suggested. 'I'm sorry but banner waving students from the home counties are never going to stop India and China using coal.'

'Gas prices shot through the roof and thousands on Benefits can't afford to put the heat on in winter. At the same time some

Council somewhere refused planning permission for an energy company to drill for gas.' Inga Larsson blew out a breath. 'You couldn't make it up.'

'Think you'd struggle to find anyone able to say what that COP26 actually achieved?' Nicky looked all around the bar. 'We're sounding like a couple of angry political activists ourselves,' they both chuckled with wide smiles.

'Another one obsessed of course had to be poor Justin,' said Inga.

'Always striving to become a partner to equal the half-brother it seems his parents sarcastically mentioned every time they spoke to him. Even Shaidy Days,' said Nicky glass in hand. 'Their fobia with the old school tie, local squire, chairman of the Hunt and secret societies the rest of the world kissed goodbye to ages ago.'

'Always possible Arbiter's favourite Italian dish is the one Adam enjoys when we go out. Spieda Bresciano. Alerick's away, she's tucking and gets spotted.'

'Mixture of meats, and somebody spotted the pair tucking in.'

'Blackmail possibly. Then we have that Georgie Conley female,' Nicky Scoley suggested, then stopped to sip her cold drink. 'That's a consuming passion to beat the lot and she got what she was after. GHB date rape drug and naive Alerick was easy meat,' she said softly.

'Slipped it in his drink somehow. Chances are.'

'Video on her phone of the fourteen minutes it took the poor sod to die.'

'Seriously?' Inga implored. 'Oh my god!'

Nicky nodded confirmation. 'Shhh,' she chided. 'Coming up in court. But what I've never understood is, why dump him in a field that close to Gorgie Hall?'

'Risky heading somewhere with a body in the boot,' the blonde DCI suggested. 'Sort of thing you do if you're a criminal mastermind, but a medical scientist?' she grimaced then sucked in a breath. 'Something somewhere tells me there's an average distance for dumping bodies. That'll be within it. S'pose Alerick taking her off some place in his diesel guzzling old Land Rover wasn't half as simple as digging a shallow grave on the edge of that field of cabbages.'

'He'd know there were bits where the planting machine never goes if anybody did. Probably more than the farmer.'

'Not sure Katherine was obsessed, just desperate to get away from him and the monotony of his addiction. Guess she wanted to be free to accept her son. Alerick hearing about him'd not be welcome. Young handsome lover in tow and holidays in her sunshine villa we imagine for a good while.'

'All gave him good reason.'

'If there ever is one.'

'Keep thinking about smarty pants Whittaker,' said the thoughtful Swede. 'Just thrown it all away,' she said glancing around the bar. 'Everything he worked so hard for. Bang gone,' she clicked her fingers. 'All for what? So he could beat his sort of brother at something, be a top dog with a malevolent organisation like Shaidy Days. As well as having real life aristocracy in tow to force their hand and enjoy in bed? When she buggered off, he changed tack. Think I'll look up obsession see what it suggests as to why?'

'Bet his KC bangs on about it being some sort of obsessive disorder. One thing's for sure now he really will be the black sheep of the family.'

'Somebody said they weren't a proper family.'

'Wonder why people do that. Favour one child against the rest,' said Nicky thoughtfully.'He wasn't even their birth child, and Justin and that Kacey weren't brother and sister.'

'Poor sod started life at the very bottom with an alcoholic waster, so we now understand. Now what sort of future has he got?'

'You don't think…no, surely not.'

'What?'

'Did these Whittakers adopt simply so they could abuse him or could she just not have any more?'

'Been known of course. How many horrific cases do we get about child abuse and killing by so-called partners?'

'If he was a naughty boy you sit him on the naughty chair, not treat him badly forever and a day.'

'Did your parents ever sit you on a naughty chair?' Nicky enquired then got on with finishing her drink.

'No of course not. Sadly Justin is a man of untold sadness, locked in bitter enmity. With no family around him at the time when he needs them most.'

'Jake reckons he was always making a play for you when you met,' Nicky suggested.

'Think he does it as a matter of course with all women without thinking,' she answered. Right there and then was not the time or place for an admission.

'For a good while we were wondering what had happened with his marriage, never imagined the brother was involved in that too.'

'You serious?' Inga gasped. 'Really?'

'Sure was, so we've been told. What's the betting his brother'll be in court? Clapping his hands when Justin gets sent down.'

'You think he'll go down?' Inga posed.

'Your guess is as good as mine in this day and age. People who know Justin tend to think it's just an all consuming compulsion by a little boy lost, when it could well be used in court as his reaction to a life of cruelty.'

She knew in time psychological assessments would get to the bottom of all his issues.

'What a terrible thing when two brothers fall out like that, said Inga. 'Blood is thicker than water but in his case of course there was no blood brother.'

'One thing I've never fathomed,' Nicky said. 'Shaidy and Day were Katherine's solicitors. How come suddenly Justin is then representing Furneaux? She was Alerick's piece on the side.'

'Think representing is the wrong word.' Inga smiled. 'Shaidy and Day are representing Katherine. They send Justin to see Alerick about something probably to do with the house and lo and behold what have we here?' she chuckled.

'Dipping his wick with both you think?'

'You know what he's like'

'He got Oliver a bollocking and wasn't even her solicitor. What a bastard.'

'What was it all about?' Inga asked then answered her own query. 'Something we may never know, but what I am aware of is unfortunately I've witnessed a wasted life.' Glass in hand she looked all about the bar.

'Justin's not the only one to throw his life away. What about his sort of sister Kacey Whittaker? We're talking Herpetologist with a BSc in Zoology with an avid obsession in reptiles and filming snakes biting. Along with expertise in Invertebrate Zoology. For Conley a Toxicology PhD, Research Council (MRS) Toxicology Unit. They worked their socks off for. All thrown away, for what?'

'Sorry to bring the o word back in. Was winning some award her obsession to add to the long list?'

'Probably a Nobel award for it.'

'They're right about this,' said Larsson holding up her glass. 'Prance in the streets with sheer delight,' she sang and sipped with her eyes closed to savour every last drop. 'From what I hear about dreary Keating-Price I find it extremely difficult to imagine a goon like him writing something that good. Delightful in fact,' she grinned.

'Fancy a coffee?'

'Good idea.'

'How you getting on with Oliver these days?'

'He's good but still a mystery man.'

'Got no better?'

'No, and Jake's a bit obsessed about it all. Reckons there's some thing cracking off behind the scenes.'

'In what way?'

'Think about it. We know the Darke boss's background with his first wife being killed. We have both met Jillie and know what she does and little Holly. We know about your background. Sweden, your dad's job move to Nottingham. Bristol, degree and a sex role here, then MIT. Connor and I meet up with Jake and Sally from time to time who we all know is a nurse. Know Jamie supports Gainsborough Trinity and so on. What do we know about Bristow? As far as Jake is aware he's never been for drink or anything with any of us except maybe a couple of times.'

'Doesn't time fly. Must be a good nine months now.'

'Jake's got a bit of a bee in his bonnet about it all. Keeps asking why he never attends a crime scene, when you did from time to time and so did Craig. We know he lives somewhere near Grantham and his mother owns a vineyard in France. Gives us a bottle or two for birthdays and stuff. We only know about the vineyard when Sandy I think it was, asked him where he could get more. What else do we know?'

'Good stuff I've got to say. Gave me a couple of bottles.'

'What about brothers, sisters, father? Girlfriend, partner, married, divorced, hobbies? Even been suggested he's distant and to a degree austere as the result of a difficult childhood.'

'That sounds like something from a psychologists handbook,' an amused Inga responded.

'Could have been subjected to child abuse as there's never a word about his father.'

'Way he is s'pose.' Inga responded with little enthusiasm. 'Probably one of those who keeps himself to himself.'

Nicky went off to the bar. 'You all set for Christmas?' she asked on her return, well aware what the answer would inevitably be as always from such an organized woman.

'Well on the way. You?'

'Pretty much.'

'You don't sound sure.'

Butterscotch Nicky Scoley blew out her breath as her face opened up. 'Moving. After Christmas we reckon.'

'To where?' her boss gasped back.

'Three bedroom house Michelle's Matthew's been doing up,' she admitted pulling out her phone. 'Look,' she said and Inga took the phone to view a series of photos.

'Hey. That looks really good. Nice big kitchen. En suite looks gorgeous. Well done you.' Inga patted Nicky's arm. 'Guess that's a whole lot better than where our Justin will be spending his time for a while.'

'Garden's a bit rough at present, but he'll sort that when the house is finished. Matt's putting solar panels on the roof to save on energy costs.'

'Alerick would be proud of you.'

'Closer to work too.'

'Connor happy?'

'Pleased as punch to be getting away from the rent rat race at last.'

'Don't forget a house warming.'

'As long as you behave yourself!'

277

STRANGER THAN FICTION

Back in the heady days of the Swinging 60s, I was involved in the management of pop singers and beat groups. One singer was invited to open a new Lord John boutique in Carnaby Street.

This involved me traveling in an open carriage drawn by a team of white horses. One of the owners of the boutique rode with us wearing a gold plated leather jacket. Arriving at the new store my singer duly performed the opening ceremony.

This was followed by a champagne reception and a galaxy of interviews with the press. I can remember personally being accosted by a reporter from the Sunday Times Magazine.

Once it was all over we made our way by taxi to Victoria Station to catch the Brighton Belle home.

Outside the station was a newspaper placard "Ringo Weds".

The journey in the open carriage and the shop opening was never mentioned at all by the media. They were obviously more interested in Ringo Starr. This of course being at a time when celebrity stories were not as frequently used as they are now these days.

What are the chances of that happening?

Two weeks prior to my last Lincolnshire Murder Mystery being released, a woman was found fatally injured at a house in North Lincolnshire.

I had been asked by local media to provide an advance copy of my book. This I had duly done. The story included a local journalist's body being discovered in a sheep trough on a farm near Hibaldstow. A location I had chosen eighteen months previous.

On the following Wednesday a well known local man from Hibaldstow appeared at Hull Crown Court charged with the murder of the woman.

The media apologized, but due to the sensitivity of the on going court case they were unable to consider my book.

Lightning you see, does strike twice.

ACKNOWLEDGMENTS

Shall we start with 'Yellerbelly'? Talk was of farm workers bending down in the field thus acquiring a brown back from the sun, with their stomach pale almost yellow in comparison.

As with so many tales from wandering minstrels there were other's who claimed to know the truth. Waistcoat colour from the Lincolnshire Regiment was one. Women keeping a secret purse for their gold coins or a special pouch for them meant in good times they had a yellow belly. The flipside is, nobody is absolutely sure.

Where do I get my ideas, is the most frequently asked question. In this case it was partially a memory from my past.

For one book, I'd read about an unusual marriage relationship in a magazine I then used. There are friends and readers suggestion naturally. People watching of course and thereby spotting the different way people behave and look. This time it was a combination of a newspaper report about a man who died while trying to kiss a deadly snake. That and pop group memories from my past I combined.

My thanks go to Keegan Gaeng from Royalty Exchange (royaltyexchange.com) from Denver, Colorado. Who confirmed you can bequeath songwriting and recording royalties in your will. Rightholders can also sell a portion of their royalties through an online bidding process. Such auctions help artistes and songwriters raise money by connecting them to private investors.

Although all the characters including police officers are figments of my imagination as is the village this time, it is obvious some readers are likely to conclude they are from the real Lincolnshire Police. Please understand, whilst they have very kindly answered many questions from time to time neither the organization itself nor their officers have any affiliation with this book.

More <u>Lincolnshire Murders</u>
coming your way soon:

HELLO THERE
PREVIEW

December

When was the last time anything really good happened to me, is a thought many people ponder from time to time. Why is it always somebody else, and usually the unworthy?

Harry Simm was exactly the same. Living a humdrum often soulless and depressing existence, was never to him a proper life. Certainly far removed from the lifestyle many people enjoy. Those who suggest life has a great deal to do with sheer luck were to his mind, spot on.

He'd read more than once how the successful and rich are not always the most talented or gifted, just the lucky ones. They experience events and situations they can then exploit to increase wealth and happiness. Such events are entirely random. Had Tuesday been such an event?

Once upon a time a busker in London spotted by sheer chance by a record producer, finished up with a chart hit. The Royal family are bestowed riches and all the pomp in their position by freaks of birth. Sandie Shaw went to an Adam Faith concert as a teenager, managed to get into the star's dressing room to sing to him. Few years later she won Eurovision.

Just the sort of things he'd read or heard about over the years but never known anybody who'd won on the Lottery unless they kept their gob shut. Proper win with odds of 1 in gotta be fifty million.

Harry'd realized ages ago if he'd put a couple of quid in a pot rather than nipping to the newsagent for a ticket, he'd have a darn sight more than the tenner he got years ago, that thirty lousy quid last year or a free Lucky Dip.

Was that what was happening to him? Thinking about it day and night had become an obsession he'd been embroiled in since that out of the blue Tuesday night in the pub. Bad weather had waterlogged the Mariner's pitch and by chance he spotted the fixture postponement on his tablet to save him trailing up on a fruitless mission.

The odds against it being anything but sheer luck were hundreds if not millions to one. Bit like the Lotto.

A good four years ago he'd jacked in the perpetual torment of a relationship with Gloria, packed his bags, moved lock, stock and barrel away from the Cornhill Market and Lincoln, out to to the coast to open his back street shop.

Thinking about it now he had to admit the decision to move'd been something good for once. Following his dream and luck had nothing to do with it. Sheer hard graft and a whole bunch of tormented worrying nights had got him through.

Had he remained with that bitch in Lincoln he'd have gone to the City match which that evening was still on. Rather than planning to head off up the coast to Blundell Park. Then at a loose end he'd decided once the shop was shut, he'd grab a bite to eat, wash, get changed before heading for the pub. Better having that easy stroll than heading off up to Grimsby in the cold.

He was sat near the window supping his pint and chuntering to himself as he waited for Malcy, late as usual. Then right out the blue this talent scout for a photographer just wandered up to the table to ask if he might be interested in doing catalogue modelling and internet video work.

His first reaction had been an astonished gasp 'Me?' and looked about to see who else it might be aimed at. 'You're joking!' and Malcy turning up five minutes later was well pissed off to have missed it all.

This was it. Lady luck it had to be and excitedly he'd taken the business card offered, called the number and tonight's the night. Sunday night for a meet seemed a bit bloody odd to him, but this was a great opportunity not to be missed and anyway he reckoned these arty types are never your nine to fivers.

Harry had literally in between customers bit by bit all day, given his flat upstairs a good bottoming. Tidied, cleaned and polished just as his dear old mum would always do for visitors. Been a good day, business had been quite brisk in the afternoon for a change for the time of year, and all his hard work was paying off. Now this cherry on top.

Being a worrier, the weather could be against him. Very cold and foggy told him there could well be a no show.

Few bunce made from this modelling business would give him a good start towards a fresh look. Had that old boy in the shop again on Friday offering hand carved Hindu Gods, but claimed that was all he made. Once more he'd come out with the same old guff about Rishi Sunak making them trendy.

Who in Mablethorpe would want one? The single one he'd taken on sale or return still sitting on a shelf told its own story. The guy could certainly carve, but why stick with one subject more appropriate to markets in Delhi, if its still called that. Could be it was all to do with religion.

Harry knew kids stuff always sold well. Billy out at Burgh le Marsh made good unicorns and fairies. He'd bought a dolls house a bit back and wished he could get more. Having it snapped up within a day or two had been good business. Harry'd sold paperbacks when he was at Lincoln Market. Ones he picked up from car boots for 10p a throw and sold for 25 was a good mark up. Might be worth trying them again.

Sharp tap on the shop door exactly on time.

'Hi,' Harry greeted his visitor excitedly.

'Hello there,' his visitor returned as he was invited into his emporium. After the usual welcoming pleasantries about the cold weather, the guest insisted on a guided tour of his stock. The choc-a-bloc hoard of quaint and curious.

A couple of big metal round wall art sculptures seemed to take this Jules' eye. Butterflies of all shapes and sizes, an old wooden wheelbarrow appeared to prove interesting but the general stuff he'd got from house clearances was simply ignored.

'I live upstairs,' he explained and gestured away from the shop in a bid to get on with it. Find out the whys and wherefores. 'Coffee, Tea?'

'Be honest it'll be fine down here,' said his visitor and sauntered towards the little cubby hole Harry used as an office come kitchen. 'Coffee'll be good.'

'You live around these parts?' nervous Harry asked to make conversation.

'Based in Nottingham, but the job as you can imagine takes me to a whole load of places. Last week I was in Wales. Bit wet I'm afraid but fortunately this job keeps me indoors for the most part.'

Harry was making two Nescafe coffees with water from the old tin kettle as they chatted.

'This what you do, just sort of approach people?' Harry asked waiting for the kettle.

'Yes, in a word. But I handle this side of things for a whole range of publications, internet and video organizations. In Wales last week on the lookout for somebody to fit a particular Rugby product image one of the other spotters told me about.'

'And me?' he asked and waited.

'General. Been on the look out for if you don't mind me saying, a person of interest. A character. Rather than a bland looking average ten-a-penny guy for some new product launch. The average short back and sides or daft haircut blokes are no good for this project. You're ideal I've got to say.'

'Gotta tell yer, this is all a bit of a shock. Not something I'm used to all this'

'Could easy arrange for some shots in the shop here,' this Jules said sat there gazing around. 'Be good for our online clothing retailer. Be different certainly, but that's up to the director and photographer.'

Pre-boiling the kettle upstairs had been a complete waste of time. Once the coffees were made the pair settled down on the two old garden chairs to discuss what he was desperate to hear about.

'Can we talk about availability first up?' Harry was asked as his visitor peered all about.. 'Is your spare time limited with this place?'

'Not really. This is not Tesco with the opening times on the internet and plastered on the door. Need to take a bit of time off now and again with the need to deliver some o'me bigger items anyway.'

'Useful.' Jules nodded. 'Tell me. Are weekends better than weekdays do you think?'

'Weekdays,' Harry replied and lifted his tin mug for an initial sip. 'Allus close on a Monday but weekends is when tourists about. Not so much this time o'year but you get a good few now

283

and again. Time then can be a bit precious.' He shrugged. 'Not carved in stone though,' he said thinking of the extra cash.

'D'you have sugar by any chance?' was so frustrating.

'Yeh. Upstairs,' Harry said, hiding a sigh.

'To be honest sweetener would be batter? Diabetes,' was grimaced up as Harry got to his feet.

Harry scanned the cupboard top quickly. 'Think there's some upstairs,' he suggested.

Back down he handed over a pink sweetener packet. 'That do?'

'Yeh fine. Thank you.'

Disappointingly so far there'd been no talk of actual money or what likely amounts, but the good news was the suggestion of a photo session actually in the shop for online clothing would prove ideal. Was this more from that lady luck? He'd get his good stuff in the background, move all the tatt out the way.

From their chat about the arrangements they moved back to a question and answer session about the variety of goods he had on offer. Not antiques by a long chalk, but certainly a good amount of rubbish alongside a number of unusual pieces. Jules had already stopped to look interestingly at what the label said were Vintage Chinese Porcelain figures, Harry knew were not vintage, not Chinese that was for sure and never Porcelain

'You okay?' Harry felt a bit odd, sweaty and had to sit down. Be all the excitement he told himself. 'Can I get you anything? Aspirin, paracetamol? Where are they? Upstairs?'

'Sorry about this,' Harry said and blew out a breath. 'Be alright in a bit.' What an absolute bugger. Lady Luck turns up and...

'Do you have to take any medicine?' Jules his visitor asked. 'Maybe you forgot with all this going on. Any pills or anything I can get for you?'

'God I feel shit!'

284

Ingram Content Group UK Ltd.
Milton Keynes UK
UKHW020744250723
425746UK00014B/341